KNIGHTS THRANIS

THE CHRONICLES OF FREYLAR

- VOLUME 2 -

by

Liam W H Young

First edition printing, 2017

ISBN 978-1-78808-703-2

Copyright © Liam William Hamilton Young 2017.

All characters appearing in this work are fictitious. Any resemblance to real persons, living or dead, is purely coincidental.

All rights reserved. No part of this book may be reproduced in any manner without written permission except in the case of brief quotations included in critical articles and reviews. For further information, please contact the author.

Cover Illustration Copyright © Liam William Hamilton Young 2017, moral rights reserved by Hardy Fowler.

A catalogue copy of this book is available from the British Library.

Printed and bound in the United Kingdom by Biddles.

SURREY LIBRARIES	
Askews & Holts	05-Jan-2018
SF	£8.99

ACKNOWLEDGEMENTS

Foremost, I would like to thank Hardy Fowler again for the excellent cover art illustration for this book. Hardy is a joy to work with, and really understands my vision for the world of Freylar.

I would also like to thank Matthew Webster once more for his enormous contribution to this book. Matt has been an amazing sounding board throughout the writing process for this book, and continues to provide his invaluable editing services.

Again I would like to thank Kevin Forster for his sage counsel regarding the correct use of medieval weaponry.

Lastly, thank you to both Tibor Mórocz and Matthew Wells for proofreading this book – your collective feedback was invaluable.

I dedicate this book to all the hard working members of the emergency services, and to the talented engineers of this world who safeguard our everyday lives with ever advancing technology.

Whilst writing this book both my son Tristan and I were involved in a road traffic accident, which could have ended tragically. Fortunately we both walked away from the incident unscathed, aside from minor cuts and bruising as well as being shaken by the ordeal – a testament to those unnamed heroes who I dedicate this book to.

TABLE OF CONTENTS

ONE Trust

TWO Burden

THREE Hide

FOUR Pain

FIVE Discomfort

SIX Encounters

SEVEN Realisation

EIGHT Impact

NINE Reality

TEN Awakening

ELEVEN Facade

TWELVE Bridges

THIRTEEN Mist

FOURTEEN Summons

FIFTEEN Collusion

SIXTEEN Displacement

SEVENTEEN Rush

EIGHTEEN Family

NINETEEN Ethics

TWENTY Goodbye

TWENTY ONE Change

TWENTY TWO Detection

DRAMATIS PERSONAE

ONE
Trust

There was a time when both Orders fought tirelessly alongside one another in combat, regardless of the adversaries they faced who threatened to end their way of life. Their bond was one forged from the shared hardships of battle, and their allegiance was thought to be unbreakable. Regrettably that time had long since passed. Now the once great notion of a glorious alliance between their Orders threatened to fade from memory entirely. He knew not the root cause responsible for the rift between the Orders, though he suspected that his predecessor was partly to blame for the damaged relationship and ongoing feud. The quarrel between their Orders had existed for as long as he could remember, it was unsurprising then that neither side could offer any real insight as to the catalyst responsible for their estranged existence. Despite the grim state of affairs reality painted, their insular thinking could not realistically continue; if he could not implement change himself, then he would find a Freylarkin who could. The recent devastating attack by the Narlakai had shattered their own Order at the grass roots level, which was likely to incur repercussions for generations to come. Ending a species was commonly achieved by targeting its offspring; the same held true for The Blades. Their enemies had known this fact well and had therefore sown the seeds of their long term ruin. Their recruitment rate would inevitably fall into decline now, as young Freylarkai took the foreseeable decision not to enlist following the terrible events visited upon those who valiantly went before. In time the horrors of the recent Narlakai invasion of Freylar would fade from memory and their ranks would flourish once more. In the meantime, he needed to fill the gaping void left in the wake of the decimated Blade Aspirants, if he was to stand any chance at maintaining the continued security of their domain. He needed the Knights Thranis. It was essential to his plans that he regained their trust prior to attempting to rebuild The Blades' relationship with the now distant Order.

'Marcus! Are you listening?' boomed the Captain of The Blades, breaking his train of thought.

Both he and Ragnar had agreed to meet openly by the arena's west gate, where The Teacher habitually trained the Order's Aspirants and Novices. It was hoped that their presence would serve to motivate the remaining Aspirants. Besides, the Captain had a keen dislike of Waystones, which were the only means of ascending to his personal quarters high up in the Tri-Spires overlooking the arena. As such Ragnar welcomed the change of venue.

'I am sorry old friend. I was lost in thought.' he replied.

Prior to the invasion the west gate had teemed with sparring Aspirants. Now only a handful of the newly promoted Blade Novices religiously practiced their martial prowess at a notable distance from others of the same rank. Those Aspirants who survived the recent confrontation with the Narlakai each wore a teardrop shaped Moonstone, gifted to them by queen Mirielle as a sign of Freylar's gratitude for the horrors each had endured whilst defending their domain. Yet in addition to their gifts, each had received the curse of a heavy burden of ill-fated memories that came from having witnessed the horrible demise of their fellow Aspirants in battle. Now the survivors – with the notable exception of Rayna – followed Anika's questionable fervent path; they each routinely pledged their devotion to the Order, as though the act of doing so was some kind of religious mantra which gave them strength. Anika had become a ringleader, or spokesperson of sorts, for the group which had disturbingly named itself The Vengeful Tears. Rayna had become their reluctant icon – as evidenced by her awkward body language towards the newly formed band of zealots. The Vengeful Tears revered The Guardian, seeing Rayna as some kind of saviour or focal point for their growing fanaticism to the Order. When recently he had spoken privately to her on the matter, Rayna had been quite blunt in her response.

'I don't like it Marcus. Their increasingly zealous behaviour is worrying.'

He understood well Rayna's concerns – indeed he shared them – though it was a difficult situation to manage; each member of The Vengeful Tears had refused to talk about their ordeal at Scrier's Post, and even Nathaniel had failed to properly connect with his students since the awful attack on their kin.

'What do you suppose is causing this behaviour?' asked Ragnar who stared intensely at the separatist Novices with his thick muscular arms folded tightly across his chest.

'Trauma I suspect. We each deal with the ramifications of battle in our own way.' he said. 'This is their chosen salvation, though I do not agree with it.'

'Fanatics are too literal.' replied Ragnar who clearly had no interest in elaborating the point.

'Agreed, though we have more pressing concerns.'
'Which are?'
'A complete lack of Aspirants.' he said whilst locking his gaze firmly with Ragnar's own.

'We will recruit more.' replied Ragnar sharply.

'I think that will be an extremely difficult task, in light of recent events brother.' he said. 'Nathaniel is a skilled teacher, however recruitment is not his strong point. Aleska may be able to help with recruitment in time, but we need to bolster our depleted numbers quickly.'

'You have a plan for this I am sure.' replied Ragnar, cocking a thick eyebrow with obvious intrigue.

'The Knights Thranis.'

'Bah, that lot. Where were they during the invasion?' said Ragnar vehemently. 'And besides, the Knights Thranis are even more fanatical than that lot over there!'

'Exactly my point.' he replied with a coy smile.

The Captain of The Blades was not renowned for his sharp mind, though Ragnar was invaluable in a fight and greatly inspired those around him in battle. He decided it best, therefore, to allow the idea to manifest in Ragnar's mind of its own volition, thus allowing the notion time to flourish of its own accord. Stating the obvious could inadvertently incite Ragnar's ire by appearing to belittle the Captain's political intellect. A short time passed as Ragnar considered his words intently.

'So you want to offer The Vengeful Tears to the Knights Thranis, in exchange for what...their loyalty?' replied Ragnar eventually.

'Correct. They need fresh stock of their own, and we would benefit greatly from restoring our alliance with them.' he explained. 'For too long the Knights Thranis have survived on the fringes of our society, their numbers slowly eroded due to their incessant hunting of the Ravnarkai. We need to reintegrate them with Freylar proper, else lose them entirely.'

'But you have tried to negotiate with them before Marcus, and what good has it done?' questioned Ragnar.

'True, but this time I do not propose a typical negotiation.' he said, before elaborating further. 'The Knights Thranis do not trust our generation Ragnar, for we are too closely linked to the sins of our predecessors. I need someone who they might look upon in a more favourable light to spend time amongst their kin.'

'And where would we find a suitable broker for such a task?' asked Ragnar.

Without uttering a word he extended his left arm directing it towards The Vengeful Tears, specifically towards Rayna who sparred fiercely against her peers under Nathaniel's watchful eye.

'Rayna?!' blurted Ragnar, who then quickly calmed his demeanour of his own accord as he contemplated the unorthodox choice of candidate.

'Still she spars with those beneath her station, despite her recent promotion. It is a sign of loyalty and respect, both of which are qualities sought after by the Knights Thranis.' he said. 'The Guardian is not like us brother. Rayna has a way with things which we do not. She speaks plainly, yet inoffensively. She has presence, and is respectful to others. She listens well to wise council, and is firm in her considered decision-making. Also Rayna is not native to Freylar, a fact that disassociates her entirely from those of our Order who have come before.'

Ragnar grunted several times whilst drawing the fingers and thumb of his right hand slowly across his long red beard. Ragnar's first encounter with The Guardian had been less than hospitable, though since agreeing to train Rayna, instructing her on the use of her ability, the

Captain's attitude towards the light bringer had mellowed considerably. One had to earn Ragnar's respect in person, preferably in the heat of battle, and Rayna had done exactly that using her boundless determination to succeed where others would likely have failed.

'I see the merit in your proposal.' the Captain replied thoughtfully after much deliberation, affirmed by further grunting. 'Let us hope Marcus, that this mad scheme of yours bears fruit.'

'Lothnar, know now that I will defeat you in that arena.'

Even now, whilst he and Krisis tracked their targets across the Narlakai borderlands, those words still echoed inside his head. It was not the words themselves which preyed on his mind, but rather the manner of their delivery. When she had first spoken the words to him there was no uncertainty in her proclamation; Rayna was unwavering and her statement resolute. It was exceptionally rare for a Paladin to be spoken to in such a manner, especially by one of lesser rank. It bothered him, like an itch incapable of being scratched. Aleska had encouraged him to provoke Rayna, thus expediting her development, having foreseen that The Guardian would aid him in releasing Alarielle from her wretched Narlakin imprisonment. Aleska's scrying of the future had indeed been accurate, though the aging scrier had omitted one significant detail; when Rayna released the soul stealer imprisoning his would-be lover, Alarielle's soul decided against moving on with the other Freylarkai prisoners released that cycle. Alarielle instead chose to return to her original body – now controlled by Rayna – content to take a back seat, therefore reintegrating with

Freylarkin society as a spectator only. Consequently Alarielle was no longer able to interact directly with the world around her, although she could still observe. Given that Rayna and Alarielle both shared the same body and were able to commune with one another, he presumed – rightly or wrongly – that Alarielle was now keenly aware of his feelings towards her. How then was he supposed to fight Rayna at the Trials? The Guardian had justifiably earned her title during the confrontation with the Narlakai at Scrier's Post, though in doing so had muddied his view of her. When Rayna first arrived in Freylar, he had contemptuously accused the interloper as being little more than a dishonourable body thief. He supposed in hindsight that he had needed someone to direct his grief towards in light of Alarielle's untimely release, but now everything had changed. What was once black and white in his mind had now become a gradient of confusion which he struggled to reconcile.

Distracted by endless spiralling thoughts, he had inadvertently allowed Krisis to get ahead of him once more; for a dire wolf Krisis was incredibly fleet-footed, and possessed an enviable amount of stamina. In order to maintain pace with his lupine companion, he made intermittent use of his wraith wings to close the gap between them. Krisis had picked up the scent of their targets with relative ease shortly after they passed Scrier's Post; the former sanctuary now looked even bleaker up close in the wake of the recent atrocities. Having acquired their scent, his instructions to Krisis were simple enough.

'*Find them!*'

For three cycles they had tracked the pair; in truth he had hoped to have located them already, however, Darlia had fled with her telepathic companion immediately after the battle for Scrier's Post, and thus enjoyed a two cycle head start. He incorrectly assumed that Darlia's retreat would have been severely handicapped by the wounded Freylarkin at her side. Despite their disadvantage, however, the fugitives had made good progress towards the borderlands, thus they continued to evade his detection. Regardless he and Krisis pressed on, determined to track down their targets. He carried with him a heavy burden, for he felt partly responsible for the ill fate visited upon those Blade Aspirants stationed at Scrier's Post. So it was that his need to corner Darlia and her renegade companion had evolved into a dangerous obsession. Although they had yet to determine Darlia's exact whereabouts, he felt sure they were close to their targets. Ragnar had insisted that he send an immediate report back to the Tri-Spires upon locating the exiled scrier and that no contact be made without support from The Blades; however, his growing obsession threatened to endanger such cautionary action. The thought of Krisis and himself charging Darlia's position bubbled fervently at the fore of his mind – he had all but convinced himself of the necessity for such an approach.

'I will end you.' he muttered, short of breath, as he continued to chase Krisis deeper into Narlakai territory.

'Marcus, Nathaniel informed me that you wish to speak with me.' she said, standing in the doorway to The Blade Lord's private quarters.

Marcus' quarters were overly modest. Except for a plain-looking writer's bench, there was little worth noting in the sparsely furnished chamber. Marcus had no interest in ostentatious accommodation; The Blade Lord was content simply to have a modicum of personal space to marshal his thoughts and a place to sleep at night. She admired the simplicity of his living arrangements; there were no distractions, thus Marcus' was able to focus keenly on what mattered. The continued security of Freylar was Marcus' primary raison d'être, all other concerns were secondary. Mirielle had charged Marcus with the responsibility of defending Freylar, a duty which he never once failed to uphold – though it was fair to say that recent events had shaken the Freylarkai nonetheless.

'You need not stand on ceremony Rayna. Come in please.' replied Marcus in his characteristically reassuring voice.

As she entered the room, Marcus turned his head away from the room's only window; he half sat across the window's sill offering her a warm smile. Marcus was extremely likable and had a way of reassuring those around him, yet despite his generally relaxed demeanour he still managed to maintain a commanding presence. In part this was due to his impressive height, well defined musculature and prominent facial features accentuated by his close shaved hair. His slate-grey eyes quickly made contact with her own before gazing deeply into her soul. The Blades held a deep-seated respected for Marcus and it was easy to understand why; The Blade Lord was both charming and pleasant, yet neither characteristic detracted from his supreme authority. Unsure where to stand in Marcus' presence and desperate to quell her nervous hands from fiddling aimlessly, she leant back against the writer's bench, planting her hands flat upon its smooth surface. Marcus' friendly smile widened further at her obvious awkwardness.

'That is the same position Ragnar favours. Are you after his job perchance Rayna?' asked Marcus playfully.

She immediately began to feel a little self-conscious following Marcus' friendly quip; she promptly straightened her back and placed her hands in her lap so as not to appear overly casual in his presence.

'Please, at ease Rayna. I did not invite you here to engage in social awkwardness.' Marcus said, clearly looking to put her at ease.

'Why did you invite me here Marcus, if I may ask?' she enquired curiously.

'Nathaniel pre-warned me several times that you ask a great many questions,' replied Marcus, who continued to tease her light-heartedly. 'But to answer your question I have an interesting mission for you, should you decide to accept it.'

'Mission?' she replied with mounting intrigue.

'You are a Blade Adept now Rayna, and The Guardian no less. I believe it is time that we take your development beyond the walls of the arena. Nathaniel can teach you much, though in order to reach the heights I believe you to be capable of achieving you need to broaden your learning. Mastering combat is only half of it. I need you to sharpen your strategic and political mind *if* you want that job?'

She considered Marcus' words and their implications, more so perhaps given the unexpected interest he seemed to exhibit towards her personal development. Although the prospect of a mission excited her, it would nonetheless draw her away from the arena; such action threatened to have a detrimental effect on her training regime during the run up to the Trials, where she was expected to face Lothnar. Marcus had mentioned the notion of broadening her learning; perhaps this was an opportunity not to be overlooked she wondered? Unwilling to commit either way without further information, she decided to press The Blade Lord on the matter, seeking further clarification.

'What exactly does this mission entail?' she enquired.

'Good, I see that I have piqued your interest.' he replied. 'Have you heard of the Knights Thranis?'

'I know little of them, other than that they are a separatist Order, having broken away from The Blades.' she replied. 'I gather they patrol the southern lands, hunting the Ravnarkai in an ongoing campaign to cull their numbers.'

'That is correct.' said Marcus shifting his body weight off the window sill before approaching her. 'Though to further elaborate, that hunt is part of their heritage. It is a long-standing tradition which extends back some three thousand passes. It is an integral part of their insular society, though I believe what was once duty has since grown into a fanatical obsession.'

'And is that your personal analysis of the Knights Thranis, or instead fact – if you don't mind me asking?'

Marcus laughed at her question, though the act itself was not a dismissive gesture. She realised the question was a bold one, and perhaps not best put to The Blade Lord. Regardless, she had no interest in dancing around the matter; if indeed she chose to accept The Blade Lord's unique offer, she would need to be apprised of the facts and not personal interpretations. She concluded from her own character assessment of Marcus that The Blade Lord was a Freylarkin capable of logical reasoning, and was therefore able to appreciate her question for what it was.

'My understanding of their Order is based solely on recorded history and behavioural observations from first-hand encounters.' replied Marcus plainly. 'Actually, I am glad that you asked the question; this mission requires a Freylarkin capable of separating truth from personal opinion. Specifically I require someone to spend time amongst the Knights Thranis. Moreover, I need said individual to earn their trust so that I can look to rebuild a relationship with them. Our Orders were allies once. I would see that state of affairs restored if at all possible.'

'But why now?' she asked, pressing her line of enquiry. 'Presumably this is not a new agenda?'

'Now is the right time Rayna.' replied Marcus. 'You witnessed first-hand what happened to the Aspirants at Scrier's Post, and the subsequent genesis of The Vengeful Tears. They have embarked on a path which we are unlikely to turn them from.'

She regarded The Blade Lord sternly as the pieces of the jigsaw slowly assembled themselves within her mind, revealing a more complex and elaborate undertaking. There was no denying Marcus' aptitude for strategic planning and political prowess; rather than tackle problems individually, Marcus had taken a step back from the minutia and had considered the Order's concerns in a wider context – The Blade Lord had cunningly found a means to resolve multiple issues simultaneously. Marcus' eyes widened with interest, as if to suggest that he saw the pieces in her mind slotting correctly into position.

'I see. The Vengeful Tears have become dangerous to our Order. Their ideals could potentially spread and take root in others of a similar disposition. You believe that their zealous behaviour would better suit the Order of the Knights Thranis. Furthermore providing a means to increase their dwindling numbers would likely cast The

Blades in a more favourable light, thus delivering the allies you desperately seek in order to shore up our own Order.' she surmised.

Marcus nodded slowly, applauding her assessment, whilst offering her another of his charming friendly smiles; the gesture confirmed the unerring accuracy of her analysis, based on the scraps of information he had deliberately served her. She had already won favour with both Ragnar and Nathanar, with perhaps even a small measure of respect from Lothnar, her greatest doubter. Although she was no sycophant, earning the respect of The Blade Lord would stand her in good stead amongst her peers, despite the bumpy nature of her arrival in Freylar.

'Though why not send a more senior member of The Blades to attempt such a gambit?' she continued, thinking aloud. 'I have no prior dealings with their Order.'

'And that is exactly what I require.' replied Marcus. 'The Knights Thranis are wary of my generation given that each of us served under my predecessor. You, however, are untainted in their eyes.'

'So my task would be to broker the restoration of an amicable relationship between both Orders, and in doing so establish a more suitable environment for The Vengeful Tears. Though what makes you think I can convince both parties to accept one another?'

'You need not convince them all. Take Anika with you, win her over and she will do the rest for you.'

'Marcus, have ever you considered that perhaps you are more dangerous than the Knights Thranis and The Vengeful Tears combined?' she replied, to which Marcus laughed heartily once more. 'Yet how does this negotiation aid me to develop my martial ability on the run up to the Trials?'

Marcus' demeanour suddenly changed; his face bore an expression of grave concern, 'Spend time amongst the Knights Thranis and you will embark on The Hunt. The Narlakai are nightmare horrors possessing little more than dull instinct, but the Ravnarkai...they are ravenous beasts, capable of tearing their prey apart. They know nothing of mercy and would eat you alive given the opportunity.'

'Delightful...so when do I start?' she asked jovially, looking to lighten the mood once more.

'You already have.' said Marcus smiling again.

'Rayna, are you sure you are ready for such a task?' murmured Alarielle from the depths of her soul.

'I *will* be ready.'

'Good. Both yourself and Anika had best start packing.' replied Marcus. 'Come the next cycle you will both commence your journey south.'

TWO
Burden

'Krashnar, open up!'

The battered makeshift stretcher bearing Lileah's wretched broken form lay crooked on the uneven ground beside her; given its hasty manufacture it was a miracle that the poorly constructed frame had remained intact during their crossing. The abhorrent fusion of bronze and flesh that was her left wrist throbbed painfully, yet without the strength of her prosthetic mechanical claw it would not have been possible to drag Lileah's prone body to Krashnar's hide. Lileah, splayed across the wooden stretcher, looked abnormally pale – as though disease had taken hold of the petite Freylarkin's damaged physique. On a good cycle Lileah typically looked gaunt and malnourished, now the body of her grievously wounded lover appeared as if its soul barely remained tethered to its decrepit physical anchor. The dead weight of the stretcher had taken its toll on her left arm; she struggled to raise her ornate claw as she sought to drive it into the rogue shaper's half-concealed door once again.

'Open up now!' she screamed, delirious from stress and exhaustion.

Even in her wildest dreams, she had never once imagined returning to Krashnar's hide. Just the sight of the familiar door to his horrid abode was enough to stir haunting memories of her past torture. Almost anything was preferable to the evil laying beyond that door, but she was desperate; there were no other options available to her. Lileah's soul clung on by a thread – her lover would not survive the extended journey to one of their more agreeable associates.

'Go away!' came a distant strained voice from behind the door. 'I told you never to return here!'

'Open this door now, else I will rip it from its moorings you callous bastard!'

She waited for a response from the exiled shaper, yet there was none. Krashnar's hide was well hidden within the cracked relief of the borderlands, though after spending so much time in the barren wilderness his presence had inevitably revealed itself to them. Their trained eyes knew well how to distinguish unusual occurrences dotted across the bleak landscape leading to Narlak – home to the Narlakai – and it was this ability which had enabled them to discover Krashnar's lair many passes ago. Her previous visit to Krashnar's hide had scarred her mind indefinitely; the nightmare memory, made manifest in the form of her ghastly flesh-metal replacement hand, made it easy for her to recall the location of the rogue shaper's abode. Krashnar was also a creature of habit, unlikely therefore to relocate his base of operations simply because others of his kind had stumbled across his location.

'Open up now else I will inform The Blades of your whereabouts, and the illicit activities it conceals!' she said vehemently as her choler began to rise.

Immediately she heard the sound of a great many locks frantically being opened; she had clearly struck a nerve, thus acquiring her unwilling benefactor's attention. The door before her swung open revealing a lanky, dishevelled Freylarkin, seemingly incapable of standing fully upright. The odd-looking shaper had long brown unkempt hair that obscured most of his face, and a crazed look about him.

Krashnar had the same pupil-less eyes as Freylar's queen, Mirielle, though his were black like polished obsidian orbs. Gazing into the shaper's eyes was like staring into a sinister black void, one which threatened to devour her soul.

Krashnar was shaking badly and from his body language she could tell that he appeared to be paranoid about something; the shaper's head twitched constantly, left and right, as he nervously surveyed the rugged landscape behind her.

'Why are you here?!' rasped the wild-looking shaper.

'Release comes for her Krashnar!' she replied, inclining her head towards Lileah's pallid prone form.

Krashnar observed her fading lover with his cold abyssal eyes; they gave nothing away regarding his visual assessment of Lileah's rapidly deteriorating condition.

'So why bring her here then? Do I look like a renewalist to you!?' replied Krashnar coldly, abruptly trying to close his door on her.

Before the uncaring shaper could seal the door tight, she drove her claw into the diminishing gap between the door and its frame, causing wood to splinter from both. She felt nothing as the faded heavy wooden door sought in vain to crush her bronze mechanical hand.

'Leave me alone!' rasped Krashnar, clearly frustrated by her action.

'Surely you can do something for her?' she implored desperately, 'You helped me, did you not?'

'Did I?!' he replied opening the door fully once more, realising now the missed opportunity to close it. 'Look at you Darlia, and what you have become – a monster...'

'And what of your own grotesque appearance Krashnar – who are you to label me such?' she replied tersely.

'I am your demon creator!' Krashnar rasped once more. 'When last we parted your lack of gratitude was boundless! Why is it then that you come here Darlia, seeking my services yet again?'

'Because I must, do you not see?' she replied as tears began to well in her eyes. 'Who else am I to turn to in this accursed wasteland?'

'Then you would have me mutilate her – is that what you want?' hissed Krashnar.

'No – I would have you save her!'

'Aren't you going to wish me good luck?' echoed a familiar voice from her left across the large study hall.

She turned immediately from her books and looked down the length of the long thick wooden bench at which she sat. Beyond the bench, at the far end of the empty study hall, stood Rayna with an infectious childlike smile stretched across her face; the recent invasion of Freylar and the horrors of Scrier's Post seemingly had little or no effect on the dogged light bringer's personality. Instinctively she offered Rayna a warm smile of her own. It was then that she suddenly recalled the time when nightmares, born from the grubby repressed memories of a previous life, first began to plague Rayna's subconscious. The revisited horrors of Rayna's former existence threatened to steer The Guardian down a dark path, one leading to overwhelming despair. Yet despite the relentless subconscious attacks on Rayna's psyche, the relatively new-born Freylarkin endured the continued assault and eventually emerged stronger in spite of the ordeal. She admired Rayna's unyielding determination to overcome such challenges and wished that she could say the same of The Vengeful Tears; instead they had lost their way, choosing to embrace fanaticism as a survival mechanism. Thanks to her position on the ruling council she had been privy to Nathanar's raw account of the events at Scrier's Post, thus she was not limited to those carefully depicted events in the official report which he had submitted as commander of the rearguard. Initially she had toyed with the idea of scrying those horrible past events, but after hearing Nathanar's stark retelling she decided it best not to burden herself with such sorrow.

Rayna strode confidently across the sparsely furnished hall and promptly sat down opposite her at the wide study bench she had chosen that morning. Rayna playfully pushed her books to one side, temporarily putting an end to her studies.

'I have not seen you in several cycles Kirika.' said Rayna. 'Is something the matter?'

'You still manage to confuse me with your bizarre choice of words.' she replied, all too analytically. 'Though in answer to your oddly phrased question, I felt sure that you would not wish to see me in light of recent events.'

Rayna frowned momentarily, with a brief look of disapproval, before reverting to her characteristically casual, even playful, demeanour.

'Look here...you are not your sister, and you are sure as hell not responsible, or indeed accountable, for her actions.'

'And yet I *do* feel accountable for Darlia's transgressions.' she replied. 'Though I had never sought to be such, I often felt that Darlia viewed me as a hurdle blocking the path towards her own success. I am convinced that my sister felt the need to push her ability to dangerous levels in order to surpass my own.'

'Oh my, so you're camped out here, alone with your dusty books, wallowing in self-pity and needlessly blaming yourself because of a sibling rivalry?' Rayna said, clearly goading her on the matter.

She scowled at her interrogator; it was the first time she had exorcised displeasure towards her surrogate sister since Rayna's arrival in Freylar. Rather than taking offence at her obvious displeasure, Rayna instead beamed once more as though believing with supreme confidence that an infectious smile would soften the blow – which it inevitably did.

'How do you do that?' she replied, after her scowl had abated. 'You insult me one moment, and then the next wash away any negative lasting ramifications with a light heart.'

Rayna simply laughed. The Guardian's ability to cut to the heart of any matter was but one of many enviable skills in Rayna's arsenal. Since her mentor, Aleska, recently retired from active service on the ruling council, she had made a secret pact with herself to become more assertive, thereby reinforcing her role as council member despite her young age. Darlia's re-emergence, however, had been a setback in her personal development; she had allowed her estranged sister's vendetta to tar her own image needlessly. Rayna was correct in her counsel; she was not Darlia, and indeed not accountable for the abhorrent behaviour of her blood-born sister.

'Look, I'm leaving soon, as I'm sure you are aware.' noted Rayna after laughing at her expense.

'Yes. You are going to be spending some time with the Knights Thranis, so I hear.' she replied.

'Indeed, I shall be spending time amongst them.' confirmed Rayna. 'Marcus has asked that I take Anika with me, and I do not wish to leave the vale with other concerns preying on my mind. I need to know that you will get past this, sister, and move on before I set out for the unknown.'

'Do not worry about me and my personal insecurities.' she replied. 'As of now I will attempt to no longer burden myself with my sisters' actions. Whilst I cannot vouch for my future success in this endeavour...it is a start at least.'

With that she stood up and proceeded to gather up the books Rayna had pushed aside. It was time she fulfilled her secret pact, rather than repeatedly doubting herself.

'Since you came all the way to see me, you may as well put yourself to use and help me file these books away.' she said with a beaming smile of her own.

Rayna returned the smile along with a casual wink. After tending to her books, both then left the deserted study hall behind them; it was time now to abandon her self-imposed shackles and move forwards, forging a fresh chapter in her life. Though Darlia remained an ever-present concern, it would no longer be one she would allow to hold her back.

After leaving the Tri-Spires' cold study hall behind them, she accompanied Rayna down into the heart of the vale, home to Freylar's forest dwellers. Rayna had insisted that they spend the afternoon together, given the early departure with Anika the following cycle; it would be some time before both would return from their mission, and so she was pleased to spend what little time remained with Rayna prior to her departure. Although Queen Mirielle had tasked her with overseeing Rayna's integration with Freylarkin society, she did not perceive the task to be a mission as such. She enjoyed spending time with Rayna, and this in turn had wrought a positive outcome on her own personality.

They strolled aimlessly through the forest, content to converse and share each other's company whilst they immersed themselves in the half-hidden community established by the forest dwellers. It was easy to overlook the important role played by the common folk of Freylar, when ensconced within in the Tri-Spires attending to matters of state. The change of pace was refreshing and allowed her to partially reintegrate with the natives, albeit temporarily. Their random path through the forest took them past several outdoor classes where younger generations paid strict attention to the wise teachings of their elders; that was at least until The Guardian was spotted. It became apparent to her that Rayna had become somewhat of a celebrity amongst the locals, especially in the eyes of the youth, though it was unclear exactly how much the forest dwellers understood of The Guardian's origin and the revelation heralded by Rayna's unique means of arrival in Freylar. Upon reflection, she decided that she was over-analysing affairs; regardless of their collective level of true understanding, most of the forest dwellers appeared to welcome Rayna's presence amongst them and that was ultimately the desired outcome of Mirielle's planned integration. Initially the fear was that Rayna's unorthodox presence would incite fear and panic amongst the Freylarkai, fortunately none of that had come to pass.

As they continued to watch the various outdoor sermons, her thoughts shifted to those of Aleska. She had not spoken with – or indeed seen – her former mentor since Aleska recently retired from both The Blades and the ruling council of Freylar. There had been an official ceremony to mark the occasion, which had both celebrated Aleska's service to Freylar and Nathanar's ascension to the rank of Paladin. To the best of her knowledge, Aleska had made no retirement plans. Presumably therefore, her former mentor was open to new possibilities in order to curb the likely boredom of official retirement. She could well imagine the venerable Freylarkin instructing the youth of Freylar, imparting vast oceans of knowledge to those yet to make their mark on the domain. She made a mental note to raise the notion with Aleska during their next early morning rendezvous, however, given that Aleska had uncharacteristically missed their last engagement, she wondered when exactly that would be.

'Over there! The Guardian!' cried an unexpected voice from one of Rayna's youthful onlookers.

'Oh no...I fear that we've lingered here too long.' noted Rayna bashfully.

'Come now, you cannot deny your youngest fans the opportunity to meet The Guardian.' she teased playfully.

'*Go on, it will be fun.*'

'Not you as well...' said Rayna.

Rather peculiarly Rayna's comment seemed directed at someone else, as though another was privy to their conversation.

'Guardian, Guardian, Guardian, Guardian...' came the sound of Rayna's hastily assembled audience.

'I fear that if you do not appease them, they could potentially turn nasty.' she continued to tease. 'I doubt that even you could handle that little lot.'

Rayna half grumbled an incomprehensible word – entirely beyond her understanding – before reluctantly descending the bank upon which they stood, towards the eager class awaiting them. Like small insects scattering before a larger presence, the children hurriedly reordered themselves into a makeshift crescent-shaped amphitheatre; the smallest amongst them kneeled in the front row, those directly behind sat on hastily repositioned wooden stools whist the taller members chose to stand at the back of the congregation alongside their tutors. Everyone, it seemed, was keen to get a good look at The Guardian up close, as she gingerly took up position before the growing throng which was now drawing the presence of several other inquisitive Freylarkai within earshot.

'Right, well...err...I cannot address you all without the presence of my good friend Kirika.' said Rayna, who then beckoned her to come forth with an outstretched hand.

'Kirika, Kirika, Kirika, Kirika...' chanted the insistent children who yearned to discover more about their enigmatic saviour.

She supposed that in hindsight she had been the architect of her own demise, which was rather ironic considering her ability to scry. Regardless there would be no denying what was now their shared audience, and thus she too reluctantly stood before their captivated onlookers with a well-practiced smile.

'What goes around, comes around.' Rayna quietly whispered into her ear.

'You have not left the vale...yet.' she whispered in return, unsure how to back up her hollow threat.

Both had been unwittingly drawn into a tricky interrogation, courtesy of their own childish behaviour, though it was a small price considering the excited and expectant faces before them.

'So then, where shall we start?' Rayna asked openly.

A cacophony of sound broke out across their gathered audience as each excited member struggled to voice their question over their raucous peers. Quickly realising the error, Rayna sought in vain to calm the over-enthusiastic crowd; the presence of The Guardian only excited their audience further. Seizing the initiative, she stepped forwards, deciding to take the first few steps on the path to bolstering her own self-confidence. She thrust her arms into the air then slowly lowered them, bringing her right index finger vertically towards her lips. At once the crowd settled down, quickly realising the merit of her actions and the need to restore order.

'If you have a question then raise your hand, and may I ask that you all patiently wait your turn.' she said with a new-found sense of authority more befitting of her role.

A sea of hands rose immediately before them. Without any real thought, she selected one instinctively, hoping to be seen as expressing no favouritism towards any one Freylarkin in particular. With barely-contained excitement, the chosen Freylarkin immediately fired off their question.

'Is it true you destroyed a whole legion of Narlakai?'

Rayna laughed politely before attempting to provide a measured response to the overly-generous assumption. 'Not entirely, and certainly not by myself, though we were significantly outnumbered during the assault on Scrier's Post.'

Keen to prevent Rayna from getting bogged down in the minutiae, she quickly asked the audience to raise their hands once more. Again, she instinctively selected another member of the audience – this time a young Freylarkin from the front row.

'My father told me that you sent the Narlakai home with your powerful light magic.'

'Did he now...? Well it wasn't just me,' replied Rayna, politely responding to the young Freylarkin's malformed question. 'I had the rest of The Blades to aid me, including some who are sadly no longer entirely with us.'

Rayna's choice of words seemed strange – to her at least – though one could argue that The Guardian exhibited many alien mannerisms when directly compared to Freylar's native population. Regardless, she quickly selected another candidate, seeking to maintain the rapid flow of questions and answers. This time she selected an older member of the audience.

'What was it like being a Sky-Walker?'

'Please excuse me. I am not sure that I heard you correctly. Sky-Walker?' replied Rayna.

'I heard that you came from up there, where the Sky-Walkers watch over us.' clarified the youth, who pointed directly towards the sky, which was just visible through a hole in the dense canopy above.

'Err...I see.'

Rayna was clearly thrown a little off guard by the leading question, especially coming from one so young. Mirielle had foretold the scenario unfolding before them when Rayna was first brought to the attention of their queen. The hope had been that the gradual dissemination of the facts regarding Rayna's arrival would soften their inevitable blow; it seemed they were about to test that theory.

'Well...it was certainly different.' replied Rayna, following the statement with a wide smile. 'What specifically would you like to know?'

Rayna had effectively thrown the question back to the audience for further refinement; it was a skilful means of avoiding the obvious trap of disclosing too much information whilst trying to satisfy an open-ended question. By forcing the children to narrow down their line of enquiry, it meant that Rayna only needed to focus on answers to questions which the audience could conceive, and thus more likely comprehend. Following Rayna's lead, she quickly selected another hand, once again from the front row.

'Are you able to fly higher than the clouds?'

'The Sky-Walkers live in a domain well beyond the reach of Freylar. The inhabitants of that domain all walk.' explained Rayna.

Quickly she selected another raised hand in a bid to shield Rayna from becoming bogged down with incomprehensible detail.

'Why did you leave?'

'I chose to come here...to help defend Freylar against the Narlakai invasion.' replied Rayna.

'Do you have friends back home?'

'Indeed I do...one of them is called Trix, however, Freylar is my home now.'

The latest response from the reluctant celebrity caused much discussion to break out amongst their audience. Clearly excited and overwhelmed by the unequivocal information directly imparted to them, members of the audience quickly began conversing amongst themselves as each discussed and digested The Guardian's words with great fascination. They had reached a natural pause in the questions and answers session, thus she decided to capitalise on the reprieve by politely excusing themselves.

'I am afraid that we have overstayed our time here and must be getting on now.' she said raising her voice enough to cut through the rapture of their audience.'

'Guardian...will you visit us again?' cried one of the children.

'Of course I will.' replied Rayna earnestly.

'Promise!'

'Oh, it's a promise.'

With the session formally concluded, they both promptly withdrew from the sound of cheers and clapping hands. They climbed back up the slope towards the top of the bank overlooking the class whilst its tutors struggled to regain control over the pupils. Their presence – more so Rayna's admittedly – had caused bedlam, though in a positive and uplifting way. Leading questions aside she felt that the session went exceptionally well, indeed far surpassing her own lofty expectations for such an impromptu interrogation.

'Well that went rather well, do you not think?' she said turning her head towards Rayna as they resumed their stroll through the forest.

'You mean the chaos behind us?' replied Rayna with a subtle hint of sarcasm.

'Come now, it was a success.' she replied. 'Now we can let them do the remainder of the work for us. By the next cycle half of the forest will know everything that was said here and you will be journey-bound for the Knights Thranis.'

'But what if I've doomed Nathaniel to a deluge of paparazzi in my absence?' questioned Rayna.

'Firstly, I do not know the meaning of this paparazzi of which you speak.' she replied. 'And secondly, Nathaniel can take care of himself. Besides, he is already renowned in these parts.'

'Fame...how I loathe that word.' replied Rayna, sighing heavily.

'Sister dearest, popularity is a useful tool. You would be wise not to run from it, or worse shun its existence entirely.' she said, attempting to impart her counsel on the matter. 'Popularity is a double-edge sword; it can easily evolve into quite the opposite if disregarded.'

'You mean I should give them what they want?' enquired Rayna.

'To an extent yes, though just enough to sate their appetites.'

Rayna considered the point for what seemed like the remainder of their meandering; eventually they rounded on Nathaniel's tree, which promptly concluded their stroll. The light was starting to fade as the late afternoon sun sunk lower in the sky, hindering its ability to penetrate the dense canopy of the forest. As expected Nathaniel was nowhere to be seen, implying that The Teacher had yet to return from the arena. She was about to break their shared silence by imparting a fond farewell, though it was Rayna who ultimately spoke first.

'Very well, I will humour them.' said Rayna turning towards her, before casually leaning against Nathaniel's tree with arms folded. 'I see your logic Kirika, though it is not my desire to become a public spectacle.'

'I understand sister and I am glad that you will ease their understanding, still...none of that is important now.' she replied. 'You are about to write a new chapter, post your rebirth. Ensure that you keep your wits about you as you travel south, and remain ever alert in the presence of the Knights Thranis.'

Rayna smiled before bringing their inevitable farewell to an end, 'So then...will you now wish me good luck?'

She winked playfully then kissed Rayna lightly on the cheek.

'Good luck, Guardian!

THREE
Hide

Three weeks had passed since the government controversially voted in its initiative to relocate the Shadow class; officially the contentious policy had been called the Exodus, however, the Shadow class referred to the programme of blatant targeted human cleansing with a more apt name – the Rout. Thus far he had managed to evade the Peacekeeper patrols tasked with escorting the Shadow class out of the metropolis. Although some of the law enforcers had swept the outer perimeter of the Wild, none had ventured into the heart of the metropolis' urban wilderness. Prior to the Rout, his fellow Shadow class members had labelled him the fool when first he declared his intent to forge a home in the Wild. Now that foolish decision was the only thing keeping him beyond the reach of the Peacekeepers. It grieved him knowing that he was unable to convince his kin to disperse and go to ground throughout the metropolis, thereby masking their true numbers. It was inevitable that those in power would eventually perceive the visibly growing number of Shadow class members as a threat; that eventuality was now being played out across a grand stage, with the government successfully curtailing their numbers. The media – as well as other controlled sources of information – reported that the Shadow class was being escorted to a new district, well beyond the metropolis' perimeter, where its members could start over; the reality – he suspected – entailed a far more sinister fate.

The air temperature had dropped noticeably over the recent weeks, signalling the inevitable arrival of autumn. Having spent the last couple of years learning to survive in the Wild, he knew well that the winter months to come would be bitter and unforgiving. Food sources would become scarce and the extreme cold would be his greatest adversary; there had been many nights when the reaper sent its cold chill to test him. Despite the bleak forecast, there was every chance that the incessant patrols restricting his movements to the Wild would peter out before the onset of winter. What remained of humanity had become comfortable, holed up in its utopian dwellings. With the obvious exception of his kin, the metropolis' inhabitants had their wants and needs catered for by their semi-automated urban host. There was no longer a need for humanity to endure adversity and suffering, in fact the Middle and Apex classes had lost all notion of the concepts. It was likely, therefore, that there would be no appetite for Peacekeeper patrols to conduct their operations in the cold. Besides, by his count there were precious few members of the Shadow class currently remaining in the metropolis; the government could not realistically continue to impose its curfews and run its campaign of Peacekeeper patrols once his kind had been visibly swept from the streets. Those savvy enough amongst his kin would go to ground; they would wait out what was essentially a siege on their way of life.

  The crisp autumnal night sky was absent of any cloud cover, allowing the moon to shine brightly, bathing the landscape in its milky silver light. He quietly pulled back the Perspex roof of his hide to better observe the night sky. The hide itself was little more than a wide hole which he had excavated during his time spent in the Wild. The shelter was by far the preferred of his numerous hideouts, all of which were strategically concealed throughout the artificial wilderness. He enjoyed sleeping in the hole; it offered excellent protection against the elements – the wind in particular – and retained at least some heat. The roof of the hide was camouflaged with an abundance of local flora, which had grown naturally across its surface with time. Although the roof was – for the most part – fixed in place, there remained one small section which could be slid back and forth, allowing him easy access in and out of the subterranean bolt-hole. Casting his gaze towards the sky, he picked out constellations recognisable to him courtesy of his books; although technically they were on long term loan from Kaitlin's library, he sincerely doubted that his literary benefactor would ask for their return. Captivated by their simple beauty, he lost himself in the vast ocean of the cosmos as his gaze languidly drifted from one constellation to the next. Andromeda, Pegasus, Aquarius, Pisces; all were visible in their natural splendour. The continuous advance of technology had introduced the world to countless wondrous new phenomena, yet none as beautiful as the stars above – in his opinion at least.

As his gaze drifted once more, this time in search of Capricornus, a sharp cracking sound echoed through the still night air. Instinctively he flinched before turning his head, directing his wide eyed stare towards the source of the sound, trying to discern its origin. The sound was reminiscent of dry wood cracking under foot – perhaps a natural predator had picked up his scent and had come to investigate the source. Worse still, had the Peacekeepers tracked him back to his hide? The light from the moon illuminated numerous shapes on the near horizon as he peered intently into the void. His trained eyes swept the landscape, picking out all manner of flora and fauna partially lit by the moon's unobscured presence. In the distance he rapidly picked out a shape clinging to the base of a thick tree. The outline of the object was foreign, suggesting the presence of something not native to the Wild. The shape moved abruptly, pushing itself away from the tree it had been using to brace itself. As it continued to move noisily towards his position, more dried branches cracked beneath its tread, causing it to stumble. As the shape began to near, its true form quickly became apparent; the shape was humanoid, much to his despair. Better to have been an animal, which would have made his situation far less complicated. At least it was not an approaching Peacekeeper, of that he was certain – the unwitting invader was clearly not comfortable with physical activity and lacked perception in low light. He briefly considered sliding the access panel to his hide shut, and waiting out the encounter, but his insatiable curiosity would not allow it. Common sense prevailing at last, he quickly grabbed a baton from the cluttered possessions strewn throughout the hide, before seeking a closer glimpse of his quarry. Deftly he crawled out of his hole, then quietly slid its access panel shut before stealthily embarking on a flanking manoeuvre towards his target.

Silently he approached from the left of his target, which continued to struggle to navigate the Wild's dimly-lit woodland. His heart pounded heavily in his chest, and he could feel a knot in the pit of his stomach. His muscles tensed up, causing him to clutch the baton tightly in his right hand; the weapon had been lifted from an isolated Peacekeeper prior to the Rout, whilst the negligent law enforcement officer answered nature's call. The weapon was his now, and one he was very much familiar with.

Advancing ever closer he readied the baton, choosing to hold it low by his side. His target continued to fumble awkwardly before him, seemingly remaining oblivious to his advance. Deciding it best to mitigate the risk of being detected, he quietly scraped up some earthy detritus from the forest floor and hurled the contents of his hand beyond the human silhouette; the loose mud and bark impacted noisily with the forest floor. Predictably his target turned to investigate the sound, providing him with the opportunity he sought. He tried to calm his nerves, before following up on his cheap trick, but the attempt was futile. Empowered by the rush of adrenaline now flooding his system, he suddenly leapt forwards, rapidly closing the remaining distance. With a single forceful swing of the baton, he contacted the back of his target's left leg behind its vulnerable knee joint. He followed through with the swing, using the momentum to pull the leg upwards. The silhouette let out an audible yelp and immediately fell to the ground awkwardly with a bass thud, landing in a crumpled heap. The prone victim immediately reached with both hands to instinctively clutch their battered leg. He dropped to the forest floor and pressed the length of the baton against the windpipe of his wounded prey.

'Who are you?' he demanded aggressively in a hushed tone.

Despite the low light, he could now partially make out the prominent features of his victim, who writhed in pain; a hard jaw line and thick eyebrows suggested his prey was male, though larger in build compared to his own physique.

'Who are you!?' he repeated angrily, pressing the baton harder against the throat of his victim.

'I'm like you!' rasped a strained voice in response to his harsh interrogation.

'Like me how?' he shot back.

'Shadow class!' rasped the voice once again, 'I can't...breathe...'

Easing his weight off the baton slightly, he pressed his victim for further information, unwilling to yield his advantage so easily.

'Prove it!'

'My arm, check my right arm.'

He adjusted his grip on the baton so that he could free his left arm, then hurriedly he pushed back the sleeve of his victim's right arm. The weak light of the moon was enough to pick out an ugly fresh scar running down the forearm, suggesting the hasty removal of a bio-key; this was the signature work of the Shadow class – he bore the same mark.

'Can you walk?' he asked, this time in a calmer manner.

'I don't think so. You messed up my leg pretty good.'

'Here, let me help you.' he replied, extending his right arm.

He hauled the stranger's dead weight upright, pulling their left arm across the back of his shoulder so that he could act as a human crutch. Working together he slowly guided their way back towards his hide, albeit noisily – his new found companion was clearly unable to take a knock and moaned incessantly with each ragged step they took.

'Shut up and keep quiet, else you will bring us unwanted attention.' he snapped.

'You brought this on yourself!' his companion shot back in return.

'You were already groping around in the dark with all the grace of an intoxicated street urchin! It's a miracle the Peacekeepers didn't follow you here, what with the ruckus you were making.' he retorted. 'Now shut up, and get moving!'

With renewed vigour they made their way quickly back to his hide. He slid back the roof's access panel and unceremoniously pushed his injured companion – who moaned loudly in protest – head first down into the hole. He quickly followed suit, before sealing the access panel tightly shut behind them. The hole was cramped with the two of them present, making it a challenge to locate a glow-tube amongst his scattered possessions in the dark. Eventually he laid his hands on one of the translucent acrylic cylinders; he shook the tube vigorously causing its contents to react. Green light began to emanate from the tube, affording him the first proper glimpse of his unexpected bunkmate. His new lodger had a larger build – compared to his own – likely due to lack of exercise, as opposed to actual overeating. He also had longish dark greasy hair, which reflected the weak light of the glow-tube, and smooth pale skin.

'Who are you?' he questioned whilst studying the fresh face opposite him.

'You mean aside from the person you just assaulted?'

'No, I mean your name you noisy idiot. What's your name?'

'Very well, since you asked so politely. My name is Austin, though people usually call me Trix.'

It was early – too early his students would say. Given his own decision to follow a routine morning commute to the arena, setting out prior to first light had become a necessity; he would not have his students arriving before himself, and he had no desire to live within the confines of the Tri-Spires. Besides, he rather enjoyed his morning hikes since they afforded him the time required to properly digest and consider current affairs and their potential implications. There had been a significant amount of change in his life lately; the loss of his daughter, Rayna's arrival, the Narlakai invasion, Lothnar's impending challenge and now the issue of The Vengeful Tears. His solitary commute to the arena allowed him to reflect on these events. Losing The Vengeful Tears had been hard to stomach. He had spent much time furthering their development and honing their skills, yet now they had unnaturally distanced themselves from him. Their shared ordeal at Scrier's Post had wrought deep festering wounds upon their souls. Physical damage he could deal with – being a master renewalist – though damage to the mind was not something he had experience with. He felt helpless, completely unable to aid his students when they needed it most. It was a feeling he loathed, and one which he had not experienced on such a scale before. Whilst it was not uncommon for individuals to drift from the core ideals of the Order, or indeed abandon it entirely, the masked sorrow which ailed The Vengeful Tears had become more like an infection. Regrettably, thus far The Blades had been unable to cure the infection; it now needed to be cut out before it could further spread. Whilst he understood and accepted Marcus' ploy to transfer his troubled students to the Knights Thranis, he desperately wished for a way to bring his students back.

The world outside was only dimly lit by the first of the sun's rays; he slowly consumed a large chunk of bread, accompanied by a bowl of assorted berries, as he gazed absentmindedly through the small window of the downstairs living space whilst he ate, watching the young light seep through the forest's thick canopy. His mind was flooded with thoughts, and yet he seemed unable to latch onto a single one. Aleska had advised him, on numerous occasions, to take some time out from the arena; perhaps a break would serve him well and maybe even help to restore his concentration. With Rayna's imminent departure, and no Aspirants currently pending induction into the ranks of The Blades, the timing for a brief vacation was opportune; maybe he would take time off after all, he mused. With all the other thoughts fighting for his attention, the notion was quickly lost in the maelstrom of his mind as he became distracted by tired footsteps gently plodding down the tree's spiral stairwell. He turned to investigate the sound, only to see Rayna half asleep at the bottom of the stairwell.

'Ah, the sleeper has awakened.' he teased as Rayna directed her tired body lethargically towards him.

'What, may I ask happened to you?' he enquired as Rayna rubbed encrusted rheum from her bleary eyes.

'Oh that wretched former life of mine, that's what happened.' replied Rayna wearily.

'Your memories are haunting you again, are they?' he replied in a more serious tone.

'It would appear that I'm now ready to learn of some fresh new horror from my past...as if I didn't have enough on my plate.'

'Although clearly frustrating, your mind is presumably trying to commune something of import; a significant event which you subconsciously chose to forget.' he offered impartially.

'But to what end Nathaniel?' questioned Rayna irritably. 'I don't sleep, they're going to freak Alarielle out and besides, that life is beyond my reach now.'

He laughed involuntarily at Rayna's agitated words.

'How is this funny Nathaniel?'

'It is not.' he replied. 'Your concern for my daughter's soul is admirable, but Alarielle will cope with your demons rather effortlessly I should imagine – given she was previously trapped inside a Narlakin. And besides, you do not have the luxury of time to sleep.'

Rayna's sluggish state of being took a moment to fully digest his words, only then did she recognise his familiar good-natured dry banter.

'Not funny Nathaniel.' replied Rayna grumpily, narrowing her eyes to slits.

'Your former life may well now be beyond your grasp, but that does not mean that you cannot learn from the experience.' he replied. 'Adversity can teach us many important lessons. Forging a better tomorrow requires understanding of the past. Do not see your dreams as an adversary, but instead an ally.'

Rayna rubbed her eyes once again then dragged her left hand across her face, fingers splayed, trying to brush aside the last of the last cobwebs clinging to her mind.

'Nathaniel, it's too early for your sermons.'

He laughed heartily at her offhand remark, though he knew Rayna well enough now to know that she would at least consider his words regardless of her tired and grumpy demeanour. Rayna had numerous challenges ahead of her, therefore he could very well appreciate her frustration due to lack of sleep. Before he could return her mild retort with a witty quip and one of his customary wry grins, there came a firm double knock from the narrow wooden door of their tree.

'Come in!' he said aloud.

The door immediately swung open revealing Anika who promptly greeted them with the same cold, distant formality that was characteristic of The Vengeful Tears.

'Teacher, Guardian,' said Anika, nodding respectfully. 'I trust you are both well?'

'Anika, lighten up will you?' said Rayna abruptly. 'This isn't the arena.'

Anika appeared somewhat caught off guard by Rayna's remark; it took a few moments for the young Freylarkin to compose herself.

'No it is not, though we are to be formal representatives of The Blades during our mission are we not?' Anika replied factually.

Rayna groaned audibly, whilst rolling her eyes in response to Anika's dry understanding of the facts.

'Indeed we shall, but at this rate I will be a thoroughly bored representative after our journey together.' noted Rayna, regaining some of her customary joviality. 'Where is the spritely young Freylarkin I once knew?' she queried, favouring Anika with a playful wink.

Anika fidgeted uncomfortably, unable to look either of them in the eye, then brushed aside Rayna's question entirely.

'We need to leave shortly if we are to beat sundown. The journey will take most of the cycle.'

He hated seeing Anika this way; devoted entirely to the Order with little or no time, or indeed desire, to engage in non-essential social interaction with her brothers and sisters. Anika's soul had hidden itself from sight behind a distant cold façade, unwilling to open itself up to others. He knew that deep down Anika was hurting from her ordeal; seeing so many of her fellow Aspirants laid low had embittered her good nature. The once spritely and enthusiastic young Blade Aspirant had become entirely consumed with notions of duty and revenge. Anika no longer cared for a life outside the Order; her life *was* the Order and those who opposed it would meet her festering wrath. Despite realising the cause of Anika's plight, he was unable to assist his fading student. He lacked the skills to break down the barrier which had rapidly formed between them. The destruction of war habitually left casualties in its wake; it saddened him deeply seeing his former Aspirants reduced to such a state.

'It is probably best that you both get going.' he said, realising the futility of Rayna's attempts to goad Anika into opening up.

'Very well. Try not to get too bored without us.' replied Rayna, along with another wink of her right eye.

'No doubt that will be a challenge.' he replied with one of his wry grins. 'Do not underestimate the challenges you will each face, and remember your combat training. I expect you both to represent The Blades favourably.'

'Yes Teacher.' Anika replied diligently.

Rayna groaned once more before responding to his request herself. 'Sure thing – provided I get some sleep.'

She watched with disgust as Krashnar carelessly poked and prodded Lileah's prone body throughout the night. Together they had pulled Lileah from the battered stretcher and laid her ruined body across one of Krashnar's thick wooden work benches within his workshop. Unlike Mirielle's chamber, which was filled with wondrous constructs that existed in harmony with their surroundings, Krashnar's own warped creations where twisted and dark; they were ugly things that were entirely unnatural in appearance. Seeing the disturbing constructs dotted around the maleficent shaper's workshop reminded her of the reason for his public exile – Mirielle had decreed that the controversial shaper be exiled due to his unwavering obsession with the darker, lesser practiced, facet of shaping which had been prohibited across the domain. Like her, Krashnar desired to push his ability in each and every direction, however, some areas of his work were deemed too uncomfortable for public consumption. When asked to curtail his experiments, Krashnar openly refused to do so and was thus exiled from Freylar.

'Why is it that you did not foresee this wretched mess Darlia?' asked the twisted shaper in a rasping voice.

'That bitch Alarielle, or whatever foreign force commands her renewed being. The thing eludes my scrying for it has no clear destiny.'

Krashnar laughed sardonically with his rough, cracked voice. Clearly the hermit knew more than she, despite living on the fringe of society and cut off from any social interaction with his former kin.

'And you find this amusing...why?!' she sneered in return.

'Because you proclaim to see everything, and yet you do not!' Krashnar shot back. 'Even an outcast wretch like me has heard talk of The Guardian.'

The condescending remark spiked her anger uncontrollably. Without any conscious thought she drove her claw towards the side of Krashnar's throat, forcing him towards the nearest wall. The sharp blades of her demonic claw dug into the wall, causing stone chippings to explode outwards from the rough surface. Some of the fragments caught Krashnar's left eye, causing him to wince in pain as he stood tightly pinned against the wall by the deadly embrace of her mechanical prosthetic claw.

'What is she?!' she screamed, barely able to contain her desire to end the wretch.

'The better question would be who.' Krashnar sneered in return, clearly unfazed by the threat of release.

'Who then?! Speak now worm or I shall indulge in some shaping of my own!' she demanded angrily.

Krashnar tried hard to turn his head to spit in her direction, however, realising the futility of his action he instead chose to slaver onto one of the blades of her claw. The fluid was reminiscent of black tar; clearly not the by-product of a Freylarkin in good health. After contacting with the bronze metal of her claw, the black substance began slithering across the smooth cold surface towards the flesh of her connecting stump. She quickly released her hold on Krashnar, then immediately swept the vile parasite away with her good hand. The back of her right hand momentarily contacted with the thing, causing a shiver to run through her body.

'So, do you enjoy the company of monsters Darlia?' Krashnar asked mockingly. 'Perhaps you care to threaten me again?'

The parasite, which had landed on the floor, began to slither its way back to its former host. The sight of the thing turned her stomach. She watched with disdain as the black fluid moved of its own volition towards Krashnar's leg; upon contact it moved upwards then promptly disappeared beneath his attire. She sneered again at the twisted shaper.

'Just help her.' she said pointing towards Lileah.

'Then stay out of my way in future.' replied Krashnar, who gingerly made his way back towards the workbench where Lileah lay.

'She is exceptionally weak. You did well to apply pressure to the wound, though she has lost much fluid and the wound is beyond my capacity to heal.' the shaper continued.

'Then what have you been doing all this time?' she said interrupting impatiently.

'Examining and assessing. Though I am no renewalist, it is plain to see that her wound is infected and that the infection has spread through her abdomen and torso. There is, however, a procedure that can save her...though you will not like it.'

'Tell me, what vile machination do you propose?'

Krashnar held up his left hand; both little and ring fingers were missing. In their place were smooth stumps which ended just below the knuckle.

'As you know, there is a price for shaping soulful objects indefinitely – flesh for flesh. Given the spread of infection, the sacrifice required to re-shape Lileah's tainted body is too great for any of us to absorb, however, there is a material I can use as a workable substitute.' explained Krashnar.

'And what is this substitute you allude to?' she asked, fearing the answer to her own question.

'Come now, you are a talented scrier are you not?' replied Krashnar sardonically, 'Look into her future and see for yourself. Moreover, look to that bladed claw you carry.'

'No! I dare not bear witness to whatever abhorrent fate you have in mind for her, for if I do then I risk shirking what must be done.' she replied, turning her head to avoid Krashnar's black abyssal gaze.

'Then we have an accord.' replied Krashnar.

A sudden chill gripped her, forcing her body to gently shake. Refusing Krashnar's proposal meant damning Lileah to imminent release, and yet allowing the maleficent shaper to work on her lover invited a fate far worse. She prayed for Lileah's forgiveness.

'Now go occupy yourself someplace else, and do not think to interrupt my work!'

FOUR
Pain

'I had not expected to see you here Nathaniel.' she said, seemingly catching Nathaniel off guard.

'Kirika...you startled me.'

It was a rare feat indeed to catch The Teacher by surprise, though the look on Nathaniel's face suggested that his mind was deeply pre-occupied; he seemed particularly concerned by the lack of a response from his continued knocking on Aleska's door.

'Forgive me, I did not mean to startle you. Indeed I am surprised myself to have caught you unawares.' she replied. 'What troubles you Nathaniel? Are you here to see Aleska?'

'Yes, though I have been knocking on her door for some time to no avail.' he explained. 'I have not seen Aleska since her official retirement and her neighbours, whom I have since spoken with, have not seen her for some time.'

'I see.' she replied thoughtfully. 'She also missed our last social engagement, thus I too had wondered if something was the matter with Aleska given her lack of presence as of late.'

'Certainly she is not here.' Nathaniel stated. 'Perhaps you could use your ability to discern her whereabouts?'

'Nathaniel, that would be an invasion of her privacy.' she replied flatly.

'Perhaps, though I genuinely have cause for concern in light of her apparent disappearance.' Nathaniel replied.

She considered Nathaniel's request for a moment, weighing up his concern against the ethics of prying into someone's personal affairs. It was entirely possible that Aleska simply wanted some personal space, and was off somewhere enjoying her well-earned retirement. Given she was no longer an active member of The Blades, or indeed the ruling council, there was no need for Aleska to inform others of her whereabouts; the venerable former council member was free to come and go as she pleased.

'I am sorry Nathaniel, but I cannot use my ability to invade Aleska's privacy.' she replied earnestly. 'Aleska could be simply enjoying the peace and quiet of retirement for all we know. Your concern for her welfare is not justification enough to scry her movements.'

'I understand, though consider this. Aleska is a significant security risk to Freylar, given the wealth of knowledge she possesses, and she is missing.'

The point was valid; more so given that Aleska had only recently retired from service. The knowledge possessed by Aleska was still current and could in theory be leveraged by Freylar's enemies. Given the recent invasion and Nathaniel's logical security assessment, she reluctantly conceded the point.

'Very well, you make a compelling case.'

She stepped past Nathaniel, who promptly moved aside, and placed the palm of her hand against the smooth surface of Aleska's front door. Engaging her second sight, she guided her vision slowly backwards through time, witnessing images of all those who recently came knocking at Aleska's door. Firstly there was Nathaniel, who in turn was preceded by a single guard. Prior to the guard came Aleska's neighbours, preceded by Aleska herself, who left her chamber carrying what appeared to be a bedroll and some other possessions strapped to her back. It appeared that Aleska had left with no intention of returning anytime soon.

'Aleska has left the Tri-Spires.' she said somewhat vaguely.

Before Nathaniel could respond, she touched the stone wall of the adjacent corridor, searching for more images of Aleska's recent past. Keying in on an abundance of fresh imagery, she traced her finger tips across the surface of the wall, following Aleska's footsteps. Aleska walked at a steady pace, on account of her age and the burden she carried across her back, nevertheless her former mentor purposefully cut a path towards the main entrance of the Tri-Spires.

'Follow me Nathaniel.' she said as she continued to track Aleska's movements.

Nathaniel followed her diligently as she travelled the series of winding corridors leading towards the main entrance of the Tri-Spires. They passed several inquisitive-looking guards en route; neither offered any explanation as to their bizarre behaviour, nor were they questioned on account of their rank. Once they left the artificial construct of Mirielle's sole design, she paused for a moment to touch the ground with her left hand, allowing her to scry fresh images which would guide her towards Aleska's unknown destination.

'She took the road north.' she said in a vacant tone as her mind began searching for the cause of such action.

'Is she headed towards the forest?' questioned Nathaniel, who had an increasingly troubled look about him.

'Unlikely. Aleska carried a bedroll and other personal belongings with her.' she replied. 'I got the distinct impression she was travelling beyond the vale.'

Nathaniel looked towards the northern horizon with searching eyes; his silvery orbs glistened in the morning light as he studied the northern ridgeline intently in hopeless desperation. Establishing a frame of reference for the passage of time whilst scrying was always difficult, therefore she could not be certain when exactly Aleska left the Tri-Spires.

'You will not find her Nathaniel. In all likelihood she left the vale several...' she began to explain before Nathaniel interrupted her.

'Please Kirika, you must help me find her.' he implored. 'I do not have the skill to track Aleska's movements, and I am concerned for her wellbeing.'

'Nathaniel, I cannot simply leave the vale on a whim due to my role of council member, however, there is one who would accompany you.' she replied, piquing Nathaniel's interest. 'If I request this of her, she will almost certainly welcome the chance to hone her ability during a sanctioned mission. That said, you would be entirely responsible – and accountable – for her safety.'

'I understand.' replied Nathaniel without hesitation. 'Make it so Kirika...and please, do hurry!'

'Are you certain?'

Krisis held his gaze with glowering yellow eyes; perhaps it was not wise to question the ability of a dire wolf to track its prey, he wondered. Although less developed mentally, compared to the Freylarkai, dire wolves nonetheless shared many of the same emotional states. He got the distinct impression that Krisis was unimpressed with his line of enquiry. His companion neither moved nor responded to his apparently disparaging query. He supposed in hindsight that the question was akin to someone asking if he had managed to commune with a mind, having been instructed to do so.

'*My apologies, we proceed with caution.*'

Krisis turned on his heel then slowly began walking towards the rocky outcrop on the horizon. He followed his lupine companion, all the while trying to stay low so as not to needlessly give away their position to potential onlookers. With supreme agility Krisis expertly masked his approach as the veteran hunter increased the pace of their advance. He tried to mimic Krisis' movements by hugging the terrain whilst they made good their swift and silent approach. Not once did he stray from the dire wolf's chosen path, which he followed diligently; Krisis had mastered the art of identifying the best paths upon which to tread, besides he had no desire to further incur the dire wolf's ire.

Darlia's telepathic ally had felt the sharp edge of Nathanar's double-handed sword at the battle for Scrier's Post, yet the vicious strike had failed to release its target – assuming the dominant telepath had not since succumbed to their grievous wound. In his experience animals were typically aggressive when cornered, even more so when injured; he wondered therefore if the same would hold true for his mysterious nemesis whilst both he and Krisis tightened their metaphorical noose. In the back of his mind he could hear Ragnar's gruff voice once again urging him against indulging in any lone engagements with the unidentified target, yet his need to repent for his unintentional role in the events leading up to the massacre at Scrier's Post all but consumed him. It was his responsibility to accurately forewarn Freylar of the Narlakai advance, yet he had allowed himself to be manipulated into doing quite the opposite by blindsiding his kin to the real threat. Regardless of the dangers, and Ragnar's repetitive warning, they pressed towards the rocky outcrop, which grew in size with each passing step. They were now well within a few hundred paces of their target; if the telepath yet lived, contact would be imminent. In light of his previous encounters, he took added precaution to shield his mind by attempting to cloak its presence – knowing now that any attempt at erecting mental blocks would likely fail. He dearly hopped that the preventative measure would afford them time enough to complete their assault. They were two hundred paces out now, yet he registered nothing of the telepath's expected presence. Tempted as he was to further question Krisis on the matter, he refrained from agitating the proud dire wolf further. Despite the uneasy silence, they continued to press forwards, now increasing their momentum. His muscles began to tense tightly in anticipation, yet still there was no contact. One hundred and fifty paces...a hundred...fifty...

Without any warning a dull scream echoed forth from the rocky outcrop ahead of them. His vision lost focus as a psychic force, unlike any he had experienced previously, ripped through his mind forcing his knees to buckle. The pain speared through his mind threatening to cleave it in two, like a metal spike being hammered into dry wood with an oversized mallet. The intensity of the pain increased to near unbearable levels, causing him to collapse onto his back whilst clutching his head. His vision faded entirely, replaced instead by thick vivid bands of rapidly changing colour, and the contents of his stomach began to churn violently. The rising levels of pain caused him to retch violently. Vomit rode up his throat before weeping from the corners of his mouth. Though barely conscious he felt his body sliding, or rather being dragged, across the dry cracked earth. His head bumped repeatedly against the uneven ground as an unseen force continued to pull at him sporadically; something was tugging at his right leather greave – he could feel vice-like pressure around his leg pulling at the dead weight of his body. The pain continued to burn through his mind, though with each fresh tug of his right leg the pain began to recede. Slowly he regained partial control of his body, and the harsh strips of colour blinding his vision began to fade. Channelling what little strength he had available, he turned his head to the right to look down the length of his body. Krisis had locked onto his lower right leg and was backing up awkwardly, dragging him slowly away from their quarry. Exhausted by the ongoing psychic attack, he had little choice but to continue to lay prone whilst Krisis struggled to tow him beyond the reach of the wretched telepath responsible for his latest defeat. Despite having been wounded by Nathanar's blade, his nemesis continued to best him at every opportunity; ultimately, he would recover from the mental damage sustained by this latest attack, though his pride would take significantly longer to heal. Twice now he had been laid low by his unseen assailant, twice he had failed miserably to counter the overwhelming power of the rogue telepath's mind. For as long as he could accurately recall his supreme mastery over his ability had never been questioned, now though his once resolute confidence began to crumble, giving rise to fear and doubt. Whether it was naivety or arrogance, he had previously assumed himself to be the most powerful telepath amongst his kin; the latest ruined state inflicted upon him by the mind of another confirmed in no uncertain terms that his assumption had been incorrect. In truth, he had acknowledged the likelihood after their first encounter, but now his inferiority was confirmed beyond doubt. Clearly minds existed which were more powerful than his own; the thought scared him, indeed it terrified him. Ragnar was right to insist that he refrain from making contact, yet even so he had gone against the Captain's wise counsel. In doing so he had not only been mentally defeated for a second time, but he had also potentially given up their position and along with it The Blades' advantage of surprise over their enemy.

Lileah's screams grated agonizingly against her soul; the cries from Krashnar's workshop were twisted and abhorrent. Each fresh scream made her shudder more violently than the last, as her nerves unravelled rapidly to the awful sound of the shaper's work. Krashnar created monsters, that fact she knew well – literally first-hand; Lileah's hapless cries, however, audibly confirmed what she already knew to be true. Given the choice, she knew not if Lileah herself would have chosen the life of a monster over that of release. Regardless, Lileah had been denied the right to choose for herself; she had instead made that decision as next of kin in light of Lileah's incapacitation. Now that decision was already haunting her. She knew Lileah's future would be forever etched with pain and suffering – she chose deliberately not to scry that particular strand of fate, for fear of what she already knew her second sight would reveal. Again, the screams came. She pressed the palms of her hands hard against her ears in an attempt to dull the worst of the hideous sound, which echoed down the corridor leading to Krashnar's workshop. The futile gesture failed miserably to mask the awful sound of torment resulting from Krashnar's metal and flesh mutilations. Unable to endure the noise of Lileah's suffering any longer, she turned on her heels and ran down the rock-walled corridor, expressly disobeying Krashnar's order not to interrupt his work. The wooden door to the shaper's workshop was locked, barring her entry. More screams rang out as Lileah's tormentor continued to mercilessly work his maniacal ability. Conflicting emotions assaulted her whilst she stared venomously at the door between herself and the horror of the work in progress being wrought on the other side. She knew well the outcome if Krashnar was unable to finish his work, and yet she could not bear the thought of what monstrosity the shaper's ministrations would breed. Unable to decide on her best course of action, she stood mutely before the workshop's wooden door, frozen with guilt and indecision. Tears gathered along the lower lids of her eyes, until inevitably they abandoned her to fall silently to the dusty stone floor of Krashnar's hide. Her mind became numb and her body rigid, yet the tears continued to flow in response to the screams from the far side of the impassable portal.

Without any warning the heavy bolts securing the door to Krashnar's workshop slid back noisily, rousing her from her numb state. The door opened partially and Krashnar's twisted visage promptly filled the widening gap. The shaper looked more crazed than usual, as though his monstrous work had unhinged his already unstable mind further.

'If you are going to lie around like a broken doll, you might as well assist me with my work.' rasped Krashnar in his characteristic cracked tone. 'That is, if you have the stomach for it?' he continued, laughing amusingly to himself.

The black obsidian orbs that were Krashnar's eyes stared vacantly at her; they were empty things, chilling to behold, and contributed nothing to the shaper's odd body language. His weathered mouth, by contrast, curled slightly at both ends forming a sarcastic grin; clearly Lileah's tormentor was pleased with his crass humour and current work in progress.

'You are a bastard Krashnar.' she said coldly.

'Darlia, I have been called far worse.' Krashnar sneered in response to her uninspired insult. 'Are you coming or not?'

'As if you need ask.' she replied dejectedly.

She clutched the side of the partially opened door with her prosthetic claw, allowing its blades to wrap around the edge menacingly. Temporarily burying her anxiety, she stepped forwards assertively pushing the door fully open, which prompted Krashnar to melt back into the dim light of the dingy workshop. Lileah lay moaning in pain, fading in and out of consciousness, splayed out across one of the room's thick wooden work benches. In her mind she had already begun to form ghastly images of the horror lying in wait for her, and yet she was completely unprepared for the sight of the disfigured form which slowly came into focus with each closing step. Stopping short a few paces from Lileah's mutilated body, she raised her right hand to her mouth in utter revulsion at the ghastly sight before her. Lileah had been stripped completely naked, even missing the odd trinkets and charms she once wore. What little colour there used to be had drained entirely from Lileah's skin, and her short, raven black hair glistened with sweat. Lileah was a petite thing, that much at least remained unchanged, though her previously gaunt features had notably worsened. Yet Lileah's emaciated state was far from the worst of it. The entirety of Lileah's abdomen and torso had been fused – or perhaps even replaced, she could not quite tell – with the same metal alloy attached to the stump of her own left arm. Lileah's breasts had been removed, replaced by dull bronze metal sheeting, giving the ruined Freylarkin an androgynous look. Lileah's body was now one of cold tarnished metal joined to pallid skin, stretched thinly over a skeletal frame. She wept uncontrollably, yet she was unable to look away from the abhorrent sight. Underneath the layers of dirt and grime Lileah had possessed a raw hidden beauty, despite the Freylarkin's malnourished appearance; now that beauty had been stripped away, replaced with metal-infused flesh wrought by the warped imagination of one who delighted in experimentation.

'What have you done to her?!' she half whispered in a solemn voice.

'Exactly what you asked of me.' replied Krashnar, who ran the remaining fingers of his left hand across Lileah's metal-infused abdomen whilst licking his dry cracked lips.

'Do not touch her you fiend!' she cried bitterly.

Krashnar laughed quietly to himself before replying, 'It is somewhat late in the cycle for that, do you not think?'

'You cannot leave her this way!' she implored. 'You have robbed Lileah of her femininity.'

'I have saved her – at your request, need I remind you?' Krashnar shot back angrily. 'If you do not appreciate my work, you are free to seek the services of another.'

Their demented creator, though clearly unhinged, did not lie; she had indeed asked, or rather more truthfully coerced, Krashnar into saving Lileah from release, knowing full well the likely ramifications of her request. She desperately sought another to lay blame against for Lileah's mutilation, yet the true architect of her lover's ruin could be found simply by looking into a mirror.

'If you are quite finished exercising your venomous tongue then perhaps you can assist me in refining the design, thus reshaping some of Lileah's "lost femininity", as you put it.' Krashnar said dispassionately.

'You make me sick.'

'Irrelevant.' replied Krashnar dismissively. 'Are you going to assist me or not?'

Still appalled by the rogue shaper's latest work, she hesitantly approached the bench upon which Lileah lay in a semi-comatose state. Her vision distorted as tears collected in her eyes once more, yet the lack of definition failed to soften the blow of what she was witnessing. She reached out to touch Lileah's chest; the tips of her right fingers contacted with the cold surface of metal. Lileah's skin was indeed no more, replaced instead by the familiar alloy used to construct her own bladed claw. She wept uncontrollably as the reality of her decision hit home. When first she met Lileah she had promised the waif both the opportunity to exact revenge against Mirielle's regime and a better quality of life. In point of fact she had failed to make good on either of her hollow promises, moreover she had played a significant role in instigating quite the reverse; they had been defeated by The Blades, courtesy of the Order's Aspirants no less, and now Lileah's quality of life was destined to take a sharp downturn. Lileah would almost certainly no longer be capable of giving birth to children; that basic right had been denied to Lileah without consent. Adding to Lileah's future misery, both pain and suffering would forever stalk the Freylarkin until the cycle came of her eventual release. She had failed Lileah completely, a fact that was inescapable.

'Now then, where shall we begin?' mused Krashnar, curling his lips whilst licking them deliciously at the prospect of further utilising his ability.

Despite Krashnar's complete lack of compassion, she would not allow the twisted shaper to leave Lileah in such an androgynous state. All she could hope to achieve now was the partial restoration of Lileah's dignity, by directing Krashnar's wretched ability more favourably. The thought of working on Lileah's body alongside the twisted shaper sickened her, for she had no right to do so. Regardless of her feelings on the matter, she was too heavily invested in Lileah's fate to consider backing down now. The time to wash her hands of the whole Mirielle affair had long since passed; she would see events through to their grim conclusion, and that included Lileah's restoration.

'We are both monsters you and I,' she said dejectedly, still sobbing, 'You her bastard father creator, and I her ill-advising surrogate mother. I pray for her forgiveness, yet I deserve and expect none.'

'You pray only for yourself, how selfish of you Darlia.' said Krashnar sardonically. 'Am I not also deserving of her forgiveness – not that I require it? After all, I am the one who saved her am I not?'

'You have damned her to a life of torment, which I condoned, however, there is a stark difference between you and I, Krashnar.' she replied scornfully.

'Which is what?' enquired Krashnar with an ugly smile stretched across his face.

'You enjoy this...ergo, you deserve nothing!'

Krashnar laughed loudly; the vile sound of his voice filled the grubby workshop, fuelling her revulsion towards the shaper.

'I like you Darlia. You are one of my greatest creations. Never before have I managed to instil so much loathing in a creature.' replied Krashnar. 'I think that I shall now pour my hatred into this latest work.' he continued before resuming his repulsive laughter.

FIVE
Discomfort

They had travelled south for the better part of the cycle; the journey had been exhausting. Though the familiar verdant flora of the vale was still present, the terrain had evolved into a mixture of rolling hills and rocky outcroppings. The constant changes in gradient and the hard ground underfoot took its toll on their legs. Her strained calves ached incessantly, despite the intermittent use of their wraith wings to reduce their journey time. There was little exchange of dialogue between them as they travelled south; the distinct lack of conversation made the strain of their journey all the more difficult, with little to distract them from the mounting pain in their legs. On a number of occasions she tried to strike up conversation with Anika, though her dogmatic responses made further dialogue exceptionally difficult. Anika was focused entirely on the mission, thus the troubled Freylarkin would not allow idle chatter to distract her in the field. It saddened her that their first encounter with the Narlakai had eroded their friendship to such an extent. She tried to raise the matter with Anika, but was met with a wall of silence.

After a short break around noon, to recover their strength, the gradient of the terrain increased sharply and a strange mist crept over the horizon. The rolling green hills gave way to an increasingly rocky landscape, littered with clear springs and narrow trickling streams which wound inefficient paths across the hard relief. Tall spindly black trees grew from rocky crags at impossible angles; their bountiful small leaves were a mixture of white, pink and red hues which danced haphazardly in the air when spirited away by the wind. Though harsh and unforgiving, the alpine landscape nonetheless possessed a raw, crisp beauty. Marcus had suggested that she broaden her learning, and he was right to do so – she needed to expand her knowledge of Freylar. Since her arrival, she had only left the relative safety and comfort of the vale once, to fight under Nathanar's command at Scrier's Post. If she wanted to achieve the levels of success both Marcus and Nathaniel hoped of her, she would need to widen her understanding and explore more of her new world.

The light started to fade as the late afternoon sun began its gentle descent towards the western horizon; realistically they had expected to make contact with the Knights Thranis before now. Anika remained insistent that they were heading in the right direction, yet their destination – known as the Ardent Gate, a confirmed stronghold for the Knights Thranis – continued to elude their sight. The rugged landscape rose and fell, making it difficult to navigate the unfamiliar terrain since landmarks routinely faded in and out of sight. After a while the ground took on a steeper decline, shepherding them towards a long narrow pass which cut a straight path between two immense opposing rock faces. She likened the ominous-looking pass to a deep cut or wound, as though a titan had buried the smile of its enormous axe into the land, carving out a path where previously none had existed. Cautiously they made their way along the pass, ever wary of potential rock falls. The light grew dimmer with each advancing step and the ambient air temperature dropped noticeably. Suddenly a dark shape flickered across the upper edge of her vision. She craned her neck back and looked up towards the summit of the rock walls, hoping for a clearer glimpse of the source of her distraction. Unconvinced that her overactive imagination was not to blame, she turned to Anika seeking confirmation.

'Did you see it too?' she enquired, realising then that Anika was also looking upwards.

'Yes,' replied Anika flatly, 'I believe we are being watched.'

Immediately she unsheathed Shadow Caster with her right hand and directed her gaze back towards the passage's southern exit. Anika followed suit, readying her falchion and shield, promptly moving to cover her rear. Together they stood silently with their backs close to one another; her senses went into overdrive as she sought to identify their anonymous stalker. Two figures suddenly stepped into view at the far end of the passage, blocking their path south. A third ominously leant out over the top of the rock wall to her right; the dark shape appeared to be wielding a drawn bow and was aiming downwards towards their location.

'Behind us!' said Anika in a foreboding tone.

'Two up front, one above.' she replied quickly.

'We have been ambushed!' replied Anika vehemently.

The dim light of the passage prohibited them from rendering the surrounding silhouettes in any meaningful detail. The distant shrouded figures remained perfectly still; content to observe their prey from a safe distance.

'Identify yourselves!' she cried, no longer concerned with the threat of loose falling rock.

'Who is asking?' a female voice cried promptly from above.

'We are Blade sisters from the vale. We seek an audience with Knight Lord Heldran.' she replied.

Her words echoed confidently across the narrow pass, yet no immediate response came from those surrounding them. She supposed that their half-seen interrogators were considering her words carefully, prior to making their intentions clear; it was possible they were communicating amongst themselves, assuming the presence of a telepath to aid them.

'Why?' the same female voice eventually responded.

'With respect, our message is for Knight Lord Heldran himself.' she replied cautiously.

'State your name and rank!' demanded the voice.

'She is The Guardian!' cried Anika fervently.

Anika's unexpected interruption made her cringe. She had a hard time stomaching the title as it was; she had no desire to publicise the label beyond the vale.

'My name is Rayna, Blade Adept.' she replied promptly, seeking desperately to stem further talk on the subject from Anika. 'My companion's name is Anika, Blade Novice.'

Again there came a lull in their sparse conversation as their interrogators considered their response.

'I am Heldran.' spoke a male voice, this time from the direction of the two silhouettes stationed at the southern end of the passage. 'You may communicate your message. If I deem your words to be ill-spoken, you will leave this place immediately.'

'Very well, and I thank you for hearing my words.' she replied cordially. 'The Blade Lord has sent us here so that we may pledge our services to your Order. It is his hope that through our actions both the Knights Thranis and The Blades can re-forge bonds of old.'

'Ha!' spoke another voice, again from the south. 'So Marcus sends us a Novice and an Adept. We are indeed privileged!' continued the voice derisively.

'Zephir finds your words amusing...as do I.' replied Heldran once more.

'My words are sincere, Knight Lord Heldran, as are my intentions.' she asserted unwaveringly.

'Perhaps, though regardless, I am intrigued to meet the saviour of Scrier's Post.' replied Heldran. 'Maybe, with the right training, you will not get yourselves released during The Hunt.'

The figure claiming to be Knight Lord Heldran was clearly well informed; given his apparent knowledge of the recent events at Scrier's Post, she wondered if the Knights Thranis had found a way to infiltrate The Blades. It then occurred to her that perhaps the Knights instead had access to scriers of their own. If her fleeting paranoia was correct, it stood to reason that Heldran already knew the real reason for their presence. Either way, she had piqued the Knight Lord's interest; better to incite interest than something less favourable. Marcus had tried previously to break bread with the Knights Thranis without success. Perhaps Heldran's curiosity would allow her the opportunity to heal old wounds, she mused.

'We would be honoured to assist the Knights Thranis in hunting the Ravnarkai.' she said formally.

Her reply did not elicit the response she had hoped. Zephir was the first to laugh at her apparently ill-chosen words, followed by the shadowy female figure above, who still aimed her bow at them. After a brief moment Heldran crossed his arms defiantly, affirming her public ridicule.

'Perhaps one of you will kindly enlighten me as to why my words amuse you so?' she continued, trying to maintain an air of confidence, despite the disparaging body language from their interrogators.

The laughter was quickly silenced, though not as a result of her retort – the raucous clamour of their social tormentors was instead abated by the sound of heavy metal treading upon the hard ground. The purposeful sound of authority came from behind her. She turned her head briefly towards Anika, confirming visually that which she had already surmised – the previously silent figure blocking the rear end of the passage now walked slowly towards them. The advancing knight approached at a slow, methodical pace, though he had yet to draw any weapons.

'That there is Knight Captain Gedrick.' the figure replied in a deep imposing voice, whilst pointing a heavy gauntleted hand towards the faux Heldran. '*I* am Knight Lord Heldran!'

Heldran's visage revealed itself slowly as the fleeting shadows of the narrow passage receded from his deeply weather-worn face with each advancing step. Heldran was clad in worn plate armour, with the exception of his face; each plate bore a scuff, dent or mark, all of which had a story to tell. A monstrous double-handed sword, with a menacing curved point, hung loosely from his left waist, sheathed in an ornate leather-bound scabbard, and he carried his tired-looking helmet grasped in an oversized gauntleted metal fist. His frame was huge, even for a Freylarkin, and easily rivalled Ragnar's; for a brief moment she imagined the two giants sparring viciously in the arena against the backdrop of a roaring crowd. Anika shifted her body weight, seeking a better defensive stance against the lumbering hulk; despite the gesture's obvious futility, she admired her Blade sister's doggedness. Remembering Nathaniel's sermons well, she tore her sight away from Heldran's dominating presence and continued to fix her gaze on Gedrick and Zephir who, thus far at least, had not moved.

'Listen well to what I am about to say little girl.' boomed Heldran against the crashing tread of his metal heels.

She felt Anika's head tilt backwards as what little light the pass afforded them quickly receded in the presence of Heldran's enormous shadow, which now loomed ominously over them. Unwilling to show any sign of weakness, she responded to the Knight Lord's antagonising remark before he could finish his words.

'I am no one's little girl. Disrespect me again and I will burn out the windows to your soul, Knight Lord Heldran.' she said fervently, no doubt in a manner much to Anika's liking.

Heldran remained perfectly still as he stood patiently, towering menacingly over them. After what seemed like an eternity of silent judgement, Heldran raised his right gauntleted fist once more; this time signalling the female with the bow to stand down.

'I admire your conviction Guardian, but know your place in these unfamiliar lands,' boomed Heldran sternly. 'As I was about to say, before you kindly interrupted me, we do not hunt the Ravnarkai...they hunt us!'

'Please come in.' commanded a distant voice from behind the arched wooden doors.

With a simple gesture of his left hand, the doors to the chamber opened enough to allow him entry. Mirielle greeted him with a warm smile as he entered the room; she was sat at a wooden bench adjacent to the chamber's large arched window. He returned Mirielle's smile as he approached casually, whilst casting his gaze over the alien-looking artefacts littering her workbench.

'Forgive me, I did not mean to interrupt your work.' he said apologetically.

'Oh, these trinkets...they are not work. More of a hobby I suppose.' replied Mirielle, looking up from her latest manipulations of nature.

'I thought you had ceased such indulgences in light of the revelation following Rayna's arrival here in Freylar?' he replied inquisitively.

'It is true that her world frequently distracts me from other thoughts, though shaping even these small personal effects helps me to focus more clearly.' explained Mirielle.

'I see.' he replied, unsure how to continue the conversation given his limited understanding of the art of shaping.

He wanted to say more, indeed he hoped that Mirielle would invite him to sit down and keep her company, yet he struggled to conceive an interesting subject of conversation beyond their professional working relationship. Rather than endure the awkward silence rapidly manifesting between them, he chose to steer their conversation, or rather lack thereof, back to matters of the domain; a more formal topic which they were both comfortable with, though one which would do nothing to further his relationship with Mirielle.

'Rayna and Anika should have made contact with the Knights Thranis by now. I expect it will be some time before we hear from them, assuming lord Heldran does not shun their offer of assistance.' he said, defaulting to the habitual tone in which he frequently delivered his reports.

'I hope that this new strategy of yours bears fruit Marcus,' she replied, smiling gently. 'However, the Knights Thranis will likely not appreciate being manipulated should they learn of your true agenda.'

He had not intended to discuss business so late in the cycle, however, he found it difficult to engage with Mirielle on personal matters. Though Mirielle had an inviting demeanour, nonetheless she continued to remain distant despite her welcoming disposition. Notwithstanding the passes he had loyally served under their queen's rule, he still remained unable to fathom the gulf which existed between Mirielle and those seemingly closest to her – including himself.

Indulging unexpectedly in a moment free of inhibition, he decided to shift the conversation in an entirely new direction; surprising even himself, he decided to embark on a line of personal enquiry which Rayna had attempted when first they had formally met.

'Mirielle, do you mind if I ask you a personal question?' he asked in a somewhat meek manner, rather uncharacteristic of his typical self.

Mirielle hesitated momentarily, before withdrawing her hands from her newest creations, then turned round fully to face him whilst remaining seated at her workbench. She placed her hands neatly upon her lap and began rubbing her fingers nervously. Typically their queen feigned confidence well, however, he had seen the nervous signs before when conversation had become personal, typically within a more intimate setting.

'Apologies if I am making you nervous, for that was not my intent.' he said calmly, trying to put Mirielle at ease. 'Would you rather I sat?'

'Oh yes, please do.' replied Mirielle, turning quickly to an adjacent vacant chair at the workbench.

He promptly sat down, hoping to dissipate some of the awkwardness between them; Mirielle continued to rub her fingers regardless.

'I can leave if you want me to?' he said quietly.

'No, please stay. I am just not used to...' replied Mirielle coyly, whilst clearly struggling to make eye contact with him. 'What is it that you wish to ask me?' she asked, cutting short her previous sentence.

'Do you remember when we first formally met Rayna – or Callum, as she was known then – in this very room no less?' he enquired.

'Indeed I do, for it was not that long ago when we all stood here, listening attentively to the fantastical retelling of her arrival here in Freylar.' replied Mirielle.

'But shortly after her story, Rayna asked you a rather curious question when you proposed to augment her sight.' he said. 'I believe the question concerned the sacrifice you made in exchange for your unique permanent gift of sight.'

Mirielle dipped her head slightly as Rayna's question became prevalent once more, though this time the words spilled from his own lips. When first asked of her, Mirielle had successfully batted the intriguing question aside with the position of authority, aided by a warm smile, to defend herself. Now that same question had been directly put to Mirielle by her closest confidant, and one of a similar station to her own. Mirielle cast her gaze towards the floor; her long white hair fell across the marble-like skin of her delicate face, and light from the arched window flashed across the smooth polished surface of her silver wreath.

'Mirielle you know me by now; all the armies I have commanded under your rule, all the battles I have fought in your name, and all the deeds I have done, for you, regardless of their nature. You have witnessed largely all there is to know of me. I am loyal to you and your rule. You know me Mirielle, and yet...I know so little about you.' he said.

Mirielle said nothing. He found it difficult to assess the impact of his words on account of her long white hair, which now obscured the entirety of her face. He thought about pulling back the curtain behind which she hid, though he had never physically touched their queen before. Using his ability instead he commanded her long white hair to withdraw slowly, consequently revealing her slender marble-like neck and soft jaw line. Mirielle gingerly looked up as he gently swept more of her brilliant white hair aside with his mind, sweeping it neatly round the back of her neck. Slowly Mirielle raised her head, eventually making eye contact with her watery pupil-less eyes.

'Forgive me my queen, I had not sought to upset you.' he said compassionately, after noticing the onset of tears.

'Marcus, you press upon a matter which is hard for me to discuss.' replied Mirielle quietly.

'I apologise.' he said, immediately regretting his spontaneous decision to broach the subject.

'You need not apologise, I just need you to understand the personal nature of what you ask.' Mirielle replied, before continuing after a long pause. 'As Freylar's newly appointed queen, I felt the need to know everything. This desire, or perhaps rather need, to understand became an obsession which steered me down a path towards self-mutilation. Once I had discovered how to enhance my sight, I desperately sought to make the change permanent as my thirst for knowledge became insatiable.'

Mirielle exhaled deeply then paused for a moment, whilst she marshalled her thoughts on the matter; her vacant stare drifted towards the sea of tiny crystals hanging from the otherwise naked branches of the gnarled stone tree within her chamber. He did not understand the significance of the tree, or indeed why Mirielle felt compelled to shape the enigmatic construct after acquiring her unique vision; he knew so little about their queen. Perhaps the tree represented one of Mirielle's visions, unveiled courtesy of her enhanced sight, he mused. Regardless, he fought back the urge to seek answers to further questions; he decided not to jeopardise Mirielle's rare moment of confession by being greedy – he was grateful for their shared honest moment together.

'Perhaps you can draw some parallels between Darlia and my own past transgressions?' said Mirielle doubting herself.

'No, the two are not comparable.' he said sternly.

'How so Marcus? Am I not just as guilty as she through my obsessive over-indulgence?' asked Mirielle.

'I do not believe so,' he replied, 'Darlia's compulsive need to manipulate the future affected us all, whereas your actions affected only yourself.'

'But did they Marcus?' replied Mirielle. 'What about the revelation I carelessly disclosed?'

'You are our queen, Mirielle. You cannot give in to self-doubt, or question your actions, for to do so would erode the Fraylarkai's faith in your leadership.'

'Regardless, I have made mistakes Marcus – ones which I cannot undo.' Mirielle replied sadly.

Mirielle's gaze returned to the stone tree opposite as her thoughts seemingly began to consume her once more. Whilst he could appreciate the complexities of the obsessive disposition shared by both Darlia and Mirielle in the pursuit of developing their abilities to the extreme, nonetheless he could not reconcile Mirielle's comparative conclusion; both were fundamentally very different individuals – in his opinion at least. He supposed that the burden of leadership had taken its toll on their queen; he wished dearly that Mirielle would confide in him her most troubled thoughts, lest they continue to fester. Still, she had finally opened up to him on this one issue at least – it was a start.

'I appreciate you confiding in me Mirielle. Know that my door is always open, should it aid you to share your burdens with another in confidence.' he said. 'I am aware, however, that you dodged my earlier question.'

Mirielle continued to stare vacantly at the tiny crystals hanging from the twisted stone tree; her face bore little emotion – on account of her pallid features – making it difficult to evaluate her emotional state. He realised that his line of enquiry would steer Mirielle down a reluctant path, and yet he pressed the matter regardless. Ragnar was his own personal sounding board; he often sought the Captain's blunt counsel when the strain of leadership became arduous. Previously Aleska had fulfilled a similar role for Mirielle, however, the venerable scrier had since stepped down from the ruling council, placing her experienced counsel beyond Mirielle's practical reach. He hoped that by coaxing their queen to open up that, in time perhaps, Mirielle would come to confide in him of her own volition. Enduring the burden of leadership alone was no easy task; a fact he knew well.

'I cannot answer your question Marcus...at least, not yet.' replied Mirielle softly, eventually breaking away from her reverie. 'Please, do not give up on me Marcus.' she continued in a cracked voice, turning to face him with eyes that brimmed with tears.

Mirielle blinked to clear her vision; a single tear slowly traced a thin line down her left cheek. His own expression became one of immediate concern, for he had not intended to cause her distress – which clearly he had done.

'I am sorry,' he replied, 'It was not my intent to rouse your grief. I sought only to ease your burden.'

'And you have...but, the rest will take time.' replied Mirielle softly, then offered him a warm smile of affirmation. 'Whilst I am not yet ready to confide all, perhaps in the meantime you might offer me a shoulder to cry on instead?'

They arrived at Scrier's post well into the night. Ordinarily the intense journey would have caused them to work up a sweat, but the crisp autumnal air staved off any perspiration. The complete absence of cloud cover allowed the Night's Lights to bathe the landscape with cool white light. Coupled with their excellent vision in low light, both were able to see quite clearly despite the sun's absence. His new companion had made the crossing with surprising ease; though Keshar did not have the benefit of his training in the arena, her endurance was impressive nonetheless. Idle conversation revealed the young scrier to be the daughter of a local farmer, whilst her brother was a renowned fisherman of whom he had previously heard talk of within the vale; he supposed therefore, that Keshar was no stranger to hard work – it pained him to admit that he had seen Aspirants with lesser fortitude, though none had ultimately progressed past that rank.

He had not expected to return to the awful site of Scrier's Post, especially so soon after their hollow victory against the Narlakai. Keshar's knowledge of the events tarnishing the site's name was limited, and he intended to keep it that way. To her credit he believed the apprentice scrier capable of consuming the sordid events with ease, though he did not wish to needlessly distract Keshar from her assignment – there was no need to burden his companion with a distasteful history lesson at this stage. Kirika had tasked the eager young scrier with re-tracing Aleska's movements, thus allowing him to track the retired Valkyrie to Scrier's Post; he had no desire to return to the awful place. Did Aleska simply pass through, or perhaps instead they would find her holed up amidst the ruins? Regardless, he was tired, and not in the required frame of mind to begin to understand Aleska's motive for visiting the defiled sanctuary.

'Why would Aleska come here?' asked Keshar inquisitively as they stared at the ominous ruins on the bleak horizon.

'I do not know. It is my hope that she simply passed through.' he replied.

Keshar raised no further questions; she motioned to press on, clearly eager to complete the assignment with which Kirika had entrusted her. He quickly placed a restraining hand on her shoulder; the act prompted Keshar to turn her head towards him immediately, fixing him with a questioning stare.

'It has been a long journey.' he explained. 'Whether Aleska did indeed pass through, or instead still lingers there, makes little difference. It is late in the cycle; we need to rest here and regain our strength.'

'Though I do not actively seek to question your judgement Nathaniel, would it not be wise to seek shelter within the sanctuary?' asked Keshar innocently.

He exhaled deeply; the recent events of Scrier's Post briefly flashed across his mind, causing his left eye to twitch involuntarily. The question was not without merit, and one to which he owed Keshar at least some explanation given her willingness to freely aid him. Nonetheless, he chose to keep his explanation brief; there was no need for them both to sleep uneasily.

'I would prefer not to. That place...haunts my soul.'

SIX
Encounters

His new lodger shuffled awkwardly within the dark confines of the shared bolt-hole, searching for comfort where none existed. As Trix continued to hopelessly slide around the cramped interior of the hide, he silently observed the curious intruder gleaning what little information he could – like a biologist studying a new organism. Trix was clumsy, that much was obvious; the self-proclaimed Shadow class member was clearly not used to 'roughing it'. Like a child, Trix made unnecessary noise with every gesture. Although far from overweight, Trix had a larger, more rounded, build than his own. He figured his newest Shadow class acquaintance was somewhat of a stranger to the concept of exercise; odd then, he mused, that Trix had somehow survived the Rout given an apparent lack of agility. Presumably Trix possessed some other skill set which had allowed the bumbling interloper to evade the Peacekeeper patrols.

'What are you doing here, in the Wild?'

'I came here to find you.' replied Trix loudly.

'Hush!' he snapped. 'Keep your voice down.'

'But there's no one else here.'

'You don't know that!' he shot back. 'Now learn to speak more softly, and be quick about it, or else get out.'

He likened himself to a parent, scolding an adolescent for doing wrong. Though he had no desire to rebuke a fellow member of the Shadow class, they could ill afford to give away their position; noise carried a long way through the stillness of the night. He had survived this long, on his own, looking out purely for himself. Now, it seemed, he also had the actions of another to manage; life was about to get more precarious, he suspected. Despite the poor light offered by the fading green glow emanating from the glow-tube, he could see from the expression on Trix's face that he had blasted a hole in his guest's confidence. Trix was probably the type who found it difficult to befriend others; perhaps it was time to mellow his attitude, he thought, convinced now that the person opposite him was no threat – not directly at least.

'I'm sorry.' he said apologetically. 'Perhaps we can start over. My name is Callum.'

'Yes, I knew that already. You're the Fox, aren't you?' replied Trix excitedly, apparently not one to hold a grudge.

'I have been called that before, by others of our social class, however, I believe the nickname is a poor attempt at sarcasm, intended to mock my decision to live...here.' he said, laughing quietly at the hole in which they sat.

Humour was clearly lost on Trix; the vacant look in Trix's eyes suggested that his unintended joke failed to register with his audience of one.

'How's the foot?' he asked, promptly changing the subject.

'It's painful, thanks to you.' replied Trix flatly.

'I see. So...why did you venture into the Wild to find me? And how did you manage to remain undetected these last few weeks?'

'The public sewer network. I hid underneath the metropolis, waiting out the worst of the Rout. Afterwards I left, to find you.' explained Trix.

'Surely the Peacekeepers sent patrols to sweep the sewer network clean of our lot?' he enquired, trying not to sound overly distrusting.

'They did, but I had altered the blueprints.' proclaimed Trix in a rather blasé manner.

The information provided freely by Trix did not add up; he was clearly missing an important piece of the puzzle. The metropolis' records were likely stored in the central data core, how then did Trix achieve such a lofty claim? Those systems were protected by sophisticated intruder prevention countermeasures. It was not possible for public citizens to gain access to such records without the relevant access credentials, unless...

'You're a hacker!'

'Don't be so crude!' snapped Trix, obviously irritated by his remark. 'I am a software engineer.'

'Forgive me for being presumptuous, but members of our class are not readily granted access to central data core records. How is it then that you acquired access?'

'Look here Fox, a *hacker*, as you put it, would have wormed their way into the system like an unwanted parasite. Do not typecast me as one of *that* lot.' replied Trix, who was clearly annoyed by the stereotype.

'Forgive my apparent ignorance, though you're avoiding the question.'

Trix paused for a moment. His new companion seemed to be considering a response; perhaps the complexity of explaining his infiltration of the systems was beyond him, or maybe Trix simply did not trust him enough to divulge such information – he could not tell.

'The security measures installed to protect the central data core were substandard. I was able to reverse engineer their design and exploit their short-comings in order to upload some enhancements of my own. The revised code addresses a significant number of vulnerabilities, which previously left the systems open to attack.' explained Trix broadly.

'Ah, but you left yourself a back door I presume?'

'Fox, you think too small. I rebuilt the main entrance!' said Trix ardently. 'It was simple enough for me to amend public blueprints to help conceal my underground activities.'

'So how come you ditched your bio-key? Surely you could have masked your active whereabouts too?' he asked.

'My identity possibly, but not my point of access; the system designed to track bio-key access is standalone. It is well beyond my reach. The work of a privately contracted developer I believe. At any rate, I am not currently able to access the Infonet anonymously, which brings me here.'

'Why here?'

'As I said, to find you, or weren't you listening?'

Trix's presence made him uneasy. He had successfully remained off-the-grid while he was alone; the unexpected presence of another complicated matters. Concealing the presence of another of his kin – even within the Wild – would be no small feat. It would have been far safer for both of them if Trix had remained underground; now they both risked exposure.

'You would have been safer remaining hidden within the sewer network. Coming here puts us both at risk. What is it you want from me so badly that warrants our potential exposure?' he asked.

'Ah, the point of my *groping around in the dark, with all the grace of an intoxicated street urchin*, as you so eloquently put it.' replied Trix sarcastically.

'Get to the point Trix.' he snapped.

'I need to get back into the Infonet, and I need your help to do it undetected.' explained Trix, completely unfazed by his retort.

'I'm no hacker, or more to the point a *software engineer*. How is it you expect me to help you?'

'I don't need a software guy. I need someone who can infiltrate and remain undetected. I need you to breach the heart of the metropolis and track down someone for me.'

'What you're proposing is madness. Why would I risk possible capture by the Peacekeepers, simply to aid you in this fool's errand?'

'So, you want to remain here, forever, in a hole – Fox?'

'Funny!'

'Help me and I will set things up so that we can both live comfortably and undetected in the metropolis – and I don't mean underground like vermin.' said Trix emphatically.

Infiltrating the heart of the metropolis as Trix proposed would be extremely risky. Without access to Peacekeeper patrol routes, shift patterns and specialist equipment, remaining undetected beyond the relative safety of the Wild would be extremely difficult. He was fast on his feet and a quick thinker too; both traits served him well, and had bailed him out of prior trouble on a number of occasions. Yet despite the obvious suitability of his talents for Trix's proposed mission, realistically his chances of success were slim. If he failed to execute the brazen plan unnoticed, whatever unknown fate became of his lost kin would soon become his own – a thought he did not savour.

'So, you want me to incur all the risk whilst you do...what exactly?' he asked flatly.

'I will back you up.' Trix proclaimed.

He sniggered, unable to control his own laughter; the thought of Trix attempting to quietly infiltrate the metropolis was delightfully entertaining. The clumsy programmer would do well to remain undetected in the Wild, let alone in the surrounding urban sprawl. On reflection he felt ashamed of his condescending laughter and apparent inability to suppress his obvious amusement.

'Obviously I had no intention of accompanying you; not in the literal sense at least.' replied Trix sheepishly. 'I should have said, more specifically, that I would assist you remotely.'

'Go on...'

Trix pressed his right thumb to a data-strap around his left wrist; a dull holographic access panel materialised before them, enhancing the dying light of the failing glow-tube.

'Disconnect that thing now!' he snapped, instinctively reaching forwards to grab Trix's outstretched arm.

'Relax!' Trix hissed in response, whilst trying to pull his arm free. 'It's standalone! It is not connected to the Infonet.'

'You shouldn't have brought tech into the Wild.'

'Calm down, I know what I'm doing' replied Trix, clearly irritated once more by his lack of willingness to accept his superior understanding of the technology he was using. 'The first thing I did was modify this strap and disable its data-link to the Infonet, shortly after the Peacekeepers started tracking us. Do you think I'm stupid, despite remaining undetected for as long as you?'

'Forgive me...I am not used to managing the actions of others.' he replied apologetically.

'Then don't. I take responsibility for my own actions. I want this plan to succeed Fox. I will not jeopardise its chance of success.' replied Trix.

Trix possessed talent – that much was clear to him now – and his fellow Shadow class member was right; he needed to let go and trust his unlikely new ally. He harboured no desire to live in the Wild indefinitely; the Wild had no future, it was a temporary retreat which, in theory, allowed him to ride out the storm currently sweeping his social class aside. Though it was difficult for him, having operated alone for so long, he needed to relax his control and allow those competent enough to aid him. Trix's proposal warranted consideration – it would be unfair of him to dismiss it out of hand.

'You make a valid point. Assuming then that I went along with your plan, how specifically can you assist?'

Trix immediately began to operate the holographic access panel single-handed at an impressive rate; his fingers danced across the ethereal display at phenomenal speed as lines of code jumped sporadically across the projection. Trix seemed to be executing a series of pre-programmed scripts designed to subjugate target systems. After less than a minute a topographical view of the metropolis snapped into view, filling the entire holographic display, overlaid with a splatter of tiny red dots. With a series of quick short gestures Trix zoomed in on the display, isolating the northern perimeter of the Wild, causing the red dots to separate and reduce in frequency. The dots were moving.

'You said this was standalone!'

'It is...from the Infonet at least. This is ghost data from a direct connection to a redundant NGDF satellite.' replied Trix.

'What does that mean exactly?'

'Look here, every weapon produced by the NGDF is tagged to prevent further global conflict.' explained Trix, pointing his index finger towards one of the red dots on the display. 'Their whereabouts is monitored in real-time. This data is buffered and sent in timed packets to redundant storage on the satellite we are currently connected to.'

'So...you're tracking the Peacekeepers?'

'Almost.' replied Trix. 'If they're unarmed then the satellite won't register their location. Also it's ghost data, so there's lag.'

'How much lag?' he asked eagerly.

'Five minutes.'

This new development changed everything. The ability to track the majority of Peacekeeper patrols presented Trix's ambitions plan in an entirely new light. Despite the challenges still present, and the obvious issue of latency, there was now a real chance that he could execute his part of the proposal undetected. Trix had already taken an enormous risk by coming to the Wild in search of a ghost. Now the ambitious Shadow class programmer had taken further risks; exposing both his plan and the tech required to achieve it. Trix was staring at him eagerly, like a child desperate to learn if its parents would buy *that* new toy. He could no longer dismiss the opportunity presented to him as wishful thinking; Trix's plan had substance, moreover it had a chance. Given the opportunity to improve his bleak outlook, would he accept a level of risk in order to achieve a better standard of living, he mused? The time had come to decide, and the options were clear to him; maintain the status quo, or instead throw his lot in with another of his kind and gamble big. He was not typically the gambling type – but things changed.

'So...who do I need to find?'

Her body still felt drained after their dogged journey to the Ardent Gate; that, and the fact it was still dark outside, should have compelled her to sleep well. Instead she lay awake. Previously forgotten memories from her past continued to occupy her thoughts, so too the events of the previous cycle when first they had met the Knights Thranis. Now these thoughts churned in her mind, denying her any chance of sleep. Eventually she gave up on any hope of beginning her slumber; she rolled out of the hammock assigned to her for the evening and quietly exited the communal resting quarters. It felt strange sleeping in the same shared space as the knights of the Order, yet this was their way of life and so she accepted it. The Knights Thranis were a close-knit community – that much was abundantly clear to her – thus they behaved much as a family would. Initially she was concerned that the knights would shun their presence, however, Heldran's quick acceptance of their pledged services resonated throughout the Order. Heldran had accepted their olive branch, if for no other reason than sheer curiosity, affording them a rare opportunity to fight alongside their former allies. Quietly she moved along a curved stone corridor, away from the sleeping quarters assigned to her; one of several communal areas, painfully excavated from the stone underbelly of the Ardent Gate. It was an odd name for the stronghold, she mused, for it resembled no gate she had ever seen. The Ardent Gate was more akin to a redoubt, albeit one half-buried in the surrounding rocky landscape. The venerable bastion erupted partially from the bedrock, exposing its upper tiers proudly. Below the surface the structure had an impressive supporting underground network of tunnelled roots; these stone roots seemed to spiral down and outwards, each ending in a large subterranean communal living space. She used her ability to manifest a small orb of light to aid her poor vision, supplementing the weak light from the ancient Moonstones studded along the tunnel wall. The orb hovered before her above head height, guiding her path with its light; by her will alone it drifted languidly along the gloomy tunnel, offering her a new perspective on what was to be her new home – for the immediate future at least. Ultimately, she would be called back to the vale, more specifically to the arena, to receive Lothnar's challenge. For the time being the Knights Thranis had permitted both Anika and herself to be their guests, however, they would be expected to earn their keep whilst in the company of the knights – specifically in battle.

The tunnel maintained a steady uphill gradient, until it eventually came to an end at the base of the Ardent Gate; the narrow passage gave way to a large circular subterranean chamber. Numerous other dark passageways connected to the chamber, along its circumference, creating an underground hub, of sorts. A winding flight of steps protruded from the chamber's circular stone wall, affording access to the upper levels of the stronghold. Upon their arrival they had entered at ground level, just above her, yet a further four or five levels rose above that. The hub's connecting tunnels were spaced equidistantly, though there was a space where one should have existed but did not. In its place was a large stone hearth, carved directly into the wall. A well-built Freylarkin sat on one of several wooden benches nearby, staring languidly into the dancing flames of the fire alight within it. Although the Freylarkin did not turn to acknowledge her, the light from her orb had clearly given away her presence.

'Trouble sleeping?'

The familiar sound of Heldran's deep voice echoed around the chamber, further enhancing its already foreboding tone. Taking the leading question as an invitation to approach, she quickly crossed the cold floor of the stone chamber, intending to sit opposite the Knight Lord. The broad-shouldered Freylarkin maintained his fixed gaze on the flickering flames in the hearth as she approached. There appeared to be no wood or coal in the hearth, instead the flames danced energetically across the surface of what looked like black polished stones.

'Throw another Firestone in there, would you?' said Heldran, absentmindedly pointing his right index finger towards a pile of the stones stacked nearby in a lone wooden crate.

She picked up one of the stones from the crate – it was surprisingly cool to the touch – and promptly tossed it into the hearth. The flames roared with renewed ferocity as they drew life from the black offering. Having done as instructed, she dissolved her orb of light and sat down on the vacant wooden bench opposite Heldran.

'Are our sleeping arrangements not to your liking, Guardian?' asked Heldran in a deep flat tone.

'They're fine.' she answered him. 'My troubled past finds it amusing to occupy my dreams, therefore I find it extremely difficult sleeping for any length of time.'

'Ha, well then I am in good company Guardian. I rarely sleep myself; such are the burdens of leadership.' noted Heldran.

'There is no need to address me as The Guardian.'

'I have heard it said that you lived amongst the Sky-Walkers, who diligently watch over us. Do you deny this allegation?' asked Heldran who continued to gaze into the stone hearth.

She sighed heavily. Even on the fringes of the domain, her past continued to stalk her present. Freylarkin society was diverse in its beliefs. Naturally there were those Freylarkai whose attitudes towards the unknown were largely pragmatic, like Kirika and Larissa, and then there were those at the other end of the spectrum. According to Nathaniel a great many of the forest dwellers believed in superior beings, who watched over them from lofty vantage points – a statement which she recently witnessed being ratified first-hand by the youth of Freylar. Yet she did not seek to actively meddle with Freylarian beliefs, nor too did she aspire to be a part of such dogma. Marcus had cautioned her of the Knights' creed; it was no surprise therefore, that Heldran might also subscribe to the same beliefs as her forest neighbours.

'No...I do not deny it, however, I do not wish to be judged according to the beliefs of the people. Rather, I hope to be regarded based on my actions here in Freylar.'

'Guardian or not, it has been many a pass since last a light bringer helped fill our ranks; perhaps you can help lighten the Order's mood?' replied Heldran, who turned his head towards her finally, flashing a weak smile.

She returned the Knight Lord's obvious humour with a broad smile of her own. Heldran was not the standoffish character she had wrongly been led to believe. Though he indeed looked the part of the separatist leader, Heldran was also world-weary; perhaps the venerable knight's previously perceived dogged demeanour had been eroded with time. Leadership invariably weighed heavily on one's soul; Queen Mirielle was no exception to the inevitability, nor was Marcus. The Blade Lord had briefly touched on the matter of timing, when last he had spoken with her; perhaps now was indeed the right time to heal old wounds.

'It must be difficult for the Order to survive out here?' she asked, looking to sympathise with Heldran's mood.

Heldran turned his attention back towards the soothing flicker of the flames, pushing back his long dark brown hair which threatened to obscure his front-row view of the hearth.

'We have adapted to the harsh beauty of the land, but our numbers are few. Many have been released during the countless passes we have occupied the Gate.' explained Heldran.

'How did this place earn its name, for I see no gate?'

'Ah, a valid question, and one which you will learn the answer to at first light, when we resume The Hunt.'

'So soon...are we not to be trained prior to joining the Order's crusade?' she asked, failing to mask her obvious surprise.

Heldran smiled weakly once more, before responding to her question. 'The two of you will learn your craft in battle, and quickly at that. We do not have the luxury of time...or The Teacher.'

'You know Nathaniel?' she asked, surprised to hear Heldran mention her mentor's famed title.

'Yes, we fought alongside one another during times long since forgotten. I was a Knight Conscript back then, newly inducted into the Order, and Nathaniel had recently joined the ranks of The Blades. This was well before Marcus joined your Order, you understand?'

'Heldran speaks of a time long before my own.'

She knew well that the Freylarkai led long lives, and yet she had never really given the matter much thought. How many lifetimes had Nathaniel lived in comparison to her own short existence? Even Kirika – although considered young by Freylarian standards – had already led multiple lifetimes. Her sudden appreciation of the passage of time made her feel small and insignificant. Was Marcus right to send her to meet with Heldran, she began to wonder? Whatever misfortunate events had previously transpired between both Orders transcended multiple lifetimes; she saw that clearly now. How then could she possibly hope to understand and rectify such long-standing resentment? There would be no accounting for truth, not without the aid of a potent scrier; time masked fact with layers of dust, and emotions played tricks on the mind. Even truthful recounts could be inadvertently distorted, unbeknownst to their narrators. Absolving past blame would therefore be a wasted endeavour she surmised, since none could be accurately attributed to either Order. Whilst The Blades could accept full responsibility for the damaged relationship, she suspected that such an act would be considered insincere by the Knights. A hollow apology – moreover one perceived as such – was no apology at all, and would be rejected outright, seen as little more than an insidious political manoeuvre as a means to an end.

She needed to find another way to earn the Knights' trust, specifically Heldran's own.

'But enough of history...tell me about you.' said Heldran, turning his head to face her once more.

'What do you wish to know?'

'I gather that body used to belong to Alarielle.' said Heldran with a gentle nod towards her. 'It is rumoured that you used to be male.'

She smiled at Heldran's choice of question. 'That is not a rumour...it is fact. Does my appearance fail to please you Lord Heldran?'

'Ha, I was told you had a sense of humour, unlike your stale companion.'

'Anika is troubled by the recent horrors of Scrier's Post.' she explained, without trying to sound defensive.

'We all have our demons to battle.' replied Heldran. 'Still, you seem unperturbed by those events.'

'Not to put too fine a point on it but, being reborn in the body of a different race and differing sex creates unique challenges, which frequently distract me.'

'I can only imagine.' replied Heldran with a wide grin.

'*He likes you! Tease him. Freylarkin males like to be teased.*'

Time and again she had been reminded of the fact that physical weapons were not her sole means of disarming opponents. Feminine wiles were a valid means of subduing others, including female counterparts. Mischievous smiles and occasional body contact could deal just as much damage mentally as a well-placed cut from a falchion. Guided by Alarielle's counsel, she give Heldran a wink and made a point of leaning forwards as she stood up.

Heldran regarded her with childlike curiosity, allowing his gaze to track her as she rose from the bench.

'I have enjoyed our brief midnight chat. Perhaps you will have another question for me tomorrow night?'

'Perhaps I will.' replied Heldran distractedly.

'Incidentally my lord, I view the past as exactly that. Though I cannot speak for others and their true agendas, I did not come here to intentionally spy or to manipulate. I was asked to spend time with the Knights Thranis, and to earn their trust. That is my intent. I will not deviate from that creed, come what may when the sun rises. Sleep well Lord Heldran.'

SEVEN
Realisation

He awoke to the dawn chorus of Sky-Skitters attempting to attract female mates; good luck with that he thought, as he rolled his head slowly to the side to better observe the bleak uninhabited landscape from their elevated vantage point. They had spent the night camped outside underneath the Night's Lights at his request. Despite Keshar's obvious desire to press on, he had not had the fortitude to reacquaint himself with Scrier's Post so late in the previous cycle; the darkness added to the site's sense of foreboding, further increasing his loathing of the events which had recently transpired there. Wasting no time now he got up, painfully, and proceeded to stretch out his back. Although his own bed, back at his tree in the vale, offered little comfort, it was nonetheless a stark improvement on the hard ground upon which they had spent the night. His cycles of sleeping rough under the Night's Lights, at one with nature, had long since passed; such adventures were better suited to those sharing Lothnar's disposition. A weak murmur came from Keshar, who was just now starting to wake courtesy of the Sky-Skitters' mating calls. He rubbed crusted rheum from his eyes then blinked a few times to clear his vision. His body ached all over, yet that was hardly surprising given his age. Keshar, however, had little trouble waking from her slumber; how he envied the vigour of youth. Seeing the young scrier now reminded him of the devastating blow dealt to the Aspirants at Scrier's Post. Perhaps Keshar could be tempted to try out for The Blades, he mused, as his mind drifted towards thoughts of recruitment.

'Morning to you Nathaniel.' said Keshar rather spritely.

'I hope you slept well?' he enquired, flashing her one of his wry grins.

'Better than you, I suspect.' replied Keshar, with an unexpected grin of her own.

He acknowledged her good-natured quip with an audible 'Humph', before stretching out his back once more. 'Well then, shall we get going? We can eat en route.'

'Yes indeed, I am eager to see Scrier's Post now that we are here.'

It was then that he recognised the dichotomy that their destination represented. To him Scrier's Post was little more than a mass grave, one which had become the untimely resting place for so many of his recently released former students. He loathed the site because of what it now represented. To him at least, Narlak was more preferable than the miserable tomb which loomed ahead of them. Yet despite his personal unease, Keshar was full of enthusiasm and clearly eager to see Scrier's Post first-hand. Perhaps the young scrier's excitement stemmed from her desire to see more of their domain, being largely untraveled as she was, or maybe she felt a connection with the sanctuary due to her ability. Either way, he could not tell. Regardless, his emotions were clearly at odds with those of his youthful companion.

Infused with the renewed vigour of a night's sleep, albeit an uncomfortable one, they closed the distance to Scrier's Post in good time. When they approached the site's perimeter wall, it looked markedly different to how he recalled. A cursory glance suggested that the site had been the subject of recent remedial works, therefore it appeared – to him at least – partially restored, thus displaying a glimmer of its former glory. The arrow slits, which Nathanar had ordered the shaping of, were now absent; no trace of their previous existence remained. Curious also was the main black gate which had also been altered – the metal bars of the blackened gate appeared greater in number, increasing the density of the vertical bars thereby making it difficult to see through the augmented construct. Was someone deliberately trying to obscure line of sight to the sanctuary he wondered.

'*Someone* has *definitely* been here recently.' he said, thinking out loud.

Keshar quickly turned her head towards him; his choice of words was clearly not lost on her. She nodded her head gently, acknowledging his concern, then proceeded to use her ability. Keshar was young and required significant development to further her ability, for the present she needed physical contact with the target of her scrying. She approached the perimeter wall cautiously and placed her left palm flat against its weather-beaten surface. After a brief period of suspense Keshar's face eventually altered in intensity as her second sight engaged, allowing her to begin processing past images of Scrier's Post. It took Keshar some time to complete her scrying, after which she turned towards him with a face etched with concern.

'Please forgive me Nathaniel, Aleska was accompanied by another. I should have seen this earlier.' stated Keshar apologetically.

'You need not apologise. You are an apprentice; I do not expect you to see as Kirika would.' he replied, trying to salve Keshar's wounded pride.

'It is difficult for scriers like me to further our training, given the sanctions imposed on our kind.' explained Keshar, who appeared frustrated with her obvious limitations. 'Still, that is no excuse. I will focus harder next time.'

'Regardless, that is not our immediate concern. We need to breach the perimeter wall undetected, in order to better assess the situation.'

The organic-looking rock wall encircling Scriers' Post was a good four paces in height – too high to simply fly over. As female Freylarkin went, Keshar was tall, though she lacked the physical strength required to provide him with the adequate leg up needed to scale the perimeter wall. Further, Keshar, in all likelihood, lacked the arm strength necessary to pull him up.

'How do we deal with you?' he mused aloud, staring up at the Freylarian-made defence denying them access to the sanctuary beyond.

'Can we not simply use the main gate?' asked Keshar naively.

'Even if it were unlocked, which is unlikely, we will give away our position entering the grounds that way. We need to gain access unseen.' he explained, before pointing towards the western section of the perimeter wall. 'Over there!'

Quietly they moved left around the wall flanking the outpost. If they could somehow scale the west wall, they would avoid line of sight from the sanctuary's long slit windows at either end of the main structure – assuming they has not subsequently been altered. With this in mind he knelt down and locked his fingers tightly together, offering Keshar a stable platform upon which to step. She regarded him with a bemused expression, clearly failing to understand his objective. He expected the daughter of a local farmer to be more practical about such things, though clearly his intent required some explanation.

'I am offering you a leg up. I will push you up so that you can grab the top of the wall.'

'Nathaniel, I will not be able to get up there!' replied Keshar defiantly.

'Of course you will. Just humour me.'

Acting as instructed, Keshar placed her left foot onto his locked fingers. Without hesitation he stood up, pushing his arms upwards, thrusting Keshar towards the top of the wall, denying the startled Freylarkin the chance to think the brazen manoeuvre through. Keshar let out several awkward groans as she frantically grabbed the top of the wall and proceeded to unceremoniously haul her body up to its apex. After a lot of awkward footwork and numerous curses, Keshar manoeuvred her body so that she lay precariously across the top of the wall.

'You could have warned me Nathaniel!' said Keshar in a strained voice. 'What now?' she continued, irritably.

'Hook your left arm and leg over the wall, then hold out your right arm. I am going to use you to climb up.' he explained.

Once more he denied the apprentice scrier the opportunity to protest through immediate action. Crouching low to the ground, he unfurled his wraith wings and launched himself upwards towards Keshar's outstretched arm. Grabbing her arm he planted his feet flat against the wall and began to pull himself over Keshar. The technique was far from elegant, yet it served their needs, allowing both Freylarkai to scale the wall and use their wraith wings to drop silently down into the main courtyard. His one regret was the stony expression etched on Keshar's face, coupled with her glaring violet eyes.

The Ardent Gate; that name now held new meaning for her. Little had she realised that the Knights Thranis had, over the passes, re-sited a number of Waystones into the heart of their stronghold, thereby allowing them to move quickly across the domain's southern lands. Though the mystical stones frequently made her head spin, they were undeniably unprecedented forms of travel and provided a significant tactical advantage by facilitating the Knights' rapid redeployment. The Gate Room occupied the entire second floor of the Knights' stronghold, and was guarded at all times through tight shift rotations. Use of the Waystones was limited exclusively to The Hunt; all other activities, such as the harvesting of food and resources, were restricted to the local area.

She scratched the right side of her head absentmindedly; it itched occasionally following her decision to shave off the sides of her shoulder length blonde hair earlier that morning. The Guardian had expressed concern, questioning whether the decision was impulsive, but for her the act was symbolic, the beginning of something new. Though The Guardian had politely rejected the same offer from Captain Gedrick, stating that she had accommodated enough change already since her arrival in Freylar, when asked herself she had embraced the opportunity for change. Many of the Knights Thranis shaved their hair, or part of it; their military lifestyle meant that maintaining long hair was a burden best forgone. Her raison d'être held new meaning after their conflict with the Narlakai at Scrier's Post; the commonly perceived beauty of long well-kept hair no longer concerned her, nor did attracting a mate of the opposite sex. Her sworn duty as a Blade Novice to protect Freylar now occupied her every waking thought. She would never again allow horrors such as the Narlakai to invade her domain. The Knights Thranis, too, had sworn an oath to protect Freylar above all other concerns, thus she felt a strong connection to their Order; shaving her hair simply affirmed her unwavering intent to lend her support to their campaign. The new cycle ushered in her first experience of The Hunt as they passed through the Ardent Gate to the southern fringe of the domain. Captain Gedrick led the latest campaign against the Ravnarkai, and with The Guardian bolstering their ranks they would not falter.

'Anika, have you adjusted to your armour?' asked Xenia judgementally.

Xenia was a staunch member of the Order – whom she greatly admired – and was the female knight who held a bow over them during their first encounter with their new allies. Xenia was tall for a Freylarkin, had short raven black hair, which too was shaved along the right side, and was an unrelenting devout Knight of the Order. Unlike Captain Gedrick, who maintained a cool head, Xenia was feisty and quick to judge. Regardless, she felt a kindred soul in Xenia who – much like her – held true to notions of duty and honour. She had learned much about the female knight during their journey to the Ardent Gate, shortly after their first encounter. The Order was everything to Xenia, as indeed appeared to be the case for the other knights she overheard talking as they had marched out earlier that morning. Their numbers were few, though accompanying them were Zephir and Knight Restorant Loredan, who was the Order's sole surviving renewalist. The revered renewalist was flanked by Knights of the Order at all times; according to Gedrick, without Loredan's ability to heal their wounds, the Knights Thranis would have long since faded from memory. The Captain had warned them, in no uncertain terms, of the dangers they would face when fighting the Ravnarkai; it was a stark warning, subsequently reiterated by other knights in their company.

'Remember, that armour is the only thing between you and the Everlife.' said Xenia, who continued to lecture her on Ravnarkai combat doctrine.

'The fit is adequate, though I am not used to the heat.' she replied.

'That will come in time. What is important for now is that you remember to lean into the charge, and let your armour and shield ride the impact.' continued Xenia. 'Only then, once your opponent's momentum is spent, will you counter with that impractical falchion of yours.'

'And what if the Ravnarkai should knock me off my feet, what then?' she enquired.

'If that happens, consider this my first and last lesson for you.' replied Xenia flatly.

Zephir, who marched directly in front of them flanking Loredan, had been listening in on their exchange. Until now the knight had remained unusually silent, abstaining from lambasting his habitual sarcastic remarks; he seemed more interested in The Guardian, who marched at the front of their column alongside Captain Gedrick.

'Do not concern yourself *petite*. The Ravnarkai only expend their energy on those who would make a worthy meal.' he said disdainfully, blatantly mocking her height.

The Guardian overheard the derisive comment and deliberately broke step until she fell back in line with the column alongside Zephir. The sardonic knight ignored Rayna's sudden presence, and instead chose to focus on Gedrick, who remained at the head of the column. Unperturbed, The Guardian lent in close to Zephir, offering counsel of her own.

'When Anika cuts you down to her height, I will be certain to pull rank and ensure that she offers you a lesson in ground based combat. Far better than all that venom you spit, don't you think?'

Zephir made no further remark and instead focused on the rhythmic step of their march. Rayna gave the belittled knight a beaming smile then quickened her pace to rejoin Gedrick's side. Though she remained nonchalant in the wake of the incident, The Guardian's unconventional rebuke made her smile inside. She was short – that fact was undeniable – yet her height would not thwart her efforts to drive back the Ravnarkai.

'Ignore him. Zephir has survived many Hunts; each one adds to the increasing weight on his soul.' explained Xenia.

'I understand.'

'Do you?!' Zephir shot back, flashing a cold dark sneer.

'I may only be a Blade Novice, but I have endured horror enough to last me a lifetime.' she replied sternly. 'Have you yourself witnessed the souls of your brothers and sisters torn screaming from their moorings, rendering their bodies withered empty husks?'

'Perhaps not, *petite*, though I have seen them dismembered and eaten instead.'

'Quiet!' commanded Gedrick in a deep voice from the front of the column. 'Whilst you bicker needlessly amongst yourselves, The Hunt already begins.'

She watched with intrigue as Krasus diligently carried out her will; the master shaper followed her direction meticulously. Mirielle's recommendation had proven to be an excellent candidate for the work she had in mind. With the aid of Krasus' expert ability, it would not take them long to restore the derelict sanctuary to working order, thus rendering it fit for purpose once more. Krasus was fastidious in his work, which arguably delayed progress, though his mastery of his ability more than made up for time spent fussing over details. Despite being younger than her, Krasus was nonetheless a mature Freylarkin; the reduced age gap made it easy for them to communicate – there were times when she found accurately communicating with the youth of Freylar irksome. She was delighted therefore when Krasus agreed to accompany her so readily; the talented shaper was keen to engage in a project far removed from his usual mundane trade, back in the vale. The opportunity to stretch his legs beyond the confines of the Tri-Spires also greatly appealed to his sense of creativity; ergo she had little trouble coaxing Krasus away from the normality of existence in the vale. Sat on the worn stone steps of the sanctuary's inner stairway, watching with admiring eyes as Krasus manipulated the long slit windows at either end of the structure. Krasus performed a series of complex hand gestures, then touched one of the northern window frames; immediately the window's lower sill rose in height, forming new rock in its wake as it rose vertically. When the sill eventually came to a halt in its new resting place, the total length of the window had been reduced to almost half of its original height. This caused a reduced amount of light to enter the room, though it had the advantage of restricting visibility to the outside world. Scrier's needed to focus their ability; moreover, apprentice scriers required isolation from unnecessary distractions in order to glean the most from their second sight.

'Aleska, what are you doing here?!'

She flinched suddenly at the unexpected question, which echoed throughout the room in its scathing tone. Startled, she quickly turned her head towards the sanctuary's main entrance. Standing in the arched doorway was Nathaniel, and another she recognised, Keshar, one of Freylar's apprentice scriers. She recalled first being introduced to the promising young scrier several passes ago; Kirika had introduced her and was singing the youth's praises at the time. Seeing the grass roots scrier again now, standing at the fulcrum of her latest ambition, amused her immensely. Given the disapproving look on Nathaniel's face, it was ironic that he should be the one to bring the first of her future students.

'Perhaps I should ask you that same question, Nathaniel?' she countered politely.

'Kirika and I were concerned about your unannounced leave of absence.' replied Nathaniel. 'Why have you come to this forsaken place?'

She knew well that her absence would not go unnoticed indefinitely; indeed she had already foreseen Keshar's arrival, though not the manner of its unfolding. Failing to make her last appointment with Kirika was bound to set tongues wagging. Still, she had not expected to see anyone from the vale so soon – there was still much to do.

Although she was deeply fond of Nathaniel, and enjoyed his company immensely, his presence now was not conducive to her plans. It was entirely likely that he would disapprove of her actions, especially given the undisclosed nature of her presence at Scrier's Post.

'There is no need for concern. I am here on official business Nathaniel.' she responded coolly.

'Why have you brought a shaper here with you?' asked Nathaniel sternly.

'Perhaps we could talk outside in private?'

Nathaniel nodded slowly before dismissing Keshar, who seemed content to indulge her curiosity further by examining the sanctuary up close – she took this as a good sign, and confirmation that her scrying still bore fruit.

The air outside was brisk; instinctively she rubbed the length of her arms, trying to generate a little warmth. She looked up, only to bear witness to the drab autumnal grey sky above; summer had left Freylar, leaving behind the firm grasp of autumn. They would need to work fast if Scrier's Post was to be serviceable for the coming winter. No doubt the drop in temperature would agitate her already aching joints – a good hearth would be needed she reminded herself. She glanced at Nathaniel as they walked towards the north end of the courtyard; his face bore a stony expression and the musculature of his exposed arms appeared tense, causing their scarring to seem more prominent than usual. Though she understood their significance, she often wished that Nathaniel would heal the ugly scars which – in her opinion – marred his otherwise good looks. In any event, Nathaniel's body language had changed; she would need to choose her words wisely in order to diffuse his obvious agitation.

'Aleska, please explain your actions here at this awful place.' asked Nathaniel, wasting no time in cutting to the heart of the matter.

'Very well, I will explain my presence here, though I ask that you hear me out fully before drawing any conclusions.' she replied flatly.

'Agreed.' replied Nathaniel, who then leaned against the perimeter wall with his arms folded.

'As you know, queen Mirielle deemed it necessary to impose restrictions upon those with the ability to scry; there were no exceptions to this ruling. The judgement was supported by the ruling council and, when necessary, enforced by The Blades.' she recounted, setting the scene for what was to come.

'Specifically, you refer to Darlia?'

'Correct, amongst other incidents. Look around you Nathaniel. What was the result of that action?' she asked, now fixing her gaze on the tiny silver orbs which were his preternatural eyes.

Nathaniel chose not to break eye contact with her. Instead he sighed heavily, before issuing his blunt response. 'War.'

'Which lead to an invasion of Freylar, followed by the regrettable and untimely release of your students.' She took a moment to let the facts sink in, before proceeding to explain the reason for her presence at Scrier's Post. 'We made a terrible mistake Nathaniel; instead of backing our scriers into a corner, we should be nurturing their ability.'

'Ha, the likely seed of yet another war Aleska. Nurturing, manipulating – whatever you choose to call it –

still denies true freedom to those cursed with the second sight.'

'But you agree that scriers cannot be allowed to operate unchecked?'

'You know my position on the matter. I supported the council's controversial decision, but exchanging one set of shackles for another is not the answer. Moreover, the act of changing that stance would be construed as indecision by the public.'

'Though I disagree with you on the former, you are quite correct on the latter point. For that reason the migration would need to be a gradual one.' she replied.

'The migration of what exactly? I ask you again, Aleska, what are you doing here?'

Nathaniel was beginning to show signs of increased agitation.

'You have your school in the arena, where you train those with heart and aggression. I intended to build my school here, at Scrier's Post, where we will once more nurture those with the ability to scry. It is here that we will mould future scriers; teaching them how to control their ability whilst keenly educating them, particularly regarding the perils prevalent when overstepping the accepted boundaries of one's scrying.'

'You cannot compare my training in the arena to this...this madness you propose Aleska!' replied Nathaniel, who now stood upright, having abandoned the brace of the perimeter wall.

'Hypocrisy, Nathaniel, as well you know it! You train your students, as would I.'

'Past and future; neither can be known fully to the Freylarkai. It is a fool's errand Aleska, the knowledge would destroy Freylarkin society.'

'And that is why we must educate them; to prevent extreme abuse of the ability.'

'You offer the illusion of freedom, whilst still controlling their actions Aleska. You will only create a build-up of pressure, which will explode once the truth is known. Better they abide by the restrictions already in place.'

'What restrictions? Do not be so naive in this matter Nathaniel; they are already breaking the sanctions placed upon them! Dare I even enquire as to how exactly you found me?'

'That was sanctioned, by your own student no less!' replied Nathaniel, whose anger was now beginning to flare.

'No, it was personal usage Nathaniel.'

'We were concerned for your wellbeing Aleska. You left the vale without informing anyone of your intent.'

'That is not adequate justification Nathaniel. Am I not entitled to my privacy?'

'You are twisting my words!'

'And you are failing to understand mine! It is not enough to make an example of scriers who cross the line. Curiosity simply cannot be curtailed; events here have taught us that painful lesson. Surely you understand this Nathaniel?' she implored, desperately hoping that the issue would not cause a divide between them.

Nathaniel turned his back on her abruptly and disengaged from their heated conversation in order to vent; he walked several paces away from her, along the perimeter wall, before coming to a halt. Nathaniel performed a well-rehearsed series of breathing techniques, which he routinely taught his students. The exercises were designed to release tension and calm the mind, thus allowing one to focus their thoughts more clearly. The techniques were not dissimilar to those taught to apprentice scriers. She decided it best to afford him the space he required, before resuming their heated exchange. After a short while Nathaniel returned. He looked calmer, yet also distant – his altered demeanour terrified her.

'Clearly we disagree on this matter.' said Nathaniel calmly. 'Your revised thinking scares me Aleska, and I am concerned as to what this means for you personally. It is obvious to me now that you intend to reinstate Scrier's Post. I cannot be a part of your ambition, and I will not be the one to break this news to our queen. That is something you alone must do. Are you prepared to suffer the consequences of your actions, or would you prefer to reconsider your position and let this be the end of the matter?'

'Oh Nathaniel...it pains me to see such matters come between us.' she replied despondently.

'It pains me also, Aleska, but you have not answered my question.'

'I value your friendship and your company, Nathaniel, but regardless, you do what you must, since my decision on this matter is final.'

Nathaniel sighed deeply before replying, 'So be it. I will escort you and your shaper companion back to the Tri-Spires where you can explain your recent actions to Queen Mirielle in person. She must be the one to cast judgement on the matter.'

'You need not trouble yourself with such action Nathaniel.'

'You are responsible for the creation of new infrastructure which will undermine Freylarian law. Queen Mirielle must be made aware of your actions here – you need to return to the Tri-Spires at once.'

'Nathaniel, there really is no need; it was Queen Mirielle who sent me here.'

EIGHT
Impact

She flinched violently, waking herself from her reverie. It had been a long night, and her attempts to get some rest that morning had been largely unsuccessful. Their fervent work on Lileah's mutilated body had run through the night. Though their efforts eventually bore fruit, the ostentatious work wrought by Krashnar, under her direction, did nothing to diminish Lileah's disability. For now Lileah remained semi-conscious, though she feared the impending cycle heralding her lover's full awakening. The changes to Lileah's body were ghastly. Her reaction to the sight had been one of revulsion, how then would Lileah respond to the sight of her own body which resembled little of its former self? Even Lileah's flesh had changed; what little fat once clung to her petite frame had since withered away, as her body exhausted its final reserves. Lileah's skin was blotched and bruised; those areas not marred had instead become unnaturally pallid.

'Eat!' said Krashnar, who tossed an over-ripe fruit into her lap. 'You will be of no further use to me if your strength wanes.'

The spoiled fruit was a fitting analogy for Lileah's current plight; something once beautiful, in its own unique way, now spoilt, bordering on rotten. She stared vacantly at the pungent fruit; her appetite had abandoned her, and Krashnar's inappropriate choice of meal did nothing to remedy the situation. The wild-looking shaper bit savagely into his own serving; juice from the over-ripe fruit spilled from the corners of his mouth, polluting the air with its sweet sticky scent. She pushed the unappealing fruit onto the stone floor where it landed with a wet thud – further proof that the meal was no longer fit for consumption.

'That was a waste of good material.' said Krashnar in his habitual raspy accursed tone.

She loathed listening to Krashnar's abhorrent voice; were it not for his mastery of his ability, she would have no reason to engage in any dealings with the insidious shaper. Previously she had been a scrier widely respected amongst her peers, and enjoyed a comfortable lifestyle alongside her kin; now she kept the company of monsters and other things best avoided. She once had everything, and now nothing. Lileah would soon abandon her – that inevitability she did not need to scry – and she no longer had a place to call home. Even her sister Kirika lay beyond her reach. Was her desire to explore the extremes of her ability worth so much loss she began to wonder? Arguably not, given her present company and the ill fate that had befallen Lileah.

'Are you even listening to me?' rasped Krashnar once more.

'I wish that I could do anything but listen to you. The awful sound of your voice, and the poison it proclaims, is anathema to me.' she replied flatly.

Krashnar gave a horrible laugh in response to her derogatory remark; the shaper seemed to feed on her loathing as though it nourished him, or gave him some sense of purpose to his otherwise wretched existence.

'Irrelevant.' replied Krashanr.

'Then what is relevant to you?!' she replied, offering Krashnar another of her familiar sneers.

'For now, at least, she needs nourishment of her own; without it her body will wither entirely, rendering my work useless.' explained Krashnar. 'Since she cannot yet eat of her own volition, we must feed her forcibly by inserting a tube down her throat.'

Prior to seeking Krashnar's aid the very notion of forcibly feeding a Freylarkin via a tube would have shocked her, but already she had become accustomed to Krashnar's twisted way of thinking. Though the idea still sickened her, once again the shaper made a valid point; she just wished that Krashnar's methods were less garish. His ghastly work ethic and constant need to experiment was distasteful. The rogue shaper seemed disinterested in anything conventional, such was his sociopathic disposition.

'And what would you have us *forcibly* feed her?'

'We may as well put that fruit to good use, which you so spitefully disowned.' replied Krashnar, staring at the spoiled fruit which lay at her feet.

'Eurgh, you are a repulsive being.'

'So you keep stating. If you find my work distasteful then you are welcome to leave. I have no time for those lacking vision, or the stomach, to see my projects through to their conclusion.'

'That is all Lileah is to you, a new *project*; an opportunity to experiment with something different. Your projects are vile Krashnar.' she replied in a distant monotone voice.

'*Your* opinion.' replied Krashnar.

For reasons she did not entirely understand, Krashnar's response resonated with her. Like a Freylarkin finally deciding to get out of bed in the morning, her mind suddenly re-engaged with her surroundings, rousing her from the numb state of being she had defaulted to since Lileah's transformation. She turned her gaze towards

Krashnar, instinctively narrowing her eyes, as she sought to probe the shaper's words further.

'And that of a great number of other Fraylarkai, presumably?'

'Ha!' replied Krashnar, who then spat more of the vile black liquid from his mouth that she had previously had the displeasure of witnessing.

The fluid landed less than half a pace from the pungent fruit at her feet. Shortly after making contact with the stone floor, the black tar-like substance consolidated its form then slid quietly across the floor towards the over-ripe fruit. Upon contact, the fluid seeped into the heart of the burst fruit, promptly causing it to discolour; the vibrant red and orange hues of the fruit's flesh turned rapidly to purple and brown, akin to the colour of bruising.

'*You* know better than most that exile is rarely the will of the people. Mirielle ordered my exile, as she did yours. Their queen alone is responsible for our unjust sentence. Remember that!'

'I recall well enough the reasons for my own downfall, it is just that...' she started to reply, before her mind quickly became lost within a turbulent sea of colliding thought.

The contaminated fruit at her feet was now beginning to wither and fade from existence because of her decision to spitefully reject it, rather than accepting it for what it was. How had Mirielle's actions been any different, she wondered?

'Where are your thoughts taking you Darlia?'

'They are none of your concern; my thoughts are my own. Now then, what further abhorrent acts would you have me perform?'

It was fast approaching dusk and the cycle's light was already abandoning them. The southern fringe landscape was littered with jagged rocks which protruded from the surrounding heathland. More of the black spindly trees which they had seen on their journey to the Ardent Gate dotted the landscape; their small plentiful leaves drifted haphazardly on the light breeze as autumn tore them free of their moorings. The strange ever-present mist which lurked on the horizon was beginning to roll in closer now, causing the fading light of the cycle to weaken further. The odd mist diluted the low sun, bathing the scrubland with a preternatural yellow-grey light. Except for the occasional rustle of leaves, as the wind swept through the dark twisted trees, the only audible sound came from the habitual clanking of their armour. Given the surreal nature of their surroundings, she felt at times as though she was wandering around inside a painting; nothing about the place seemed real – to her at least.

Most of the cycle had been spent patrolling the landscape, though Captain Gedrick had insisted on frequent breaks to ensure they remained fresh. They kept their patrol simple, repeating the same circular route time and again; Xenia assured her that knowledge of the landscape was a useful tool when combating the Ravnarkai. She learnt from Zephir that the Ravnarkai were fickle pack hunters, however, when the mood for battle did finally prompt them to attack, she was assured that such engagements were furious affairs and invariably bloody. However, according to Zephir, it was extremely rare for the Ravnarkai to attack so late in the cycle.

'Perhaps they figured that *petite* here is just not worth the bother?'

'More likely they got bored of listening to your unimaginative insults Zephir.' retorted Xenia, who was clearly beginning to tire of the sardonic knight's quips.

'No, it is not that.' said Loredan, finally breaking his silence since leaving the Ardent Gate. 'They have been stalking us for some time now.'

'If you knew that, Knight Restorant Loredan, why did you not inform us sooner?' she asked, curious as to why he had previously withheld his counsel.

Loredan was lean for a member of the Knights Thranis; she presumed, given his ability, that he engaged in less combat than the other knights. Yet despite his leaner build, his muscle definition was nonetheless still impressive; she recalled the knight's physique well from their arming that morning. She had been studying the Knight Restorant's meticulous application of his arming doublet at the time, which included mail voiders to protect any gaps in his plate armour. The obviously well-practised ritual was slow and methodical; though it was likely that Loredan could have sped up the process, he took his time, ensuring that nothing was unaccounted for. Xenia's earlier words returned to her once again, causing her stomach to churn. 'That armour is the only thing between you and the Everlife.'

'The timing of my warning now seems appropriate.' replied Loredan, who nodded his head towards a dark shape, half-obscured by a large jagged rock protruding from the mist on their right flank.

The shape was completely motionless. At quick glance it could have been mistaken for an extension of the rock behind which it lurked. It seemed – to her at least – to be watching them. Its outline was beastly in appearance; even at a distance she could make out the well-defined musculature of the lean arms and legs which supported its oversized head and body. It was hunched over menacingly, like a wolf preparing to charge down its prey, yet it remained perfectly still as it continued to observe them.

'Barbutes on!' barked Gedrick.

She immediately pulled at her helmet, which was hooked by its strap over the long hilt of her falchion. In her haste to wrestle the barbute free, she fumbled the head armour, which dropped to the hard ground, promptly rolling away from her.

'Ready your ardent swords!' barked Gedrick again.

Instinctively she unsheathed her falchion and readied her shield. She thought about retrieving her barbute, but the dark shape was already advancing towards them with incredible speed; it had since dropped to the floor, and was using its arms as an additional pair of legs for increased velocity.

'Three more on our left flank!' cried Zephir, who now gripped the hilt of his ardent sword menacingly with both hands.

She turned her head back towards the shape on her right, which by now had already covered half of the original distance between them – its speed was astonishing. Another shape burst into view behind the first, leaping out from the cover of the protruding rock which had masked their collective presence.

'First one is mine!' cried Xenia, who immediately nocked an arrow to her bow.

Xenia drew her bow sharply and released its arrow straight into the front left limb of the advancing shape. The shot was clean, causing the beast to collapse to the ground; it kicked up dirt and heather as it rolled off course, carried by its own momentum. Astonishingly the Ravnarkin rolled over several times, before subsequently regaining its feet in one fluid motion. Seemingly unperturbed by the attack, the Ravnarkin continued its charge towards Xenia along its new trajectory, with only a fraction of its momentum lost. Xenia was already preparing to release another arrow, though she could ill afford to observe the outcome of the combat with the second Ravnarkin already bearing down on her. Turning from Xenia, she readied herself for the oncoming Ravnarkin charge. Heeding her companion's words, she adjusted her footing and shifted her body weight accordingly. She tightened her grip on her shield and pulled it in close to her armoured torso. Even without her barbute, she could hear the sound of her own heavy breathing as she steeled herself in readiness for the imminent impact.

Moments prior to contact, the Ravnarkin burst into visual clarity. The beastly looking form had slanted black oval eyes and a powerful crooked maw which protruded forwards like a muzzle. The Ravnarkin's jaws were wide open, exposing a dual set of foul jagged teeth. The muscle definition across its hunched body was grotesquely pronounced, causing its ailing ruddy pink skin to appear stretched across its lumpy frame. The creature's muscles seemed fit to burst, particularly across its limbs, despite their lean appearance. The beast suddenly dipped its head as it charged down the final few paces between them. It slammed violently into her shield. The Ravnarkin's brutal impact instantly winded her and caused her vision to momentarily black out, whilst her body struggled to cope with the shock. Her legs became weightless and she felt her body rise upwards. The creature's momentum saw it pass beneath her as it took out her legs; her body was thrown across its back like a rag doll, left to crash hard against the ground in a crumpled heap. Her senses went numb and she could feel the accelerated thump of her heart pounding in her chest. Without a moment's thought, or any regard to her present condition, she clambered back to her feet and tried to re-orientate herself whilst gasping for air. The Ravnarkin had overrun her and was skidding wildly in an attempt to circle back for a fresh charge. Her left arm was missing its shield, though her right still retained its strained grip on her falchion. None of her training in the arena had prepared her for a foe which clearly held no regard for its own wellbeing; the Ravnarkai seemingly possessed no qualms about using their bodies as effective battering rams – their solid bulk made them worthy juggernauts. Her attacker eventually regained traction with the hard ground and renewed its charge towards her, albeit lacking the momentum of its initial attack. Its pace had slowed considerably affording her time to potentially counter the renewed attack, despite her bewildered state. Cognitive thought played very little part during the remainder of her duel with the Ravnarkin; the only forces governing her actions now were instinct and Nathaniel's ingrained training, fuelled by the adrenaline flooding her system – there was no time for anything else. She spun round on her left armoured heel to perform a discus-like slash, aimed at where she instinctively predicted the beast would be based on its current speed and trajectory. She brought her falchion round in a vicious arc injecting as much power as she could into the attack. Hoping to strike the Ravnarkin across its flank, the timing of the attack was premature, causing her blade to instead slash diagonally down across the side of its face. The creature's right eye exploded on contact with her falchion, releasing watery black fluid. Stained teeth and ruddy flesh were torn from its maw as the weight of her blade cut deep. The impact momentarily stunned the creature, causing it to fall onto its left flank. Whilst the frenzied Ravnarkin began to right itself, she followed up the attack by stepping forwards and bringing the sharp edge of her falchion up and under the Ravnarkin's muzzle; the blade sliced deep into the already ruined flesh of the Ravnarkin. Defiantly the wounded creature stood up unsteadily on its legs, despite her devastating attack. It hissed loudly with the remains of its bloody maw stretched wide, revealing a long slender tongue which hung loosely from the ruined side of its mouth. It slashed with its left arm towards the right side of her torso; its sharp claws caught her between the plates of her armour, digging deep into the mail of her arming doublet. The ferocity of the blow caused her to cry out in pain as the force of the creature's claws broke the surface of her skin. As she stumbled backwards, reeling in pain from the attack, the Ravnarkin pressed forwards, slashing at her face with its right arm. She felt the sting of the tips of its claws rake across her face, narrowly missing her left eye. The attack wrong-footed the Ravnarkin, exposing the blind side of its right flank. She rolled forwards across her right shoulder then, using the momentum to regain an upright position, she channelled her remaining strength into bringing her falchion round in a last deadly swing. She struck her attacker flush across its right flank. The razor-sharp edge of her blade scored a deep gash across the side of the beast's torso, sending it crashing to the ground once more. The Ravnarkin hissed in pain and writhed on the ground as dark purple blood poured from the fresh wound. Her strength finally waned, causing her legs to give out on her; she dropped to her knees, still gasping for air, watching intently while her fallen attacker rapidly bled out from its fatal wounds.

It was only after the fallen Ravnarkin's final death throes that her body began to relax; the earlier rush of adrenaline began to fade fast, allowing the pain of her battered body to announce its presence. The right side of her torso ached terribly. She looked to where the Ravnarkin had caught her with its wretched claws; blood was seeping through the mail voider, between the plates of her armour protecting the right side of her torso. Instinctively she tried to apply pressure to the wound with her free arm, refusing to abandon her falchion, though her armour thwarted her efforts. She drove her falchion into the ground, using it as a crutch to regain her feet. Quickly surveying the battlefield she counted the corpses of at least five Ravnarkin. The conflict around her was reaching its climax. Another Ravnarkin promptly fell to the deadly arc of Gedrick's ardent sword; the enormous blade tore into the right side of his attacker's neck, spraying the ground with more of the Ravnarkai's blood. Two more Ravnarkai were still standing, though Zephir and The Guardian had their measure – the surviving beasts would soon join their fallen kin.

Falkai, who had been marching at the rear of their column prior to the ambush, lay badly wounded on the ground, though fortunately Knight Restorant Loredan was already tending to the fallen knight's wounds. She tried to reach Zephir and The Guardian, to lend them support, but the pain in her torso held her back; already unsteady on her feet, she was beginning to feel giddy and light headed.

Before losing her balance entirely, she careened towards the nearest tree, using it as a brace. Though the battle was effectively won, she refused – this time – to end the confrontation on her back. She closed her eyes and employed breathing techniques, taught to her by Nathaniel, to help regulate her breathing and make attempt at masking the throbbing pain of her wounded torso. In those peaceful moments of still darkness she could feel her soul beginning to drift away, carried by the gentle sound of her controlled breathing. However, the familiar sound of Zephir's derisive voice soon roused her from her reverie.

'Falkai, get up!' shouted Zephir. 'You are making us look bad in front of *petite* here.'

She opened her eyes to see Zephir and Xenia walking casually towards her. Zephir had removed his barbute, which he now carried in his left hand. He had a wide grin stretched across his bruised face, which was a rarity for the sardonic knight.

'Looks like you made a mess of that one.' he said, nodding towards the fallen Ravnarkin behind her. 'You share Xenia's heart I see, and have perhaps earned yourself a place at the dining table tonight *petite*.'

'My name is Anika.' she replied flatly, having finally grown tired of Zephir's continued mocking of her height.

Zephir smiled; it was the first time she had witnessed the veteran knight express any such pleasantries since their first encounter. He extended his arm towards her, which she gladly accepted.

'I am afraid that is the best you can expect from Zephir.' said Xenia light-heartedly, as Zephir pulled her away from the tree.

'Loredan will get you patched up, after he is done licking Falkai's wounds over there, though you may end up with a scar on that pretty face of yours. Loredan is no *master* renewalist, like your Teacher, but he can get the job done.'

'I did not come here to look pretty.' she replied in her familiar flat tone.

'Ha!' replied Zephir. 'That I can see for myself, though I suggest you go find your barbute and perhaps consider using it next time eh?'

'Sure. And since I clearly do not need a shield either, perhaps you could show me how to swing that giant toothpick of yours?'

Zephir laughed hard, though his laughter was free of its usual venom. Perhaps she had misjudged the veteran knight she mused? The Knights Thranis were a tightly-knit Order, with strong bonds of fellowship bred through countless battles endured together. She began to understand now why they had been so chiding and reticent towards herself and The Guardian during their first encounter. To the Knights Thranis, both she and Rayna *were* outsiders, yet to prove their worth. However, now they had bled on the field of battle – or at least she had – in service to the Knights' Order; that act alone meant something. The Guardian had provided the crucial foot in the door they needed, and their subsequent service to the Order had potentially ushered in their acceptance. When Zephir offered her his hand, she could sense that it was intended as more than simple aid; his change in body language had confirmed as much. The act itself was symbolic, and a firm sign that they had taken the first few steps down a long road which, hopefully, would bring both orders closer together. Initially she had seen their mission as little more than an opportunity to cement her commitment and fealty to The Blades. Having spent little over a cycle with the Knights, her perception of their mission had altered somewhat. She admired their fealty to their own Order; who amongst The Blades would freely offer themselves as bait, to draw out an opponent, she wondered? The Knights Thranis were clearly skilled warriors, who led a disciplined lifestyle. They lived to serve their Order, enjoying only the pleasures offered through service well executed and the company of those sworn to their campaign. She admired the simplicity of their existence and the solace – to her at least – their way of life offered.

Zephir stepped closer, and in doing so his demeanour suddenly took on a more serious tone. 'Once we return to the Ardent Gate, you can have your choice of toothpick. After which, Anika, I will train you!'

NINE
Reality

He woke suddenly. Slowly the familiar sight of the Night's Lights came into focus. He was lying on his back, out in the open. Krisis was licking the side of his face; the loyal dire wolf had clearly succeeded in waking him from his slumber. He sat up abruptly. Instinctively he clutched his head, which ached painfully; evidentially he had not yet fully recovered from the psychic scream which had temporarily paralysed his body. Krisis had been the one to drag him away to a safe distance, though he must have subsequently lost consciousness entirely. He tried to stand but his body was stiff and ached all over, forcing him to stay down. Absentmindedly he licked his lips; they were dry and cracked. He wiped the back of his hand across the corner of his mouth to dislodge some dirt; he was surprised by the amount of stubble he felt on his chin. How long had he lain unconscious, he wondered? Turning to Krisis for answers, he opened up a conduit to his mind which he then linked to the dire wolf's own. Though dire wolves were only capable of basic thought, and had even less concept of time than the Freylarkai, nonetheless they recognised well the passing of the moon.

'How many moons have passed?'

Krisis barked loudly in response to his telepathic enquiry; the dire wolf barked precisely three times, suggesting that the same number of cycles had passed since the encounter with his nemesis.

'Damn it, you idiot! Why did you not listen?!' he said, chiding himself aloud.

For a brief moment he thought about dispatching Krisis once more, as he had done previously when alerting the vale to the impending Narlakai invasion. Circumstances were different now though; Darlia and the rogue telepath would be long gone. Despite the wound inflicted by Nathanar, the pair would almost certainly now be beyond his reach. Allowing revenge to cloud his judgement, he had recklessly compromised their tactical advantage through his impetuous actions – The Blades no longer possessed the element of surprise. Returning to the vale with news of his failure would only worsen his less than perfect standing with Marcus. He had already been made to look the fool, courtesy of Kirika's estranged elder sibling; another public setback would likely cast doubt over his ability, and possibly even his rank. At any rate, he would not be returning to the vale immediately given his weakened state; there was still time to consider his options.

'Damn you!' he said aloud, cursing towards the black sky.

It was glaringly obvious now that he simply could not defeat the rogue telepath alone. He offered Krisis a sidelong glance, as he contemplated his own failings – something he was not accustomed to doing. His faithful lupine companion sat tentatively, awaiting further instructions. Others would judge him based on his actions, though Krisis would not; the trusted dire wolf knew only loyal service, and would not question his master. He smiled affectionately at Krisis and offered his right hand; the large dire wolf quickly moved to his side, gladly accepting the opportunity to have its thick black fur stroked.

'*You have done well.*'

It was late evening and, with the exception of those tasked with sentry duty, all of the knights were gathered in the Ardent Gate's mess hall for their evening meal. The gathering was habitual; every evening the knights would rally around one of four enormously long wooden tables stationed in the mess hall. The tables were arranged such that they almost connected with one another at either end, forming a large square arrangement. The Knight Lord had insisted that the three empty tables remain in situ as an ever-present reminder of the losses the Order had sustained over the passes. They served as a stark reminder, to those still engaged in The Hunt, of the very real danger the Ravnarkai posed to Freylar. Without the knights' incessant culling, the Ravnarkai would flood the southern lands unopposed. If left unchecked the Ravnarkai's numbers would swell uncontrollably, driving them further north. Due to their tribal mentality, the beasts were extremely territorial; each sect distanced itself from its neighbours, causing them to spread out across their domain. Occasionally sects would come into contact with one another and these were often bloody encounters, resulting in heavy losses on both sides. For the most part the Ravnarkai maintained a good distance between their neighbouring kin. That said, the beasts were extremely aggressive; those outside of their sect were met with ferocious hostility, more often release.

A number of cycles had passed since their introduction to The Hunt. In that time both she and The Guardian had accompanied Captain Gedrick on two more sorties. However, the Knights' most recent staged incursion was deemed beyond their current ability; she and Rayna had remained behind at the Ardent Gate, training with the other reserves. Following their first engagement with the

Ravnarkai, she had chosen to forgo her familiar falchion in favour of an ardent sword, the Knights' preferred weapon of choice. She found the long blade awkward to wield at first, however, after careful one-on-one instruction from Zephir, she quickly learnt the correct hold and use of the weapon and subsequently welcomed its increased range. Xenia had offered to further train her bow skill, though engaging one's foes at range was not her strong point. Although courting release through direct melee with the Ravnarkai was a frightening experience, she secretly enjoyed the rush and the discipline of close combat with the beasts; the fear and anxiety of release helped her to bury the memories of her recent encounter with the Narlakai. Fighting against the Ravnarkai was typically barbaric – they were savage creatures, eager to tear at flesh and spill blood. Yet despite their innate savagery, she preferred fighting these beasts to the Narlakai. The soul stealers were largely incorporeal things; fighting against them was disconcerting. The Ravnarkai, by contrast, were far simpler opponents to evaluate. They were tangible creatures which fought instinctively with tooth and claw, combined with their superior strength, speed and agility. Despite their preternatural movement, their moves could be anticipated. The Narlakai, however, were entirely unpredictable – their eerie disposition terrified her.

The mood around the long wooden table was jovial, despite the empty tables and chairs that surrounded them. Knight Lord Heldran sat at the middle of the table, with his enormous back to the wall, facing towards the centre of the squared table arrangement. Knight Captain Gedrick sat to Heldran's right, with Knight Restorant Loredan occupying the Knight Lord's left flank. She sat near The Guardian, who in turn sat opposite Heldran. Flanking her were Knights of the Order whom she had already fought alongside during The Hunt, including Xenia and Zephir. The Knights Thranis were much like an extended family. Each contributed to the maintenance and general cycle-to-cycle running of the Ardent Gate, regardless of their ability. Indeed, she and The Guardian had helped to dress the table at which they dined, whilst others diligently prepared their evening meal. There were those of the Order tasked with hunting game, and others who routinely took shifts on sentry duty. Popularity and rank played no part in the community; everyone helped. Even Gedrick and Heldran routinely engaged in mundane errands, entirely beneath their station – there were simply not enough Freylarkai stationed at the Ardent Gate to justify able bodies taking a back seat when jobs needed doing. The change of pace was refreshing, and a complete departure to the stuffy rigid hierarchy of The Blades. The Knights Thranis had only a basic hierarchy. Aside from Gedrick and Heldran, those Freylarkai stationed at the Ardent Gate all held the same rank of Knight – though only once they had proven their loyalty and tested their mettle during The Hunt. Loredan was the only member to hold the title of Knight Restorant, due to the countless number of Freylarkai he had saved from release during The Hunt. Though an honorary title, the Knights Thranis held a deep-seated respect for Loredan; if required to do so, each would welcome release to ensure that no harm came to their revered renewalist. For the most part they were equals, brothers and sisters in arms, and respected one another accordingly – despite their banter occasionally suggesting otherwise.

She watched with interest as those gathered around the table ate and socialised with ease; she envied the casual manner in which they interacted with one another. Since the attack at Scrier's Post, she found it difficult to converse freely with others. The incident had left its mark on her psyche; she found it hard to let her guard down, even during social gatherings. Curiously the same incident had seemingly not affected The Guardian. Rayna had an almost permanent mischievous smile etched on her face, as she conversed enthusiastically with Heldran across the wide table.

'You envy them, do you not?' asked Xenia, who sat next to her.

She sighed heavily before responding, 'Yes, because I used to be like them.'

'What, you...a prolific conjurer of dialogue?' interjected Zephir, who sat opposite them, looking up from his food in amusement.

'Unlike you then?' replied Xenia playfully.

'Point well made.' Zephir replied, before turning his attention back to his meal.

'It is true. I never used to be so...guarded.'

Zephir's eyes languidly followed her plate as she gently pushed it aside then leant back in her chair. Absentmindedly she cast her gaze towards the mess hall's high wooden ceiling. She was not particularly hungry, and memories of her past distracted her from the prospect of a good meal. Zephir's greedy right hand latched onto the abandoned plate; she had barely touched her food.

'Sure you do not want this?'

'No, you eat it. I am not hungry.'

'Regardless of your appetite, your strength will abandon you if you do not eat regularly.' Xenia lectured.

Abandon – the word resonated with her as she continued to gaze upwards. Ever since the souls of her fellow Aspirants were released during that ill-fated night, she too had felt abandoned. She could still hear Kryshar's screams, though they were faint like a distant echo in her mind. Where did their souls reside now, she wondered? Prior to The Guardian's arrival in Freylar, she had been a firm believer in the Everlife; a domain vigilantly watched over by the Sky-Walkers, who were also the Freylarkai's guardian benefactors. However, things were different now since Rayna's enigmatic arrival. Aside from her presence, The Guardian offered little to validate the existence of the Sky-Walkers. Her world had changed, and in doing so had forced her to change with it, as her perception of Freylar and its inhabitants altered in line with her experiences. Her friends had abandoned her, and along with them her once spritely disposition. The Vengeful Tears temporarily filled the void in her soul, yet she still felt hollow inside; their zeal alone was not enough to sustain her – she longed for *something* more.

'That necklace you wear...does it hold meaning? I see that both you and Rayna wear one.' asked Xenia politely.

'They were a gift, from Queen Mirielle, for our service during the recent Narlakai conflict at Scrier's Post.'

'Is it a Moonstone?' Xenia enquired curiously.

'Yes, one shaped by the queen's own hands. Its tear-like form is a reminder of the sacrifices made during that sordid engagement.'

'You lost a lot of friends, did you not?'

'More than I care to admit. However, those of us that survived the horror lost something greater that cycle – we lost part of ourselves. Fitting then, I suppose, that we call them soul stealers. I wrongly assumed in my naivety, that only those whose souls are ensnared by the nightmares are affected by encounters with them. I now know that is not the case.'

'Sometimes, when you lose a part of yourself, it creates space for something new and wonderful – like tending to a garden, removing unwanted weeds.'

'But what if something good is lost?' she asked, turning her gaze back towards Xenia.

'Then something wondrous might take its place, like pruning a tree. It is healthy for the old to make way for the new. How can you grow if you never change?'

'But those around me do not like what I am becoming.' she said, followed by a sigh.

'I like you.'

Xenia smiled warmly at her. She could not recall when last a Freylarkin had offered her such warm affection. She felt herself blush unexpectedly, as heat rose in her face. Suddenly she became extremely self-conscious, yet there was no need for such insecurity. The gathered knights in the mess hall paid no attention to their private conversation; they continued to enjoy the jovial social interaction with their peers. Even Zephir seemed content, devouring her meal.

'You are wrong, incidentally.' Xenia continued, still wearing her exuberant smile.

'Hmm...about what exactly?' she replied curiously.

'About you being guarded – you just showed me part of your true self.' explained Xenia. 'Do you mind if I ask you a personal question?'

'Not at all.' she replied, still trying to compose herself. 'What is it you wish to ask me?'

'I am curious to know...where do you plan on sleeping tonight?'

She lay awake, fidgeting in her hammock, unable to sleep yet again. Eventually abandoning the notion of sleep, she silently ascended towards to the hub, using her inner light to guide her way. As expected, Heldran maintained his quiet vigil over the chamber's hearth, however, he was busying himself with work as opposed to indulging in his habitual fire-gazing trance. He looked up from his work the moment her light caught the periphery of his sight.

'Could not stay away eh?' said Heldran with a smile in his characteristic deep voice.

The Knight Lord was tending to the knights' armour; he was meticulously polishing each plate, removing the grime of The Hunt.

'*You should sit next to him this time.*'

Following Alarielle's advice, she chose to sit adjacent to Heldran, this time sharing his wooden bench – what little free space remained of it. The immense frame of the Knight Lord dwarfed her own physique; until now she had not fully appreciated Heldran's actual size. She wondered now if in fact he was bigger than Ragnar.

'You wish!' she responded jovially. 'Would you like a hand?'

Heldran passed her a pair of greaves, along with a cloth and a ceramic pot which contained a dark substance that he was using to polish the knights' armour. The greaves were tarnished and scuffed in places; they had seen better cycles. Still, the Knights Thranis wasted nothing. Everything within the Ardent Gate was maintained and restored to working order, be it an intricate piece of armour or a simple bucket.

'See how you fair with that. Should you meet my lofty standards, perhaps I will afford you something more taxing, like a breast plate.' said Heldran, followed by an amused laugh.

'Forgive me Knight Lord, for I had not realised that the task of polishing one's armour was so challenging. It comes as no surprise then that you are taking your sweet time to work through that pile of armour over there.'

Heldran suddenly went quiet, locking his gaze with her own. For a brief moment she wondered if perhaps she had overstepped the boundaries of their early friendship. Alarielle had been the one to suggest that their fledgling friendship be pushed further; now she was testing that advice. Despite feeling awkward, she maintained her playful charismatic grin, which she knew had the uncanny knack of charming her audiences. Slowly the corner of Heldran's rough lips began to curl gently upwards. Without warning he slapped her heavily with his right hand across her back, almost knocking her clean off her wooden perch. The Knight Lord let out a thunderous laugh, which echoed round the chamber.

'How did I endure my solitary nights prior to your arrival I wonder? I can see why Marcus sent you.'

'I'm glad that I amuse you Heldran. I hope that our ability to fight the Ravnarkai is equally acceptable?' she enquired whilst reseating herself.

'Hmm...I have yet to decide what I am going to do with you both. Though I must confess, it pleases me that Anika is starting to show signs of life. I thought for one moment there that you had sought to enamour my opinion of The Blades with yet another stuffy member of your Order.'

'She's had a rough time of it recently. Her first sortie was a horrific experience, one which came too early in her development. Anika is angry. She needs an environment where she can vent her frustrations, rather than allowing them to fester whilst they feed on her soul.'

'Ah, it is clear to me now. You, or rather Marcus, believe that the Knights Thranis can provide such an outlet? Is that why you are truly here Rayna?'

Heldran's jovial mood quickly dissipated and his expression once again bore a look of distrust as his mind began to slot together Marcus' underlying agenda. She knew the full extent of their assignment would eventually surface; her response now would be crucial to the success –

or failure – of their mission.

'Play to your strengths. Now is not the time to experiment.'

'I have already explained to you why I am here my lord. Marcus has his agendas, I have never insulted your intelligence by suggesting otherwise. His machinations do not interest me. I am here to earn your trust, even if I have to court release to do so.'

'Hmm...and what if The Blade Lord's agendas do not coincide with our own? No amount of flirting with a tired Freylarkin like me will aid you if we are at an impasse.'

'The Ardent Gate has three empty tables in its mess hall. Do you want to start filling those seats or not? It bothers me not either way, for that is not why I am here.

And besides, old Freylarkin enjoy flirting – it keeps them young.' she said with an over-exaggerated smile and a playful wink.

'Ha! Your new found feminine wiles are anything but subtle Rayna. I do not find tricksters agreeable, but...you seem to have an honest way about you, even if those you serve do not.' he replied. 'You can share my bench for a while longer, whilst I decide what to do with you.'

'Shame, and there was me thinking that a blow from your right fist would be the answer to my sleeping woes.'

Heldran laughed again. It was apparent to her now that the Knight Lord was an honest and simple Freylarkin, who valued plain speaking and hard working. Heldran clearly had no time for subterfuge and double-meanings. She would need to put in the effort to implicitly earn his trust.

'The night is still young Rayna. Incidentally, I am not old. World-weary might be a more appropriate description.'

She smiled politely before changing the subject to a matter which grated on her.

'May I request greater clarity regarding a matter over which you have already passed judgement?'

'You really are desperate to sleep.' replied Heldran jovially. 'Speak your mind Rayna.'

'Why is it that we were not considered *able* for the Order's recent sortie? Both Anika and I are here to lend our sword arms, regardless of the potential dangers faced.'

Heldran did not answer immediately. He finished his current work then reached for a set of dirty vambraces from the pile beside him. He spat on the cold tarnished metal and began to apply a generous amount of the black substance from the ceramic pot she held. After privately assembling his thoughts, Heldran turned his attention back to her.

'You raise a valid question. We are currently executing a high risk strategy, one designed to bring neighbouring Ravnarkai sects into contact. If successful, the manoeuvre will become the catalyst for a significant culling of their numbers. Conflicts between neighbouring sects are extremely infrequent; they are haphazard occurrences at best. Given our Order's dwindling resources, we have decided to increase the frequency of these conflicts in order to level the playing field.'

Astonished by Heldran's words, she was momentarily taken back by the lengths the Knights were prepared to go to in order to succeed in their campaign. Marcus was indeed correct; The Hunt *had* become a fanatical obsession for the Knights Thranis. Yet the Ravnarkai were a threat, if they remained unchecked. In light of their gradual erosion, the Knights needed to evolve their tactics in order to continue their campaign.

'That is a bold strategy!'

'Aye, one not taken lightly either.' replied Heldran, who had since turned his attention back to his work.

'How does this strategy work in practice?' she enquired.

'Two detachments of knights each patrol the common perimeter of neighbouring sects. As they repeat their patrols, the knights gradually come together, drawing the neighbouring sects towards one another.'

'So you bait the Ravnarkai...again. Does the Order employ any tactics which do not involve using its own knights as live bait?'

Heldran laughed heartily once more.

'Perhaps you understand now why I did not want you and Anika engaged in these *meat grinders,* as we affectionately call them. You both lack the necessary experience required for such sorties. In time I will review that decision, though in the meantime you are both expected to continue your training at the Ardent Gate.'

Heldran had made his decision and presented valid reasoning for it. Attempting to sway the Knight Lord on the matter would likely incite irritation; she accepted his decision and nodded in agreement, though she could not fully mask her look of discontent. She sorely wanted to aid the Knights Thranis in their crusade; waiting behind at the Ardent Gate was not what she had in mind. Still, Heldran's decision on the matter was final – she would accept it as such.

'I sense your disappointment Rayna. Know that it is a good thing! If you *had* come here purely to offload Marcus' damaged Blades, you would have little desire to court release so readily.'

'I want to help, Heldran, and to earn your trust...that is all.' she said honestly.

'If that were truly the case, you would have started cleaning those greaves already.' replied Heldran, followed by another of his deep thunderous laughs.

They spoke little to one another for the remainder of the night; both were content to simply share each other's company, along with the warmth of the well-lit hearth. After they had completed their work, she turned in for the night – for the second time. Heldran remained by the hearth, claiming that he would follow suit shortly. Given the burden of responsibility which rested firmly across his broad shoulders, she wondered if indeed the Knight Lord ever truly slept; perhaps the sorceries of the Ardent Gate's resident shaper – who she had yet to meet – had somehow mitigated Heldran's basic need to rest. In any case, she *did* require sleep, even though the slumberous art frequently haunted her with her grubby past, or worse still eluded her entirely. When at last she returned to her hammock, she was surprised to see Anika's own completely empty. For a brief moment she considered tracking down her Blade sister, though her now overwhelming need to sleep quashed any concerns. In all likelihood Anika too was having difficulty sleeping, she convinced herself; after all, they were still adjusting to sleeping in what were essentially hanging nets.

TEN
Awakening

It took them over a week to prepare for their operation. Trix was meticulous in his planning. The self-proclaimed software engineer spent hours analysing the ghost data from the redundant NGDF satellite. Trix's primary concern was establishing identifiable patterns in the numerous Peacekeeper patrol routs currently active throughout the metropolis. In addition the questionable hacker was keen to learn situation response times in the unlikely event that their operation went bad – Trix left nothing to chance, including weather forecasts and lunar phases. After the mass accumulation of data, Trix devised a simulation of predicted patrol routs which they used to overlay the NGDF's laggy ghost data. The delayed real-time data combined with Trix's own predictive data gave them a heuristic overview of Peacekeeper patrol routs. Armed with this new information, his chances of infiltrating the metropolis undetected increased significantly. Each additional day spent planning put his mind further at ease. Initially he had been quite apprehensive about the mission, however, now he was keen to get on with it. The matter of his departure date had been the subject of a heated debate between them recently – their shared frustration increased by their cramp living arrangements; he had not designed his bolt-holes with lodgers in mind, especially clumsy software engineers. Trix was far from tidy and had a habit of spreading out – this he found to be incredibly irritating. How could one so methodical in their thinking be so untidy, he mused? The dichotomy of Trix's behaviour vexed him on more than one occasion.

'If we wait much longer, there is an increased risk of the Peacekeeper patrols changing. Even you must subscribe to that logic?'

Trix sighed heavily.

'Fox, must you be so impatient?' replied Trix tersely.

'Yes, I must. I grow tired of living amidst your squalor in these cramped conditions. Can't you at least tidy up after yourself?'

Trix ignored his frank remark; that or the comment simply did not register. He found it difficult to discern whether, on occasion, Trix was actively ignoring him, or instead failed to understand his point of view and therefore dismissed it out of hand entirely.

'Look, I get your thinking, and I don't disagree, but we need to wait for optimal conditions.'

'Which are what now, exactly? What are we waiting for this time Trix?' he replied agitatedly.

'Two days from now there will be a new moon. That is when we will commence the operation.'

'There will be barely any light from the moon tonight. Waiting another two days for the dawn of a new lunar phase will not adversely affect my chances of success.'

'You mean *our* chances of success! I have been painstakingly planning this operation for some time now. I am not prepared to take any risks at this stage.' Trix replied vehemently.

He dragged his right hand slowly down the length of his face, signalling his obvious frustration. Trix's behaviour was too rigid; that would need to change once the operation got under way. They could not afford to be inflexible once he was in the field. Decisions would need to be made fast and decisively else he would not remain undetected for very long.

'Fine, but once we get underway this approach will not work for us. We will need to be fast and fluid, since I will only have around five hours of night cover to work with. If we dally around in the field, we may as well abandon the entire operation now.' he said pointedly.

Trix paused for a moment to consider his words – at least he was not being ignored. After a long moment of silence, Trix conceded the point.

'Fine, but until then, stop pestering me! There is still a lot of outstanding preparation to do.'

Given they had covered every likely scenario in detail, he found it difficult to believe Trix's words; though having struck an accord, he now needed to uphold his end of the bargain. Trix had, however, been uncharacteristically vague regarding their course of action once contact was made with their target in the metropolis. They intended to remain in contact at all times, through a secure communications channel, therefore he assumed that Trix would relay further instructions upon contact with their target. Yet he was eager to learn who exactly the mysterious individual was, and why Trix had placed such importance on meeting with the enigmatic resident. He therefore decided to push his luck and give Trix a little nudge, one last time, in order to extract the final piece of the puzzle.

'Fine, though I do have one final question.' he replied. 'Who exactly am I going to be tracking down?'

Trix looked up and stared at him blankly. For a moment he wondered whether the odd programmer intended to speak at all. Perhaps this was one piece of information Trix was not prepared to share. Although Trix had been relatively forthcoming when asked questions directly, nevertheless his gut feeling suggested that something was amiss.

'You will be locating a retired software developer; a former private contractor who – for a time at least – worked for the government.' replied Trix after an awkward period of silence.

'And the name of this individual is?'

'If I tell you, will you please shut up and let me work in peace?' replied Trix grumpily.

'Sure, I can do that.'

'Your target is a Mr L. Cameron.'

They remained at Scrier's Post for several cycles. He had hoped to use the time to sway Aleska from her intended path, yet he had failed miserably to do so; indeed his presence only served to further agitate Aleska. He tried desperately to understand her point of view, though he could not see the logic in her maddening proposal. Reneging on ruling council policy and educating newly empowered scriers, in the hope that they would not abuse their ability, was a perilous venture in his opinion. As he understood it, scrying was like a drug which preyed on the weak minded. Offering scriers the illusion of freedom and subsequently insisting that they manage their likely addiction would only lead to greater crisis. He recognised the failings of the current policy, which clearly needed refinement, but Aleska's proposal – allegedly sanctioned by Queen Mirielle no less – was both reckless and irresponsible, in his mind at least.

'Nathaniel, why are you still here?' enquired Aleska as she approached him from across the courtyard. 'If you value our friendship, please return to the vale and allow me to continue my work here.'

'I cannot abide by what you are doing here Aleska.' he replied sternly.

'And I am not asking you to do so. However, you need to voice your concerns to Queen Mirielle.'

'Bah, you are using Mirielle as a shield, knowing full well that I do not readily have direct access to our queen.'

'Then take your concerns to the ruling council. Seek their guidance on the matter.'

He sighed heavily, confounded by Aleska's maddening response. It was uncharacteristic of her to be so obstinate; typically Aleska was sympathetic to differing points of view, however, on this particular matter she was clearly resolute and not about to change her mind. He knew Aleska would find stepping down from the ruling council hard, despite her public statements to the contrary; was this course of action a direct result of Aleska seeking to re-establish her place in Freylarkin society once more, he wondered. She had the queen's ear, therefore could the real driving force behind the controversial decision in fact be Aleska herself?

'Tell me honestly. Are you doing this to create a new authority role, one specifically suited to your own talents, now that you have stepped down from the ruling council?' he enquired boldly.

Aleska's expression turned stony; her eyes narrowed, making her cheekbones appear more prominent, and what little colour there was rapidly drained from her face. She parted her lips, as though about to speak, but instead raised her right hand and slapped him lightly across his left cheek.

'How dare you!' she replied, both angry and upset by his remark. 'This has nothing to do with...status, or clinging onto power. How could you think me capable of such?'

'Aleska you have made a career from politicking and the manipulation of others to suit the ruling council's agendas. I may be a simple unambitious Freylarkin, but I see these things for what they truly are. I care for you a great deal Aleska. It was my hope that you would distance yourself from such machinations in your retirement. But instead you endorse this...foolishness.'

'So you think Mirielle the fool?!'

'I think our queen doubts her own policies, which we have paid dearly to uphold.' he explained. 'The greatest test of courage is to hold one's nerve during times of strife. We are being tested, each of us, and now is not the time to renege on policy which, until now, has sufficed. We cannot afford to retreat, due to this one setback. If we falter now then Darlia has already won!'

'Nathaniel, Darlia is a symptom of the dogged enforcement of our inflexible policy towards scrying.' Aleska implored.

'No, that Freylarkin is the cause of all this. She *chose* to defy our laws and test the limits of her ability, and in doing so lost her way.'

'But if we closely monitor and educate scriers, we can avoid future recurrences of the disaster which took place here.'

'Aleska, if you offer scriers a taste of freedom, they will want more!'

'You are wrong Nathaniel.'

'How can you be certain?'

'I am certain because I have seen it!'

'No! We cannot allow a possible future to shape our actual present. You of all Freylarkai should know this.'

'The Blades can ill afford a repeat of the tragedy which took place here Nathaniel.'

'On that point we agree entirely, but I cannot condone what you are doing here Aleska.'

'As I said to you before, you must do what you feel is right and raise your concerns with the ruling council.' replied Aleska dismissively.

'But you have Mirielle's ear, and Marcus will likely have no desire to challenge our queen on the matter.' he said wearily. 'You asked me why I am still here...I am here because of you!'

'I will not go against Mirielle's wishes Nathaniel, with which I am in complete agreement.'

'Is this poor decision the will of the ruling council, or Mirielle's alone? Kirika was seemingly unaware of your reason for leaving the vale unannounced; was she consulted on this matter?'

'Speak to the ruling council Nathaniel.'

'Aleska...this is wrong! Mirielle is not thinking straight. Our queen spends increasing amounts of time brooding in that tower of hers, disconnecting herself from the Freylarkai under her rule.'

'Careful Nathaniel, such words invite civil unrest.'

'This decision will undermine Mirielle's ability to rule, you know this!' he implored.

'Not if carefully managed.' replied Aleska.

It became clear to him that Aleska would not be swayed from her path. Their verbal exchange was heated and ultimately served only to erode their relationship in part. The divide between then was now widening. Initially he had hoped to contain the matter, though that was no longer possible. He had always been on the outside, looking in, regarding maters of state – he accepted this. He was not a politically driven Freylarkin, but he could not allow Aleska's work to go unchallenged.

'Clearly we are at an impasse.' he said despondently. 'I will return to the vale with Keshar and consult the ruling council.'

'So be it.' replied Aleska quietly. 'However, I believe you will be returning to the vale alone.'

'I do not understand.'

'Keshar has informed me that she wishes to remain at Scrier's Post and commence studying under my tutelage.'

Unable to mask his emotions, he exhaled angrily. He valued Aleska's friendship dearly, thus her recent actions cut deeper than any of his visible scars. The shrinking world around him felt as though it was pushing back against him, slowly backing him into a corner. He despaired at the thought of being alone in his analysis of the situation.

He marched purposefully across the courtyard towards the main sanctuary where he presumed he would find Keshar, along with Aleska's appointed shaper. Both were inside the main structure. Keshar sat on the previously worn stone steps, leading to the open roof space above; now the steps were perfectly level and each was highly polished to mirror shine. Keshar's head was buried in a leather-bound book, no doubt pertaining to techniques used when scrying. Krasus, however, sat on the ground floor, with his legs crossed, and continued to make further alterations to the sanctuary; the master shaper busied himself with the creation of stone seating, conducive to the art of meditation and introspection. Although he loathed the sight of the master shaper at work, Krasus had done a fine job reworking the interior of the sanctuary. The internal architecture of the sanctuary no longer mirrored its original gothic design; Krasus' continued efforts were modernising the sanctuary's interior through the introduction of sharp lines and organic curves. The structure's worn stone finish was slowly being erased, replaced instead by sleek glassy surfaces. The deliberate modernisation of the sanctuary was no doubt in accordance with direction from Aleska; it was clear that she sought to put some distance between the site and the stain of its past.

'Keshar, may I have a moment of your time?'

'Of course you may Nathaniel.'

Keshar promptly snapped her book shut, then silently jumped down from her perch.

'Have you concluded your discussions with Aleska?' she asked.

'Yes, indeed I have.' he replied with a weak smile. 'I intend to return to the vale this cycle.'

'Oh, I see.'

Keshar was clearly feeling awkward. He knew that she would expect to be asked to return with him, yet he could already see, from the look in her violet eyes, that she had no desire to resume the life of a farmer. Kirika had allowed Keshar to aid him so that the young Freylarkin could expand her horizons. Now he threatened to bring about an abrupt end to the apprentice scrier's development. This was the danger he had failed to convince Aleska of. The allure of exploring her ability further had already taken hold of Keshar. Although taking her back to the vale was – in his mind at least – morally the right thing to do, he could tell from Keshar's body language that she would resent him for that decision. In all likelihood, Keshar would later return to Scrier's Post of her own volition, in spite of being dragged back to the vale. He had dallied too long at Scrier's Post, and in doing so he had lost Kirika's protégé to the dangerous path offered by Aleska; he cursed himself for allowing the predictable scenario to play out.

'You are welcome to remain at Scrier's Post, however, if you decide to do so you must follow my teachings.' proclaimed Aleska, who had quietly followed him into the sanctuary.

Aleska's interference immediately raised his choler. He tried desperately to mask his growing anger; allowing his frustration to surface would be unfair on Keshar, who was now a political pawn caught in Aleska's web. If only Kirika had been able to accompany him, the outcome of his visit would have been very different. His best move now was to remain level-headed and focused. Aleska had cast her stone, but it would take some time for the ripples of her actions to affect others. Therefore he would play the long game – he vowed to return, once his position was stronger.

'Whilst I would prefer to see you return with me to the vale, you must ultimately choose the path upon which to tread.' he said plainly.

Keshar's expression was torn following his words. It was clear that she longed to remain at Scrier's Post and learn from Aleska, though she sought not to offend him by doing so. The opportunity to learn from the venerable scrier was no doubt an intoxicating prospect given her ability – he could not hope to rival Aleska's offer. With no desire to see Keshar caught in the middle of his differences with Aleska, he decided to offer the young scrier an easy exit.

'I will not judge you based on your decision. You must decide what *you* believe is in your own best interests.'

'I am sorry Nathaniel, but I wish to remain here and further my studies.' replied Keshar softly.

'There is no need to apologise.' he replied. 'Should you change your mind, send a Sky-Skitter and I will return for you.'

He gave Keshar a weak smile then turned to face her new mentor. Losing the young scrier would only strengthen Aleska's cause, though he convinced himself that this was only a temporary setback. His primary focus now was to return to the vale, where he would seek Kirika's counsel on the matter; assuming Aleska's successor was indeed unaware of the developments at Scrier's Post.

'Kirika entrusted me with Keshar's wellbeing; that responsibility now falls to you.' he said sternly.

'I will take care of her Nathaniel.' replied Aleska sincerely.

He chose not to respond to Aleska's questionable assurance of Keshar's welfare.

'Do me at least this one courtesy Aleska: ensure that Krasus erects a suitable memorial to honour the newly released. Their sacrifice should not be forgotten.' he said aloud, ensuring that their audience overheard his request.

Aleska had no choice but to sanction his request – there would be no justification to the contrary. Though she clearly sought to erase the sanctuary's grubby past, he would not allow her to do so entirely. The memorial would survive Krasus' remodelling, reminding those visiting the site of the sacrifices made by The Blades. Though Aleska would likely insist the memorial be low-key, any ambiguity in its appearance would only serve to raise further questions. He loathed using his own students in politics, especially those released in service, but he would not permit their actions to pass into the history books unnoticed. The memorial would also serve as a stark reminder that he had unfinished business with Aleska, who now regarded him with a stern expression of her own.

'So be it.'

During her time holed up within Krashnar's hide, she lost track of the cycles, which seemingly merged into a single continuous nightmare. Lileah's remaking had proceeded extremely well – according to Krashnar – though the process had left her feeling empty inside. She began to understand the reasons for the insidious shaper's uncaring disposition; sympathy and emotion played no part in the abhorrent acts they wrought upon Lileah's body. The maleficent actions she helped carry out during the process of restoring Lileah to health haunted her, thus she found it difficult to sleep. She recounted the numerous times they had forcibly fed Lileah, by inserting a tube down her throat deep into her stomach. The crude act caused Lileah to gag involuntarily as they injected puréed fruit and other liquefied nutrients. At first she wept uncontrollably, though as time marched on she became desensitised to the necessary clinical procedure. Still, the results were irrefutable. The blotches on Lileah's skin began to recede and the bruises had faded entirely now. In addition, the previously raw colour of Lileah's flesh where it fused with the bronze metal alloy of her newly forged abdomen and torso, was now significantly less so. Visibly, Lileah's skin looked much healthier, despite the fact that she remained unbearably thin. It would take some time for Lileah to regain her full strength. Krashnar had warned that in the interim it was likely, following her inevitable awakening, that Lileah would lack the strength to mobilise her new body, given its increased weight.

She lay beside Lileah now, running her fingers through the telepath's short raven-black hair. At her request they had moved Lileah from the shaper's grimy workshop into marginally improved sleeping quarters. Since Krashnar only had one spare serviceable bedroom in his compact hide, she chose to sleep with Lileah, who continued to slip in and out of consciousness. Although Lileah was not fully aware of her present situation, she fancied that both her own presence and the familiar sound of her voice served as welcome comfort. As she continued to lightly comb Lileah's hair with the slender fingers of her organic right hand, Lileah began to stir once more. She paid little attention to the stirrings at first, but when Lileah began to pant rapidly she promptly sat up, concerned that something was wrong.

'Krashnar!' she cried loudly. 'Come quickly!'

Lileah's eyelids began to flutter rapidly and her head tossed left and right, as though she was experiencing extreme discomfort.

'Krashnar, get in here now!'

Shortly after her terse repeated summons, Krashnar lurched into the room with his abyssal black eyes wide open.

'Something is wrong.' she said, looking to the rogue shaper for guidance.

'This is not unexpected.' replied Krashnar, licking his cracked lips gleefully. 'She is having difficulty breathing, since her chest cavity will no longer expand and contract as it once did. She will soon adapt to shallow breathing.'

'But why is this happening now?!'

'Because she is waking up!' explained Krashnar pointedly. 'Until now her body has been operating reflexively. Now her awakening mind is interfering, insisting that her body behaves as it once did.'

'What can we do?'

'Nothing.' replied Krashnar dismissively. 'Just leave her to get on with it.'

The uncaring shaper was about to leave the room when Lileah's eyes suddenly opened wide. The room was dimly lit by a small solitary Moonstone, mounted in a twisted metal cradle, which sat atop a small trunk adjacent to the bed. Despite the Moonstone's feeble light, Lileah's pupils were fully dilated, causing her to turn her head from the weak light. Although still quite light outside, there were very few windows allowing natural light to enter Krashnar's hide – the exiled shaper valued his privacy, likely on account of his ugly experiments.

'Lileah, it is me, Darlia.'

'Dar...lia...why...can I...not...'

'Calm down Lileah.' she replied compassionately. 'Try to focus on your breathing.'

'Where...am I?'

'You are safe. I have brought you to Krashnar.'

'What...you mean...your hand.'

'Yes, the very same.' she said, swallowing the lump in her throat. 'You were injured at Scrier's Post. I did not know what else to do, so I brought you to Krashnar.'

Lileah tried to move, but the weight of her now metal-infused torso held her in place. Quickly realising her lack of mobility, Lileah tried to raise her head to better understand the reason for her restraint. She placed her left arm behind Lileah's partially raised head, careful not to contact the back of Lileah's head with her claw. With the aid of her arm supporting Lileah's neck, Lileah gingerly raised her head further and regarded her new body for the first time. Krashnar promptly drew closer; the deviant flesh worker was eager to see Lileah's reaction to his latest achievement. Lileah said nothing at first. With the exception of her rapid breathing, Lileah remained silent; the frail telepath simply stared in mute disbelief at her reworked body. Slowly, gradually, Lileah's face became twisted and vengeful; she clenched her jaw tightly, instead breathing quickly through her nose, as raw anger slowly began to take hold of her. Lileah was impetuous by nature, but the visible rage consuming her lover now was difficult to stomach – for her at least. However, Krashnar seemed to delight at the scene unfolding before him. The shaper's black obsidian eyes widened even further, reminding her of insect life native to Narlak. Admittedly Krashnar had – visually at least – transformed Lileah's ruined body into a horrifyingly beautiful work of art; her torso was awash with wonderfully intricate ornate details, and the proportions of Lileah's reworked body were anatomically pleasing – this she had personally insisted upon. However, none of that altered the fact that Lileah was now disabled; there was only so much freedom of movement the talented rogue shaper could engineer into Lileah's new body. Lileah's rage rapidly turned to fury, and her head began to shake at the ghastly sight of her own body, witnessed for the first time.

'What...have you...done!'

'Darlia brought you to me on the cusp of release. You had all but bled out from your wound, and your chest and abdomen were heavily infected.' explained Krashnar factually. 'I have fused the damaged areas of your body with a metal alloy, thereby ridding you of the infection.'

'You have...mutilated me!'

'Incorrect.' replied Krashnar dismissively. 'I have restored you to health, and in doing so have made you stronger. Your enemies will find it difficult to run you through with a blade the next time you meet.'

'But I...cannot...move!'

'You are impatient, like Darlia. Your body lacks the strength required to manoeuvre your increased density. You need to eat and exercise your muscles. In time you will be able to function once more.'

She glanced to where her own left hand used to be, replaced now by the bronze metal claw fashioned also by Krashnar. The suffering which lay in store for Lileah was no stranger to her; the painful rehabilitation process of learning to use her prosthetic claw still haunted her. Now she would relive those awful memories once more through Lileah's own arduous rehabilitation.

'You had...no right!'

'Oh, so you prefer release then? That can also be arranged, if you so desire!' rasped Krashnar tersely.

'Who caused...this?' demanded Lileah.

'Nathanar. He was the one who cut you down.' she replied solemnly. 'After our defeat, I dragged your ruined body back here....I did not know what else to do.'

Her vision began to blur and tears involuntarily spilled from her eyes. They fell upon Lileah's raven-black hair, glistening in the weak light of the Moonstone. She quickly wiped her eyes with her remaining good hand, hoping that Lileah would not witness her unexpected display of emotion. Regrettably her moment of weakness did not go undetected by Krashnar who studied her intently.

'Take me...to him.'

'Take you to whom?' she replied hesitantly, confused by Lileah's request.

'To *him*...Nathanar!'

'Lileah you must rest. You are in no condition to go anywhere. We can talk about this later.'

'*Take me!*'

She fell off the bed involuntarily, landing in a crumpled heap on the dirty floor. Lileah's telepathic communication was brutal, like someone screaming directly into her ear. It violently jarred both herself and Krashnar, leaving them shaken. She clutched her head which throbbed painfully. Although Krashnar was also badly affected by the attack, he was nonetheless the first to recover despite his wretched appearance. He stood back up uneasily, ready to address Lileah whilst still grimacing profoundly – his face was even more twisted than usual.

'I will take you. But first you will regain your strength. And you will refrain from doing that again! Those are my terms.'

'And if I...refuse your...terms...shaper?'

'Then you will remain here, you ungrateful wretch, until release comes for you.' replied Krashnar angrily.

'I am...subservient...to no one!'

Krashnar coughed up more of the vile black fluid within him, which he spat vehemently from his mouth. The putrid substance landed on Lileah's metal torso, where it immediately began to slither towards the base of her neck.

Lileah tried again to move, but the increased weight of her new body fixed her firmly in place. Lileah tried to raise her head once more to better observe the parasitic fluid slithering towards her head.

'Stop it...you win!'

Having partially recovered from the shock of Lileah's telepathic rebuke, she quickly rose to her feet and swept the vile substance aside with the back of her claw. The metal of her prosthetic clanked loudly against Lileah's own, reminding her again of the sacrifices her actions had wrought.

'Unappreciative bitches, the pair of you!' rasped Krashnar tersely. 'You demand my aid, only to repay my unique services with complete disrespect. *Should* you see sense, we will discuss your return to Freylar, and what specifically that entails, once you are able. Otherwise, have your despondent lover here drag you away from this place. I have no time for your childish insolence.'

Krashnar promptly left the room. Lileah turned her head away and began to whimper, which further hindered her breathing. Seeing Lileah defiantly laid low eroded her soul. Although their failed invasion of Freylar was a mutual endeavour, the fact remained that she had been their primary driving force. Although Lileah resented the inhabitants of Freylar for shunning their existence, she alone was responsible for cultivating her lover's bitter loathing and directing the resulting hatred towards their former kin. She had played a prominent role in the events leading to their present demise – she hated herself for that fact.

ELEVEN
Facade

They had been training for most of the cycle as part of their reserve duty. It still irked her that they were left behind, though she appreciated Heldran's reasons for doing so. In total, a good third of the Knights had passed through the Ardent Gate that morning. The chosen members of the Order were now actively engaged in a meat grinder; the product of the latest choice of tactics utilised by the Order in their tireless campaign against the Ravnarkai. Specifics of the mission had not been made public knowledge, however, given the number of knights committed to the sortie, she assumed that the stakes were high. Captain Gedrick, Zephir, Falkai and Xenia were but a few of those knights called upon to lend their service to the mission, as well as revered Knight Restorant Loredan. It frustrated her immensely being left behind along with Anika and the other reserves, though Heldran had made it quite clear to her that only veterans of The Hunt were to engage in meat grinder operations; thus they remained, honing their skill. Regardless of her annoyance, their predicament afforded them the rare opportunity to learn from Knight Lord Heldran himself, who currently oversaw their training. Initially the Knight Lord had regarded her unwavering commitment to practice with dual falchions as questionable, however, Heldran's attitude towards the unconventional practise mellowed after she explained the reasons behind her choice of weapons. The Knight Lord seemed genuinely interested in her impending challenge versus Lothnar at the Trials, even more so after she unsheathed Shadow Caster; the enigmatic blade quickly attracted Heldran's keen eyes.

Though tempted to dig a little into Heldran's past, to establish whether a relationship existed between the Knight Lord and the blade, etiquette managed to stave off her insatiable curiosity – for the time being at least.

'Do not be afraid to close the distance, uncomfortably so, with your opponents Rayna.' Heldran instructed her. 'Your weapons are not limited to your blades. Kick your opponents' knees, sweep their legs, or even headbutt them if you must. You do not yet possess the skill to rival a Paladin, however, become unpredictable – as Nathaniel wisely advised you – and Lothnar will have a rough time of it.'

'What about respect for my opponents?'

'Bah, there is no respect in combat Rayna. Release your opponent and do it quickly, any way you can, lest they do the same to you! Combat is not an art form, as some might suggest; it is brutal, savage and short.'

Heeding Heldran's counsel, she reversed the grip on her falchions and leapt forwards towards Morin, her opponent. Morin reacted swiftly to her unexpected advance, using his acute reflexes to bring his ardent sword round in a wide arc towards her upper torso. She tucked her head in tightly and rolled forwards beneath the ardent sword's deadly swing, which missed her entirely. As she came out of her hasty roll, she used her momentum to drive her right shoulder forwards into Morin's abdomen. The manoeuvre was far from elegant, but it got the job done. Her untidy impact winded Morin and sent the knight crashing to the ground. She promptly kicked the knight's hands, causing Morin to loosen his grip on his ardent sword; the enormously long sword fell from Morin's grasp, where it landed on the floor a good pace from where he fell with an audible thump.

'Using the weight of his weapon against him – good!' boomed Heldran, whilst clapping his heavy hands.

Formally signalling the end to the fight, she lightly pressed Shadow Caster against Morin's exposed neck. Faint wisps of grey smoke rose gently from the falchion's sharp edge; they clawed at the fallen knight's throat, as though seeking to rip out his larynx. Heldran moved closer to better observe the curious behaviour of the forged-Dawnstone blade; his eyes widened with obvious interest as he watched the translucent ephemeral smoke seek desperately to wrench the soul of her opponent from its moorings to sate its hunger.

'The blade imprisons the soul of a Narlakin, does it not?'

'Yes, so I am told.' she replied. 'Shadow Caster has been starved of souls for quite some time. See how it clings desperately to Morin's mortal coil.' she said, winking playfully at her concerned opponent. 'I am surprised that you are familiar with the blade.'

'When you have lived as long as I have Rayna, you come to witness a great many things – such as that one's twin for example.' replied Heldran, who pointed his right index finger towards Shadow Caster.

Unable to suppress her curiosity any longer, she seized the opportunity to glean further information from the Knight Lord regarding the blade. She had tried previously to learn more about the blade's origin from Nathaniel, though – for the time being at least – The Teacher maintained a tight-lipped stance on the subject, for reasons unknown to her. With a fresh opportunity to better understand the blade now presenting itself, she gladly released her grasp on the leash of her own insatiable curiosity.

'Nathaniel informed me that the blade is part of a set, though he has not since elaborated further on the matter.'

'Well, that must be quite maddening for someone of your curious disposition Rayna?' replied Heldran with an obviously amused smile.

'Oh, not you as well!' she replied, frustrated by his evasive response. 'You should never leave a *girl* hanging.'

'Err...perhaps I could get up now?' requested Morin sheepishly, who continued to lie on the hard ground at the mercy of their subject of conversation.

'Ha! Release poor Morin there and perhaps I will feed your own starved hunger for knowledge.'

She withdrew Shadow Caster as requested. The mesmerising smoke, emanating from the surface of the blade, immediately receded following its withdrawal from Morin's neck. She handed the falchion to Heldran who appeared eager to inspect the sinister blade more closely. Free now of the alien weapon, she extended her arm to Morin who gladly accepted her assistance in righting himself.

'Morin, perhaps you could knock Anika down a peg or two. She seems to be having her own way of it over there, and we would not want her ego swelling too quickly now, would we?'

Morin nodded with an agreeable smile. He promptly retrieved his fallen ardent sword then jogged off to train alongside the other reserve knights, leaving her alone with the Knight Lord. Heldran's gaze was now consumed by Shadow Caster entirely. He cut the air repeatedly with the falchion, watching closely as more of its translucent smoke trailed from the flat of the blade.

'It may surprise you to know that I have fought the Narlakai myself on several occasions.'

'But how is that possible? I was led to believe that they exclusively inhabit the north. How then would the Knights Thranis come into contact with the soul stealers?'

'You incorrectly assume that our Order is tied to the south Rayna.' revealed Heldran.

'What?! But The Blades would have seen--' she began to respond, before breaking off into a moment of deep thought. It was then that the obvious dawned upon her. 'The Ardent Gate!'

'Indeed. Rayna, The Hunt is very much part of our heritage, and a necessary tradition at that. It is not, however, the reason our Order came to be. The Knights Thranis' true raison d'être is to guard the Ardent Gate, at all times. We exist to ensure that it is never left undefended.'

'Marcus never mentioned this to me.'

'That is because Marcus is not aware of our true motives. His perception of our Order is derived from his own limited contact with the Knights Thranis, that and the insidious tongue of his predecessor Blade Lord Caleth.'

'So...where exactly have the Knights Thranis been?'

'Everywhere! The empty tables in the mess hall are not solely the product of casualties incurred during The Hunt. We have sent expeditions through the Ardent Gate to domains far from here. Not all of those expeditions have returned! We have visited Narlak, Ravnar and places well beyond our understanding.'

'Then what about...'

'What, the domain where you were born? The domain of the *Sky-Walkers*.' replied Heldran sceptically.

'You don't believe in them?'

'Rayna, I believe in what I can see with my own eyes. In truth, I do not know what you are. Guardian, outworlder, deity...body-thief – take your pick. But I do believe that I can trust you, which is why I am telling you this.'

'But the Gate Room houses, what, some twelve Waystones perhaps?'

'Ah, but you have not seen the entire Gate Room. You must have learnt by now that our Order cannot be judged on initial appearances alone.' replied Heldran cryptically.

'Ha, clearly I needed to be retaught that particular lesson. The Knights Thranis are quite the illusionists are they not?'

'We try our best.' replied Heldran with a wry smile.

Heldran cut the air with Shadow Caster once more; the Knight Lord seemed to be evaluating the weight and balance of the blade, though given his recent proclamations she no longer remained certain about Heldran's true motives. Perhaps that was in fact the Knight Lord's true objective, she mused: to confuse and confound his Order's onlookers. In light their recent discussion, she needed to re-evaluate her perception of Heldran. The venerable leader was clearly not as two-dimensional as perhaps she had been led to believe.

'Regardless, I digress. You are keen to learn more of this blade's history, are you not?'

'You know that I am,' she replied eagerly, 'Stop teasing me Heldran.'

'Oh, and I thought you liked to tease?'

'*Heldran is quite perceptive.*'

'Indeed.' she replied sheepishly.

Heldran paused for a moment's thought, after which he reversed his grip on the blade before passing Shadow Caster back to her.

'That weapon has a sordid history. I sincerely hope that the light you bring to Freylar will prevent you from following its dark path. I believe that Nathaniel handed you this blade in the hope that you would absolve its past, and therefore – to some extent – his own actions.'

'*What is this?!*'

'How could you possibly know that this weapon was passed to me by Nathaniel? Do you possess the ability to scry Heldran?'

'No, nothing like that, indeed I have no *ability* to speak of. I know because that weapon previously belonged to The Teacher himself. I have witnessed the blade's ravenous hunger and what it can do to a soul.' replied Heldran factually. 'Shadow Caster...do you know why it was named as such?'

'No, I do not. Nathaniel has told me little about the blade, only that it was forged from Dawnstone and traps the soul of a Narlakin.'

'That is correct, but there is more that you must understand. The Narlakin imprisoned within that blade traps the souls of many others...indeed it has devoured one soul of particular note. I believe you have heard the name already: Caleth.'

'Are you saying that the Narlakin trapped within Shadow Caster was responsible for releasing Caleth?'

'Ah, but you misunderstand me Rayna.' replied Heldran, whose weathered face now bore a grim dark expression. 'I am saying that a former wielder of that blade released Caleth.'

'What?! He cannot mean my father?'

'Nathaniel?! Are you certain?' she replied, struggling to mask her obvious shock.

'Rayna, I am certain. I was there!'

Her head began to swim at the implications of the Knight Lord's words. It was clear to her now that she had underestimated Heldran. He *was* a master illusionist, despite the lack of an ability, and had a wealth of knowledge at his disposal. She tried to block out the world around her in order to process Heldran's words, though for the first time since their union Alarielle's thoughts clouded her own. The psyche of her symbiotic host began to unravel as Alarielle's perception of her own father was fiercely challenged. Although Heldran collated and withheld information to safeguard the wellbeing of his Order, neither she nor Alarielle suspected the Knight Lord capable of lying or deceit; indeed, Heldran had nothing to gain by lying about Shadow Caster's past. Presumably he expected her to discuss the matter with Nathaniel, therefore what did Heldran hope to accomplish by disclosing the past, she mused.

'Why? I do not understand Rayna. Please, you must challenge Heldran's words.'

'Do you need time to digest this information?' asked Heldran sincerely, placing his colossal left hand on her relatively petite shoulder.

'Thank you, but no.' she replied. 'What I need is to understand your words more clearly, and the motive behind them.'

'Rayna please sit, and I will endeavour to explain.'

'You came to our Order asking that we trust you – specifically that I trust you. Now, I am asking that you reciprocate. This you must do, if we are to successfully build upon our tentative new foundations.'

'You are asking me to accept the unthinkable Heldran.'

'As are you, Rayna. You expect much from me, hoping that I will open my arms once more to The Blades. Why is that? Simply because you vouch for them?' questioned Heldran. 'As I said to you earlier I trust *you*, but that new-found trust does not extend to your peers by default. You cannot expect me to wash aside a lengthy and sordid history of distrust so easily.'

'I suppose this new body of mine has filled me with an unrealistic sense of optimism.' she said, followed by a weak smile.

Heldran returned her smile. Once more he slapped her unexpectedly across her back in good spirits.

'Do not think poorly of Nathaniel. He did what was necessary to prevent outright conflict between our Orders.' explained Heldran. 'You need to understand that Caleth was poisoning The Blades against us. Of course these are my words. Perception is easily distorted over time, and often dictated by which side of the fence one stands.'

'Nathaniel once looked into my eyes to discern the truth of my arrival in Freylar, and you yourself seek truth with your own eyes. When I look at you Heldran, I do not see deceit or subterfuge – though perhaps a degree of caution.'

'Ha, a wise assessment. I become increasingly wary with each pass Rayna.' replied Heldran thoughtfully. 'I can see that you have much to think about. Consider my words carefully. When finally you return to the vale, there is a conversation waiting for you with Nathaniel, however, please ensure that you speak with him objectively.'

'You need not worry on that account. I owe Nathaniel much; the least I can do is listen to his own account of past events with an open mind.'

'Good!' boomed Heldran, who slapped her heavily across the back once more. 'Now then, let us resume your training. You have clearly expressed a desire to engage in one of our meat grinders. As such, it is high time you pushed your combat ability to the next level. I suggest that you take the remainder of the cycle to prepare yourself Rayna, for the next opponent you will spar against will be me.'

She knocked loudly on Marcus' door; there was no answer from The Blade Lord. Placing the palm of her left hand against the door's smooth wooden surface, she pressed against it, gently confirming what her unique sight had already informed her – the door was unlocked. She peered gingerly through the widening gap between the door and its frame; there appeared to be no one at home. She supposed that perhaps Marcus was busying himself down in the arena. Since the incident at Scrier's Post, and increasingly more so during Nathaniel's sudden request for a temporary leave of absence, The Blade Lord had spent much of his time in the arena with Captain Ragnar; their presence was deemed necessary, to help bolster the shaken morale of The Blades, in light of the Order's recent losses. Convinced now of Marcus' absence, she pushed the door to his private quarters wide open and walked silently into the chamber. It dawned on her then that there was actually little need for Marcus to lock the door, given its sparse furnishings. Aside from his armour, and the large bastard sword he habitually carried, she wondered if in fact Marcus owned any treasured personal possessions. Marcus seemingly had no hobbies or interests outside of the Order; The Blade Lord devoted all of his time to the defence of Freylar, and his unwavering support of her rule. Thinking back, she could remember at least two separate occasions where she had found herself wondering what Marcus would *do* without The Blades.

She walked quietly across the chamber towards its single large window and proceeded to make herself comfortable on its worn sill; it was Marcus' favourite place to contemplate anything and everything. She had often seen him perched against the window, high up in the Tri-Spires, deep in private thought whilst the world below went about its business. As she stared down from the elevated vantage point into the heart of the vale, she began to fully appreciate the reason why Marcus habitually favoured the spot for his quiet contemplation. Spying upon the vale from so high up, with nothing but a light breeze to accompany her, saw her troubles – momentarily at least – melt away in the warmth of her newfound serenity. For a brief moment she forgot entirely about the burden of leadership, and the mistakes she had made during her reign which continued to trouble her. Sadly the moment could not last. The feeble sun disappeared once more behind the abundant broken cloud cover, causing the autumnal sky to darken again along with her mood. Thoughts of Marcus' gambit with the Knights Thranis, Darlia and the inevitable reaction to Aleska's foray at Scrier's Post preyed on her mind once more.

'Enjoying the view?'

Startled by the unexpected voice, she flinched violently, causing her to lose balance on the sill entirely. Her heart leapt into her mouth as she sensed her body slip from the window's smooth frame. Adrenaline flooded her body as it tipped towards the opening, seemingly of its own volition. Sensing her muscles tense, she frantically snatched at the polished granite frame, desperate to save herself from toppling out the window; from such a lofty height, there would be no easing her descent with her wraith wings. Convinced that she would indeed fall, an invisible force suddenly gripped her tightly then promptly drew her steadily back into the chamber. The invisible caress lowered her gently to the ground and quickly released its hold. Her legs wobbled uncontrollably from shock, causing them to give way unexpectedly, ushering in the promise of a second fall. This time, however, strong arms gripped her torso, pulling her upright again. She opened her eyes – realising that she had involuntarily shut them. Marcus held her tightly, with his well-defined semi-naked arms. Realising now that she was in fact safe, the muscles in her neck quickly relaxed, causing her head to gently fall back whilst she exhaled deeply with relief. Marcus quickly slid his right hand around the back of her head then moved his left hand to support the small of her back. She felt weightlessness once again, however, this time she was carried safely over to The Blade Lord's bed. Marcus laid her still-trembling body neatly upon the stiff bed, then gently swept her long white hair clear of her face.

'I am so sorry.' said Marcus earnestly. 'Please forgive me Mirielle.'

She did not reply at first. Still shaken by the ordeal, she focused on regaining her composure and attempted to regulate her breathing. She closed her eyes and focused on relaxing her body, in addition to slowing down her breathing. When she opened her eyes again, Marcus was staring intently at her with obvious concern; he was clearly anxious about her current wellbeing.

'Are you OK?'

'I will be absolutely fine, I just need a moment.' she replied eventually.

'You had me worried there! I have no desire to see you fall from the top of the Tri-Spires.'

'It happened because of my own carelessness. I have been on edge lately. You startled me that was all. Besides, I should not have invaded your privacy.'

'I believe I mentioned to you previously that my door is always open. Though perhaps I should shut my window in future?'

Feeling somewhat awkward, she sat up. She placed her bare feet on the cold floor and began to test their returning strength.

'Perhaps you should rest a little while longer?'

'I will be fine.' she said, rising unsteadily from the bed.

'Were you looking at the lattice in the sky again?'

'Actually no – not on this occasion at least. I am ashamed to admit that curiosity led me to your window, despite my better judgement.'

'Then...what *were* you doing, if I may ask?'

She smiled gingerly at The Blade Lord; in that instant she felt like a young Freylarkin again, one who had been caught performing a forbidden act. Like a bewildered parent, Marcus looked to her for answers, though she felt embarrassed at the prospect of confessing her true motive.

'I wanted to know why it is that you spend so much time perched in your window.'

'Well...feel free to simply enquire next time. I gather that asking questions is safer than falling through windows.'

'You should not tease your queen so.'

'As always, you are wise in your counsel.' Marcus replied, using the full extent of his charm. 'Did you manage to satisfy your curiosity, with your near untimely release?'

'As it happens, I did. I had not expected the simple act of looking down across the vale to be so...calming. I understand now why it is that you enjoy sitting there.'

Marcus smiled, then gently grasped her right wrist and lead her gingerly back towards the site of her near misfortune. Marcus hopped onto the wide sill, instinctively adopting his favoured position. Then, without warning, he lightly spun her round and lifted her onto the sill so that she sat comfortably between his legs. She had known Marcus for a long time; never once during their time together had he been so forward with her physically. Once again she felt a rekindling of her youth in Marcus' presence; his uncharacteristic impulsive action prompted her to rediscover body chemistry thought to be long since lost to her. Marcus slid his arms around her thin waist, prompting further adolescent bodily reactions due to his close proximity. She felt a mixture of apprehensiveness and nervousness, and yet she did not wish the moment to end. Sensing her illogical anxiety, The Blade Lord drew his arms in more tightly around her waist, though not uncomfortably so.

'Relax...try to forget about Freylar, if only for a fleeting moment. Our domain will still continue to be, regardless of how often you choose to angst over it.'

'You are right of course, though it is difficult for me to forget the inescapable – my enhanced sight forbids it – more so given our recent illumination caused by Rayna's arrival.'

'I am afraid that I do not understand.' replied Marcus softly.

'Not now, but shortly you will. Behold my blessing, or rather my curse; judge for yourself, either way.'

She raised her right hand and lightly touched Marcus' temple. Pulses of warm light raced up her slender marble-like arm towards her fingertips. The light caused Marcus to groan in pain, though his torment did not last. With his temporary metamorphosis complete, she waited silently for The Blade Lord to fathom his newly acquired perspective of their domain. She had considered enlightening The Blade Lord on numerous occasions in the past, though until Rayna's unorthodox arrival in Freylar, she had been unable to reveal her secret – to anyone. Marcus exhaled deeply as she sensed his wondrous bemusement at what he was witnessing. Curiosity clawed at her mind, attempting to turn her head so that she could witness Marcus' reaction first hand, however, this time her better judgement prevailed; she assumed that Marcus was not currently in the right frame of mind to prevent them both from toppling out the window.

'Is that where...The Guardian comes from?!' enquired Marcus, whose awestruck gaze focused exclusively on the moving giant lattice layers criss-crossing the sky. 'This is incredible!'

'Yes – so I once thought. However, if you stare at it long enough, it will take something from you. It is a greedy thing, feeding indirectly on the souls it nurturers. I wonder sometimes if the Narlakai are more honest.'

'What exactly do you mean by that Mirielle?'

'I mean that the Narlakai *are* what they are...they make no attempt to conceal their true nature, the fact that they feed on the souls of others. But that *thing* up there behaves very differently. It deceives us all. Each of us seemingly remains trapped within it, yet few of us even realise that fact. You wanted me to let you in, so that you can better understand why I am the way I am. Now you know the maddening truth of it. And to think that I sacrificed part of myself, if not my entire soul, to learn of this inescapable reminder; that we are each of us, unwitting captives of our own deities.'

'If the arrival of Rayna has altered your perception of the lattice and its true motives, how then do you now perceive Rayna herself? Do you suspect Rayna's own motives, and if so why would *it* send her here?'

'I do not know why Rayna's fate is now tied to our own. Perhaps she wronged the Sky-Walkers and has been sent here to atone, or maybe...we are just mere playthings to them.'

She could sense that her idle speculation caused unease in Marcus. He relaxed his hold around her waist and sighed wearily. Being the sole Freylarkin charged with the overall responsibility of Freylar's security, Marcus already had enough weight bearing down on his broad shoulders. She feared now that perhaps she had unnecessarily added an additional load, one which even The Blade Lord would struggle to manage.

'Mirielle, is that what you *truly* now believe?' enquired Marcus, after a quiet moment of shared contemplation.

'Maybe, perhaps. Marcus, in truth I simply do not know. I have more questions now than answers. How then can I lead the Freylarkai with so many unanswered questions? Moreover, how can I lead our people into the future, when I do not understand the present?'

Unbeknownst to Marcus, her question was rhetorical. She already knew what had to be done. In order to successfully navigate the many complex strands of fate fast unravelling before them, the Freylarkai needed more than their wits about them; even her own enhanced sight would not be enough to guide her leadership along the correct paths ahead. She needed more – she needed her people's second sight, and Aleska would be the one to provide it for her.

'Mirielle, I have faith in your ability to lead us into the future. You *will* find a way, of that I am certain. And, should you require my aid, I will be here for you – always.'

TWELVE
Bridges

Despite the obvious threat to Freylar, he was in no hurry to return to the vale. He required more time to fully recover from the latest attack on his mind. Furthermore, he needed to take stock of the situation and collect his thoughts before issuing his formal report to Marcus. He decided to report back his findings in person, rather than employ the services of an airborne courier – as was his habitual mode of communication. Delivering word to Marcus first-hand had its risks. The Blade Lord would easily be able to read his body language; any discrepancies in his verbal account, or slip-ups on his part, would be more easily discernible than from a stale written account. However, relaying the minimal intelligence first-hand would stress the lack of urgency, and reinforce the uneventful nature of the report he intended to deliver. Subconsciously he had already decided to omit his second encounter with the rogue telepath from his formal report. However, he was still struggling to justify the omitted truth in his own mind; he had never once lied to The Blade Lord, intentionally or otherwise – that was about to change.

He disliked travelling across the Bleak Moor – it was far too exposed for his liking – therefore he had chosen to take the lesser travelled but more direct route south-east. Just visible to the left, on the darkening horizon, was Scrier's Post, which continued to stand eerily alone. Regardless of what the site represented to others, to him it was a mass grave and a loathsome reminder of his own personal failings. They pressed on past the abominable stain on Freylar's landscape and continued their journey south. They would not make the vale before nightfall, thus he decided that they would make camp for the night out in the open, beneath the Night's Lights.

'*We will rest here tonight.*' he said, communing telepathically with Krisis.

Rather uncharacteristically, Krisis began to growl deeply; the faithful dire wolf sat down firmly on its hindquarters and stared intently at the southern horizon. Following Krisis' gaze, he quickly picked out the dire wolf's cause for concern with his acute vision; a dull light flickered in the distance against dusk's encroaching gloom. Krisis continued to growl fiercely at the distant light. They were clearly not alone, but who amongst the Freylarkai would choose to make camp beyond the relative safety of the vale, he wondered. Certainly not one of his own scouts, for they were currently garrisoned; The Blade Lord had ordered them to return to the vale, in light of the Order's recent losses. Besides, his scouts knew better than to give away their position so easily. Who else then would be so bold?

'*Go quickly. Make haste to within one hundred paces, then approach with caution.*'

Wasting no time, he unfurled his wraith wings and set off immediately towards the distant light, trailing Krisis; the fleet-footed dire wolf had already taken an early lead, and would likely maintain it, courtesy of his seemingly boundless lupine stamina.

He was no expert at making fire. Though his efforts had finally borne fruit, the process of building a camp fire had increased his current stress level. He cursed one final time at the poorly constructed fire pit, as he tossed another branch onto the greedy fickle flame. He was about to try to relax and enjoy the warmth of the dancing flame, when a sudden deep growl emanated from the surrounding darkness. Instinctively he stood up and immediately drew his falchion; the flickering light of the flame flashed across the blade as he drew it deftly from its worn scabbard. A pair of yellow eyes winked into being from the darkness before him, quickly followed by the outline of a lupine head – too big to be that of a normal wolf, he quickly realised. Cautiously, he adjusted his footing, in case the animal decided to strike. He cursed himself for allowing his distracted mind to lower his guard; had his opponent the sense to immediately charge, he would have already lost the unexpected encounter.

'You will swiftly become a slave to your own construction Nathaniel, if you keep feeding it twigs.'

He recognised the voice from the darkness; it belonged to Lothnar, who promptly stepped forth from the darkness to his left. The yellow eyes before him suddenly drew closer, revealing their host's true identity.

'This is Krisis, whom I gather recognises you Nathaniel.' said Lothnar casually.

He realised now that the dire wolf before him was in fact the same one used by Lothnar previously to deliver word to the Tri-Spires, forewarning the recent Narlakai invasion. Aleska had subsequently taken the animal under her wing, though he did not recall seeing the animal at Scrier's Post. In any event, he knew now that Krisis was unlikely to attack him. He sheathed his falchion, signifying that he meant the dire wolf no harm. Krisis reacted in kind by sitting firmly on the ground.

'I was never any good at building fires.' he replied, turning his attention now to Lothnar.

'I see that.' replied the loner Paladin. 'We need to get something of substance on there to burn, plus some more kindling, else the flame will burn itself out.'

Lothnar busied himself with rectifying the pathetic attempt at a fire, whilst Krisis' piercing yellow eyes continued to regard him mutely. Feeling like a spare part, he decided to prepare some food, presuming both Lothnar and Krisis had yet to eat that evening. He laid an assortment of nuts and berries on the ground, intended for the dire wolf, which Krisis greedily consumed. Lothnar caught sight of the meagre meal, prompting the Paladin to reach for the worn hessian satchel strapped across his back. Lothnar subsequently tossed the released body of a large rodent before them, causing the impressive dire wolf to bark enthusiastically at the sight of an improved meal.

'Let us eat properly, shall we?' said Lothnar with a wry grin. 'I assume you can skin that Nathaniel?'

'I forget this is your domain Lothnar.' he replied, flashing a wry smile of his own.

Lothnar slid a throwing knife out from a sheath strapped to the underside of his left arm. The Paladin flicked the small blade with astonishing alacrity; it flew from his hand and embedded itself into the belly of their intended meal, causing the rodent to roll onto its opposite side, facing towards him.

He pulled the knife from the lifeless animal and set about cleanly skinning the large rodent. Though he lacked the skill to build a decent camp fire, his mastery of the blade was never a subject of debate.

'It is not wise to construct a fire on your own. The light draws too much attention.'

'Would you rather we put it out?'

'No need. With the three of us present we can rotate a watch throughout the night.'

The fire was burning steadily now under Lothnar's watchful eye; the rekindled fire brought the unlikely companions closer as they shared its generous warmth, seeking to stave off the chilling autumnal air. He unsheathed his short blade from the belt around his waist, and impaled the freshly skinned rodent on the tip of the blade. He passed the plain looking weapon to Lothnar, assuming the Paladin would do a better job at cooking their meal.

'Nathaniel, what may I ask lures you from the arena – out here of all places?' enquired Lothnar curiously.

He sighed heavily in response to the question, as though the act would somehow alleviate his woes – which it did not. Though he had intended to consult with Kirika first, he desperately sought the counsel of another regarding Aleska's recent actions. Despite their past differences, Lothnar was pragmatic – when not consumed by emotion.

'You do not need to answer that question, brother. I appreciate that we do not always see eye to eye on matters.' continued Lothnar, who slowly turned the rodent above the flame.

'Lothnar, let us agree now to bury the past – for good! Do you think that we can both agree to such an accord?' he replied, extending his right hand.

Lothnar slid the blade across to his left hand then grasped his own in a firm grip. They nodded respectfully to one another; a positive sign that perhaps their relationship might improve in the wake of their chance encounter.

'Agreed. I grow tired of the friction between us. Let us bury it.'

They shared a moment of comfortable silence. He had longed to set aside his differences with Lothnar; the act of finally doing so relieved some of the stress harboured by his tired body. The moment ended when Lothnar suddenly broke into quiet laughter, as though amused by a private joke which had suddenly become clear. He failed to mask his look of confusion at the amused Paladin cooking their meal. Krisis, by contrast, was uninterested in Lothnar's change in demeanour; the dire wolf continued to salivate at the sight of their meal, turning above the flame.

'Nathaniel, why is it that we waste time bickering amongst ourselves, while others plot our downfall?'

'I suppose it is our nature.' he replied wearily.

He ran his fingers through his shoulder length hair, which had become knotted during his stay at Scrier's Post; it would be some time before the sanctuary could be deemed habitable.

'Lothnar, I need to inform you of a recent development, however, I can only do so in complete confidence. You understand?' he said looking Lothnar directly in the eyes. 'What I am about to say must remain strictly between us – for the time being at least.'

'You have my word that this conversation will go no further. What troubles you Nathaniel?'

'I need to speak to you...about Aleska.'

'Trix, can you hear me?' he said, whispering so as not to attract any unwanted attention.

'*Speak louder. You're very faint.*'

'Err, have you forgotten where I am right now?' he replied sarcastically, with a slightly raised voice.

'*No, but you seem to have forgotten who's covering your backside out there.*' replied Trix over their low-tech medium-range communications link. '*If you don't speak louder, I won't be able to hear you clearly.*'

'Maybe this was a bad idea.' he said thinking aloud.

'*Shall we abort?*'

'No, no way! I was only kidding.'

The last thing he wanted to do now was call off their operation. Waiting for the green light from Trix to proceed with their meticulously planned incursion had been particularly painful. The rogue software engineer, or rather hacker-programmer, had insisted that their preparations be perfect before sanctioning their sortie, and yet Trix had clearly overlooked the simple act of talking. He wondered whether practical common sense was a trait sorely lacking amongst Trix's ilk. Despite the obvious technical difficulty, he had no desire to postpone the commencement of their operation; spending another day cramped amongst Trix's squalor was not an option – for him at least – and their bolt-hole was beginning to smell.

'*If you're done complaining, shall we proceed?*'

It was Trix's idea to transmit analogue communications as opposed to a digitally encrypted signal. Though he was convinced that digital encryption would be secure, Trix's main concern was outright detection of their signal, so instead the software engineer decided to simply employ an obsolete analogue mode of communication. Although the signal would be unencrypted, Trix was confident that Peacekeeper patrols would fail to even detect their public broadcasts. Better to remain completely invisible than well protected – according to Trix at least. Archaic technology was now their ally, or so he hoped.

'I still don't understand. Why not just give me the data?'

'*You wouldn't know what to do with it. Besides, there is always the possibility of a back-hack. We're going to be connected to the redundant NGDF satellite for quite some time.*'

'You could have improved your tactless response simply by informing me of the latter part.'

'*What?*'

'Oh forget it. I'm moving out.'

'*Say again. Speak louder!*'

Choosing to deliberately ignore Trix's last broadcast, he exhaled deeply as the full realisation of what they were about to do suddenly hit home. He sensed a pit in his stomach as anxiety momentarily got the better of him. Infiltrating the metropolis was typically a non-event for someone of his streetwise talents, but doing so in the wake of the Rout would be an entirely different matter. Peacekeeper patrols would be rife, and security would no doubt be heightened generally. Offering one final prayer to no one in particular – being an atheist – he regarded his home with one final sidelong glance before breaching the perimeter of the Wild, taking a leap of faith into the unknown.

Seeking out every available recess, he slipped silently between the dark cracks of the metropolis, melting effortlessly between the shadows unseen. He was no stranger to the shadows, which had become his allies over the years; he found the relative safety of their dark embrace comforting. Regrettably, his route took him through the metropolis' derelict former business district. The entire area had become home to the Shadow class, who illegally moved in after big business moved out. He knew the area well, having lived amongst its shanty dwellings himself for two years in the wake of his government-run – and, more often, charity funded – children's homes. Ordinarily the abandoned business district was a welcome sight, though now it was one of foreboding. The once teeming hive of illegally occupied dilapidated former office buildings, and poorly constructed lean-to dwellings, was now desolate; the bleak former business district had been scoured clean of its former inhabitants. Seeing the empty dwellings first-hand struck him hard; the sight offered grim confirmation of the Rout's immoral success. The metropolis' cruel government, backed by its uncaring populous, had signalled the death knell for his class. There remained little now of his previous live, save for the eerie silence of the decaying uninhabited buildings. It would not be long before previously tar pitted government programs were reinstated, ushering in the complete demolition of the district and its subsequent redevelopment. This final, inevitable, act would see the stain of the Shadow class erased from the records, and along with it troubles which had long since plagued the metropolis. He could not argue with the ruthless efficiency of the policy, however, its execution was heinous and immoral. Though he had been actively chided and ridiculed by his peers for making a new home within the Wild, none of their past taunts and disparaging remarks warranted the outcome fate had dealt them. On reflection, fate had not been the architect of the Shadow class' ruin – humans had. The sight of the desolate streets made his stomach churn.

'How does it look?'

'Terrible. Trix, there's nothing left. The Shadow class is gone.'

The pit in his stomach returned at the sound of his own voice, as though uttering the words aloud somehow confirmed the existence of the lifeless landscape before him. Though he had not witnessed first-hand the global decimation of the planet, he wondered if similar scenes were commonplace during the century of hell documented by historians. Some had argued that the successive global conflicts were a necessary evil, which ultimately paved the way for an improved human race. The metropolis, and others hives across the globe like it, were intended to be embryonic vessels for that learned race – a platform from which it could rise again. The crime scene before him, however, spoke volumes to the contrary, despite its deathly silence. How could a supposedly enlightened society allow such heinous acts to take place, he mused in disgust. The glaring impact of humans and their actions was well documented across the Infonet – provided you knew where to look – yet no holographic rendition could ever do justice to the reality of such horrors when witnessed first-hand by one's own eyes. Digital renditions habitually removed the grime and grit from any travesty; being *there* and experiencing the moment was entirely different. A chill suddenly ran up his spine; he had lingered in the mass grave for too long.

'Trix, I'm moving on.' he said solemnly. 'Are there any patrols in this area?'

'Not for at least another two hundred metres. Patrols are few in number across the outskirts.' replied Trix.

He pressed on towards the heart of the former business district, whilst trying hard to filter out the sadness around him. Eventually Trix's dull voice crackled in his ear, warning him of the aforementioned danger. He wanted to continue moving forwards; loitering amidst the decrepit structures ate away at his soul, though he had little choice but to follow Trix's command and wait out the patrol. He stared up at the depressingly black sky, whilst patiently waiting for the Peacekeeper patrol up ahead to pass. His curious mind began to wander again as he stared quietly into the crisp autumnal void. Where did they go, he thought to himself. In all likelihood, the varnished truth to his question was already circulating the Infonet, but without access to a bio-key that information would not be forthcoming. Besides, he had no interest in the government's propaganda; he desperately sought the truth of the Rout, and his class' mysterious disappearance. The forced relocation of so many people could not go unnoticed; he clung to the hope that morally correct Apex class citizens still existed, and that one such individual would possess the required conviction to leak the truth of it onto the Darknet. In any event, without access to the Infonet neither he nor Trix would be able to access that information. It depressed him further not knowing what preordained fate those in power had directed for the Shadow class.

'Callum, get moving; the patrol has passed.'
'Understood.'

He was thankful to be moving again; if nothing else, moving staved off the cold touch of the night air. Despite winter still looming on the distant horizon, he already felt its chilling grasp speculatively clawing at him. Allowing the cold to bite at him too frequently would only hinder his agility. Ultimately once he reached his destination he would be fine, though in the meantime he tightened the cord around the base of his hood, attempting to prevent further loss of body heat. He continued to move silently along the empty streets, clinging to the shadows at all times to obscure his presence. Trix routinely checked in, warning him of both imminent and present patrols, allowing him to adjust his pace accordingly. There were numerous occasions when Trix instructed him to hold his position again. Despite voicing his desire to take alternate routes in order to maintain his momentum, the stubborn software engineer disregarded his proposals, choosing instead to stick with the originally planned route. Trix disliked variables; everything needed to be meticulously planned and calculated. Regardless of their difference of opinion, now was not the time to challenge his obstinate ally. Reluctantly accepting Trix's inflexibility, he continued to wage his private war against the elements, trying his best to keep the cold at bay. Eventually he left behind the depressing former business district, which gave way to the outer layer of the urban core. The abundant shadows started to recede as the many lights of the metropolis swallowed them whole. Although pockets of darkness were still present, he was now forced to routinely break cover when darting between the dark sanctuaries.

'I'm starting to lose the dark. Things are about to become difficult.'

'*Noted.*' replied Trix unemotionally.

The way forward was no longer clear to him; he would need to spend increased amounts of time planning his future movements. He also needed to move faster now, in order to limit his exposure time. No longer would his movement be fluid and graceful; thus began his dangerous game of cat and mouse.

'Morning, how was your bed?'

He faced away from the camp, yet his keen hearing detected The Teacher's awakening long before Nathaniel stood up to approach him.

'The ground was hard.'

He laughed in amusement before responding, 'Yes, the approach of winter will do that. But forgive me, I sometimes forget what it is like to sleep in an *actual* bed.'

'My back is stiff, but at least my belly is full.' said Nathaniel, offering their smouldering fire pit a sidelong glance. 'Do you normally rise so early?'

'Frequently, yes, though I freely admit that your disturbing news kept me awake during most of your watch, thus I never really slept.'

Nathaniel moved to sit beside him. It had been a long time since both had sat alongside one another. He had forgotten the degree of scarring present on The Teacher's exposed arms; each of the ugly scars represented a valuable lesson taught to the members of their Order – except in his case that was. The venerable arena master released a weary sigh shortly after sitting down, neatly summing up their downcast mood. The possibility of Aleska, and their queen no less, reneging on Freylarian law was unthinkable. According to Nathanial, however, this notion was now very real. Granted, The Teacher played his cards close to his chest, but Nathaniel was no liar – that much he knew for certain. Their domain knew conflict well, having endured numerous conflicts with other species over the passes, but under Mirielle's rule Freylar had at least enjoyed a level of stability wrought by the solid foundation her regime had instilled. For the first time during Mirielle's rule, that foundation was now revealing signs of an ugly crack. Though he respected the venerable scrier, Aleska was known to manipulate the actions of others – his own included. Was it conceivable therefore, that Aleska had somehow steered Mirielle towards such a controversial path? Regardless, the timing was poor. With Darlia and the rogue telepath still in the wind, and the hurt of their recent losses still fresh in their minds, Freylar could ill afford further conflict; moreover, an internal struggle had the potential to rip their society apart, and could well be far more damaging than any external strife.

'We must tread carefully Nathaniel. This is a delicate situation, more so given the nature of the pieces in play.'

'Agreed. You realise of course that this very conversation between us could be perceived as an act of treason?'

'Yes, I am keenly aware, though it surprises me that you approach me with this knowledge. I incorrectly assumed that your trust in me was...thin.'

'Lothnar, I find you to be most pragmatic, when not consumed by your emotions. Out here is your domain. This is where you are most dangerous, and hopefully sharpest. I need your pragmatism now, to help me see clearly. You know my own thoughts on this matter – are they misguided?'

He chose not to immediately answer Nathaniel's question. He looked towards the breaking dawn across the horizon, seeking his own clarity of mind. It was common knowledge that he was wary of scriers, and their witchlike ability, though he did not abhor them – unlike Ragnar who vehemently distrusted their kind. He recognised the potential usefulness of their ability, but also the danger of the siren's call. He needed to set his caution aside, and logically think through the facts The Teacher had brought to his attention. He separated out Nathaniel's own personal views and carefully analysed the facts. Kirika was unaware of Aleska's unannounced disappearance, thus it stood to reason that the ruling council had indeed not been consulted – in its entirety at least. Aleska's foray was also being conducted in secret; further substantiating Nathaniel's claim that the assignment had not been sanctioned by the ruling council. It was possible, he supposed, that Aleska was operating alone, and that Mirielle's alleged changed stance was little more than a tactic designed to stall Nathaniel's investigation; indeed, Aleska had not been in a hurry to dismiss The Teacher from Scrier's Post. But why would Aleska operate alone, he mused. Aleska rarely chose to engage in activities where the outcome was not already assured.

His expression became grim as his quiet contemplation drew him ever closer to Nathaniel's own worrying conclusion. He continued to marshal his thoughts, during which time Nathaniel said nothing. The Teacher did not judge, nor did he make any attempt to pollute his thinking. His unlikely companion simply allowed him to assess the facts for himself. After some time, he finally turned to Nathaniel, ready – in his mind at least – to offer his own personal view on the matter.

'Nathaniel, I have considered the facts of the matter and nothing else. Regrettably, my conclusion matches your own.' he replied flatly. 'This development could be disastrous for our people.'

'The fact that we are in accord is bittersweet. Whilst I no longer feel alone and adrift, the very real prospect of subversion scares me Lothnar. Know that I am not easily scared!' replied Nathaniel earnestly.

'I understand. The prospect of exile, if we are wrong in this, does not concern me; this is my domain, like you say.' he replied, tipping his head towards the horizon. 'Though I do not share the same connection to our people as you, I am now concerned for their safety. The past and the future Nathaniel; neither should be known to us fully. Supreme knowledge of both would consume and destroy our society.'

Nathaniel grunted in agreement before replying, 'I said something similar to Aleska. She agreed with my words, and then promptly twisted them to justify her actions. It is common knowledge that I care for her Lothnar, but I cannot abide by what she is doing. Though she is clearly at ease with her actions, I cannot absolve her of them.'

'How do you suggest that we proceed?'

'Kirika is in the dark on this – she needs to know.'

'Nathaniel, informing Kirika will be dangerous.'

'Agreed, but then which course of action will not invite danger? Lothnar, we need to confirm that the remainder of the ruling council is indeed unaware of these events. Besides, although Aleska's ability wanes, she is nonetheless still powerful, and is actively gathering other scriers, of varying ability, to her. If we are to navigate the perilous road ahead, we will need a powerful scrier of our own to counter the threat.'

'So you propose fighting fire with fire?'

'Indeed.'

'And therein lays the trap.'

'You need not remind me of the hypocrisy of my proposal Lothnar.' replied Nathaniel with a dark expression of his own. 'However, I speak only of use within the already accepted boundaries of Freylarian law. I have always understood the value of scrying, despite my unease. Without this ability to guide us, how can we possibly hope to respond to this threat? I also suggest that I speak with Kirika alone – initially at least. If our conversation goes badly, I need you safe.'

'Very well, I understand the logic. Go quickly then and consult Kirika, though be sure that you tread carefully – brother!'

THIRTEEN
Mist

Heldran's ardent sword clashed violently against her falchions. Her hasty block intercepted the blow, but did not succeed in completely deflecting it; the force of the brutal impact violently jarred her body, forcing her backwards several paces. Heldran offered her a broad smile; visible in spite of his red-plumed barbute, courtesy of its wide vertical slit. The Knight Lord was in no immediate rush to press his obvious advantage, and instead taunted her further with his immense weapon. Heldran towered before her – it was the first time she had seen the Knight Lord fully armoured. His massive gauntleted hands gripped his ardent sword, which he held high, close to his barbute. The blade's extraordinary length further exaggerated the perception of Heldran's monstrous height.

'You cannot block my attacks Rayna, they are too powerful.' boomed Heldran from behind his barbute. 'Find another way to create your opportunities.'

She recalled the Knight Lord's previous sermons about fighting etiquette, or rather lack thereof. Heldran's attacks were indeed too powerful to redirect; she needed to find an alternate means of countering the armoured leviathan's advances, preferably before he backed her into a corner.

'You mean *opportunity* of course – I only require the one!' she replied, deliberately seeking to goad the Knight Lord.

'Ha! Rayna, you cannot rile me.' replied Heldran. 'Though I admire your spirit. Try again.'

Around them other knights of the Order watched with obvious interest, eager to witness The Guardian cross swords with their esteemed leader. Anika too observed from the sideline with keen interest; the troubled Blade Novice had integrated surprisingly well with the Knights Thranis, leading her to wonder whether in fact Anika favoured Heldran as the victor in their intriguing encounter.

Without giving her actions any real thought, she rolled fluidly across her left shoulder towards Heldran. As she came out of the roll, on her opposite hip, she temporarily released her grip on Shadow Caster. Using her body to obscure her true intent, she snatched at the ground with her free hand gathering a handful of loose dirt and other miscellaneous detritus. She hurled the contents of her hand at the wide vertical slit of Heldran's barbute. Most of the grit bounced harmlessly off the Knight Lord's armour, however, her cheap distraction paid off; some of the dirt found its way into Heldran's barbute and into the Knight Lord's eyes, temporarily blinding him. She grasped Shadow Caster and pressed forwards with her attack. Although blind to her actions, Heldran sensed her approach and guarded his upper torso whilst trying to blink his vision back into focus. Using the distraction to her advantage, she drove her right greave into the side of Heldran's calf, causing his right leg to buckle. The Knight Lord's leg gave way, forcing him down onto his knee. Heldran continued to maintain his guard, despite the further disadvantage. She followed up with a wide slash of her dual falchions, seeking to deprive Heldran of his weapon. The impact of her blades clattering against the Knight Lord's own rung out across the crowd, yet the vicious strike failed to disarm her opponent. Despite the force of the attack causing Heldran to lower his guard, nonetheless the Knight Lord maintained an iron grip on his ardent sword. Pressing her advantage, she stamped down hard on the blade's cross-guard with her armoured left heel, desperately seeking once more to dislodge Heldran's weapon. Defiantly, Heldran stood back up, rising to the full height of his menacing stance; the explosive nature of his sudden movement sent her tumbling backwards. She broke her fall by swiftly converting it into a backwards shoulder roll. Upon exiting the roll, she regained her feet, ready to meet the glowering stare of Heldran's watery eyes. The Knight Lord growled thunderously, like an angry bear whose slumber she had just disturbed.

'Good!' boomed Heldran. 'Again! Come at me Guardian!'

'My lord!' cried a sudden voice from the growing throng, clearly entertained by their vigorous sparring.

'What is it?!' thundered Heldran tersely without turning his attention away from her. 'Can you not foresee the lesson I am about to impart to this one?'

'Please excuse me, my lord. I have an urgent message from Knight Captain Gedrick.' replied a single harried knight, who had since pushed his way to the front of the eager spectators.

'What message?' demanded Heldran, still maintaining his unflinching stare.

'Received by Sky-Skitter, just moments ago.' the knight continued. 'The detachments led by Knight Captain Gedrick have come under ferocious attack from the Ravnarkai. My lord, they are cut off!'

'Humph, it appears that you will engage in a meat grinder far sooner than I had anticipated, Guardian.' replied Heldran, still regarding her with his flinty stare.

Silence descended across the gathered knights as they looked to Heldran for fresh orders. Without warning, the Knight Lord tossed his ardent sword effortlessly to the messenger – who deftly caught the blade by its thick hilt – and removed his barbute. Heldran turned on his heels and immediately commenced barking orders.

'Rayna, assemble half of the reserves and ensure that each is fully armoured! Vorian, the remainder of the reserves will remain here to guard the Gate under your watch! Morin, retrieve my great sword and...bring me the other one too'

The Knight Lord's words tasked every reserve in earshot with fresh purpose, including herself; she was about to commence the task assigned to her when Heldran spoke once more.

'Rayna, a quick word if I may?'

She sheathed her falchions and removed her barbute before approaching Heldran inquisitively, eager to learn what additional information the Knight Lord intended to impart to her specifically. Despite the physical exertion of their sparring, Heldran appeared entirely unfazed by their encounter; even his armour looked untouched, unlike her own which had attracted dirt and dust from rolling around on the ground.

'What else do you require of me?' she asked curiously.

'You can answer a question for me.' replied Heldran in a more reserved tone. 'You could have blinded me far more effectively with your inner light, yet you resort to methods employed by those without your ability. Why is that?'

'Beating you by using a skill that you cannot match would be no victory at all. I can beat you in a fair fight

Heldran.' she replied, offering her newest mentor a playful grin.

'Ha!' boomed the Knight Lord. 'Not yet you cannot, but...perhaps in time you will succeed in validating your lofty claim. In any event, do not engage the Ravnarkai in a fair fight! Is that understood?'

'As you command, my lord.' she replied.

'Good! You are dismissed. Oh, and Rayna...do not think for one moment that we are finished here!'

Her grin rapidly morphed into a wide smile. Their brief encounter had been insightful; the next time she faced the Knight Lord, she would not be so easily dismissed.

Several cycles had passed before Lileah was able to make an attempt at her first steps with her altered physique. Krashnar had unexpectedly shaped a pair of lightweight hollow stone crutches to aid Lileah's movement; a surprising show of kindness from the otherwise uncaring shaper. She assumed the act was in fact a selfish one, and that their abhorrent benefactor merely sought to literally shore up his recent investment – the rogue shaper would be in no position to gloat if his latest work remained bedridden. Despite Lileah's generally healthier visage, the frail telepath had a number of bed sores from her time spent immobilised, even after her best efforts to tend to Lileah's needs in spite of the atmosphere between them growing increasingly tense. The relationship they once enjoyed had now soured – as she knew it would – yet she struggled to accept the growing distance between them. Lileah had always been impetuous and quick to anger; oddly they were traits that she once admired. She saw herself as a calming influence over Lileah, offering the formidable telepath the much-needed guidance necessary to navigate their uncaring world. Since her miserable awakening Lileah had grown increasingly insular and withdrawn, often ignoring her counsel entirely. The influence she once held over Lileah waned as her lover became increasingly defiant and difficult to communicate with, despite the obvious physical disability – a disability which Krashnar refused to acknowledge. In the mind's eye of the rogue shaper, Lileah's new form was superior; her newly forged body no longer exhibited any of its former weaknesses.

'Imagine the look on their stupid faces if they tried once more to run you through with a blade Lileah!' Krashnar had proclaimed unhelpfully, shortly after gifting Lileah the new walking aids.

Lileah's first attempt to walk had gone entirely as she had foreseen; her ability to scry was not necessary to predict the impatient telepath's frustrated reaction, when learning to walk again. Despite the aid of Krashnar's stone crutches, Lileah had collapsed painfully to the floor when attempting her first few steps. Barely containing her obvious anger, Lileah had nonetheless remained surprisingly calm and allowed herself to be raised back to her feet; she had had to prompt the heartless shaper to assist her when lifting Lileah, due to the increased weight of the telepath's body. Again, Lileah had tried to walk, resulting in the same fruitless outcome.

'Darlia, this is pointless!'

'No, it is not.' she had replied patiently.

'I cannot walk! I am too heavy, that much is obvious.'

'You are not even trying!' Krashnar had rasped, whilst watching disdainfully with obvious annoyance.

An argument had promptly ensued between all three, which lasted for some time, after which Lileah conceded and agreed to try again. Lileah's third attempt had shown signs of promise, thus they had continued pushing Lileah regardless of her frequent insults and generally negative attitude. They had given Lileah time to rest mid-morning, by which time Krashnar had grown bored of their limited progress and retreated to his workshop. Although Krashnar's presence had clearly riled Lileah, the impatient telepath nonetheless cursed the abhorrent shaper for abandoning her. She had spent the remainder of the morning with Lileah despite Krashnar's absence. As she had watched Lileah grow increasingly frustrated, trying again and again to walk but a few paces, her mind had wandered; she had questioned her real reason for remaining by the telepath's side – was it out of love, she had mused, or instead a means to absolve her own guilt. It was not until late morning when Lileah finally enjoyed some success, travelling several paces across the room. It had taken Lileah most of the morning to adjust to the weight of her altered body. With the aid of Krashnar's unconventional crutches, Lileah was able to walk extremely short distances before requiring rest – it was a start.

'Lileah, I think you should stop now and have something to eat.'

'No! I want to continue.' Lileah snapped.

'But you need food to maintain your strength.'

'I said no, Darlia! Now either help me, or go join Krashnar in his wretched workshop.'

Part of her wanted to snap back at Lileah, yet she knew there would be little point in doing so. Besides, she no longer had the mental fortitude to engage in heated debate.

Since their defeat at Scrier's Post, she recognised that she too had become withdrawn. Whereas Lileah had filled the resulting emptiness in her soul with venom and hatred, she herself felt numb, and seemed to have an increasing loss of control over everything that mattered to her; like a fallen leaf dancing in the autumnal breeze, she no longer felt connected to the world around her, thus she now lacked the motivation or ambition to pursue their original goals. Despite surviving the unforeseen turn of events at Scrier's Post, mentally she was utterly spent. The fire which once fuelled her conviction had been completely extinguished; no amount of kindling would reignite her desire to invade Freylar – they had tried and failed. Their time spent at Krashnar's hide had given her ample chance to reflect on her actions and – more importantly – their ramifications. She stared vacantly now at where her left hand used to be. Prior to their defeat, she regarded her ornate bronze metal claw with anger and disdain; now though, the sight of the monstrosity made her feel empty and sad. She wondered if perhaps she would be better served by asking Krashnar to remove the wretched mechanical prosthetic; the cursed bronze talon was now a continuous reminder of everything she had lost.

'Darlia, are you going to assist me or not?' demanded Lileah, in what was fast becoming a habitual scathing tone.

'Apologies, my thoughts distracted me for a moment there. Here, let me aid you.' she replied before sliding her arms around Lileah's ornate metal waist to provide additional support.

It was mid-afternoon when Lileah finally decided that a proper break was indeed required. She prepared them both a tolerable meal – quite the achievement given the state of the produce which Krashnar kept in his cold store. Despite previously lecturing the shaper on the poor quality of his provisions, Krashnar had paid little attention to her words – what little fruit he possessed was overripe, and the bread was now stale. She made a mental note to venture out of the hide to acquire fresh edible goods the following cycle, assuming Lileah did not take a turn for the worse during the night. For the time being at least, they were forced to make do with Krashnar's unappealing wares.

'Where is the...wretch? Still skulking around...in his workshop no doubt!' asked Lileah, who reached for another morsel of overripe fruit.

'I do not know for certain, though you are probably right.'

'Well, when he is finished working...on his latest abhorrent creation...tell him that I wish to speak with him.'

'About what exactly?'

'The invasion of course...what else?!'

'Lileah, the invasion is over.' she replied sombrely.

Like a spoilt child failing to get their own way, Lileah hurled the fruit in her hand towards the closest wall. The overripe fruit burst upon impact, the skin promptly flopping to the floor leaving behind its sweet sticky juice to slowly run down the already stained wall.

'It is not over! That bitch Mirielle started this war and I will be the one to end it, with or without your support!'

Little time was wasted after the knights' received word from their Captain; Gedrick required their immediate assistance and they would not leave him wanting. Having barked his orders, Heldran waited patiently for Morin to retrieve the monstrous great sword which the Knight Lord favoured in battle. Typically, such weapons were reserved for ceremonial use, yet Heldran's strength and size meant that the practical use of such a weapon was plausible; she could only imagine the terrifying sight of the blade sweeping deadly arcs, courtesy of his formidable grasp. It was not long before the knight hurriedly returned, wielding the oversized sword along with a curious second blade, both of which – unbeknownst to her – had been ensconced within the depths of the Ardent Gate, their location known only to a few. Although the enormous sword presented by Morin was hugely impressive, it was the other weapon, diligently carried by the knight, which caught her attention. The lesser-known blade was far smaller than she expected for a weapon employed by the Order; its shape resembled that of a falchion – the weapon of choice she herself had once used prior to adopting the Order's habitual ardent sword. Heldran promptly took both weapons from Morin then ordered the knight to join their ranks, thus increasing their detachment to nine members. Most were already armoured from their vigorous morning sparring, though there was a quick reassignment of arms as the detachment ordered itself following Heldran's hurried mission briefing. Heldran strapped the enormous great sword across his back and attached the sheathed smaller blade to the right side of his thick waist. Her heart began to pound with excitement at the prospect of fighting alongside the Order's leader. Heldran caught a glimpse of her wide-eyed stare and gave her a wide smile, reciprocating her own subconscious grin. She realised then just how caught up in the fervour of preparing for battle she had become. Having caught her eye, Heldran confidently strode towards her, all the while maintaining his warm smile. The heavy tread of his armour resonated with the rhythmic thumping in her chest. If the Knight Lord's intent was to embolden her soul, he had already succeeded. Words of encouragement were superfluous as she stood quietly in awe, eclipsed by the shadow of the magnificent armoured behemoth. Though Heldran ran a tight ship, his true calling lay on the field of battle, of that she was certain.

'Anika, I have it on good authority from Gedrick that you have earned the respect of your fellow knights during The Hunt. I expect you to earn my own when we engage the Ravnarkai this cycle.'

'And you shall, my lord.' she replied fervently, standing to attention.

'Good. We number few, but we shall release many!' affirmed Heldran, affectionately placing his heavy gauntleted left hand upon her right pauldron.

Though she respected The Blade Lord's ability to effectively motivate members of her own Order, she firmly believed that Heldran's ability to do the same was more sincere. There was something tangible about the Knight Lord's affections towards the members of his Order. Marcus was an icon, who represented an ideal – like a standard on the field of battle. Heldran, however, chose to cement bonds of fellowship with his kin through tactile interaction and grounded dialogue. She sensed no hidden political agenda or subterfuge from the Knight Lord, but instead the honest actions of a simple Freylarkin commanding his Order to the best of his ability. Once more she felt the presence of strong surrogate family bonds throughout the Order. Although a notion already familiar to her, due to her shared experiences with The Vengeful Tears, the feeling now was different. Prior to arriving at the Gate, she was driven by barely contained anger and despair. Now, however, her soul no longer felt empty. The emptiness within her, caused by her harrowing encounter with the Narlakai, had been subsequently filled by the knights' camaraderie.

Heldran turned to join the others who were diligently preparing for the battle to come. As he had done with her, the Knight Lord approached each member of the detachment in turn, offering words of encouragement. She cast her gaze towards the teardrop-shaped Moonstone given to her by Mirielle; the Order's artisans had fashioned a socket in her breast plate, which now housed the unique gift. It was an unexpected act, commanded by the Knight Lord himself; a way of honouring her past, whilst creating a degree of separation. Previously she had worn the tear around her neck, and had become accustomed to its constant presence. In truth, however, the wondrous creation was akin to poison; an ever-present reminder of an experience she would sooner forget. The Knight Lord maintained that one did not turn their back fully on the past, claiming that to do so would be like plucking out an eye. Though she now understood the dangers of clinging to the past, it would indeed be foolhardy of her to abandon the knowledge acquired from her experiences – regardless of their nature.

Shortly after their preparations, the detachment passed through the Ardent Gate. They emerged from a Waystone located within an isolated glade in the heart of a gloomy forest of dark twisted trees, mostly bare of leaves. The air was crisp and a light autumnal breeze filtered through the trees, disturbing the few remaining dried leaves still clinging to their spindly hosts. Although it was fast approaching mid-cycle, the light from the sun remained weak due to the strange mist which habitually surrounded them on their sorties; the phenomenon frequently compelled the knights to tighten their spacing, despite the risks this entailed. In the unlikely event a knight got separated from their detachment, standing orders were to fall back to the Ardent Gate, as opposed to groping around in the strange mist alone or inviting unwanted attention with rallying cries. She was informed by Xenia that the ever-present mist was a characteristic of the southern lands – most likely due to their high altitude, according to Rayna's bizarre 'science'. Regardless of its origin, the irksome mist increased the danger of their already hazardous environment. Despite those born during the winter season being generally blessed with good night vision, no such Freylarkai were able to visually penetrate the strange mist. Their best defence therefore was their hearing, ergo the detachment moved slowly and carefully through the eerie wood in order to minimise their own noise.

After eventually clearing the wood, the landscape opened up as the trees quickly thinned out giving way to rocky outcroppings, fields of heather and occasional clear narrow streams which cut paths haphazardly across the land. The lack of cover allowed the breeze to gather momentum; the chill air bit at the exposed skin of their faces, reminding them of the inevitability of winter. As the landscape opened up, the infuriating mist partially receded, affording them the luxury of quickening their pace. They cut a direct path across the heath lying between them and the Captain's last known location – according to Gedrick's hastily scrawled message. The thick heather masked the pot-holed landscape and occasional puddle, wrong footing some of the knights and putting them off balance, due to the uneven ground. Fortunately, the deceiving flora claimed no casualties, and aside from the occasional stumble they crossed the tussocky landscape unharmed.

With the heather fields behind them, they started to descend towards a natural depression in the landscape's surface. The straggly heather quickly receded, giving way to more dense and abundant plant life. The basin itself felt vast, yet it was difficult to validate her gut feeling with the ever-present mist lurking on the near horizon. The ground beneath them now felt invitingly soft with its thick coverage of lush verdant foliage. As they continued their descent into the basin, the crisp breeze dissipated and more of the spindly twisted black trees they had passed earlier could be seen dotting the area. The harsh landscape of the southern lands held an undeniably surreal beauty, yet she was mindful of the hidden dangers it also concealed.

Littered across the basin stretching out before them were numerous dark shapes, which she found difficult to identify. The knights maintained their silent approach, but it was clear from their body language that each had spotted the unusual sight. Heldran was the first to draw his weapon; the Knight Lord reached for the immense great sword strapped across his back, choosing to forego the curious blade still attached to his waist. She promptly followed suit, reaching for her ardent sword, as did the remainder of the knights, including Rayna, who unsheathed Shadow Caster in addition to her falchion. They continued their quiet approach whilst intently observing the ominous shapes which now began to acquire definition.

'What are they?' she whispered, eager to understand the potential threat.

At first she wondered if the shapes were natural rock formations, but as they began to snap into focus she quickly recognised the bestial forms scattered before them.

'Ravnarkai,' whispered Heldran, whose voice sounded like quiet thunder. 'A great number of them!'

FOURTEEN
Summons

She stretched her shoulders back, trying to alleviate their stiffness. It had been a long morning sat working at her desk in the inner sanctuary of the Tri-Spires; she had predominantly spent the morning catching up on various admin duties, which had mounted up since Aleska's departure. In particular she had spent a notable amount of time reviewing preparations for the forthcoming Trials, which were now the talk of the domain; idle gossip regarding Lothnar's – now public – challenge versus The Guardian was close to fever pitch.

Following Aleska's retirement, Marcus had charged her with an increased number of duties which she was now learning to manage effectively. She began to appreciate just how much administrative work Aleska had previously performed for the ruling council. Though she found the new tasks assigned to her largely mundane – and wholly unexciting – it was nonetheless insightful acquiring an overview of the inner-workings of their domain and how it functioned as a whole. She began to understand the wealth of knowledge Aleska previously had access to, and just how involved the venerable scrier had been in the development of Freylarkin society.

Unable to relieve the increasing stiffness in her joints, she stood up from her desk and began executing several well drilled exercises, taught to her by Nathaniel during her time spent as an Aspirant training in the arena. The tried and tested series of movements quickly began to alleviate the tension in her neck and shoulders, allowing her to relax her muscles once again. Before she could complete the ritual, however, a loud knock came from the door to her quarters.

'Come in.'

One of the Tri-Spires' sentries strode purposefully into her room then waited silently for her to finish her exercises.

'Is there something I can help you with?' she asked whilst continuing her routine.

'The morning watch received a message. It was delivered by Sky-Skitter.'

'Oh...and what did it say?'

'I do not know. The message scroll is marked private, and has your name on it – I believe it is intended for your eyes alone.'

The curious news from the sentry was enough to distract her from completing her exercises. She turned to the sentry, who passed her the tiny message scroll. Having completed his assignment, the sentry offered her a courteous nod and then promptly left the room.

She stared ponderously at the miniature scroll, wondering who might be responsible for sending her the curious message. Nathaniel seemed like the obvious candidate, though he rarely used Sky-Skitters, preferring instead to relay messages directly in person. Perhaps Aleska had decided to reach out to her, she mused. Either way, the tiny scroll piqued her curiosity. Eager now to learn the contents of its message, she carefully unravelled the tiny scroll, fully expecting it to contain a single line of script. Instead, there was nothing – the scroll was blank. Instinctively she checked the back of the unravelled scroll, wondering if perhaps she had missed something on its reverse side – again nothing. Momentarily perplexed by the blank scroll, she stared vacantly at it – musing over its true purpose.

'Hmm...I wonder...' she said aloud.

She closed her physical eyes and immediately engaged her second sight. Jumping backwards through time, she witnessed the sentry knocking at her door, followed by the route the guard took to reach her quarters. She saw the message scroll being handed to the sentry by the Tri-Spire's falconer, who in turn received the scroll following its rapid flight courtesy of one of Freylar's sleek black corvids. The message had indeed come from Nathaniel, who curiously spoke directly to the scroll prior to attaching it to its airborne courier. Strange also that Lothnar was in attendance! She slowed the passage of time down to an abrupt halt, before allowing it to flow slowly forwards once more. As she reviewed the images assaulting her mind, she focused intently on Nathaniel's lip movements and the words they formed.

'Meet...me...Rayna...inception...'

She disengaged her second sight, allowing the world around her to snap back to the fore once more. 'Rayna's inception?' she whispered inquisitively to herself, 'What are...ah, but of course.'

Hurriedly she gathered up several personal effects strewn across her chamber, including a thick dark hooded robe and a sturdy pair of thick-heeled long boots. She quickly changed into the garments then promptly headed out, after locking the door to her quarters. Despite her best efforts to quell any rash erroneous thoughts, her mind began to churn of its own volition as the unusual nature of Nathaniel's summons preyed on her subconscious. Had both Rayna and Anika already returned from their trip, she wondered. Moreover, had their assignment concluded badly – after all, why else would Nathaniel summon her to the Cave of Wellbeing through such means? She knew well the dangers of idle speculation, and the needless worry such conjecture often wrought, yet despite knowing better she was unable to shake the pit forming in her stomach.

'Curious. They're not moving.' she said quietly, turning to Heldran for answers.
'Hmm...it is because they have already been released. Look there, traces of blood stain the surrounding heather.'
She tried intently to pick out the details of the ominous scene they were witnessing, though the weak light penetrating the surrounding preternatural mist of the basin worsened her already poor sight. Without good light she could not hope to match the visual acuity of her peers. She tried hard to focus on the distant shapes – identified now as corpses by Heldran – but her poor sight continued to hinder her visual understanding of the scene unfolding before them.
'I do not understand.' whispered Morin. 'If the Ravnarkai have been released, why would the Captain request our aid?'
Heldran continued to survey the landscape as they slowly pushed forwards. More of the bloody scene revealed itself as they continued their quiet approach. Although some of the corpses were still whole – albeit with ragged gouges of flesh missing from their hides – significantly more were mutilated and strewn across the basin. On closer inspection, the bulk of the Ravnarkai had been literally shredded and torn apart. Bits and pieces of their ruddy pink flesh lay everywhere, cut to ribbons and carelessly

discarded to litter the landscape. The Knight Lord clearly seemed desensitised to such macabre scenes, the remainder of the knights, however, were notably disturbed by the display of barbarism before them. Regardless, each maintained their own silent counsel as the full horror of the carnage slowly revealed itself to them. Except for the sound of their armour, and the soft crunch of heather beneath their heels, the basin remained eerily quiet – so quiet, in fact, that she could hear the heavy breathing of the knights around her. The tension throughout the detachment increased dramatically as the mist continued to recede with their every advancing step, revealing more of the mutilated Ravnarkai remains. Despite wearing full plate armour, she fancied she could hear her heart pounding in her chest. The rhythmic thump grew louder and she began to feel hot and sweaty. Her anxious unfettered imagination started to re-enact the violence which surely must have taken place before them. She felt faint and began to lose focus as the imaginary re-enactment of battle assaulted her senses. Her head felt fuzzy and a familiar darkness clawed once more at the periphery of her mind, which began to un-tether itself from the world around her. She recognised well now the inception of one of her waking dreams, yet she was powerless to prevent it.

At last he was in the heart of the Metropolis. Progress would be painfully slow now – the ubiquitous light and increased patrols made it difficult to move undetected. The immediate concern now occupying his thoughts was running out of night. In addition, he was now entirely dependent on laggy ghost data, served up by one of the NGDF's redundant satellites, overlaid with Trix's own predictive heuristics; the lack of control made him feel uneasy. Trix, however, seemed quite comfortable with the current state of affairs.

'*Stop, wait...OK, go!*'

He loathed having his strings pulled like a hapless marionette, whilst Trix guided him fastidiously through the inner maze of the starkly lit metropolis. His time spent in the Wild had given him a true taste of independence; now that freedom had been abruptly taken away, replaced instead by the deadpan commands issued by Trix over their low quality means of communication.

'*Go right at the next junction.*'

The height of the surrounding pristine white and glass buildings was daunting; he felt like an insect scurrying around beneath their immense presence. Yet his new environment felt artificial; he missed the Wild – ironic really considering the false wilderness was itself an artificial construct, wrought by humanity.

'*Wait!*'

Reacting almost immediately to Trix's newest command, he quickly crouched behind the corner of a low-level wall. He gazed up at the clear sky above. There was zero cloud cover, just the perfect void of the night – exactly as Trix had predicted. The clumsy awkwardly-social software engineer had left nothing to chance, except perhaps for himself; he was determined that Trix would not dictate his every move, indeed he had already vexed the untidy hacker on more than one occasion during the early stages of their incursion. However now his situation was entirely different, and thus he was utterly reliant on Trix's dull navigation.

'*Cross the road, straight ahead, go!*'

After another forty-five minutes of erratic silent sprinting, he eventually infiltrated the metropolis' ostentatious residential district, which was clearly targeted at high-net-worth individuals. The district's buildings were almost entirely composed of glass and metal. Each floor within the buildings was like a penthouse suite in its own right – such was the grand minimalistic splendour of their construction. The gargantuan structures were immensely tall, reaching impossibly high towards the crisp black autumnal sky. The metropolis' architecture was impressive – in terms of sheer size – though it lacked uniqueness; virtually all of the buildings followed the same tired template design. The pretentious residential structures before him now were the first – that he had witnessed at least – to even slightly deviate from the standard architectural doctrine which plagued the metropolis.

'What can you see?'

'Residential habs.' he replied. 'Judging by their appearance, this is where the Apex class resides.'

'Good. You need to approach D-zero-zero-three, level zero-two-nine.'

He quickly scanned the nearby structures; D-zero-one-four, one-three and one-five – he needed to press onwards in order to lay eyes on their target. Staying low, he continued swiftly forwards, all the while blindly assuming that Trix would alert him to any imminent dangers. With the local residents currently under Peacekeeper-enforced curfews, the clean wide streets were eerily quiet. Even at such an early hour the metropolis habitually thrummed with the sound of night-life, as intoxicated merrymakers slowly made their way home. However now there was nothing, as though the cold autumnal chill had swept the streets clean of their human revellers. Despite the empty streets, he repeatedly glanced over his shoulder ensuring that no one followed him; it was a habit he had developed during his residency in the Wild. He continued hurriedly down the long wide street before him, until eventually he spied the immense high-rise that was D-zero-zero-three in the distance.

'I can see the target.'

'*Good. Make your way to emergency exit zero-five. It is located on the right side of the building.*'

'Acknowledged.'

Without pause for thought, or indeed any real assessment of the situation he was about to engage with, he bolted towards the ominous structure, obediently following Trix's command. Remaining low, he maximised the use of what little cover there was stationed in the street, whilst making his final approach. Swiftly and silently he moved from vehicle to vehicle as he vectored towards D-zero-zero-three – such an uninspiring designation for a structure; beautifully sterile, like the vast majority of the metropolis. Only the derelict former business district, previously home to the Shadow class, possessed any real character; ironically that particular district was destined to be regenerated, and would no doubt adopt the same template design seen throughout the remainder of the metropolis. When finally he reached his destination, he slowed to an abrupt halt, crouching adjacent to the designated emergency exit. The emergency exit's door was made from thick glass and had the numbers zero and five neatly stencilled across it in large black font.

'How do I access the building without a bio-key?' he asked anxiously, frustrated by his current lack of control.

'Look for a manual holographic access panel near the bottom of the exit.'

'I see it.' he replied, promptly bringing up the display.

'Good. Enter the pass code six-three-two-three-three-four-four-five.'

'How did you acquire the code?' he asked, unable to suppress his need to understand.

'Just enter the code before the Peacekeepers triangulate your position.'

'But how could they possibly do that? We evaded their patrols.'

'Because they've no doubt picked you up on surveillance feeds scurrying around the inner core of the metropolis.'

'What? And you're only just telling me about this now?!'

'Enter the bloody code!'

'Piss off!'

'OK fine...I probably deserve that. But just enter the damned code Callum; we need you off the streets.'

Although relatively forthcoming with information, Trix never chose to divulge all the details. Despite knowing full well that Trix had glossed over some of the minutiae of the plan, regardless he loathed operating in the field without all the facts. It was clear that Trix was desperate for the plan to succeed; obviously the software engineer had no long term survival mechanism in place, and thus needed his infiltration to bear fruit. However, he wondered if indeed there were any such surveillance feeds; surely the metropolis relied exclusively on bio-key access to track civilian movements, else why the need for patrols to flush out members of the Shadow class, he mused. He considered that perhaps Trix's words were purely those of a threat, intended as a means of tightening his new leash. Despite his growing suspicions, there appeared to be genuine concern in the low quality babble broadcasted from Trix across their antiquated communications link. Venting his annoyance on the non-tactile display, he punched in the sequence of numbers provided by Trix. The word *invalid* flashed up across the display. He tried the code once more, whilst trying to keep his growing annoyance in check. *Invalid!*

'The code doesn't work.'

'*Try it again.*'

'I already have – it doesn't work!'

His heart began to thump loudly in his chest, and his breathing became shallow. He could sense the onset of adrenaline about to flood his system as his frayed nerves fed his growing anxiety.

'*Shit. Give me a minute.*'

'What do you mean *give me a minute*, you're the one now ushering me off the street at the eleventh hour! You said you had all this covered.' he replied angrily.

'*I've been disconnected from the Infonet in the wake of the Rout. The guard's credentials I loaned may have since expired.*'

'You said you would back me up on this mission, but with what exactly – old and laggy data, shored up with a few hunches?'

'*Shut up, I'm trying to think!*'

The rhythmic pounding of his heart grew increasingly louder, and his head began to spin as he sensed the plan quickly unravelling. Hindsight taunted him, suggesting that he was a fool to have trusted Trix; now he would potentially pay the price for his possible poor judgement of character.

'Rayna!' growled Heldran quietly.
'Concentrate Rayna – focus on the here and now!' snapped Alarielle.
'Apologies...I was distracted.' she replied.
'We need to focus our attention, now more than ever.'
Beyond the disturbing scene of the mass mutilated corpses appeared to be an unusual rock formation protruding from the opposite slope of the basin. Again her eyes failed her as the dwindling light and infernal mist hindered her already lacklustre vision, making it difficult to properly identify the seemingly natural structure ahead of them.

'Over there!' whispered Morin, who pointed his left hand towards the rocks. 'Looks like a narrow cave entrance, cutting into the landscape.'
'Halt!' said Heldran abruptly.
She turned once more to Heldran, this time seeking the reason for their sudden halt. Something had the Knight Lord spooked, though she could not discern what specifically troubled the giant Freylarkin.
'This hasn't played itself out, has it?'
'No.' replied Heldran bluntly. 'I see only one possible Alpha amongst the newly released, and the numbers do not add up.'
'Do not add up how?' she asked.
'Based on our reconnaissance there should be more corpses – significantly more in fact. Tribal encounters are typically bloody affairs; we know this from our recent incursions. We should be seeing the release of an entire

tribe, in addition to casualties incurred by the vanquisher. Instead I count barely a tribe's worth of released Ravnarkai here.' explained Heldran ominously.

'Heldran, what are you suggesting?' she asked hesitantly. 'Were the survivors subjugated?!'

'What!?' enquired Morin, who was clearly taken back by her words.

'That is a possibility. There is much we have yet to learn about the Ravnarkai and their behavioural patterns.'

Before any amongst them could speculate further, a weak light flashed in the distance from the cave entrance identified by Morin. Though nothing was said, each of the knights – including her – noted the distant light, which continued to flash at a steady interval.

'What is that?' whispered Anika. 'Ravnarkai?'

'No.' replied Heldran, quickly dismissing the wild speculation. 'Standard operating procedure; you are witnessing one of our methods of communication, designed for use across short distances. It is a form of short hand, used to relay brief messages.'

'It has to be the Captain! They must be holed up in that cave.' proclaimed Morin.

'Why?' she asked.

Morin gathered up the decorative red loincloth of his armour and hurriedly used the material to wipe the length of his blade. The knight then adjusted his grip on his ardent sword and began to angle the long blade, such that it caught what little light penetrated the basin. Skilfully Morin tilted his weapon, sending a signal of his own, presumably in the hope that Gedrick and the others would receive his crude means of communication. Morin continued to adjust the angle of his weapon thus varying the degree to which the blade caught the light. The low-tech, highly skilled technique required Morin to adjust the intensity of the light reflected off his weapon.

'Analogue communication.' she said aloud unintentionally.

'Rayna, I do not understand your words.' replied Heldran in his habitual low rumbling tone.

'Ignore me.'

Silently they watched as Morin skilfully relayed the entirety of his message. There was a brief pause after the knight finished sending the communication. Each of them stared intensely at the distant cave, waiting for confirmation of receipt and more besides. It was not long before the distant light began to flash purposefully once more.

'They have partially sealed the entrance to the cave.' Morin translated.

'How and why?' she said, unintentionally interrupting Morin's report.

'Falkai is a telekinetic.' replied Heldran. 'As for the *why*...Morin, please continue your translation for Rayna and Anika.'

There was a brief pause as Morin and the other knights digested the cryptic flashes of light emanating from the mouth of the cave. Abruptly, and without warning, each of the knights – except for Anika and herself – adjusted their stance and immediately raised their weapons.

'What did they say?!'

'The Ravnarkai...Rayna, they are still here!' replied Morin uneasily.

'They are watching us!' growled Heldran. 'They are stalking us like prey, from the safety of the mist.'

'Cowards!' sneered Anika who also readied her weapon, taking her lead from the knights.

'We must link up with the others, now!'

'Rayna, if we attempt the crossing they will charge us down.' replied Heldran.

'Can they not abandon their armour and fly over the beasts?' she enquired respectfully.

'There is little chance that scenario would have a happy ending.' replied Heldran. 'I have seen Ravnarkai leap as high as four paces, Rayna. Without armour, they will be cut to ribbons.'

'I understand. Though if we try and fight them with just the nine of us, we will be overrun.' she countered with conviction.

'If you have an alternative suggestion Rayna, now is the time to voice it.'

'We form up defensively, moving slowly towards the cave. When they begin their charge, have Gedrick and the others counter and in turn charge the Ravnarkai.'

'If we move deeper into the basin Rayna, we will be exposed on all flanks!' replied Morin. 'Our fallback corridor will be cut-off.'

'No we won't. I have an ace up my sleeve.'

'And what is that exactly? You recall vividly that your fate is tied inexorably to that of my own, I hope!'

'Ace what?! Rayna, your proposal makes no sense – this is madness.' replied Morin.

'Heldran, you said that you trusted me! Do not lose sight of that trust now.'

'My lord...'

'Quiet Morin.' thundered Heldran. 'Your counsel is both noted and appreciated, however, it is time for The Guardian to live up to her name. Barbutes on!'

Morin donned his barbute and nodded to her respectfully, 'Rayna, I meant you no disrespect.'

'And I took none, despite your understandable reservations, though I ask that you trust me Morin.' she replied authoritatively. 'I once informed my fellow Aspirants that *I didn't get out of bed this morning simply to hand my soul to my enemies* – that notion still stands!'

'With respect Rayna, you climbed out of a hammock this morning.'

She offered Morin a wide grin then feigned giving the knight a good-natured slap across his barbute, before donning her own. Surprisingly the Knights Thranis had already warmed to Anika, readily accepting the troubled Blade Novice into their ranks – perhaps aided by the fact that Anika had quickly earned the respect of Zephir, who seemed to hold some influence over his fellow knights. Her own circumstances, however, were quite different. She sensed that the knights viewed her as more of an authoritative figure, though despite releasing her share of Ravnarkai on the battlefield during previous Hunts, she had yet to demonstrate her worth as a leader to the Order. She understood their likely concern regarding her ability to lead – indeed she had little past experience to draw from – however, she knew hardship well, along with the determination necessary to overcome unfavourable odds. In part, Marcus had sent her to the Knights Thranis to further her insight and to take on fresh experiences – she had no intention of deviating from the Blade Lord's directive now.

'Column formation, loose spacing!' ordered Heldran. '*When* we receive their charge, I do not want the Ravnarkai spearing through our ranks. Ensure that you each have room to manoeuvre.'

'Heldran, if I may, please take the head of the column; after we link up with Gedrick you will be at the heart of the fighting, which is where we need you. I will take the middle. Morin, signal our intent to Gedrick.' she said with authority.

Heldran approved her bold strategy with a simple nod of his head. Immediately the knights formed up behind the Knight Lord, with the exception of Morin who diligently relayed their strategy to Gedrick and the others.

'After the Captain's counter charge, I propose an orb formation around the Knight Lord and Loredan. Heldran, you will defend the inner circle and protect Loredan, who will likely have his hands full.'

Heldran signalled his approval once more with another brief nod of his head, before reaching for the mysterious blade still strapped to his waist. He unsheathed the enigmatic weapon, revealing it to her for the first time. As she had previously suspected, the blade was indeed a falchion. What she had not anticipated, was bearing witness to a second blade forged from the same raw material used to construct Shadow Caster – Dawnstone.

'Here, take it!' commanded Heldran, who effortlessly tossed the curious weapon down the column towards her.

She deftly grabbed the blade by its hilt and marvelled at its ornate construction. Although the weapon shared similarities with Shadow Caster, being wrought primarily from the same material, nonetheless it differed significantly. Two curious stones were fused into the weapon: one of the stones resided just below the falchion's cross-guard, along the top of its grip, whilst the other was located towards the tip of the blade. The stones themselves seemed familiar in design, yet she failed to immediately place their origin.

'What is this?'

'The answer I cruelly denied you during your training. That is the twin you seek to learn of – The Ardent Blade.'

'How long have you had this blade?' she enquired whilst studying the alien weapon intently.

'Long enough...indeed prior to Caleth's release; understand that I used The Ardent Blade to aid Nathaniel in his *task*.' replied Heldran.

The Knight Lord's unexpected words immediately broke her concentration, forcing her to relinquish her gaze over the blade. Thoughts exploded in her mind as she began to speculate as to the specifics of the distasteful event staining the weapons she now carried.

'Why give this to me?' she replied. 'Why now?'

'I never did like that weapon, or the acts it compelled me to do. The devious power it grants needs to be tempered by a heart purer than my own; the blade opens doors to its wielder, offering temptation where none should exist. Besides, those weapons you hold are a set – they have been separated for too long. I believe, Rayna, that you will overcome their evil nature, perhaps even put them to *good* use.'

'Thank you.'

'Ha! Best you reserve judgement with your thanks. But know this: those stones you were studying are in fact Waystones; each one is inexorably bound to the other. Touch the stone above the blade's grip and it will transport you a short distance, effectively mirroring your final position around the tip of the blade.'

'You mean to say that if I slash my opponent with this weapon, that I could appear behind them!'

'Yes...though you would still need to pull the blade from their back!'

FIFTEEN
Collusion

Krashnar slid silently into her room, forgoing the courtesy of announcing his presence by knocking on her door. Without bothering to explain his intentions, the uninvited shaper lingered by the door and proceeded to visually examine her; he stared intently at her with his black abyssal eyes, examining every section of her body. In particular, he seemed interested in the parts of her body where the foreign metal he had wrought fused with her flesh. After leering over her for some time, Krashnar turned to survey the room and its contents. He sneered at the fruit she had spitefully thrown against the wall, which now rotted on the floor, emitting an unpleasant pungent smell.

'Clean that up.'

'Do it yourself!' she said derisively.

'So be it. This conversation is over, along with your invasion of Freylar.'

'Wait!' she blurted out as Krashnar turned to leave the room. 'I will do it...later.'

'Better.' rasped the twisted shaper, who regarded her with a sardonic grin. 'Your dejected lover lays asleep outside. I thought it best you and I talk in her absence.'

With enormous effort she rose from the grubby bed, upon which she had lain throughout her initial recovery, with the aid of the unconventional crutches fashioned for her by Krashnar. Her flesh ached painfully as she slowly rose from the lumpy bed, causing her eyes to water uncontrollably. She tried to fight back the pain racking her body, yet it would not release her from its agonising grasp. She felt her face contort whilst trying desperately to hold back the tears in his presence; she was loathe to display such signs of weakness in front of the wretched ill-mannered exile.

'Go on.' she said, her words barely audible due to her broken voice.

'You failed to foresee the actions of one who intrigues me, thus your invasion was short-lived and ultimately resulted in failure.'

'You refer to...Alarielle, or whatever it is...that inhabits her body?'

'Correct. Darlia's plan was flawed; she spent too long trying to control all the pieces on the board.'

'And what do you...propose shaper?' she said, still failing to mask the pain in her voice.

'I propose their complete and utter release. You and Darlia had the right idea, yet you both faltered through your lack of conviction by wasting time manipulating Lothnar, masking your advance and sending a flanking vanguard into Freylar. Subterfuge and guile are tools employed by politicians and members of the ruling council of Freylar, not those seeking to wage war on their kin.'

'You talk much...Krashnar.'

'Yes, but you have the mind to back it up.' he said, gleefully rubbing the smooth stumps on his left hand where both his little and ring fingers once existed. 'Although your body has changed much Lileah, your mind has not. You can still gather the Narlakai – their numbers are vast and they roam Narlak like cattle, begging to be herded once again. Their mindless existence lacks purpose, but you can enslave them to your will alone, to serve your own agenda.'

'I can hardly move...let alone gallivant across Narlak! Besides, there is the...matter of Alarielle, or have...you conveniently forgotten?'

'Irrelevant. I have a solution to both problems.' replied Krashnar confidently.

'What solution?'

'Agree to join me in this, and I will share such knowledge with you.'

'Why do you care...about bringing Freylar to its knees?'

'You think I want to live here – like a hermit – unjustly exiled to live amongst the dusty crags of the borderlands?'

'I did not think...you cared.'

'You did not ask. Instead you came here only to insult my work, the work which ultimately prolonged your bitter existence.'

'I did not choose...to come here.' she replied, offering Krashnar a cold hard stare.

'Nonetheless you are here, in my hovel.'

Krashnar suddenly lurched towards her. The feeble light emanating from the Moonstone, on the trunk adjacent to her bed, revealed more of Krashnar's wild visage. The shaper's unkempt long brown hair appeared to twitch with life of its own. His face was grubby and worn, and dirt lined his broken fingernails. It was unclear whether the miserable looking shaper's way of life dictated his unpleasant appearance, or whether Krashnar simply paid no attention to his personal hygiene.

'You have a choice Lileah. You can choose to remain an outcast, scratching around for a meagre existence beyond Freylar. Or you can choose to align yourself with me, and together we will forcibly take back what is rightfully ours.'

'Krashnar...I do not trust you.'

'Irrelevant. We do not need to trust one another.' replied Krashnar before coughing up a small amount of black watery fluid which he promptly spat onto the floor. 'I need you to herd the Narlakai. You need me to help you round them up, and to remove Alarielle from the board. Trust, acceptance, love...these things are irrelevant.'

'And what of Darlia?'

'Darlia is *your* problem.' rasped Krashnar. 'She sinks further towards depression with each passing cycle. Get her back on board and refocus her mind; this undertaking has no place for those of her current disposition – she is a liability in her present state.'

Though she shared Darlia's loathing of the unpleasant shaper, her growing anger and hatred towards Mirielle's regime eclipsed such trivial emotions. Behind his dishevelled appearance and ill-mannered tongue lurked a cunning and dangerous intelligence. Krashnar was many distasteful things, but he was also right. Darlia's soul had fractured, due to her lack of conviction; repairing the damage to the scrier's spirit would take time – something they lacked. The Blades had sustained heavy casualties as a result of their failed assault on Scrier's Post, yet the Narlakai still numbered many despite their abortive invasion – their losses were acceptable. They needed to strike now, before The Blades redressed their ranks, thus she had little time for indecision and self-doubt. She owed Darlia, as a courtesy at least, an attempt at reigniting her lover's previous raison d'être, however, the time for subtlety had long since passed. Krashnar told the truth of it; she desperately needed his assistance, and they could ill afford to waste time dallying.

'I will speak...with Darlia.' she replied at last, having considered the shaper's cutting words. 'If she cannot move forwards...then...there will be no place for her...at my side.'

'Good. Then we have an accord?'

'Agreed...though do not fail me Krashnar. Do so and I will obliterate...your mind!'

The dizzying heights of the Tri-Spires stood impressively before him. He gazed up from the surrounding sprawl with its routine commerce and hubbub – the very reasons he disliked loitering in the heart of Freylar for any length of time. Nathaniel had the right idea; better to live amongst the forest dwellers and remain tethered to the land. Those living within, or amongst, the sprawl emanating from Mirielle's artificial construct were no longer connected to Freylarian heritage; their standard of living, whilst arguably more sophisticated, had evolved into something less honest which failed to enrich their existence. Yet there was still hope for their capital, and those choosing to dwell within it. Reassuringly, the arena continued to stand defiantly in the shadow of the monolithic trident rising above it. The crescent-shaped amphitheatre – proving grounds to his Order – spread out magnificently as though entirely unaware of the unnatural thing which rose out of the rock face above. It was rare that he returned to the nucleus of his Order, choosing instead assignments which took him far away from the vale. Yet despite the distance he habitually maintained, returning home to The Blades helped him to reaffirm his connection to the Order. Though his true calling came from the wild beyond the perimeter of their domain, he could not remain parted from The Blades indefinitely – an Order to which he remained loyal.

Languidly he meandered through the ever-changing maze of outbuildings and alleys surrounding the arena, with Krisis ever-present at his side, until instinctively he navigated his way successfully to its west gate. The habitual clash of sparring blades greeted him warmly as he passed nonchalantly through the impressive stone archway marking the arena's west gate. Some of the more observant Adepts, Masters and Mistresses detected his unexpected arrival within their periphery; they promptly ceased their training to observe his surprise homecoming. It was a rare sight indeed to witness Paladin Lothnar returning to the fold – if only for a short time – and accompanied by a dire wolf no less. Typically he spent most of his time patrolling the borderlands alone, and on occasion alongside his scouts when they were not deployed in the field carrying out their own assignments. Rarely did he have cause to return to the heart of Freylar. Despite his frequent long leaves of absence, his rank of Paladin still afforded him a level of respect amongst the Freylarkai, in particular those within the Order. That respect was once again evident; his peers nodded respectfully to him as he made his way slowly across the main combat area of the arena, towards the tiered stone seating adjacent. Casting his gaze upwards, he spied Marcus and Ragnar; both appeared to be keenly observing The Blades practicing in the main combat area below. Ragnar was the first to visibly react to his unannounced arrival. The hulking Freylarkin slowly rose from his seat whilst forming a wide smile that quickly spread across his stern face. He smiled warmly in return, then began to climb the rows of tiered seating, used almost exclusively by audiences during the Trials.

'Brother, you are a welcome sight!' boomed Ragnar cheerfully. 'No doubt you come to relieve me of my boredom?'

'Well met brother! Marcus not keeping you busy?' he replied jovially.

Ragnar stood on the next row of seating, towering above him; the impressively built Freylarkin's height was accentuated by virtue of standing on the higher stone tier. Ragnar leant towards him offering his right arm, which he clasped firmly. The Captain of The Blades pulled him upwards abruptly, so that he stood adjacent to the red-haired light bringer. Both promptly gave one another a firm pat on the back, signalling their deep respect for each other.

'He tries his best, though I grow increasingly weary of administration.' grumbled Ragnar in his gruff voice. 'But enough of this boring talk – tell me about your recent adventures.'

'Indeed.' added Marcus, who nodded towards him respectfully. 'We did not expect to see you back here in person so soon.'

'I hear there is a shortage of Sky-Skitters along the borderlands; something about a strike – grown tired of delivering this one's reports no doubt.' said Ragnar jovially, followed by a guttural laugh.

'I see your new role of *Secretary* of The Blades has not diminished your sense of humour.' he replied sarcastically.

Marcus looked intently towards him, wondering whether perhaps he had overstepped the boundary of his friendship with Ragnar. Marcus' concerns were promptly dismissed, however, as the Captain began to laugh heartily.

'Ha...I have missed your misguided quips Loth, though be careful, for I am carrying my axe.'

'It looks blunt.' he replied with a wry grin.

'Ah, but I will sharpen it – just for you.' replied Ragnar enthusiastically.

The Captain was like a previously caged animal which had now been allowed to roam freely, as was evident by the wild mischievous glint in the Paladin's eyes. In that instant part of him regretted leaving their domain so frequently, though he knew well that he could not remain confined to the vale for any length of time. Whilst still content to serve the Order, he could not do so shackled to the vale; like a Sky-Skitter he sought the freedom to stretch his wings and roam the land unfettered.

Krisis bounded up the tiered stone seating to join them, having diligently marked his territory in the main combat area below.

'So then, did you manage to track down the scrying witch?' asked Ragnar, cutting to the chase.

'Judging by your relaxed demeanour, one would presume not.' suggested Marcus, who knelt down to affectionately stroke Krisis.

'Unfortunately not brother; her trail went cold – probably the rain.'

'Rain?! I thought you could track anyone and anything. Getting rusty in your old age perhaps?' Ragnar bantered in return.

Though Ragnar conveniently drew his sight from Marcus, he was nonetheless keenly aware of The Blade Lord's questioning gaze at the edge of his periphery. Never before had he outright lied to either Freylarkin, yet he could ill afford another public failure on his record. Besides, things were different now; he needed to remain in the vale, close to Nathaniel. If he knew the truth of it, The Blade

Lord would almost certainly have him reassigned to the borderlands chasing Darlia's ghost – along with his available scouts. Ordinarily he longed to return to his life of solitary adventure beyond the vale, though recent word of Aleska's collusion with Mirielle dictated otherwise. He agreed vehemently with Nathaniel's position on the matter and would not abandon The Teacher to tread the precarious path before them alone.

'It would appear so – no doubt the same reason you were side-lined behind a desk brother.'

The mischievous glint in Ragnar's eyes quickly ignited with wild rage. The Captain of The Blades inhaled deeply, causing his chest to notably expand, further enhancing his already intimidating physique. He offered Marcus a quick sidelong glance, thus affirming the compelling distraction; Ragnar was a proud Freylarkin, the notion of becoming rusty – or worse, obsolete – would never sit well with the hot-headed light bringer.

'Oh how I have looked forward to this. You, me, down in that arena now brother, and I will show you rust!'

'Are you sure you can keep up?' he replied, further goading Ragnar.

'The time has come for you to reacquaint yourself with my axe brother, for it has been too long.'

'Well, at least you are no longer bored.' he said as he deftly slipped a knife from the sheath strapped to the underside of his left arm.

'Marcus, keep score!'

The Blade Lord offered them both a deadpan stare then turned to Krisis; the dire wolf sat expectantly on his hind quarters awaiting further affections from Marcus.

'Come on then.' Marcus said to Krisis, followed by a deep resigned exhale. 'Let us watch these two massage their egos for a time.'

He grinned wryly in light of the sanctioned contest of skill, thereby remaining in character, but in truth his grin marked an early success, having won the first of many political battles to come. Knives were not his only weapons; though he rarely needed to resort to it, he also had a knack for misdirection when required.

They moved cautiously and silently towards the barricaded cave entrance at the opposite end of the basin. The sound of her own heavy breathing was pronounced due to the presence of her barbute; she had not yet warmed to wearing the protective head gear, though she fully appreciated the necessity of doing so. Whilst the Knights favoured solid defence, and the heavy hitting blows and increased range of their brutish weapons, nonetheless she remained true to her core training in the arena – speed and agility were her preferred means of combat, regardless of the foe. Her secondment to the Order, however, demanded that she expand her experiences and further her combat training, thus she wore the Order's armour as expected of her. She was though fortunate in that Heldran had curiously sanctioned the use of her dual falchions – a likely courtesy so that the Knight Lord could better observe Shadow Caster in combat. She glanced at the blade, which continued to bathe gently in the ever-present grey wisps of smoke emanating from its trapped Narlakin resident. The inherently evil blade had little in common with the one in her left hand – The Ardent Blade – which remained coldly inert. Visually she expected more from Shadow Caster's twin, though its unique ability – as described to her by Heldran – piqued her insatiable curiosity. Secretly, she wished that the Knight Lord had offered her the blade sooner; learning to use the weapon in battle was far from ideal, though since her arrival in Freylar very few of her experiences had been *ideal*. Once again she found herself needing to adapt to ever-changing circumstances.

Whilst they continued their approach, she observed the surrounding mist slowly converging on their position, as though controlled by some invisible force. She felt the tension rise throughout the column as each knight undoubtedly saw the ominous sign as a bad omen, more so given the distinct lack of wind in the heart of the basin.

'Stay alert!' she whispered, trying to maintain the knights' concentration despite the strange occurrence.

'They are coming – be ready!' spoke Heldran quietly, in a suitably foreboding tone.

Strange shapes began to form in the closing mist surrounding them, which now seemed less than a hundred paces from the column. The shapes were ephemeral at first, though with each advancing step the ubiquitous looming forms grew darker in colour as each became more cohesive. Heldran was right – they *were* being watched, or rather, they were being hunted.

'Rayna, they are everywhere.' whispered Morin nervously.

'Keep moving.'

'But there are too many of them!'

'I said keep moving!'

Heldran quickened their pace at the head of the column; the Knight Lord knew well the importance of linking up with the other knights. Alone they numbered too few, and would be quickly overrun; without the others, they did not constitute a large enough force to repel the increasing numbers of dark shapes lurking in the surrounding mist. She fought hard to steel her nerves as the closing shapes continued to multiply. It became clear to her that the Knights Thranis had underestimated the Ravnarkai – twice now. Not only did the Ravnarkai recognise the importance of strength in numbers, but they also understood the importance of fear and how one fashioned that dread into a weapon itself.

'Rayna, we must fall back!'

'Morin, knock it off! They are preying on your fear.'

'Rayna is right. The Ravnarkai are tormenting us – they *want* us to break!' said Heldran scornfully.

'Then it is working!'

'Morin get your shit together now!' she said coldly, scolding the knight for potentially inciting panic. 'Now focus on the cave. We need the support of the others.'

'On the right – incoming!' cried Anika suddenly.

She glanced quickly over her right shoulder, following the direction of Anika's intense stare. Two of the shapes had broken through the mist and were bounding towards them at breakneck speed, carried forwards by their slender, but muscular, limbs. She felt a sudden rush of adrenaline as three more shapes burst through the mist to the left of the leading pair. Already they could hear the awful hissing of the enemy as the Ravnarkai opened their crooked maws, revealing rows of jagged teeth which glinted in the weak light penetrating the basin.

'Run! Get to the cave!' she cried, turning her attention back to the column. 'Move – now!'

Immediately the knights quickened their pace, despite the weight of the armour each of them carried. Staring down the length of the column towards Heldran, she saw more of the dark shapes tear through the infernal mist on their left flank. The fresh wave of grotesque looking quadrupeds lowered their crooked maws and gathered speed ready for their charge. At the same time, more of the beasts ruptured forth from the mist on their right – everywhere she looked now, more and more Ravnarkai were bearing down on them. Meanwhile the bizarre weather phenomenon continued to sink into the basin, masking the true extent of the Ravnarkai ambush; the mist seemed to be following their attackers, as though inexorably bound to the enemy.

'Rayna, I think now...would be a good time...to use this ace of yours!' cried Anika, who struggled for breath, clearly unaccustomed to sprinting in full armour.

By her speedy estimate they were now less than one hundred paces from the cave entrance, yet the gathering Ravnarkai charge had rapidly closed to half that distance. In a single well-practised move she slid Shadow Caster into its scabbard at her waist. Her right hand now unencumbered, she tugged at the tied point securing its gauntlet with her left hand whilst struggling to maintain her grip on The Ardent Blade. Eventually the metal-fingered glove loosened, allowing her to use its weight to violently flick it free. The discarded gauntlet quickly disappeared into the thick verdant foliage, likely never to be retrieved.

'Alarielle, I need you!'

'I am here, always.'

'What?!' cried Anika from a short distance behind her.

'When I give the signal...dive to the ground and close your eyes – all of you!'

'You are not serious?!' cried Morin.

'Not up for debate!'

Focussing intently on her inner light, she channelled its energy through her right hand, which she clenched tightly into a balled fist. Brilliant white light began to spill forth through the gaps between her fingers, which she dug painfully into her palm, determined to contain the increasing amount of trapped light manifesting within. Her hand started to shake violently, and the barely-contained light threatened to explode outwards. Offering the Ravnarkai bearing down on their right flank one final sidelong glance, it was clear to her that the devastating charge was about to reach them.

'NOW!!'

Immediately the knights dived to the ground as she had instructed, Heldran included. Sliding to an abrupt halt, she released the caged light, allowing it to explode violently out of her right hand, sending an expansive wave of pure white light outwards across the entire breadth of the basin. The brilliant light cut through the surrounding mist effortlessly, wiping it clean from the basin. The Ravnarkai charge immediately faltered, promptly collapsing on all fronts, as the blinding light seared the beasts' slanted black oval eyes. Her ears filled with the mass hissing of pain as the disabled Ravnarkai stumbled and crashed hard into the ground, before thrashing blindly around in the foliage desperate to re-orientate themselves after the stinging attack. Her own eyes filtered out the worst of the scathing light, yet even she struggled to find her balance in the wake of its purifying touch.

'Gedrick, CHARGE!!' she screamed, testing the limits of her feminine vocals for the first time.

Though she could not fathom the details – on account of the recent attack and her inherently poor vision – the mouth of the distant cave appeared to explode outwards, scattering lumps of rock around its entrance. Their armoured brethren promptly scrambled single file through the newly formed breach; each was eager to join the imminent skirmish, commanded to battle by the familiar yet distant sound of Gedrick's deadpan voice.

'Get up!' she cried, still struggling to find her footing in the wake of her own disorientating attack. 'I didn't get out of my hammock this morning simply to hand my soul to the Ravnarkai.'

'Crazy bitch!' said Morin, who was amongst the first to his feet. 'You really are The Guardian!'

'Careful Knight, we are in danger of an accord.'

Heldran was also back on his feet; the giant Freylarkin promptly bounded towards the nearest Ravnarkin still thrashing wildly on the ground, not more than three paces from his position. Showing no mercy, the Knight Lord drove his monstrous great sword cleanly through the head of the fallen Ravnarkin with horrifying ease.

'Press the advantage!' thundered the Knight Lord vehemently.

Heldran's command set those already back on their feet to immediate purpose. A short distance behind her, one of the knights swung their ardent sword with devastating effect into the flank of another fallen Ravnarkin, slicing through muscle and shattering bone. Anika too was now upright; the zealous Blade wasted little time bringing release to those Ravnarkai closest to her. Yet they needed to work faster; the fallen Ravnarkai were already regaining their lost sight, and they still remained separated from Captain

Gedrick and the other knights. With her vision now fully restored, she reached once more for Shadow Caster, which thrummed energetically in anticipation of a fresh harvest. More of the beasts descended from the lip of the basin, no longer obscured by their fortuitous mist. By her hasty count they were still outnumbered, despite the localised culling. However, the Ravnarkai attack was now disordered and scattered hopelessly across the basin, offering them the first glimpse of hope.

SIXTEEN
Displacement

'The last time you and I met here, it was under very different circumstances. You were wasting away, slumped adjacent to that plinth over there, drowning in grief and sorrow. Rather an odd place to meet, considering...'

Nathaniel's preternatural silver eyes glinted fiercely against the subdued mauve, violet and sapphire hues bathing the interior of the cave's main sanctum. Unlike their previous encounter at the Cave of Wellbeing, Nathaniel's lean muscular definition had since returned to form. His posture was more confident now, and his silver mane was groomed; the master renewalist was a handsome Freylarkin – it was not hard to see why Aleska thought so fondly of him. She, too, thought fondly of her former mentor, though for entirely different reasons; her relationship with The Teacher was more akin to that of a father and daughter – the father she never had.

'Thank you for agreeing to meet me here Kirika.'

'You owe me no thanks. Had you summoned me to Narlak itself, I would have still come. Though...why this place?'

'My lofty rank amongst the renewalists affords me certain privileges here; chief amongst them being privacy and discretion.'

'Could you not speak to me even in my own quarters?' she enquired curiously.

'Absolutely not! What I have to say potentially has profound implications for both of us, and Freylar. The information I have to impart must remain between us, that is at least until we can agree upon the manner in which it is to be disseminated – on this I need your word Kirika.'

'Nathaniel, what troubles you so badly that you need call me back to this place?'

'First I need your word Kirika. You will not like what I have to say, therefore I need your assurance that you will not bolt from the stable on this matter.'

'Perhaps it is best that we sit?'

'Kirika, your word...please.'

'Nathaniel you have it – as do you always.' she replied emphatically.

Leading the way, she guided Nathaniel slowly towards the stone plinth upon which Alarielle's soulless body once lay. It was a strange feeling, returning to the site of Rayna's rebirth; the enigmatic Freylarkin had abruptly entered their world, bringing with her revelations and an ever-expanding wave of change – Rayna was a catalyst, if not a complete enigma. She wondered how Nathaniel himself interpreted the experience, being – in a sense – Rayna's biological father.

'Do you think you will ever forget that cycle?'

'Ha, I think it unlikely. As a father I dearly wish to exclude her from what I am about to inform you. Yet the reluctant activist in me requires her support during the dark times ahead.'

'Nathaniel, such talk concerns me. You speak as though we are about to commit treason.'

'That is because I sincerely think that we are...'

'They are regaining their sight.' cried Anika, pulling her ardent sword from another of the fallen Ravnarkai.

'Fall back to the others.' she cried.

'Go, now!' thundered Heldran, reinforcing her command.

Although still separated from their Captain, Gedrick's knights were charging rapidly towards them as they raced to close the ever-diminishing gap. Fresh Ravnarkai frantically bounded towards their position, yet their charge was chaotic and poorly executed. The explosion of light had created disorder amongst their attackers, turning what should have been a clean ambush into a messy skirmish. Though the knights still remained fewer in number, advantage would ultimately go to the side first to redress its ranks. Determined to link up with Gedrick, she channelled all of her strength into her legs and began to pull away from the others – with the exception of Heldran; the Knight Lord's enormous stride made him a formidable cross-country sprinter.

'Gedrick...orb around Loredan!' she cried, hoping once more that her voice would travel the remaining distance.

Reassuringly the Captain immediately began to coordinate the supporting knights sprinting towards them, through a series of hand gestures and battle cries. One of the knights behind her went down hard; a lone determined Ravnarkin speared through their column, seizing its prey. She heard the short-lived screams of the fallen knight fade into the distance as she and the others continued to run forwards.

Twenty paces from contact she cried once more to the others, 'Brace for impact!' She then rapidly slowed to a halt and readied her weapons. The remaining knights promptly spread out, forming a loose circle, and braced for impact as the disordered Ravnarkai charge reached its fearsome climax.

Several of Gedrick's knights, including the Captain himself, smashed into the flank of the charging Ravnarkai, using their armoured momentum to derail a number of the assailants. Those unfortunate enough to receive Gedrick's masterfully timed counter charge immediately crashed to the ground, and were sent barrelling away through the lush foliage. Some of the knights missed their mark entirely, yet their sudden presence added to the confusion, further hindering the disordered Ravnarkai charge. Others became victims themselves, and were propelled violently across the ground. Several more of the charging Ravnarkai unexpectedly crumpled to the ground short of impact; their front legs mysteriously giving out, seemingly of their own volition. The downed attackers rolled brutally across the ground, one of them smashing hard into a small outcropping which abruptly released the battered assailant with an awful wet thud. She recalled mention of Falkai's telekinetic ability, which she presumed had an invisible hand in the chaos unfolding around them. Two more Ravnarkai were suddenly launched into the air, thus confirming her suspicion; their hind legs were seemingly pulled backwards from beneath their lumpy bodies and wrenched violently over their thick bird-like heads, causing the beasts to spin madly through the air. She heard the unmistakable sound of arrows behind her, whistling through the air, followed by the ugly noise of their fleshly impact as each found its target with expert accuracy. The initial damage caused by both sides was devastating. Agonising moans and hissing pain filled the air as survivors from both sides felt the wrath of their broken limbs and ruptured organs.

'Form up! Orb formation now – protect Loredan and the wounded!' she cried.

Those still on their feet quickly broke into pairs and hurriedly dragged their fallen comrades towards the centre of the circle rapidly reforming around Loredan and the recovered wounded knights. The revered renewalist had already discarded his gauntlets and immediately began tending to the worst of the casualties.

'Gedrick, centre now and protect Loredan at any cost.' thundered Heldran, whose eyes burned fiercely within the shadowy recess of his plumed barbute.

'Heldran?' she said respectfully, querying his decision.

'My place is out there Rayna!' he replied firmly, whilst striding confidently through the perimeter of the newly reformed defensive circle.

'Tell me Guardian, do the Sky-Walkers have a name for that dark place where the souls of the damned congregate after their release?'

'Some of us refer to it as *Hell*.' she replied.

'Ha, how appropriate. Watch now as I fill that *Hell* of your with the souls of our enemies, which I shall gladly reap from their bestial forms!'

Like a savage animal released from its shackles, the Knight Lord eagerly received the beginnings of a renewed Ravnarkai assault. One of the beasts hurled itself at Heldran, attempting to knock the heavily built Freylarkin off his feet. The impact had little effect, as the Knight Lord skilfully anticipated the impromptu attack; Heldran dipped unexpectedly then drove his shoulder upwards into his assailant. The Ravnarkin rose up off the floor, carried by Heldran's upwards momentum, and was then savagely smashed back down to the ground courtesy of a violent headbutt from the enraged Knight Lord. Heldran drove his left heel into the side of the fallen Ravnarkin's head, causing the beast's cranium to collapse inwards, splattering jets of watery dark purple fluid and gore up his left greave. Watching Heldran violently release his foe with apparent ease seemingly emboldened the Knights Thranis in that singular moment. She felt renewed hope as the battle-hardened knights reacted vehemently to the Knight Lord's bloody precedent, each raising their ardent sword in unison ready for the next wave of attackers. She stared again at the inert falchion in her left hand, briefly musing over the possibilities it represented. If the enigmatic blade indeed possessed the ability to displace its wielder, Heldran would not be the only Freylarkin readily damning the souls of the Ravnarkai to the underworld.

'Nathaniel, this is a lot to take in, you understand.' she said, still reeling from his detailed account.

Her mind was drowning in thought, making her feel a little lightheaded. She stood up abruptly and made her way slowly towards the cave's entrance.

'I need some fresh air Nathaniel.'

'Please, take your time.'

A refreshing gentle breeze greeted her upon exiting the cave. The crisp autumnal air quickly worked its magic, sweeping aside the fog of confusion clouding her mind, allowing her to focus more clearly on the implications of Nathaniel's words. She stared in silence towards the distant vale in the south-east, quietly considering the sensitive information brought to her attention. The very notion that Mirielle might act outside the ruling council was unfathomable, yet her own stunned reaction disappointingly validated Nathaniel's treasonous claim; she was indeed unaware of the alleged unsanctioned developments taking place at Scrier's Post. Her heart sank, realising fully now that the Freylarkai potentially now faced a crisis of leadership; how could Freylarkin society accept an individual who operated outside the stricture of laws they themselves helped to cement. Whilst the acceptable boundaries of scrying was a single issue – albeit an important one – if Mirielle circumvented existing law, by effectively re-writing it without first seeking consent from the ruling council, what then prevented their queen's rule from evolving into a dictatorship, she mused worriedly. Moreover, reneging on established policy would incite uproar amongst the Freylarkai – the best-case scenario was that the people would become divided over the matter. She was loath to imagine the possible extent of such division; there was no need to scry the future to know that the recent turn of events would almost certainly fracture the ruling council.

'Would you like me to leave?' asked Nathaniel politely, who now stood beside her.

She sensed his uneasiness; clearly the veteran Blade Master was unsure of her own view on the matter.

'At ease Nathaniel; you have my full support on this matter.'

'Are you certain?' Nathaniel questioned emphatically. 'At best I propose treason. This matter could have profound ramifications if we choose to oppose Mirielle's rule – she can ill afford further indecisiveness. We could be released, or worse exiled, should we ultimately decide to go against her wishes. I have done my best to protect you Kirika, and have trained you well to protect yourself. If you join me in this, I will have actively coaxed you down a path fraught with danger.'

'Nathaniel, you do not coax me. I am no longer the naive little Freylarkin who stepped into your arena. I am a member of the ruling council and one of the domain's most potent scriers. I have both accepted and abide by Freylarian policy on scrying, but you will need my influence and help with this matter. Though her ability wanes, Aleska is nonetheless a potent scrier and you will need a capable Freylarkin with the ability to counter her machinations.'

Uttering the words aloud somehow made the matter seem real. She was not blind to the way in which Aleska *motivated* others to further her agendas, however, the venerable scrier's intentions – be it her own or those of Mirielle – were no longer in the best interests of Freylar. As a scrier herself, she understood more than most the dangers of inadvertently allowing the Freylarkai to become obsessed with engineering their own destiny. Current laws meant that there was little or no temptation to do so; the punishment for such transgressions was abundantly clear – her sister was testament to that fact. Encouraging scriers to explore their ability hoping that in return they restrain their likely addiction and thirst for knowledge was folly. It was one thing to restore the wounded or to erect impossible structures from organic material, but unravelling the past and potentially eliminating freedom of will by pre-determining destiny was dangerous.

'Kirika I urge you to speak with Aleska on this matter, to validate my accusations. There is also the possibility that you can reason with her, where I have clearly failed.'

'She will not go against Mirielle's wishes, of that I am certain. The bond Aleska shares with our queen is not unlike the one I share with you. Meeting with her will only tip our hand, assuming she has not already scried this outcome. As for validation, you would not lie to me on this – of that I am certain.'

'Then do me the courtesy of confirming my own account. I must be certain about what has already transpired – there can be no ambiguity in my verbal account.' implored Nathaniel.

She narrowed her eyes as she considered Nathaniel's request. She sensed conflict within The Teacher, and for good reason – ultimately the matter would involve The Blade Lord; without glimpsing into his future, there was no telling on which side of the fence Marcus would sit. Their esteemed leader was loyal to Mirielle's rule, yet he also enjoyed a strong relationship with Nathaniel, who had previously mentored Marcus himself. The path ahead of them was grey and would require extreme cunning and guile to successfully navigate. She too shared Nathaniel's unease and sense of conflict; the same conflict fermented in her own mind, as she struggled to reconcile Aleska's actions.

'Very well – there must indeed be no mistake in your account.' she said, engaging her second sight.

Knowing precisely where to start her investigation, she focused intently on Nathaniel, leaping back in time to the point where they had parted ways shortly prior to his temporary leave of absence from the vale. She watched with interest as Nathaniel and Keshar journeyed north to Scrier's Post, where they unconventionally breached the perimeter wall of the sanctuary. Her expression hardened as she witnessed first-hand the changes wrought upon the site, courtesy of Mirielle's sanctioned shaper Krasus. She jumped back and forth, focusing on Nathaniel's numerous confrontations with Aleska during his time spent loitering around the sanctuary. Her scrying mentor's discontent was plain to see; it both frustrated and saddened her to see Aleska's vehement point of view on the matter spill directly from her lips. Though she had not doubted Nathaniel's words, witnessing the events as they had unfolded wounded her soul. She exhaled deeply as the stark details continued to unfold in her mind with unerring clarity. Once again she moved forwards in time, towards the end of Nathaniel's stay at the sanctuary. The final images permitted to assault her mind depicted Keshar's decision to remain at the sanctuary. The young scrier's ill-advised chosen path stung – more so than Aleska's own questionable actions – causing her violet eyes to water.

'I have seen enough.' she said, disengaging her second sight. 'Aleska has chosen a path of madness which could irreparably damage Freylarkin society, whether opposed or otherwise.' she said wiping her tearful eyes.

'There is more that you should know Kirika.' Nathaniel said, placing his arms comfortingly around her shoulders.

'Be gentle Nathaniel, I have seen rather enough for one cycle already.' she replied dejectedly.

'Lothnar knows too.' said Nathaniel, cutting to the chase. 'He saw me camped outside of the vale during his journey back from the Narlakai borderlands to report to Marcus directly.'

'What does he know? And did he find my sister?'

'He knows everything Kirika. I was feeling low; I desperately needed to confide in someone. Strangely enough the issue has helped us to heal old wounds. He is with us Kirika, and agreed to me meeting you in person. I had to leave Lothnar out of this meeting, as a precaution you understand – I did not know how you would react to this damning insight. I hope you can forgive me?'

'Of course, and I understand. But what of Darlia, did Lothnar manage to track my sister and her accomplice?'

'For a time, though both he and Krisis apparently lost her trail in the borderlands.'

'Your tone suggests that you do not entirely believe his account?'

'There may be more to his story, and our wounds are only just beginning to heal. However, he is with us entirely on this matter – he has made it clear to me that he will not follow Mirielle down the path along which she already treads.'

'If you believe he is with us then I accept your judgement on the matter. With that said, we need to be supremely cautious going forwards, whilst we gather further support in this matter.'

'I agree. I will apprise Lothnar of our meeting, then resume my teachings in the arena – we need to continue our duties as normal. In the meantime, see if you can determine indirectly whether Marcus is aware of Mirielle's new direction.'

'Leave it with me. I will signal you once I know more, and we shall meet back here with Lothnar to discuss any new information.'

'Agreed.' replied Nathaniel.

She offered Nathaniel a weak smile then turned her gaze back towards the vale. For the most part, Mirielle's rule had been relatively untroubled; the Freylarkai had enjoyed many peaceful passes under their queen. However, it appeared now that dark clouds were gathering on the horizon. There was a time when the Freylarkai only had to concern themselves with external attacks upon their domain, however, now they potentially had an internal threat to contend with – themselves.

More Ravnarkai crashed hard into the perimeter and their formation buckled as several knights were brutally knocked to the ground by the impact of the savage beasts. Xenia and one other – also favouring a bow – joined Gedrick and Loredan in the centre of the orb; their deadly arrows whistled towards the charging Ravnarkai, cutting deeply into the ruddy flesh of the oncoming juggernauts. Some of the projectiles found their mark, severing tendons and disabling limbs, causing the lumpy creatures to crash hard into the ground, whilst others seemed to have little or no effect on their rabid assailants. Caring little about his own safety, the Knight Lord continued to cut a bloody path through the enemy with his immense great sword leaving a trail of ruined flesh in his wake. A number of Ravnarkai tried to single out and blindside the lone knight, though Falkai was quick to spot the attempts; the adept telekinetic horridly bent and dislocated the limbs of Heldran's attackers, leaving several mangled Ravnarkai thrashing and hissing on the ground nearby. She too lent her support, assisting Falkai in preventing the Knight Lord from becoming overwhelmed. Summoning forth her inner light once more, she channelled more light energy in the form of a solid beam of pure white light, which she directed towards two more Ravnarkai bearing down on Heldran's left flank. Her targets veered wildly off course, blinded by the light, however, one of them unwittingly barrel rolled into their defensive cordon, knocking Zephir off his feet. The blind Ravnarkin breached their formation, momentarily distracting Loredan from his duties. Captain Gedrick – ever alert to the changing battle conditions – saw the threat and dived towards the blind attacker, using his own body to shield the revered renewalist. After absorbing the blow, Gedrick quickly regained his footing and promptly drove his ardent sword through the beast's skull, ending its blind torment.

She quickly turned to Zephir, 'Are you OK?' she cried, hoping to learn that the knight's soul remained tethered to its mortal coil.

Zephir struggled to find his breath, clearly heavily winded by the sudden attack. The downed knight no longer wore his barbute; the force of the unexpected impact had completely dislodged his helmet, sending it rolling into the thick foliage. Zephir winced in pain as he tried to regulate his breathing, before raising his left hand and sharply pointing its index finger beyond her. He tried to give voice to his warning, but lack of breath ensured his silence. Regardless, Zephir's wide-eyed mute stare was all she required. She spun round quickly to witness another hulking Ravnarkin bounding towards her. Its crooked maw was stretched wide open, revealing its dual set of jagged teeth, which had lumps of rotten flesh lodged between then. Reacting instinctively, she raised her left arm towards her attacker, pointing The Ardent Blade squarely into the path of the oncoming Ravnarkin. The unfazed creature closed its ugly maw and dipped its head, charging headlong into the tip of the blade. The blade penetrated the beast's ailing skin; she felt her arm immediately buckle under the force of its impact. Without conscious reason or thought, she swiped her left thumb over the Waystone embedded into the grip of The Ardent Blade just below its cross-guard. The chaotic landscape behind her attacker immediately blurred and stretched into a streak of fast moving light. Her body became light and she felt the familiar sense of displacement incurred when using the Ardent Gate's own Waystones as her body was pulled through the fabric of reality. The experience was unlike any of her previous encounters, however, as pressure rapidly built in her head and her vision started to fade. Rather than the swift exponential acceleration she was accustomed to, the Waystone transition was raw and unrefined – the rough displacement jarred her entire system, causing her vision to ultimately blackout entirely.

SEVENTEEN
Rush

'Trix open this bloody door now!'

'*OK, try this one instead: Four-two-nine-eight-one-two-three-seven.*'

He punched the new code quickly into the holographic access panel. This time the word *approved* flashed up across the display. Several locks running down the length of the emergency exit immediately disengaged, and the door slid open quietly. He exhaled deeply as his body relaxed a little, relieving some of his anxiety, though his muscles remained tense and the sound of his heart continued to thump loudly. Without bothering to inform Trix, he deftly slipped past the open door into a poorly lit emergency stairwell beyond. The emergency exit's door promptly closed behind him, sealing him in. He crouched for a moment in the gloom reciting the successful eight-digit pass code inside his head. He did not possess the luxury of a photographic memory, and if things went badly again he would no doubt require the code once more; he disliked relying on Trix to support him, thus he made a point of memorising the successful code.

'*Did it work?*'

'I'm proceeding to level zero-two-nine.'

Although Trix never said as much, he could hear the software engineer's audible sigh of relief, courtesy of the analogue communicator which crackled uncomfortably in his ear. Choosing not to scold Trix further for the incident, he began to ascend the impossibly tall stairwell, the summit of which disappeared into the rising darkness above. The stairwell's lighting was minimal; no doubt emergency lighting, designed to reduce unnecessary power consumption. The feeble light exaggerated the shadows, obscuring his ascent, for which he was very much grateful; no longer was he exposed by the stark lighting of the metropolis' inner core.

After a good ten minutes of climbing, he reached level zero-two-nine. Pausing for a brief moment to regain his breath, he felt his strained calf muscles burning uncomfortably as they ached from their abrupt workout.

'OK, I'm at level zero-two-nine.'

'*Good. Go through the door ahead of you. Use the same access code. Four, two, ni...*'

'I'm in.'

'Err...right, OK, *go along the corridor. Look for hab unit one-seven-one.*'

He made his way swiftly along the starkly lit corridor servicing the floor's six hab units. The entrance to hab unit one-seven-one was just over halfway along the corridor, on the right, and was – as expected – locked.

'Will the same code work again?' he asked whilst quickly studying the door's holographic access panel.

'*Yes. The...has...rights – access all areas, in...building security need to...access.*' explained Trix over their failing communications equipment.

The quality of their analogue signal was worse now. For a short while, in the stairwell at least, their signal had improved – possibly due to his increased altitude – but now Trix's words were horribly garbled, making them difficult to understand; he wondered if his unlikely ally had anticipated the frustrating interference during his meticulous planning. Regardless, he hoped that their signal would clear up upon gaining access to one-seven-one; the hab's windows would in theory reduce the current unacceptable level of interference.

'Trix your message is breaking up. I am proceeding as planned.' he replied on the assumption that his own transmission was also garbled.

'...*repeat your...*' his ear peace crackled once more.

'I'm going in, repeat, I'm going in!' he said, trying hard not to raise his voice too loudly.

Steeling his nerves, he entered the now familiar passcode into the hab's holographic access panel. Immediately the gloss white door to hab one-seven-one slid quietly open. Gingerly he peered into the dark gloom within the hab from behind the outer wall in the corridor. The space before him was dark; only the soft glow of electronics and the distant low-level lighting marking the boundary of the spacious room provided any source of light, for which he was extremely grateful. Silently he stepped into the room, which he presumed was the main living space. The entrance door closed quietly behind him. He paused for a moment, allowing his eyes to adjust to the dark. The black silhouette of furnishings obscured the broken outline of the room's boundary floor lighting. The room itself was overly spacious; an unnecessary indulgence for any one individual. It galled him knowing that the metropolis' Apex class members were afforded such high standards of living, whilst his own kin were forced to live in squalor. Through the eyes of many, the metropolis was seen as a utopian paradise, rising from the ashes of a world ravaged by the mistakes of its previous inhabitants. To him, it was little more than a cancer; an ode to humanity's continued poor judgement. In his mind, no self-respecting species would force its own kin to live in ruin when comfortable living space was clearly plentiful; at least two families could live in the space before him now. It sickened him knowing that hab one-seven-one belonged to a single individual – Mr L. Cameron.

Cautiously he crept towards the centre of the room. He used his left hand to gently feel the way ahead, careful so as not to disturb any of the room's contents. His pupils dilated further, allowing him to pick out obstacles in his path more easily; the years spent living in the shadows served him well, affording him better vision than most in low light.

'What's your status?'

Trix's signal was clearer now. The reassuring monotonous tone of the software engineer's voice helped to ease his jangled nerves – without communications their plan was dead in the water.

'I'm in the main living space.'

'Good. There should be a door along the left wall towards the far end – open it.' replied Trix.

He picked his way past several high-backed chairs and a large metal table, until the fingertips of his outstretched hand contacted with the cold surface of a wall. The wall was smooth; he likened the sensation to touching glass. Looking down, he saw the dull reflection of the perimeter floor lighting along the bottom of the glossy wall. He wondered if perhaps the hab's inner walls were indeed composed from tinted glass, or some such material. Following the wall with his hand, he slowly traced a path towards the far end of the room whilst staring intently into the void searching for signs of Trix's elusive door.

There was a sudden swoosh; Trix's hidden door slid open to his left, as he neared the far end of the room, revealing a narrow black corridor beyond. He froze immediately, desperate to conceal his position, having been caught off guard by the door's proximity sensor. To his relief the corridor appeared empty. With the exception of further weak perimeter floor lighting, the corridor too was dark and devoid of any occupants. Prior to commencing their operation, they had made two critical assumptions; that Mr L. Cameron was both present and asleep – thus far at least, they had no cause to suspect otherwise on either account.

'There's a narrow corridor.'

'There are two doors on your left. The first leads to a wash room, the second to the master bedroom. Take the latter – the target should be there, asleep.'

'Acknowledged.'

His heart pounded loudly in his chest once more as he closed in on their target. Trix had been vague on the plan's details beyond making contact with their target. He prayed that the retired software developer was more amenable than his current ally; if contact went badly he would be forced to flee the metropolis, though Trix had assured him that scenario would not come to pass.

'What am I doing once I gain access?'

'I will inform you after the target is confirmed.'

'Damn you and your need for secrecy.'

'It's a surprise.'

'More like an inconvenience. Whatever, I'm going in – get ready!'

The door to the master bedroom slid open, prompting the room's lights to suddenly illuminate. Before him stood a large metal bed. The bed's clinical design gave it an imposing feel – it looked hard and uncomfortable – and yet the individual sleeping upon it appeared content.

'Shit! *Lights off...end lights...kill lights.*' he whispered frantically, desperate to turn off the bedroom's stark lighting.

A wave of relief washed over him as his final desperate voice command prompted the room's lights to extinguish just as quickly as they had manifested. His muscles were tense and his heart thumped louder now than before. Yet what little respite he had earned was quickly cut short when he detected movement coming from the direction of the bed. The unconventional configuration of the room's automated lighting system had inadvertently disturbed its resident sleeper. Whoever lay in the room's generously over-sized bed took a moment to adjust their position. Their movement was sluggish, and their breathing laboured, as they subconsciously sought a more comfortable spot. He remained perfectly still whilst the unknown individual continued to fidget in search of a more favourable sleeping position.

'*What's going on?*'

'Quiet!' he whispered sternly in response to Trix's poorly timed question.

After some time, the restless sleeper fell back into a deep slumber, permitting him to move freely once more. Quietly he crept round the side of the bed with the hope of visually identifying the sleeper despite the near dark. The soft glow of the room's lighting dimly lit the sleeper's profile, highlighting the worn features of someone in their twilight years. The individual – now clearly a man – had a well-trimmed beard and thick eyebrows. His lips were rough and misshapen, and his sole visible ear looked old and stretched.

'Target is an elderly gentleman; must be in his late seventies, or thereabouts. He has a beard – well trimmed.'

Confident now that the elderly gentleman was indeed caught in a deep slumber, he approached closer still, keen to identify any potential distinguishing features.

'He appears to have a minor scar on his left cheek, and his hair is thinning on top.'

'It's him!'

Silently he pulled away, before retreating back towards the foot of the bed.

'Are you certain it's him?' he enquired in a hushed whisper.

'I'm certain.' replied Trix.

'OK great, so what now?'

'Now...you kill him!'

The chaos of battle snapped back into focus once more. Her arm remained outstretched; to her surprise she retained her grip on The Ardent Blade, however, the blade's tip no longer penetrated the frontal lobe of her Ravnarkin assailant. Instead the enigmatic blade was now lodged in the back of the creature's skull. Having lost none of its momentum the beast continued towards her prior location. The Ravnarkin pulled inadvertently at The Ardent Blade, almost wrenching the weapon from her grasp as it fell away from her. Reluctantly, the curious blade withdrew from the rear of the beast's cranium, tracing an arc of dark purple fluid in its wake. The Ravnarkin crumpled to the ground where it remained perfectly still in light of the fatal wound dealt by Shadow Caster's twin; there was neither hissing nor the thrashing of the beast's final death throes, instead just the unerring silence of a swift release. The blade had cut deep into the creature's brain; more purple fluid – thicker this time – oozed from the lethal exit wound caused by the weapon's displacement. She understood now the extent of the weapon's devious nature, and its potential capacity for evil and other illicit acts. The Ardent Blade cheated its opponents, robbing them of a fair fight. She recalled Heldran's counsel vividly now; those words which he had spoken to her shortly after their sparring encounter back at the Ardent Gate: 'Do not engage the Ravnarkai in a fair fight!'

Zephir was back on his feet now, though the winded knight was still doubled over in pain, struggling to regain his breath. He raised his head towards her, offering her a brief smile of gratitude.

'Now go...put that weapon...to work!' Zephir said vehemently, with what little breath he could snatch.

She winked casually at Zephir, then grinned mischievously at the wounded knight. It was easy to imagine the potential for release and suffering that could be wrought by the evil twins she now possessed, though she could ill afford to succumb to the temptation of their powerful allure. In that brief moment she recalled more of Heldran's words, as the turmoil of battle ensued around her: 'I believe Rayna, that you will overcome their evil nature; perhaps even put them to *good* use.' Heldran believed in her, that she could in fact wield the weapons without being corrupted by their touch. Upon further introspection she recalled the darker emotions she had experienced more recently at Scrier's Post, in particular her past anger and despair previously buried by her mind. These unwanted and dangerous emotions had resurfaced in light of her reacquainted past, haunting her shortly after her arrival in

Freylar. The unstable emotions had threatened to consume her, but instead she had learnt to control them, tempering them into a weapon of her own mental construction – her wraith blade. She vowed once more to take the inherent evil she now wielded and bend it into submission, as she had previously done with her darker emotions. As with her unwanted emotions, the murderous weapons would serve her – not vice-versa.

Fresh cries of pain ended her momentary pause for thought, prompting her to refocus her attention on the horrid displays of brutality taking place behind her. She turned rapidly to witness Falkai lying on the ground a short distance to her left. His right leg was bent awkwardly, suggesting a possible dislocation. Despite his debilitating wound the obstinate knight continued to battle the Ravnarkai with his mind, sending two more of the grotesquely muscular creatures spinning through the air. Distracted by his – now airborne – assailants, the competent telekinetic failed to notice another of the beasts charging down his left flank. With renewed urgency she sprinted towards the fallen knight, desperate to intercept Falkai's newest assailant. She leapt over the distracted Freylarkin and swung The Ardent Blade towards the bounding Ravnarkin. Once more she felt the familiar buckling of her left arm due to the frenzied creature's headlong charge onto the blade's point. The Ravnarkai cared little for their own self-preservation; charging down their prey, to then tear it asunder, was reason enough to use their own bodies as hulking battering rams. Were she left unaided by the blade's ability to displace its wielder, her inherited body would have surely been destined for release, trampled to ruin under the weight of the ferocious juggernaut. Yet that would not be her fate. The Ardent Blade missed the Ravnarkin's head, and instead buried itself into the roof of the beast's hideous open maw. She swiped her thumb across the Waystone beneath the blade's cross-guard once more, again triggering the disorientating jarring transition she had previously experienced. Once again her body was wrenched abruptly from its moorings and displaced instantaneously behind her opponent, mirroring her original facing. The Ardent Blade ripped savagely from the rear of the beast's neck, sending jets of purple liquid shooting up her left arm. Unlike her previous encounter, the wounded Ravnarkin was still moving; the enraged beast trampled over Falkai's left arm, causing the maimed knight to cry out in pain. The wounded Ravnarkin then skidded sideways to a gradual halt whilst thick purple blood poured from its maw. It then bounded wildly back towards her the instant its gangly muscular limbs regained traction with the ground. With her opponent's momentum spent, she slashed at her attacker with Shadow Caster; the evil weapon tore across the Ravnarkin's slanted oval eyes, causing them to burst upon impact. True to its nature the cruel falchion cut deep into the Ravnarkin, seeking more than just a blood price from its victim. The greedy blade clawed at the creature's soul, drawing out and devouring its spirit. Her soulless blind attacker crashed into her greaves with the last of its momentum, causing her to stumble over its lifeless frame. She turned her fall into a shoulder roll and quickly rose back to her feet.

Their orb formation was failing. The disordered scattered charge of the Ravnarkai had eroded their defensive formation. Their casualties were mounting, and more of their fallen were being hurriedly dragged towards Loredan for aid. She ran towards Falkai and grabbed the knight by his remaining good arm.

'Gedrick, help me!'

The Knight Captain sprinted towards their position to provide assistance. Together they aided one another in dragging the battered telekinetic to the centre of the knights' formation.

'Loredan, you must help him.' she cried.

The tired renewalist turned towards Falkai and began his visual assessment of the knight's condition. Loredan appeared utterly spent; the relentless use of his ability had drained the revered knight's own soul.

'He is not a priority.'

'What do you mean?!'

'Falkai's soul is not going anywhere.' replied Loredan candidly.

'Gedrick, I can still fight. Go join Rayna and the others. I will protect Loredan.'

'Rayna, with me!' affirmed the Captain. 'This meat grinder is just getting started.'

She woke abruptly to the sound of Lileah's voice. The side of her face lay on the floor of their reluctant host's hovel; she had fallen asleep in the small gloomy corridor outside of Lileah's room. Instinctively she tried to lift herself up from the cold and dirty floor, though her body resisted, painfully reminding her of the drawbacks to sleeping rough on a hard and unforgiving surface. She tried once more, this time pushing through the pain of her aching body. Lileah stood in the corridor, dolefully watching her with obvious disapproval.

'Finally, you are awake.' said Lileah disdainfully.

Predictably her bronze metal claw ached more than the rest of her body; she wondered if Lileah too suffered the same ongoing torment, perhaps to an even greater extent. Since Lileah's rehabilitation, her impetuous lover had become increasingly irritable. Lileah was now consumed by her bitter hatred towards Freylar; the powerful telepath no longer thought clearly, driven instead by an unyielding need for revenge – not unlike her former self.

'How long have I been asleep?' she asked, still feeling groggy.

'Long enough – it is noon.'

Lileah was standing at the entrance to her room; she continued to lean on Krashnar's unconventional crutches and – given the changes wrought upon her body – would likely require their aid for the foreseeable future.

'Recent events have clearly caught up with me. I do not recall the last time I slept uninterrupted for so long.'

After rising slowly to her feet, she carefully brushed away the remnants of dried earth and other unidentifiable grime still clinging to her fitted brown garment. Her questionable place of rest had not been conducive to her visual wellbeing, although mentally she felt refreshed – the long overdue rest had served her well.

'We need to talk.' said Lileah abruptly, wasting no time on morning pleasantries.

'Apparently so...but perhaps I could eat some breakfast first?'

'Krashnar and I are leaving this place.'

'What?! You have barely recovered from your ordeal. Where would you go?'

'Freylar, where else?!' replied Lileah scornfully.

'Lileah no, stop it, please! That path leads to ruin, surely you know that now?' she implored.

'You cannot know that Darlia. You yourself said that The Guardian clouds your scrying.'

'To wage a blind war against The Blades is folly. We have lost our advantage, and besides...what good came of our failed attempt?'

Her own words left her crestfallen; seeing Lileah's changed form was a stark reminder of her mistake, one which she could never correct. Lileah was angry – an emotion she understood all too well – and that raw emotion clouded her lover's judgement. When Marcus severed her hand, events were set in motion which she was powerless to prevent; now the same was true of Lileah, and that sudden realisation terrified her.

'I understand your desire for revenge against those who did this to you – really I do. I, more than most, fully appreciate the anger and suffering that weigh heavily upon...'

'You know nothing Darlia! You defied their rules, and for your transgressions they took your hand as punishment. As for myself...they just abandoned me, left me to starve and rot. They cared not if I survived, or whether release came looking for me. I was nothing to them – insignificant! Then, when at last they were forced to acknowledge my existence, they robbed me...robbed me of who I am Darlia!'

'Lileah, I get it! They took from you, and now you want revenge. But if you choose this path it will almost certainly end you, and us!' she said emphatically.

'It will not! Krashnar has agreed to help me in this. Why are you unable to do the same?'

'I saved you Lileah, yet in doing so I have damned your soul. I should never have brought you to this forsaken place; everything that shaper touches becomes corrupted by his evil.'

'Krashnar is the one who saved me!' replied Lileah vehemently.

'Look at me Lileah! Moreover, look at yourself! He creates monsters. Both of us were nothing more than experiments to him; wretched amusements for his twisted mind.'

'You are wrong! Mirielle creates monsters. She set events in motion when she imposed her self-righteous will and exiled you. You wanted nothing more than vengeance yourself – to release them all! I remember well the first cycle we met.'

'And I was wrong! Violence only breeds more violence or – at best – a sham peace, sowing the seeds of future conflict. I know this now. We have each other Lileah, surely that is enough?'

'Ha, one setback and your conviction is broken. I thought you were stronger than this. Clearly you are not as I once thought. You are weak Darlia. It is the strongest who survive. As for the rest...they are insignificant, as I once was.'

Hearing Lileah's words shattered her soul; she sobbed, unable to hold back the pain she felt. She no longer recognised the vengeful bitter Freylarkin standing before her. Her lover was changed, but not just her body; Krashnar's influence on Lileah – both mentally and physically – had poisoned of her soul.

'You can barely walk.' she replied in a feeble cracked voice. 'Even if I were to join you in this madness, you cannot possibly hope to rebuild an army.'

'Krashnar has agreed to assist me.'

'The Guardian will stop you Lileah; you underestimate Alarielle's vessel and the entity controlling it – we both did.'

'She is but one Freylarkin.' Lileah replied flatly.

'Marcus has become complacent and weak. But The Guardian is a dangerous catalyst, inciting the Freylarkai and changing them in the process. That thing is unpredictable!'

'Krashnar has a solution to the problem.'

'You cannot trust him, he *will* betray you Lileah! Both of us, we are nothing more than amusing pastimes to him. Do not allow yourself to become a puppet for his sadistic personal amusement.'

'Enough! You are either with me on this Darlia, or you are...insignificant.'

'How can you say that?! I took you in, gave you purpose – I care for you!'

'You have lost sight of that purpose. Now join us, or stay here and sink further into your self-imposed state of depression.'

'Lileah, I *cannot* follow you down the path you propose. It is madness – it will destroy you!'

Lileah paused for a moment. She desperately hoped that her own decision on the matter had given her lover cause to re-evaluate her own position. She tried to read Lileah's face, but the telepath's grubby porcelain visage and stony-faced glare gave little away. She thought about scrying the outcome of their miserable encounter, but in her heart she already knew that their time together was coming to an end. She started sobbing once more, realising then that she had been unsuccessful in swaying Lileah's point of view.

'So be it.' Lileah replied woefully. 'I love you Darlia, but you have become weak. I cannot afford further distraction from you on this matter. We will reclaim Freylar as our own, and perhaps then you will return to me. Regrettably, I must now do what is necessary – forgive me.'

Without any warning, her mind screamed in pain; it was the same pain she experienced when both she and Krashnar first refused to take Lileah back to Freylar. The searing agony ripping through her mind was unbearable. She retched uncontrollably and her legs gave out from underneath her. She fell down, banging her head hard on the grubby floor. Lileah faded rapidly from sight as her vision went dark and the world around her ceased to be.

EIGHTEEN
Family

    The fighting was chaotic and ugly now; with the Ravnarkai charge successfully thwarted, pockets of fighting broke out around their crumbling formation. Loredan continued to aid their wounded at the centre of the maelstrom, but their casualties were mounting and the struggling Knight Restorant could barely cope with the demand upon him. Their bleak situation struck a chord with events at Scrier's Post; the Knights Thranis needed to quickly end the current conflict, for they lacked the numbers to weather a prolonged encounter. She twisted her ardent sword abruptly, flicking fresh purple blood from its edge onto the ground. Taking a moment to survey the hazy battlefield, she noticed further flashes of light to her left; The Guardian was fighting fiercely alongside Captain Gedrick, and was using her ability to blind more of their attackers. Inexplicably, Rayna appeared to move with impossible speed across the battlefield, allowing her to release the Ravnarkai with devastating alacrity. Rayna's fighting style was nothing if not unconventional, though she had never before witnessed The Guardian fight with such preternatural speed. Regardless, she glanced now to her right, confident that their left flank was holding. Xenia, Morin and a number of others were attempting to repel yet more of their attackers. Curiously, Xenia was shooting past her fellow knights, and appeared to be targeting a lone Ravnarkin whose body mass dwarfed that of its surrounding kin.

    'Alpha!' she said aloud, reaffirming her belief.

'What?' cried Zephir, who was now back on his feet and had moved to accompany her.

'There!' she replied, tipping her head towards the oversized Ravnarkin. 'Xenia has the Alpha targeted. We must help her to end this conflict now!'

Without waiting for Zephir to acknowledge her statement, she broke into a sprint towards the hulking Ravnarkin. The beast was now advancing towards Xenia, who had clearly drawn its murderous attention. There were few remaining arrows in Xenia's quiver, and the skilled archer only possessed a long dagger for close quarter fighting. Though Xenia's vicious arrows repeatedly found their mark, the Alpha's toughened hide mitigated the worst of their damage; their impact seemed more of an irritation to the hulking juggernaut. The realisation that Xenia would not bring down her assailant before it closed the distance fuelled her determination, increasing her speed across the uneven ground. Unaware of the beast's charge, Morin inadvertently stepped backwards into its path whilst drawing his blood-soaked blade from the fallen remains of a newly-released Ravnarkin. His unwitting intervention momentarily hindered the Alpha's advance; the enraged beast was forced to expend part of its momentum running through the hapless knight. Morin's armoured body was violently batted away by the beast's thick cranium, tossed aside like a discarded rag doll. The knight's battered form bounced and rolled through the soft foliage, before eventually coming to rest. There was no time to check on Morin's condition; she dipped her head and pulled the hilt of her weapon to the right of her waist. Angling the blade's point towards her opponent, she leant into her left shoulder and crashed hard into the advancing Ravnarkin's flank.

Her ardent sword drove deep into the side of the beast's muscular torso, causing it to hiss in pain. The blade's penetration, coupled with her own sudden impact, forced the creature to veer off course towards its left. She was dragged unceremoniously alongside the wounded Ravnarkin as she clung desperately to the grip of her weapon; her ardent sword remained part buried in the creature's thick torso, refusing to dislodge. Her head and legs bounced around violently whilst the enraged beast kicked and thrashed ferociously, trying its best to displace her. There was a sudden violent yank, which finally wrenched her ardent sword clean from her grasp. She rolled a short distance across the ground, before hurriedly scrambling back to her feet. The Alpha had cleverly rolled away from her, thereby dislodging her blade, which was now lost to the foliage. Xenia shot the last of her arrows into the side of the Alpha's head. One of the projectiles buried into its cranium and the other tore through its right masseter muscle. The frenzied creature rose up onto its hind legs and hissed loudly, stretching its foul maw wide open to reveal the bloody head of Xenia's last arrow. Despite the first arrow protruding from its head, the visible damage they had both caused the Alpha seemingly had no ill effect on the hellish brute now bearing down on her. Dark purple blood oozed from its torso and thin dark watery lines trickled from the wounds to its head, yet despite the damage inflicted they had only succeeded in exacerbating the beast's savage rage. Now its focus was directed at her; being the closest target of opportunity, and the sole Freylarkin to render it any damage of note, the Alpha focused its brutal intentions towards her. With no weapon to aid her and with very little chance of evading the beast's imminent charge, she was suddenly reminded of the same feeling of helplessness that she endured at Scrier's Post when the Narlakai curtailed the Blade Aspirants' final charge. The familiar touch of dread clawed at her mind, desperate to ensnare her in its debilitating grasp, however, experience now taught her well that nothing good came from the inevitable paralysis of fear. She clenched her teeth, causing her face to grimace, and fought hard against the pit forming in her stomach.

'Think damn it! What would The Guardian do?' she said aloud, determined not to give in.

She still wore her gauntlets, and with enough force even they could be used as weapons. Then it dawned on her, as she stared vengefully at the Alpha whilst it circled back languidly for its inevitable charge towards her. If she closed the gap between them she would reduce the force of its impact. Furthermore – like most creatures – the Ravnarkai needed to *see* their prey, they did not hunt through sense of smell alone. Casting her gaze towards her gauntlets, she flexed her armoured fingertips and prepared herself mentally for the insanity bubbling at the fore of her mind. The Alpha hissed again, this time signalling its murderous intent to run her down. She mouthed a hasty prayer of hope then screamed in return before breaking into a sprint towards the hulking behemoth.

It was odd not to find Mirielle in her chamber; typically during those rare moments of downtime their queen could be found alone, shaping magnificent constructs in her personal quarters away from the prying eyes of onlookers. Although unrivalled in her field, Mirielle no longer indulged in public demonstrations of her ability. Since her construction of the Tri-Spires, Mirielle habitually chose to retreat to her chamber in order to work on small-scale projects which were more intricate in their design. Most believed that their queen had nothing left to prove, and that her pastimes were mere personal indulgences. Yet he often wondered if there was more to their queen's solitary shaping; perhaps Mirielle had found a better way of honing her ability, or maybe instead she sought hidden truths concealed within her fantastical creations, he mused.

He checked in with a number of sentries, one of whom had seen their queen headed towards the arboretum. Following the breadcrumbs laid out for him, he made his way to the kink in the third spire. The spire's unusual bend allowed plenty of natural light to enter the angled space from above, creating ideal conditions for nurturing flora within the polished granite enclosure. As he had been reliably informed, Mirielle was indeed ensconced within the arboretum, where she sat quietly by herself seemingly lost in thought. Deciding it best not to startle her a second time, he approached slowly, ensuring that she heard his approach. Mirielle looked up from her perch and smiled cordially; she was sat on one of the many steps running up the centre of the well maintained garden, flanked by fantastical colourful plants and fluorescent vines which clung to the shade. Light from the many sloped windows above speared down into the botanical sanctuary, creating pools of light where beautiful things grew to their full potential, safe from natural predators and the inadvertent tread of the Freylarkai. The arboretum was managed by the renewalists, who maintained the space ensuring its majestic beauty remained ever-present over the passes. It was a popular space, well suited to quiet contemplation, and where one could admire the natural beauty of their domain condensed into a single public space for convenient viewing. It was rare to see so few Freylarkai within the tranquil space, though he suspected that their queen's presence was the likely cause of the unusual emptiness. It was likely that those visitors who had glimpsed their queen in the arboretum had subsequently chosen to postpone their visit, thus affording Mirielle a moment of quiet solace.

'One of the sentries informed me that I might find you here.'

'They meticulously watch my every move Marcus.'

'Indeed, as I have instructed them to do so.' he said in his most charming manner.

'Sometimes I feel like a prisoner of my own creation, and by that I refer to more than just these walls, you understand?'

'As our queen you are free to come and go as you please.'

'You mean without an entourage?' questioned Mirielle with raised eyebrows.

'They are intended for your personal protection, but the ruling council can easily overrule me on the matter. I am sure Kirika will be happy to lend her support to such a vote.'

'Though you would not?'

'My primary concern is your safety Mirielle, and the protection of Freylar. Whilst I could never formally endorse such action, know that you have my blessing nonetheless.'

Mirielle gestured for him to sit on the stone steps adjacent – which he did. It was rare that he met with Mirielle outside her council chamber. Although he rarely visited the arboretum, its majestic beauty enthralled him every time he witnessed it – more so now with Mirielle's own presence. They sat for a while enjoying the comfortable shared silence, save for the occasional sound of trickling water nurturing the arboretum, supplied by a network of thin channels etched into the walls. Eventually he woke from the pleasant reverie, remembering his reason for seeking out Mirielle.

'I almost forgot to mention that Lothnar has returned.'

'So soon?' replied Mirielle with obvious interest.

'Yes. I was surprised myself, more so to receive his report directly – he strolled right into the arena with Krisis, through the west gate.'

'Ragnar was pleased I assume?'

'As always – I left the pair to massage their egos.'

'What news does Lothnar bring?'

'Sadly, very little. Both he and Krisis lost Darlia's trail – rain apparently – and there is no word on her wounded accomplice either.'

'The one Nathanar ran through?'

'Yes...that one.'

According to Lothnar the unknown female Freylarkin was somewhat of an enigma amongst the Freylarkai. Although there were those amongst them who possessed an ability to a lesser or greater extent, never before had he heard tell of a Freylarkin – aside from Mirielle – who had mastered the use of their ability to such an extreme; indeed, The Vengeful Tears knew first-hand the power wielded by the mysterious Freylarkin. Though Nathanar had seemingly dealt with the menace, the fact that Lothnar failed to recover the culprit's body gravely concerned him. Without solid evidence of the telepath's demise, the Freylarkai were still potentially at risk from further attacks. He felt helpless knowing that the Freylarkin was potentially still out there, holed up in the Narlakai borderlands, licking their wounds whilst plotting further attacks against them. Maybe he was just being overly cautious – in all likelihood Nathanar's blade *had* released the threat. Still, the lack of a body irked him.

'Do you think they are still a threat?'

'The lack of a body disturbs me. There may be more to this which I am yet to understand, but...that is for me to angst over and not you.' he replied. 'Besides, you have an even greater concern to worry about, do you not?'

'What do you mean?!' Mirielle replied rather suddenly, with an anxious look on her face.

'You implied that you wished to disband your entourage.' he replied in his characteristically charming manner. 'Unless I am mistaken, you therefore have a vote to rig do you not?'

During their short time together in the arboretum, Mirielle had seemed unusually relaxed in his presence. His final jesting remark, however, had potentially undone their queen's recent unperturbed demeanour. Although he had grown closer to Mirielle since Rayna's departure, she nonetheless continued to hold back, as though unable to take the final step towards cementing their mutual trust. There were clearly other concerns still preying on Mirielle's mind, though until she opened the door fully he could only hope that such matters were less significant than his own.

She screamed again whilst rapidly closing the remaining distance to the Alpha bounding directly towards her. She knew well that the impact would be violent, likely shattering every bone in her body, but she was determined not to give in or succumb to the fear of her own demise. The ever-present memory of the events at Scrier's Post ate at her soul, however, now she had a new family – one which she would not fail, even if that meant inviting her own ruin. With only several paces left between herself and the behemoth charging headlong towards her, she raised her hands in a claw-like fashion and directed her thumbs towards the creature's slanted black oval eyes. Even if the sudden impact of her armour failed to render the beast unconscious, the zealot in her would see its sight obliterated in the process. She would not walk away from what would likely be her final encounter – that much she knew – though she would make damn certain that her mangled body was the last thing the Ravnarkin ever saw.

Moments prior to impact, the Alpha's hulking body lurched violently to her right – smashed off course by the brutal impact of Heldran's armoured bulk. The Knight Lord crashed savagely into the beast's lumpy frame, driving his massive great sword cleanly through the Ravnarkin's thick neck to emerge on the far side. Unable to stop her momentum she crashed hard into the beast's hide, tripping over Heldran in the process. Despite his enviable size, the Knight Lord bounced off the Alpha and landed heavily on his back. Dark purple blood gushed from the wound inflicted by Heldran's immense weapon; gouts of the creature's blood splattered against the right side of her face, and down her arm. The beast hissed loudly in pain, flicking its horrid long slender tongue, and promptly fell to the ground writhing in pain. Heldran took the worst of the impact and was slow to recover, however, her own glancing blow allowed her to recover more readily. She scrambled back to her feet once more then ran towards the bloody creature, which continued to thrash wildly amidst the foliage. She clasped her gauntleted hands around the enormous grip of Heldran's great sword – still protruding from the beast – and wrestled the monstrous blade from its moorings. The weapon was heavy – too heavy – making it difficult for her to wield, yet she had enough strength still remaining to bring the enormous blade around high above her head before savagely raining it down on her opponent one last time. The massive blade struck the Ravnarkin's bloody neck, severing the remaining muscle and sinew with ease courtesy of Heldran's previous blow. The Alpha's bulbous head fell away from its neck, sending further gouts of dark purple blood in her direction. Her armour was covered in gore and she struggled to see as more of the creature's foul blood filled her eyes. She released her grip on the great sword before stumbling backwards, falling flat on her back. Though blinded by her blood-soaked eyes, her ears still functioned and were filled with the horrid chorus of mass hissing as the remaining Ravnarkai collectively acknowledged their Alpha's release.

Groping around blindly, she tried repeatedly to loosen the tied points securing her gauntlets, yet each attempt resulted in both failure and her growing frustration. She was about to try for a fourth time when big strong arms abruptly hoisted her clean off the ground. Her unknown benefactor promptly stood her upright, then used their large calloused hands to wipe away the blood still clinging to her eyes. She blinked repeatedly, trying to clear her vision fully, and found the Knight Lord towering before her. Heldran had removed his striking red plumed barbute, and bore a wide stretched smile from ear to ear. He placed his heavy hands on her pauldrons and nodded respectfully to her.

'You are one of us now Anika.'

She stood quietly bemused before Heldran, still trying to clear the last of the alien fluid obstructing her vision. Her obvious confusion etched itself across her face as she failed completely to understand the meaning of the Knight Lord's words.

'Ha, look around you Anika – witness the consequence of your actions.'

Heldran released his grip on her, allowing her to take a few steps back. Slowly she surveyed the surrounding battlefield in an attempt to understand what her sightless moments had lost her. The Ravnarkai were scrambling haphazardly towards the mist, which was now receding rapidly towards the edge of the basin. Given the recent intellect demonstrated by the Ravnarkai, she expected – in the unlikely event of a victory – the beasts to execute a co-ordinated tactical withdrawal; instead the Ravnarkai appeared to be in complete disarray, as though utterly routed by the knights' counter offensive. She spun around quickly and saw more of the creatures rapidly retreating in varying directions towards the horizon.

'Do you see now what you have done? This was your doing.'

'I did not do this my lord – the Knights Thranis did this.' she replied fervently.

'Yes, but you *are* a Knight of the Knighs Thranis.'

She turned her attention back to Heldran, who was still beaming down at her.

'We played our part, and we played it well. It was The Guardian who made it possible for us to rescue Loredan,

Gedrick and the others; it was *she* who broke the Ravnarkai charge...but it was *you,* Anika, who ended this! You came to us with the burden of your past weighing heavily upon your shoulders. You pledged your services to the Knights Thranis, under strict orders from The Blade Lord. Yet I no longer see that same Blade Novice standing before me now. Instead I see a Knight of our Order; a knight unafraid of self-sacrifice, so that we may continue to survive out here on the fringes of Freylarkin society. We offered you nothing, besides the courting of your own release, and yet you freely offer us your soul. It will be a long trek back to the Ardent Gate for you, for you have much to consider. I understand that you once swore fealty to Marcus and The Blades, however, I am now offering you a fresh chance to start over – much like The Guardian when she arrived in Freylar. I urge you to forget the past, and instead to think about the future – think about what *you* want.'

Instinctively, her gaze drifted towards one of the approaching knights, obviously keen to hear first-hand the Knight Lord's words – it was Xenia. The feisty warrior still carried her bow in hand, though her quiver was now empty. Xenia stopped a few paces away from herself and Heldran, where she remained perfectly still. The female knight had no need to speak; her mere silent presence was enough to reaffirm Heldran's words.

'Now go!' said Heldran, with a firm slap of his heavy hand across her back. 'Go and join your fellow knights.'

They marched slowly back to the glade in the gloomy leafless forest where they had first arrived via Waystone. Their progress was slow, on account of the many injured knights who nursed various cuts, bruises, fractures and –

more commonly – broken bones. Knight Restorant Loredan had done his utmost to patch up the battered knights from all three detachments, yet the dogged renewalist still had much work to do in the cycles to come – once he had regained his strength. For now, Loredan was utterly spent, and had barely the strength to walk unaided. Regrettably, not every member of the Order made it through the botched meat grinder – notably Morin, who no longer marched with them. The fallen knight's lifeless broken body was instead carried between herself and Zephir, upon a makeshift stretcher hastily constructed from branches. Katrin – carried alone by Heldran across his broad shoulders – was also counted amongst those lost during the encounter. Their loss cast a sombre mood over the knights, despite the knowledge that their fatalities could have been significantly worse. Although she had never spoken with Katrin at length, the knight's release stung her nevertheless – more so the release of Morin, whom she knew well. She had spoken with Morin enough times to realise that he was a true cynic. Though his pessimistic outlook prompted Morin to question her every command, nonetheless she had finally managed to get the knight on board – with a little nudge from Heldran. Now Morin no longer walked amongst them; a fact that wounded her more than any of her physical injuries.

'*You cannot blame yourself.*' whispered Alarielle in her mind.

'I caused this!'

'*Morin was a Knight, and besides...release comes for us all eventually.*'

Heldran saw her quiet angst and had a curious look on his face; the Knight Lord promptly quickened his pace, pulling up close alongside her.

'Do not let recent events eat you up.' said Heldran, trying miserably to soften his deep voice.

'This is my fault.'

'You cannot cheat fate indefinitely – none of us can – although scriers may *think* that they can.'

'He trusted me, and I failed him!'

'It was I who ordered Morin to come, and besides we all trusted you Rayna. As a result of that trust, all but two of us are returning home. Aside from those with the ability to scry, who can say with any certainty that we will not – all of us – be released within ten cycles of now?' Heldran replied emphatically. 'I for one am glad that we defied the odds this cycle. This was a massive victory for our Order Rayna; we now know for certain that the Ravnarkai do in fact possess tactical awareness and the ability to organise themselves. In addition, we have confirmed that they do indeed have a natural hierarchy. That knowledge is far more useful than any weapon, including those which you yourself wield. We can use that knowledge to break them!'

Heldran's words helped, but seeing Morin's lifeless body carried before her, between herself and Zephir, only worsened the deepening pit in her stomach. During her previous life she had cried very little; perhaps male physiology did not readily lend itself to such acts, or maybe her repressed memories masked the worst of her past pain. Perhaps it was even related to the difference in species. Since acquiring her new body, however, she sensed that her emotions had become heightened, thus it was difficult for her to suppress any emotional hurt. Tears fell from her eyes and her vision became watery as she watched Morin's head rock in step with their sombre march.

'Listen well to Heldran, he speaks the truth of it.'

'I know.' she replied dejectedly. 'But it still hurts.'

'As it should!' Zephir abruptly interjected, having clearly overheard their exchange. 'Any good leader should feel the pain of their kin when released from this world. But understand this well Guardian; I was against the Knight Lord's decision to invite both yourself and Anika into the Ardent Gate. The Blades are estranged from our Order, and are tarnished by a history of mistrust. I admit now that I judged you both poorly, and that I was wrong to do so. Each of us within this Order is indebted to the other; that is the unbreakable bond we share. Whilst I still do not fully trust The Blades per se, know that should you require my aid in battle...I *will* be there.'

'As will I.' replied Falkai, who limped slowly behind her, assisted by Captain Gedrick acting as a crutch for the injured telekinetic.

'Aye.' concurred Gedrick, in his typical brief fashion.

'I will too.' replied Xenia, also within earshot.

'And so will I.' Heldran affirmed with a warm smile.

'But know that there is one thing that will not change, Guardian.' continued Zephir.

'Would that be your derisive attitude?' she replied, offering the veteran knight a tearful wink as he turned his head to sneer at her.

'That indeed. And the fact I reserve the right to address the Alpha-slayer as *petite*.'

Zephir's habitually dour and sarcastic statement raised their spirits, prompting those nearby – including herself – to laugh quietly in amusement.

'You are a moron!' replied Xenia jovially, the words spoken with obvious affection.

She smiled tearfully at the good-natured sounds of Zephir bickering with the others which promptly ensued.

'Morin would have wanted this, not for you all to stand around mourning his release. They are his family...and now they are your family too.'

NINETEEN
Ethics

'What?!' he replied instinctively, whilst silently praying that his mind was playing tricks with his hearing.

'*You need to kill him. That is the only way this works!*'

He felt numb hearing those words again – *kill him*. For a moment he said nothing; he stood quietly in the dark, completely dumbfounded by Trix's words. After his brain eventually finished playing catch up, his confusion rapidly turned to anger. It took all of his self-restraint not to rise to the atrocity proposed by his so-called ally. Though he was committed to a war of words, Mr L. Cameron's bedroom – of all places – was hardly an ideal choice of battlefield. He was not a killer, nor did he harbour any desire to become one. He quickly withdrew back to the main living space, though his retreat was sloppy; he found it difficult to concentrate in the immediate wake of Trix's proposed madness and stumbled several times before completing his hasty retreat.

'Are you crazy?! I am not killing him!'

'*Callum, you have to!*' implored Trix, demonstrating what sounded like actual emotion, which was typically unknown to the Shadow class hacker.

'Piss off Trix! If you want him dead then get off your arse and do it yourself. I am not a killer, and I am definitely not your assassin!'

'*Look, I get it. And this is why I deliberately never divulged this part of the plan to you.*'

'You have the audacity to call this a plan?! This isn't a plan – this is murder!'

'*It's necessary.*'

'Why do you specifically need *him* dead? Trix, he's an old man! Granted from what I have seen he lives a self-indulgent lifestyle, even decadent perhaps, but regardless, that does not warrant assassination!'

'*Callum, we need his bio-key. Without that bio-key everything I promised you remains a dream.*'

'But why do you specifically need *his* bio-key?'

'*Because he built the system Fox; the same system that allowed them to round us up like hapless livestock!*'

'Are you saying that L. Cameron created the bio-keys? I thought you said he was a retired software developer?' he replied, still failing to deduce the missing part of Trix's accursed puzzle.

'*No, not the keys – he developed the software to track them!*'

That was it – the final missing piece of Trix's ruse; as he had reverse engineered the security protecting the Metropolis' central data core, so too would he unravel the code used to locate the bio-keys. That was how Trix planned to execute their new lifestyle within the Metropolis; indefinite anonymous access to all of its systems. With that power, they could live comfortably amongst the Metropolis' Apex class members as ghosts – unnoticed by the system, yet still fully connected to it. Yet in order to circumvent the system, Trix first needed to gain access to it – L. Cameron was that means of access. He began to feel lightheaded as the significance of the previously hidden minutiae bubbled at the fore of his mind. They did indeed need L. Cameron's key, though surely killing him was not the only solution.

'We can find another way.'

'*There's no time!*'

'We could coerce him. Clearly you've researched the man, there must be something we can use as leverage to force his cooperation?'

'I found nothing like that Callum.'

'Family, friends – there must be something we can use against him. Trix I can't kill him!'

'He lives alone – always has done. L. Cameron is responsible for the forced relocation of our kind Callum. He made the Rout possible. How can you offer this man any form of compassion?'

'We don't know that was his intent. You said yourself that he was a private contractor; in all likelihood he was unaware of the misguided application of his technology.'

'You're splitting hairs. He knew the technology was intended to control the populus – don't pretend to be naive on this matter.' said Trix vehemently.

'Maybe you're right. But, regardless, they would have found someone else Trix.'

'But they didn't!' replied Trix angrily. *'You think the bastard will atone for his sins and actually help us? Or perhaps he will lie still on his bed whilst you cut his bio-key out of his arm – as we were forced to!'*

Trix's words cut deep – they were true. It was an impossible dilemma; kill the one responsible for heralding the Exodus of the Shadow class and live well, or go back to a life of uncertainty and squalor. Yet despite the ill effects of L. Cameron's work, he could not bring himself to murder the elderly gentleman. He understood well that sometimes life needed to be viewed in black and white, but sometimes the shades of grey mattered. Taking a life, regardless of the circumstances, was always grey – to him at least. Perhaps Trix would feel differently standing over the elderly gentleman with knife in hand, he mused. Either way, he was many things – there were no wings on his back – but a killer he was not.

'You cannot ask me to do this Trix.'
'Please don't make me force your hand.'
'What?!'
'Fox, just kill him!'
'Fuck you Trix! Do it yourself!'
'Noted.'

A siren abruptly sounded from the analogue communicator lodged uncomfortably in his ear. The sound was deafening at first, prompting him to instinctively wrench the outdated technology from his ear before discarding it carelessly on the floor. It took him a moment to recover from the sound blasting directly into his ear. Away from his ear the siren was quieter now, yet it was still loud enough to disturb the hab's other occupant. He dropped to his knees and fumbled around in the dark, attempting to locate the communicator by running his hands across the floor's smooth surface. Whilst he groped around haphazardly in the dark, the device began to steadily increase in volume.

'Shit! Damn you Trix!'

He finally located the device and clasped his right hand around it in an attempt to muffle the noise of the siren. The worst of the sound quickly abated, though he still needed to turn the wretched thing off. He thought about crushing the communicator under something heavy, but destroying it meant severing his link with Trix entirely. He was still in the heart of the Metropolis; dawn was fast approaching, and wishful thinking that he could evade Peacekeeper patrols alone indefinitely was naive. He despised Trix for his chosen course of action, yet he still needed the able hacker's assistance.

Light suddenly spilled into the main living space from the corridor leading to the master bedroom. The sound emanating from the retro communications device was no longer relevant; Trix's siren had served its purpose, its damage was already done, the elderly gentleman was awake. Trix had played his ace well in a desperate attempt to force his hand. Now fate would decide the outcome of his impromptu encounter with L. Cameron.

'Krashnar, what is the...meaning of this?' she demanded irritably.

'I thought that your speech had improved, yet still you struggle.' retorted the wild shaper.

'Is it any surprise after...you insist that I drag myself back down...to your filthy workshop?!'

'Stop your whining, child. If we are to achieve our goals you will need to walk more than a few paces, however, I do have something down here which will further aid your mobility – until you fully recover.'

'I will *never* fully recover.' she replied soberly. 'In any event, what heinous monstrosity...do you have to show me now?'

'I am glad that you ask.' replied Krashnar, whose eyes widened as he licked his cracked lips.

She knew the twisted shaper well enough now to understand the meaning of his disgusting mannerisms. His ugly body language was no doubt in anticipation of some new perverse pleasure, yet to be revealed to a reluctant audience. It was clear that Krashnar delighted in displaying his fiendish works to others; she wondered if the borderline sociopath actually enjoyed the obvious disgust of those who silently critiqued his work in mute horror. He turned his back to her and shuffled eagerly towards the rock wall at the far end of the dingy workshop. Krashnar ran his mutilated left hand across the rough surface of the wall in search of something. His remaining thumb and fingers eventually contacted with a loose stone, to which he applied pressure. Without warning the entire rear wall of the workshop began to recede into the dark stained floor. Grit and dust fell gently from the stone ceiling of the workshop, and a deep tremor resonated across the room. She felt the vibration run up her spine. All the while, Krashnar kept his back to her, staring into the manifesting gloom of a large passage which lay beyond the receding wall. She noted the shaper's obvious excitement; Krashnar's fingers twitched in anticipation of his latest – no doubt horrific – unveiling. She paused as Krashnar began to move down the dark corridor, wondering what lay beyond.

'Are you coming, or would you prefer to stay here and whine some more?'

Krashnar groaned and his head reeled backwards momentarily as she pricked his mind with the power of her own – a curt reminder of the boundary he once again dared to cross. It seemed that the insidious shaper required a frequent lesson in her ability, and a reminder of who was in command of their new found alliance. Though she was content for the shaper to indulge in his unorthodox initiatives, ultimately she was in control of their renewed plans for the invasion of Freylar.

'Calm down, and set those crutches of mine to purpose.'

She smiled cruelly at Krashnar's obvious discomfort, yet the minor attack on his mind did nothing to dampen his perverted enthusiasm. Krashnar promptly lurched forwards, allowing the foreboding darkness of the passageway to consume him. Fear of the unknown clawed at her soul, and for a brief moment she considered breaking off their engagement. However, casting her gaze downwards, she was quickly reminded of the architect of her current demise; her course was set and she would not deviate from her chosen path, at least not until she had Nathanar's severed head on a spike and Mirielle's rule lay in ruin. Steeling her nerves, she set her body to purpose and hobbled painfully towards her dark destiny.

The passageway was dark as the night when cloud cover greedily obscured its Night's Lights. She could hear Krashnar shuffling in the distance; the sound of his movements echoed along the passageway, which descended gradually into the void. Other than the sound of his accursed shuffling and the familiar rhythmic tap of her crutches, there was nothing – only a foreboding silence. What atrocities and twisted perversions of nature did the exiled shaper harbour in such a place, she mused. She was reluctant to contemplate the answer to her own question; she wondered nervously if there were any limits to the depravity of the manifestations shaped from Krashnar's insidious imagination. She flinched as the unexpected sound of water echoed around her as droplets fell from the ceiling, startling her; the sudden noise caused her to instinctively tighten her grip on the stone crutches she bore. Anxiously, she continued to follow the sound of Krashnar's movements. Though her night vision served her well – being a child of winter – she wondered how it was that

Krashnar found his way in the dark with apparent ease; shapers were not typically renowned for their ability to see in low light, though perhaps his changed eyes lent themselves to nocturnal viewing, she thought. Or perhaps he simply felt his way using the remains of his mutilated hand. Either way, his comfortable relationship with the darkness came as no surprise to her.

After advancing slowly for some time, the once still air around her became unsettled. She could hear a faint rush of what sounded like wind up ahead. She pressed forwards regardless, grateful to put the eerie silence of the passageway behind her. With each advancing step, the sound became increasingly loud. Unperturbed, she continued down the passageway, until the sound ahead amplified to such an extent that it resembled that of mighty bellows. The passageway suddenly turned sharply to the right, beyond which she could no longer hear the familiar scuffle of Krashnar movements between the mysterious periodic sounds of rushing wind. She stepped gingerly around the corner, completely unprepared for what was to come.

'I thought for a moment that perhaps you had gotten lost.' said Krashnar, who lit a torch attached to the rock wall.

Gentle flames flickered into being from the lit torch, forcing the darkness to retreat like the break of dawn. Standing dolefully not more than eight paces in front of her was a creature, unlike any she had previously borne witness to. The horrid aberration was some kind of unnatural construct; an amalgamation of multiple creatures, their composite body parts fused together to produce an abhorrent hybrid. The abomination had three heads, all previously belonging to dire wolves. Two of the heads joined the front of the creature's body off-centre, either side of a central third which was attached slightly higher. The secondary heads appeared fully autonomous, though each was hung low and appeared subservient to the other. All were grotesquely enlarged – far larger than those of typical dire wolves – and had foul diseased-looking maws which salivated insatiably. The many-headed eyes were black as night, bearing a distinct similarity to Krashnar's own. Its thick powerful legs – of which there were four – were dotted with islands of thick matted fur, where its ruddy skin had been stretched courtesy of its deformed bone structure. The mangy fur carpet continued piecemeal along the beast's underbelly, before promptly giving way to a thick armoured chitin carapace, affording the creature greater protection across the top half of its body. The chimera also had a prehensile tail – again covered in chitin – which clearly did not belong to any of the mutilated dire wolves. The end of this tapered to a sharp point, which dripped some kind of acidic fluid; the liquid fell to the floor – some rolling down the length of the beast's tail – where it vigorously reacted, producing an acrid smoke. Apparently Krashnar had felt it necessary to graft the rear of some other unfortunate monstrosity onto the back of the vile construct.

'Come child, witness my Meldbeast. It is quite content – for the time being at least – for it has recently fed.' said the sadistic shaper, who bore a stretched smile from ear to ear.

Whether due to the aberration before her, or the sight of Krashnar's dirty stained teeth visible behind his wide smile, regardless her stomach lurched painfully, causing her to retch violently. She instinctively raised her left hand towards her mouth, hoping to contain the bile rising up her throat, though it was a feeble gesture given the inevitable. She vomited repeatedly over her hand and onto the floor, whilst trying to avert her gaze from the ghastly visions assaulting her. Her left crutch clattered to the floor, only to receive the same injustice inflicted upon her hand. The smell of her own vomit and the rasping of Krashnar's foul tongue heightened her aversion, and she realised then that the sound she had heard earlier was in fact the abomination's laboured breathing.

'So...what do you think of my work?' asked Krashnar, who was clearly delighted by her obvious revulsion.

She spat the remnants of her last partly-digested meal onto the floor, then tried to clear her throat. Her loathing towards the insidious shaper had reached a new level; until now she had not believed it possible to harbour so much disgust towards anyone Freylarkin. Indeed, she started to wonder if in fact Krashnar truly was born of Freylar; perhaps he had simply stolen the identity of one of their kin and adopted their way of life.

'It is a grotesque perversion of nature!' she spat, still trying to clear her throat. 'What compels you to create such horrors?'

'Interesting...' Krashnar pondered momentarily. 'I suppose it is curiosity; the same curse which compels most of us with great ability, do you not agree?'

'You do this simply because...you are curious?!'

'Yes...frequently.'

'There are others?'

'Failures, all...in truth, this is my fourth rendition. It is my hope that it will survive longer than its predecessors.'

replied Krashnar, who turned his attention back to the beast, having grown tired of her vomiting.

'Where are the others?'

'As I said they were failures. In my naiveté I tried to work with too many materials. I was too ambitious and thus my previous works did not last very long. This fourth generation Meldbeast, however, is a far simpler thing; gave it more of a bite along with a bit of a sting – elegant simplicity, no?'

'You are sick!'

Krashnar laughed in his habitual raspy tone.

'Ironic, considering...' replied the shaper, offering her floor decoration a brief glance.

'Regardless, one does not adorn their abode with failures. Mirielle certainly does not – or did you think she was perfect?' the shaper continued. 'In any event, most of the failures fed their successor – no wastage of raw material. You see, I am good at recycling.'

'You disgust me.' she said vehemently.

'Now you sound like Darlia. I have no interest in what is socially acceptable, or indeed your personal morals. This creation – my Meldbeast – is necessary for our invasion.'

'I find it difficult to believe that we need this thing. Anyway, what was the required flesh sacrifice to create this monstrosity?'

'Is that not obvious Lileah? What do you think happened to the bodies of the other two dire wolves?'

'And the *thing* covering its hide?'

'Some sacrifices are more demanding than others, especially when shaping such...beauty.'

His final words on the matter made her skin crawl; Krashnar seemed genuinely infatuated with his own opus, the realisation of which made her shudder. Casting her gaze down at her own body, she realised then how restrained the abhorrent shaper had in fact been with her. However, the knowledge of his hands having mutilated and repeatedly touched her body left her feeling numb and empty. It dawned on her that Krashnar was now familiar with every part of her body; her privacy had been violated in one of the most terrible ways imaginable – she no longer held any physical secrets from the flesh worker. She turned her sight back towards the Meldbeast, which appeared to be fairly content. She saw the bones of other creations littering its closed pen against the flickering light; all were horribly deformed and stripped clean of their meat. Yet despite the Meldbeast's horrific countenance, she harboured some sympathy for the creature, given that it too had been a victim of Krashnar's crimes; they were both mutations, conceived by a common creator.

'You should thank Darlia for your current visage; had she not coerced me into helping you, it is entirely likely that you would have become this one's next meal – if not its successor.'

'Are you implying that you would mutilate a Freylarkin in such a way?'

'Ha,' rasped Krashnar amusingly, 'I suggest nothing which I have not already done.'

The now familiar feeling of revulsion washed over her for a second time, causing her to expel what little remained in her stomach. She was right; Krashnar was not a Freylarkin – she realised now that the sadistic shaper was a demon no less. Though she now despised him in every way possible, there was no disputing the fact that he would make a formidable ally. The exiled shaper clearly hated Mirielle

– for reasons he had not fully elaborated on – and had mastered the extremes of his ability. All she needed to do was unleash him upon their enemies, along with the Narlakai, and their success would be assured; she no longer required a scrier to waste time scheming her path to a victory of which she was now certain.

'In any event,' she said clearing her throat once more, 'We need your Meldbeast why?'

'The answers to these questions of yours, are they not obvious? How is it that you expect to rally your fleeing Narlakai? Surely they are in Narlak by now?' said Krashnar in a patronising tone.

'This *thing* is to be our means of transportation?!' she replied, disgusted at the thought of mounting the creature.

'Yes, though not entirely.'

'Meaning what?'

'Get on and you will see for yourself.'

Krashnar turned his back on her and moved slowly towards the metal pen holding the Meldbeast captive. The creature stirred from its contented slumber as the shaper quietly approached. Carefully, Krashnar slid free a large metal lock pin securing access to the pen, after which he confidently opened the door to the enclosure. The Meldbeast reared its deformed heads, all of which snarled as Krashnar slowly entered its pen. At first she thought the creature would release its creator there and then, but instead the Meldbeast recoiled in Krashnar's presence, suggesting that it in fact feared its maker. She wondered what terrible genesis would cause such a beast to fear its own father; was it fully conscious during its own bastard creation, she considered. Certainly she was largely unaware of the procedure resulting in her own deformity – only the agonising pain of metal alloy fusing with her flesh clung to her mind. However, she had been close to release during the procedure; it was possible therefore that the Meldbeast's own experiences were entirely different to her own.

'Back or front?'

'You are not putting your fingerless hand around my waist!'

'Back then.'

Krashnar pulled down hard on a metal chain fastened to a large iron collar clasped tightly around the Meldbeast's left head; the creature growled in brief protest, before lowering its grotesquely over-enlarged body to the floor of the grimy enclosure.

'Get on.'

It took her some time to mount the beast; reluctantly, she was forced to accept Krashnar's assistance in doing so, given her reduced mobility. She thought about taking her crutches with them, however, Krashnar insisted that she no longer required the hollow stone walking aids. After painfully mounting the Meldbeast – aided by Krashnar – she quickly discovered that its carapace armour was hard and uncomfortable, though her primary concern was potentially falling off the wretched creature. Unsurprisingly, Krashnar had an answer to the problem, though his solution was far from conventional; by now she expected nothing less from the twisted shaper. Instead of fashioning a seat, or a harness of some description, Krashnar instead pressed his hands against the Meldbeast's flank and set to work reshaping the creature's skin so that it wrapped around her legs. The grotesque procedure caused the Meldbeast's central head to howl in pain, the sound of which echoed across the creature's pen. The beast's torment made her shudder once more. Krashnar's methods were habitually brutal and hard to stomach, though she found it difficult to find fault with their effectiveness. Before climbing onto their mount himself, Krashnar used his ability once more to significantly widen the entrance to the Meldbeast's pen, thus allowing them to pass freely through it. Their creator then worked a series of levers located at regular intervals along the perimeter wall of the rock chamber housing the pen. Thick dust fell from the ceiling as an aperture noisily formed above them, allowing light from outside to bathe the chamber's interior. The Meldbeast recoiled at first from the light, no doubt unaccustomed to seeing the world rendered in vivid colour. After acclimatising itself to the light, the Meldbeast required little coercing from Krashnar to leave its filthy birthplace. She groaned in discomfort as the mutilated creature vacated its pen, before pouncing on top of the metal cage with a single powerful leap propelled by its rear muscular legs. The force of the upwards momentum jarred her body, causing her to wince in pain; although Krashnar had provided them with a means of transportation, the shaper seemingly cared not for the ongoing agony it would inflict upon her. The Meldbeast hesitated briefly whilst its three heads sniffed curiously at the outside world. Satisfied that the allure of freedom was in fact not some cruel illusion wrought by its insidious master, the Meldbeast leapt once more from the top of its filthy pen towards freedom, carrying them violently with it.

TWENTY
Goodbye

Their return to the Ardent Gate had been a sobering affair. Guards posted in the Gate Room by Vorian were the first to greet them; they promptly rushed to assist the walking wounded, including Loredan who was on the verge of collapse due to physical exhaustion through extensive use of his ability. Most of the battered knights were taken to the communal resting quarters, which fast became makeshift infirmaries for the wounded. Although half of those committed to the meat grinder simply required bed rest and time to heal, the remainder were fashioned crude splints to tide them over until they could receive Loredan's aid. The bodies of Morin and Katrin were left in the Gate Room; both were destined for public cremation the following morning. That night she tried desperately to sleep, but as usual the promise of a peaceful slumber eluded her – not helped by the constant moans of pain from the weary knights sharing her quarters. She left her hammock twice during the night and wandered up to the base of the Ardent Gate in search of Heldran. She had hoped to find Heldran sitting alone in the hub by the stone hearth, however, the Knight Lord was not there. The first time she waited for some time, hoping that Heldran might put in a tardy appearance. Upon finding the stone hearth empty for the second time, she left the confines of the redoubt and sat outside peering into the dark, with only Alarielle and her own light to accompany her. She enjoyed conversing with the former Blade Adept, though she could only ever do so alone, in private, away from the prying eyes of those who might label her insane – or worse, reveal her secret.

'Perhaps Heldran is in his quarters, sleeping?'

'He has a lot on his mind right now, with the loss of Morin and Katrin. I felt sure that he would be beside the hearth, searching for answers amidst those flames.'

'Maybe he needs some space.'

'You're probably right.'

'He is ultimately responsible for them, and they are like family to him – as are you now.'

'I've never really had a family.'

'You have me. Am I not family to you Rayna?'

'Yes, I guess you are...'

'You realise it is time, now?'

'Time to go back you mean?'

'No, it is time to go home.'

'The Trials....'

'Yes, amongst other things.'

'Speak plainly sister – we have no secrets.'

'We need to speak with my father.'

'Alarielle, are you sure?'

'I must know for certain.'

'Very well....'

Eventually she grew tired and retreated back to her hammock, hoping dearly that sleep would eventually come – which it did. When finally dawn broke, she rose early from her hammock and ascended to the very top of the Ardent Gate. There she performed a series of stretching exercises, attempting to ease her bodily aches, whilst savouring the gentle caress of the weak autumnal sun rising in the east. She smiled at the breathtaking alpine landscape stretched out before her towards the distant horizon. Although the vale too was a sight to behold, there was something wondrously raw about the crisp clean surrounds of the southern lands. In her heart she knew there would be precious few opportunities left for her to behold such outstanding natural beauty, therefore she decided to relieve the current sentry and take over the remainder of the knight's watch. Throughout the morning, she watched with interest as several of the knights below assembled a large pyre in front of the Ardent Gate. The knights worked tirelessly to assemble the wooden construct, which she assumed would bear both Morin and Katrin. It was noon when the knights finished the pyre's construction and the next shift change took place; one of Vorian's eager charges ascended the Ardent Gate to relieve her of duty.

'Your presence is requested Guardian. They will be commencing shortly.'

'Understood.' she replied.

She relinquished her watch and descended the Ardent Gate. The knights appeared to be assembling in the mess hall; she followed the herd, unsure of the correct procedure when bidding farewell to released comrades. She saw Anika waiting in the mess hall along with Xenia and Zephir. It made her smile, seeing the Blade Novice standing comfortably alongside the others; she had not seen Anika so at ease since the events at Scrier's Post. It pleased her seeing that the previously troubled Blade had at last moved on. Although Anika had changed much during their time spent with the Knights, including her physical appearance, she was nonetheless encouraged by her evolution. Anika had matured; she was no longer the inexperienced spritely zealot she first met in the arena, shortly after her arrival in Freylar. Anika had been tested in battle numerous times since, and had toughened up considerably as a direct result. Yet it pleased her to see some semblance of her former disposition only now beginning to resurface, like fresh shoots tentatively breaking through newly cultivated soil. She attributed the latest change to Anika's new-found ease amongst the knights. It dawned on her then that she could in fact be returning to the vale alone; the now very real prospect of parting ways with Anika saddened her, and yet the scenario had always been one of the mission objectives tasked to her by Marcus. She began making her way towards Anika and the others, when the familiar sound of Heldran's voice boomed out across the mess hall demanding the attention of all those present.

'Thank you all for attending; both Morin and Katrin would have appreciated your presence. Rayna, you and I will lead the service which will now take place outside.' said Heldran with authority.

The Knight Lord strode towards her whilst the other knights, including Anika, promptly formed up in a column behind him. She joined Heldran at the front of the procession and together they marched in lockstep out of the Ardent Gate and assembled in front of the pyre. The timber construction was much bigger than she had previously thought, from her high vantage point perched on top of the Ardent Gate, making its rate of construction even more impressive. The bodies of both fallen knights had already been laid neatly on the top of the pyre across a flat wooden platform – Falkai's doing, no doubt – suspended just above the tinder pile below. Both had been stripped of their armour, though each was granted the honour of cremation whilst in the possession of their chosen weapon; both knights had been arranged so that their hands were clenched tightly around the grip of their downward pointing ardent swords. It was customary to reclaim such weapons afterwards, or prior to their complete destruction, so that they could be hung in the training hall in honour of their owners' sacrifices for the Order – according to Heldran during one of their many late evening soirées. Captain Gedrick was already outside and stood next to a lit brazier adjacent to the pyre. The remainder of the knights shuffled into a crescent formation around the front of the pyre, with both herself and the Knight Lord at its front and centre. Heldran was the one to commence the proceedings.

'On this cycle, we honour the release of our fellow Knights; brother Knight Morin, and sister Knight Katrin. Each was committed to the Knights Thranis, and both were well respected and liked within our Order. We will miss their companionship as now they leave us to make their passage to the Everlife.' proclaimed Heldran sombrely. 'Would anyone else like to speak on their behalf?'

Although Heldran did not address her specifically, her joint command of the previous cycle's struggle against the Ravnarkai warranted that she contribute verbally to the service. She tried to steel herself, hoping desperately to abate the butterflies in her stomach, yet she felt more nervous now than during any of her previous encounters with the Ravnarkai. Even so she could sense the mounting expectation from the knights at her back.

'I didn't know Katrin,' she said, trying hard to fight through her cracked voice. 'But there was always a mutual respect between us in passing. Morin, however, I came to know well enough during our final cycle spent fighting beside one another. To be frank, he was a cynical pain in the arse.'

Her unexpected words prompted a hearty laugh from both Zephir and a number of other knights gathered around the pyre; most surprising of whom was Gedrick, who typically maintained a cool demeanour. Nonetheless, her words resonated with their habitually stone-faced Captain – even Knight Lord Heldran smiled at her candid prose.

'Even so, I respected Morin, and I respected his point of view. He challenged me, when others did not, and was not afraid to do so. He made me pause for second thought, which was no bad thing. Although I – as well as others amongst you – question the nature of the Everlife, that word is nonetheless entirely appropriate. Both Morin and Katrin will live on in our memories, and so in a sense they will indeed live forever – within us.'

Heldran turned his head towards her and nodded in appreciation of her words, before signalling the Captain to light the pyre. With a swift boot of his right foot, Gedrick kicked the lit brazier onto its side towards the base of the pyre. The pile of assorted tinder immediately caught light and within moments the entire construct was ablaze. It did not take long before the flames licked greedily at the base of the wooden platform supporting the bodies. The knights remained perfectly still, and watched mournfully as the pyre continued to burn fiercely; none took a step back, despite the intense heat from the flames. Before the flaming mass could claim the bodies entirely, Falkai hobbled awkwardly through the gathered knights towards the front of the congregation. His right leg still required attention, though in the interim he chose to make good use of a makeshift crutch, which he held tightly with both hands. The adept telekinetic plucked the ardent swords with ease from the hungry flames, with the sole aid of his gifted mind. Unexpectedly, Falkai then turned to her, presenting her with both of the recovered blades.

'It is tradition to adorn the training hall with the weapons of our fallen. Their presence helps us to remember those knights released in service to the Order.' explained Falkai. 'I knew both Morin and Katrin well. I believe that both would have appreciated The Guardian laying their weapons to rest.'

She took the ardent swords offered to her and nodded respectfully to Falkai in return. Both blades appeared undamaged and each was still relatively cold to the touch, despite their recent caress by the flames.

'It would be an honour.'

After delivering the weapons, Falkai smiled in appreciation then turned his attention back to the pyre. Together – all of them – they stood quietly, looking on as the merciless flames consumed the remains of their fallen comrades.

It was late in the afternoon when she finally regained consciousness following Lileah's brutal mental attack. She picked herself up groggily from the – now familiar – dirty floor of the gloomy corridor, outside of Lileah's room. Her head ached painfully. After regaining her bearings she immediately left the hide; she spent the remainder of the afternoon angsting over her conversation with Lileah alone in search of solace. When finally she decided to return to Krashnar's hide, she immediately went looking for Lileah. She clung to the desperate hope that she could yet sway the young telepath's decision from resuming their war, in which she wanted no further part. She ran from room to room, eager to locate Lileah so that they could resume their earlier conversation. At first she thought that she had overlooked the petite young Freylarkin resting in one of the dirty rooms, however, searching a second time proved equally fruitless. Krashnar too was nowhere to be found, causing her to suspect that both were ensconced in his horrid grubby workshop. Although she abhorred the rogue shaper's place of work, she anxiously pushed open its door, hoping to find both Lileah and Krashnar standing beside a grimy workbench discussing his latest atrocity. To her dismay the room was empty, yet it had changed since last she laid eyes on it; a large dark passageway now connected to the room at its far end, where previously she had pinned Krashnar to a wall with her ornate bronze metal claw. She approached the tunnel cautiously, concerned by its devious presence; exactly how big was Krashnar's hide, she thought pensively. She peered gingerly into its foreboding darkness, attempting to discern any signs of activity. Aside from the sound caused by the occasional droplet of water, echoing in the distant dark, the tunnel appeared desolate. Prior to stepping into the breach, however, she pressed the palm of her good hand firmly against its right wall and engaged her second sight. Immediately she saw Lileah – leaning heavily on her crutches – and Krashnar, who shuffled confidently into the gloom. Curious to learn their present whereabouts, she traced their path slowly through the darkness until the passageway veered sharply to the right. Without any warning, the uncomfortable sight of Lileah retching upon the floor rooted her in place. Krashnar seemed to enjoy Lileah's revulsion, as was evident by his familiar debauched smile, which regrettably she recognised all too well. The depraved silent imagery continued to assault her mind. Something nasty had taken place here, demanding she pause for thought; she began to question whether in fact it was smarter simply to turn back, and yet she felt a strange horrifying compulsion to continue forwards. Seeing Lileah again now, clearly disgusted by what she saw, reminded her of their last heated exchange of words. The spontaneous recollection of their unfinished conversation set her mind to purpose once more, instilling in her the courage necessary to press on in spite of the knowledge that more of the shaper's evil lurked in the past – soon to be her present.

Seeing the patchwork monstrosity filled her with dread, though it was not the hideous beast's abhorrent visage which tore deep into her soul. Watching haplessly as the insidious shaper aided Lileah to mount the foul abomination finally ripped her soul from its moorings. She collapsed to the filthy floor in front of the monstrous beast's pen, weeping uncontrollably whilst staring vacantly towards the darkening sky above. Her heart broke, no longer able to bear the weight of her regret. She had lost her lover, with all certainty – that much was clear to her now. Lileah was truly lost to her, consumed by the need for revenge. The realisation of this crushed what little remaining hope she had desperately clung to and shattered her soul. The depraved images of Krashnar's ghastly construct escorting her lover away from her was more than she could bear. The sky grew dark and the cold air descended into the chamber, filling the growing emptiness inside her. Her once insatiable desire to know everything had in fact been the architect of her downfall. She had but a single friend remaining to her now, one which beckoned to her with its siren call. Its promise of eternal peace lapped at her like an advancing wave, offering her the sweet mercy of release.

After the ceremony they all gathered in the mess hall where an impressive meal had been prepared for the knights, as was tradition when honouring their fallen, according to Xenia. She took her habitual place at the fully laden long wooden table, next to both Xenia and Zephir. Since being reunited with the Knights, she felt a sense of ease which had eluded her back in the vale after her failure to reconcile the aftermath of the Narlakai invasion. Her time spent with the Knights Thranis had afforded her the opportunity to start over, as such she no longer felt alone or out of place. The words spoken to her by the Knight Lord, shortly after severing the Ravnarkin Alpha's head, occupied her thoughts once again. She found herself unexpectedly smiling at Heldran's glowing appraisal of her development since her arrival at the Ardent Gate. Heldran was right; she was indeed a Knight now, and was treated as such. Both The Blades and the vale seemed like distant memories to her now. How could she return to her previous life, she mused. It was then that she realised that in fact she could not. Impulsively, she abruptly stood up – just as those around her had found their seats – causing her heavy chair to scrape noisily across the flagstone floor. All eyes were immediately upon her, drawn by her unexpected action. She suddenly felt nervous, yet when she turned towards Heldran's beaming weathered face, any concerns she had melted away.

'Anika, you have our attention.' said Heldran warmly. 'Have you made your decision?'

'I have.' she replied, conscious of the fact she was still smiling.

She promptly turned to The Guardian, choosing at last to reveal her innermost thoughts.

'Guardian, you have helped me much during the short time that you and I have been acquainted. You helped me through an extremely dark time, and together our journey has led us here. It has been an honour to be your Blade sister, and know that I would fight alongside you versus the impossible if you so asked. You are a good friend Rayna, and I remain loyal to you, but my place is here now with the Knights Thranis. I cannot return to the vale; my time with The Blades has come to an end. I hope dearly, sister, that you think no less of me for wanting to stay.'

All eyes shifted from her to Rayna; The Guardian seemed entirely nonchalant in the wake of her sudden proclamation. True to her playful demeanour, Rayna took an overly long drink from her wooden cup, purposely prolonging the moment. Rayna then slammed the emptied cup down on the wooden table and turned towards her with an uncharacteristic stern look.

'You think The Blades would want you back with your hair looking like that? And besides, I find it difficult to believe that Nathaniel will want any competitors in the arena vying for his title – Master of Scars!' replied Rayna with a mischievous grin.

All those gathered around the table turned their attention back towards her; some were grinning from ear to ear, a few laughed quietly to themselves, whilst others feigned fear – widening their eyes and biting their knuckles playfully. She glanced towards Heldran, who cocked one eyebrow in anticipation of her response. She knew The Guardian well enough now to realise her game; she was no longer the guarded aloof Freylarkin who made easy prey for Zephir's sardonic taunts. Rayna knew that, and had handed her the opportunity to silence any remaining critics for good.

'Well...they let *you* in!' she replied, winking in return.

The mood in the mess hall suddenly lifted; some of the knights tapped their fingers jovially upon the edge of the wooden table, building to a crescendo, and others howled at her response. Xenia touched her right hand gently and grinned feverishly up at her. Rayna abruptly stood up from her seat and strode confidently towards her. Both opened their arms and embraced one another affectionately.

'I will miss you!' said Rayna emphatically.

'And I you, sister.' she replied tearfully, finally allowing her emotions to once again permeate her regimented exterior.

After numerous cheers from the gathered knights, Heldran himself rose from the table and outstretched his burly arms, brining swift silence to the raucous ensemble. He clasped his right hand around his relatively tiny cup, and raised it high above his head.

'We welcome you to our Order Anika, hair 'n' all!' boomed Heldran to the sound of cheers from all those gathered. 'As of this cycle, do you pledge fealty to the Order of the Knights Thranis? And do you swear to protect the Ardent Gate, along with its secrets, with your very soul?'

'I swear it!' she replied fervently, before reaching for her own cup.

'Then sit, Knight Anika, and feast in the honour of both Morin and Katrin as a Knight of this Order.'

The gathered knights drank vigorously from their cups before slamming them down hard on the table, signalling their acceptance of her induction into the Order. Heldran did the same, and would have sat, if not for a moment's hesitation swaying his course. Once more the Knight Lord demanded silence, this time to address her former Blade sister.

'Guardian...Rayna...whilst I am no scrier, it is clear to me that your destiny will take you beyond the Ardent Gate; you do not intend to stop here, and nor do I wish to see it – greater things lay in store for you, of that I am certain. You came to me with a proposal, or rather...an idea; a renewed alliance between the Knights Thranis and The Blades. I still do not trust The Blades, and yet, as I mentioned to you previously, I trust you – implicitly – for you have earned it! We have heard Knight Anika speak of her loyalty to you; since she offers it freely, so then shall I – this I *now* swear. We owe you a debt, one which I intend to repay. Should you require my aid, know that you shall have it. I would gladly fight alongside you in battle once again, Honorary Knight Rayna.'

The mood amongst the gathered knights suddenly became serious, as each carefully considered the Knight Lord's words. According to Xenia it was not unheard of for the Knights Thranis to swear personal oaths, whilst remaining loyal to their Order. Judging by their body language, however, she got the impression that it was extremely rare for the Knight Lord to do so himself.

'As would I...Honorary Knight Rayna.' said Captain Gedrick, who until now had remained seated.

'And I.' said Falkai, struggling to stand with his makeshift crutch.

'I too swear this.' said Loredan, who promptly stood and raised his cup for the second time.

Around the table, each knight took it in turn to echo the oath sworn by Heldran. Although the Knight Lord had not asked this of them, each recognised the leadership and valour demonstrated by The Guardian during the rescue of Gedrick and his knights. Although Heldran had rejected Rayna's offer of an alliance, in a curious way The Guardian had ultimately achieved her intended goal.

'It has been an honour to fight alongside each of you during The Hunt.' said Rayna, who now stood clutching the back of her chair. 'And you honour me further with your oaths. As a final parting gesture of comradeship, before I return to the vale, I present to you all an offer. Most of you are aware of the – speaking frankly – *massacre* at Scrier's Post. Those few Blade Aspirants who survived the ordeal are left troubled by the horrific events that they endured. They are struggling to connect with their Order, since the ordeal, and would – I believe – benefit from a change in direction. Anika was one of those survivors – they call themselves The Vengeful Tears – but her time spent at the Ardent Gate has seen her exorcise her demons. I do not ask this of you, instead I offer this proposal purely for your consideration: should you wish to swell your ranks, I will speak to The Vengeful Tears personally, on your behalf, about joining your Order – should you decide to accept them. Whilst I am no scrier myself, and thus cannot predict their destiny, they are nonetheless good fighters. They look up to Anika – she can guide them – and I firmly believe that each would prove their worth if given the opportunity. Sadly the Order of The Blades is not the right environment for them, and it will be exceptionally difficult for us to pull them back from the darkness consuming them. They need a fresh start, one which I believe you can give them. However, should you choose to accept my offer, you will need to dust off a second table.'

Heldran smiled warmly at Rayna before promptly offering his response, 'Your offer is greatly appreciated, Honorary Knight Rayna. We will convene the next cycle to discuss the merits of your proposal in full. But for now, I ask that you all sit and feast in Morin and Katrin's honour.'

TWENTY ONE
Change

That evening she chose to stay up late, savouring what might be her last time sat gazing languidly into the ephemeral flames of the now familiar stone hearth. Once again, the spritely flames danced energetically for her personal amusement, fuelled by a fresh Firestone, now consumed by the mesmerising conflagration. She felt a sense of calm watching the flames lapping against the inner walls of the hearth, destined never to escape the confines of their stone overseer. Later that evening Heldran joined her; the Knight Lord chose his habitual perch adjacent to her upon the wooden bench opposite the hearth. Neither spoke of her proposal, nor did they discuss the loss of Morin and Katrin, or Anika's decision to remain at the Ardent Gate. Instead they sat quietly together, content simply with their comfortable shared silence. During her time spent with the Knights Thranis, the hearth had become a place where both she and Heldran could forget their troubles – if only for a short period. Eventually, tiredness came looking for her; she yawned loudly, unaware of the noise she made.

'It is time that you found your hammock for the night.' said Heldran.

The Knight Lord gave her a heavy pat across her back, sending her firmly on her way to the communal resting quarters deep within the Ardent Gate. As she made her way silently to her hammock, she noticed again that Anika's own was once again vacant; she smiled to herself, pleased that her former Blade sister had found purpose once more. For the first time in a long time, she closed her eyes without reliving the darkest parts her former life, content in the blissful ignorance that all was right with her world – the world she had chosen.

The following cycle the knights gathered to discuss her proposal concerning the Vengeful Tears. Although the Knight Lord had not specifically asked her to do so, she chose not to attend the meeting. In order for her proposal to bear fruit, the Knights Thranis needed to accept the Vengeful Tears of their own volition – any attempt at coercing their decision on the matter would fail, therefore she decided it best not to interfere.

Whilst the knights discussed her proposal, she packed her things ready for her return to the vale. It felt strange preparing to leave the Ardent Gate, but her time with the Knights had run its course. Though she looked forward to her inevitable return to the vale and reconnecting with Nathaniel, Kirika and Marcus, she felt less prepared for the awkward conversations ahead. She was uncertain how Marcus would react to the Knights' sworn oaths – to her specifically – and then there was the issue of Caleth; whilst Alarielle was desperate to learn the truth of her father's involvement, she was far less eager to do so. Still, further knowledge of the events leading up to the release of The Blade Lord's predecessor would perhaps enlighten her as to why Heldran distrusted The Blades. After packing her possessions, she decided to venture outside and practice her swordsmanship. Nathaniel had been the one to insist that she work on her unpredictability in combat, as opposed to mastering set routines, in light of her impending challenge against Lothnar. She could not rival the Paladin's skill in combat at such an early stage in her own military career, though she was able to think fast on her feet. In addition, fighting alongside the knights had expanded her martial prowess – as Marcus had predicted – and she had since increased her arsenal of tricks. She used the time wisely to work on her feints and rolls; she was not afraid to dirty her attire in combat, though Kirika would likely take a dim view of her garish style.

It was noon when the meeting between the gathered knights finally concluded.

'You cannot return to the value looking like that! Marcus will likely send you back to us.' boomed Heldran, catching her by surprise.

She had not noticed the arrival of Heldran and Gedrick, such was her level of concentration on her training. She sheathed her blades and brushed away the grit clinging to her clothes.

'Your hair needs fixing as well.' said Gedrick in his habitual deadpan tone.

'Since neither of you feel the need to comment on my fighting technique, can I therefore assume that your collective teachings have not been entirely wasted on me?'

'Not entirely,' replied Heldran jovially, 'Though we are not here to critique your skill with a blade.'

'You have reached a decision then?'

'We have, and it has been decided – after careful consideration – that we shall accept your proposal.'

Initially she was taken aback by the decision reached by the knights; given their entrenched distrust of The Blades, she had not expected such a positive outcome. But then she reminded herself that the Knights Thranis were also pragmatic; their numbers ultimately needed replenishing, and they had few recruitment options available to them.

'You look surprised.' said Gedrick.

'I suppose that I am – in part at least.'

'Our reticence towards The Blades is overshadowed by the need to maintain our Order and – although you were not present at the meeting – Anika can be equally as persuasive as you.' replied Gedrick. 'Anika has convinced us that the remainder of The Vengeful Tears could indeed become valuable additions to our Order. We are therefore confident now that with Anika's guidance they too will find a new home here within the Ardent Gate.'

'I am genuinely pleased with the Order's decision. I will speak with The Vengeful Tears upon my return to the vale and inform you via Sky-Skitter as to their decision.'

'Please do. But before that can happen, we need to show you how to get back.' replied Heldran.

'That shouldn't be necessary, I believe that I am able to recall the way. If I travel through the night I should make short work of it.'

'Ah, but you mean to take the slow route. Surely you must realise by now Rayna, that there is a faster way?'

Controlling the creature was far easier than she had expected. Naturally she had assumed the need to subjugate all three of the Meldbeast's feral minds, which in itself might have posed a minor challenge – let alone trying to get them to work in unison. However, she had subsequently learnt that although each operated independently from the other, only the central head controlled the remainder of the chimera's warped body. Whether by design or instead a limitation of its constituent parts, the remaining two heads were little more than aggressive passengers, forever tied to the fate of their common host. Regardless, the Meldbeast now answered to her – not Krashnar – though she suspected the loss of control over his pet was not high on the shaper's list of priorities, having already extracted his amusement from the creation.

Although she could telepathically commune with and impose her will upon others, she found it difficult to forcibly extract information from their minds. In particular, it was arduous trying to glean anything useful from the shaper; Krashnar's mind was far from conventional – there were bits missing and other areas which felt abnormally bloated. However, through his quirky body language and anti-social mannerisms alone she sensed that the vile shaper had fresh atrocities occupying his twisted thoughts. Krashnar's relentless twitching and fidgeting suggested that he was excited about something yet to come. After abandoning Darlia at Krashnar's hide, she held sway over the Meldbeast's course whilst it bounded across the barren landscape carrying them both with it. Although she was not privy to their final destination, Krashnar had barked the occasional new heading, prompting her to set the Meldbeast to purpose along its new bearing. The creature's pace across the cracked relief of the borderlands had been supremely impressive; it took them very little time to reach their destination. Propelled by its muscular legs, and fuelled with the desire to explore the world beyond its filthy pen, the Meldbeast had sprinted across the rugged landscape at near breakneck speed.

'Why bring us here, and at night? We have swapped one hole for another!' she had snapped irritably, due to the pain wracking her body; her new form had not lent itself well to their unorthodox means of travel.

'Get some sleep.'

'You have brought us to a cave, in the middle of nowhere – you expect us to sleep here?'

'Yes. Stop complaining.'

At Krashnar's behest, she had reluctantly allowed him to assist her in dismounting the Meldbeast. She recalled the hideous abomination's awful howl of pain when Krashnar unmade the flesh straps securing her legs to the creature. After chaining the beast to the cave's entrance, they had spent the night sleeping uncomfortably on the bedrock waiting for dawn to break, whilst the Meldbeast stood sentinel.

It was morning now and her body screamed in pain again as she tried to lift herself unaided off the cave floor. Krashnar was already awake and watched her unsuccessful attempts to right herself with sadistic amusement.

'Why is it that you enjoy...watching others suffer?!' she spat venomously, whilst struggling to control her shallow breathing again on account of her raw anger.

'Do you not find it delightfully amusing watching Fan-Fish attempt to swim upstream?'

'You are a sadist!'

Krashnar released a bored pantomime sigh, 'Sadist, monster, demon, sociopath...which is it you prefer? I lose track of all the nasty quips which spill from your venomous tongue, as you needlessly try to classify something which you will never truly understand.'

'Help me!'

'Please...hmm...?'

She wanted desperately to destroy his sick twisted mind – no one would miss it – though such fanciful thought would never work in practice. As much as she despised the wretched shaper, she needed Krashnar and he knew it.

'Fine...*please* help me!'

'Better.'

Despite becoming more accustomed to her new body, it still continued to regularly torment her; she found it irksome being unable to stand upright unaided – a simple action which she had previously taken for granted. After Krashnar helped drag her to her feet, she tried to calm her volatile anger and regain some control over her restricted breathing.

'Why did we come here?'

'Ah yes, the inevitable question.' replied Krashnar sardonically. 'We came here because there is a Waystone hidden in this cave.'

'And that is significant why?'

'Because Lileah, it leads to the vale.'

'What!? And you have been aware of this all this time?' she replied pointedly, unable to mask her shock.

'Yes.'

'Why tell me this now and not before? Besides I thought we were heading towards Narlak, to round up the fleeing heard?'

'No, *we* are not. That is your job.'

'You mean to travel to the vale alone?'

'Yes. The cave narrows into a passageway, at the end of which is the Waystone chamber. After so many long passes languishing in exile, I will return to the vale and deal with The Guardian. You will press onto Narlak, gathering what remains of your mindless flock, after which you will assault the vale. I will then rejoin you as we strip the self-righteous from their place of decadence. If the herd is still intact, speed will be our route to victory; The Blades will be unable to react quickly enough.'

'And what if the herd has fractured – what then?'

'Take your time. Gather as many Narlakai as you dare with that mind of yours. Lothnar's scouts will see you coming, but we will have numerical supremacy.' Krashnar explained. 'Take our provisions; they should see you through ten cycles easily. I will meld you to the beast once more, so that you do not fall from its back.'

'But how am I supposed to...'

'Supposed to what?'

'Relieve myself!'

'The Meldbeast will not mind; its carapace is easily cleaned – the rain will do the rest.'

Bidding her final farewells to the Knights Thranis was far more emotional than she had expected. She felt empty inside after Heldran released her from his enormous embrace, worse still after Anika finished hugging her affectionately; both of them had tears in their eyes, knowing that it would be some time – if at all – before they would see each other again. She wiped the tears from her eyes and smiled affectionately at those who had gathered for her imminent departure. They had assembled in the Gate Room, which previously she thought contained only twelve Waystones. Her apparent ignorance regarding such matters was made abundantly clear when Vorian pulled one of the room's concealed levers; the entire room rotated slowly anti-clockwise, driven by a system of complex gears and pulleys. As the room rotated, the alcoves housing the existing twelve Waystones disappeared from sight, promptly revealing twelve more. The Knights Thranis, it seemed, had access to an enormous network of Waystones, completely unbeknownst to The Blades.

'I trust you will guard our secrets Rayna?' asked Gedrick as she picked up her belongings ready for her departure.

'You have my word,' she replied, 'Also, I will be sure to speak with The Vengeful Tears at the earliest possible opportunity.'

Heldran raised his left hand and pointed towards one of the newly-revealed Waystones. She turned to observe the curious stone, only to feel the familiar thump of his other hand firmly upon her back one final time. The weight of his enormous hand pushed her towards the Waystone, which lay inert upon its waist-high stone plinth.

'I hate long goodbyes.' the Knight Lord said, 'Go now, and remember us fondly.'

'I shall...oh, and that oath you each swore to me; it goes *both* ways, whether you like it or not – never forget that!'

She walked towards the Waystone and held out her hand, just above its colourless crystalline surface. She glanced sidelong at the Knight Lord, Anika and the others, offering them one final grin, followed by a characteristic wink of her left eye as she allowed her hand to drop.

'Hold your breath!' boomed Heldran, who had a curious grin on his weathered face.

The Gate Room and its occupants stretched and elongated before slipping from her sight completely. Suddenly her body felt light, and the air around her became heavy, before giving way entirely to water! She panicked and thrashed around instinctively, causing her body to spin. The water around her was clear and she could hear a muffled sound coming from above. Frantically she kicked her legs and dragged her arms down several times, pulling herself upwards. She broke the water's surface gasping for air. Her eyes were filled with spray and the sound of crashing water assaulted her ears. It took her a moment to gather her bearings before realising that she was in the pool at the base of the Eternal Falls. She swam awkwardly towards the edge of the pool, encumbered by the weight of her waterlogged clothes and possessions. She dragged her sodden body – again – onto the shingle at the water's edge; twice now she had been dumped at the base of the falls – once by Nathaniel during her training, and now by the Knights Thranis.

'Just you wait Heldran!' she said aloud.

She stood up and immediately began to shiver in the cool air. Autumn was starting to fade, and with it the onset of winter approached. She knew the path back home well and chose to make quick work of it, desperate to get out of her wet clothes.

By the time she made it to Nathaniel's tree, a number of local Freylarkai had already acknowledged her return to the vale. Though she tried her best to avoid any contact without seeming rude, her increasing popularity made anonymity extremely difficult. Out of courtesy she knocked loudly on the door, announcing her arrival. There was no response. Unsurprising, she thought; it was mid-afternoon, Nathaniel was therefore still training in the arena in all likelihood. She entered the tree, wandered upstairs to her room and took off her – now semi-dry – clothes, discarding them casually across the floor. She caught a glimpse of her body in the dresser mirror, which sat on top of the table adjacent to her bed. Her body was dotted with bruises from her last encounter with the Ravnarkai, despite wearing full armour during the battle. She still found it strange seeing Alarielle's body – now her own – reflected back at her.

She wondered if there would ever come a time when she would fully accept her new physique. Sometimes she would forget, particularly when engaged in a mission or training in the arena. Yet there were other times, typically when alone, where she would become incredibly self-conscious of her stolen female form. Although she had become comfortable with others seeing her in Alarielle's body, she had yet to fully accept the change herself; perhaps knowing her previous identity made it difficult accommodating her new one, she mused. Either way, she felt detached seeing her long slender legs riding up to her altered genitalia. Without any real conscious thought she touched her body with her slender fingers; she traced them slowly across the contours of her body, as though examining herself – again – for the first time. Her fingers felt as if they touched the skin of somebody else, rather than her own inherited form.

'You've fought both the Ravnarkai and the Narlakai; how can you still be wary of your own body?' she whispered quietly to herself.

'*If you have questions, I can answer them.*' replied Alarielle, catching her off guard.

All of a sudden her face flushed with embarrassment, realising now that she was being watched. Indeed she was foolish to have ever assumed otherwise. Alarielle was a part of her, ever-present, thus she could never truly be alone; a small price to pay, she mused, having stolen the body of another.

'*Do not be embarrassed Rayna. This must still be confusing for you – it is confusing for me too. It has been a while since I last saw my – our – body. I forgot how easily it bruises.*'

'Sometimes I wonder if I will wake up, back in the Wild; maybe I'm bleeding out, and this is all lurid imagination from my oxygen-starved brain?'

'*Freylar is very real, as is the body we both inhabit – do not shy away from it Rayna.*'

'I won't – I just need more time.' she said, whilst failing to fight the urge to spontaneously yawn.

'*And sleep, so it would seem. My father will not be back for some time; perhaps it would serve you well to get some rest before his return?*'

She was yawning heavily now; lack of sleep had finally caught up with her and was determined to make itself known.

'You're right of course – after all, you know our body better than I.'

'*For now perhaps, but I do not believe that will always be the case.*'

'What do you mean by that Alarielle?'

'*That is not important right now. What is, however, is that you get some sleep!*'

TWENTY TWO
Detection

'Shit, shit, shit!'

The siren continued to sound. Hurriedly he stuffed the alarming analogue communicator into his right pocket in a continued bid to muffle its drone. He ran towards a dimly-lit side cabinet, stationed against the wall to the right of the corridor's open door. Hurriedly, he grabbed the first object of note remotely fulfilling his requirements, before racing back towards the corridor. He took two steps into the short passageway then froze abruptly; a semi-naked elderly man stepped out of the master bedroom, directly into his path. For a brief moment both stood perfectly still, dumbfounded by one another's presence. The man was thin and drawn, as though the passage of time weighed heavily upon him, or perhaps instead the senior citizen suffered from a medical aliment responsible for his frail appearance. The retired programmer parted his withered lips, as though about to speak, but instead turned his head.

'No, wait!'

His desperate cry fell on deaf ears as the elderly man scurried back to his room, sealing the door behind him. Fuelled by a sudden rush of adrenaline, he sprinted down the corridor and called up the door's holographic access panel to override the lock. Frantically he punched in the code: four-two-nine-eight-one-two-three-seven; the door slid open. Mr L. Cameron was standing in front of another holographic access panel at the foot of the bed; the elderly man was clearly shocked by his abrupt entrance and froze in horror.

'I am not here to hurt you, but you must step away from that access panel.'

There was no response from the elderly man, who was clearly scared and confused by his unauthorised intrusion. He glanced towards the access panel; it appeared as though Mr L. Cameron was attempting to establish an outbound connection. The startled man saw his divided attention and began to slowly shift his balance.

'Do not touch that panel!'

Again the man said nothing. He could sense the programmer's mind analysing the situation, assessing every possible outcome of their unexpected encounter. Instinctively he tightened his grip on the foreign object weighing heavily in his right hand, snatched from the side cabinet back in the main living space. The object was an ornament of some description, though in his haste he had paid it little attention. Regardless, it felt hard; it would be sufficient – if needed – he affirmed to himself. However, he hoped dearly that the elderly man had the sense to back away from the holographic access panel, and yet worryingly Mr L. Cameron continued to stare mutely at him. Suddenly the muffled siren emanating from his right pocket ceased. Without warning the man resumed his interaction with the holographic access panel.

'Stop!' he cried as he darted forwards.

The elderly man raised his right arm, desperate to block his advance, which he grabbed and tried to twist away. Despite the man's frail appearance, Mr L. Cameron was deceptively strong; the elderly man pushed back aggressively whilst trying desperately to work the panel with his free hand.

'Stop it!' he cried once more.

He wrestled with Mr L. Cameron's right arm, trying in vain to push the man away from the holographic access panel. His opponent refused to give any ground, and instead thrashed his arm wildly towards his face, catching him flush on the cheek.

'Help!' screamed the old man, finally breaking his silence.

'I'm *not* going to hurt you!'

'Intruder! Help!' cried the elderly man once more.

'Be quiet!'

The man thrashed wildly again, this time scratching him across his forehead with rough edged nails. Desperate now to silence the elderly man, he took a step backwards and used his strength to knock Mr L. Cameron to the ground using his left shoulder. The old man grunted as he toppled and fell, dragging him down for the ride. He fell awkwardly on top of the elderly man, whose head hit the hard floor with a sickening wet thud. He quickly pushed himself up from the prone man's crumpled body, and gasped at the sight of blood rapidly pooling around the back of Mr L. Cameron's head.

'No, no, no!'

Panic gripped him as the shocking reality of his unforeseen actions quickly set in. Desperately, he leaned down and shook Mr L. Cameron's left shoulder, hoping dearly for signs of life, but instead the prone body reacted mockingly to his prayers as it went into cadaveric spasm. Seeing the elderly gentleman's disturbing final movements was almost too much to bear. He withdrew his hand slowly, gasping once more, this time at the sight of his own blood soaked fingertips.

'Oh shit! Fuck! What have I done?!'

His breathing was shallow now and his mind went blank as a strange numb paralysis gripped him. His muscles tensed unbearably and he could feel his hand tightening its grip painfully on the ornament still in his right hand. He could feel the pressure building inside his head, ready to explode, when suddenly a stray thought pierced his chaotic mind. He released the ornament, causing it to drop noisily to the floor, and snatched the analogue communicator from his pocket. Frantically he reattached the communicator to his ear and screamed hysterically, hoping desperately that Trix would hear him.

'Trix! Trix! Where are you, damn it!'

'*Callum, what's going on?*'

'Trix, he's dying, he's fucking dying on me!'

'*What?!*' replied Trix, clearly confused.

'It's the old man – he's bleeding out; his head is bleeding!'

'*How?*'

'I pushed him. He cracked his head. What the hell do I do now?'

'*OK, just calm down.*'

'Don't patronise me Trix, this is your fucking fault! You triggered that siren.'

'*I did what was necessary – you can blame me later. Right now we need to extract his bio-key.*'

'Please tell me you're not serious?! The man's dying! We need to help him!'

'*Callum, I'm a software engineer, not a bloody surgeon! We can't help him, and if the authorities learn of his death – which they will if you don't remove that key – then you'll have a team of Peacekeepers battering down his door within the hour.*'

'What the hell? Trix, I've fatally wounded an innocent man, who you now want me to carve up; I'm not your butcher damn it!' he replied angrily.

'That man is far from innocent, and besides, you need to realise the very real shit you're in right now Fox!'

'Shit which you created!'

'Irrelevant. This is the only way you and I get a shot at a life within this wretched metropolis. You do this or you take your chances with the rest of our kind – oh and incidentally, where are they exactly, hmm?'

He did not respond to Trix's verbal tirade. His body was a torrent of emotion; anger, rage, shock, grief, despair...denial – emotionally, he was a mess. Sure, he had been in a fight before – many times in fact – but never had he actually killed anyone. Now a man lay dying before him, as a direct result of his actions, and he was powerless to prevent it. He wanted to scream, but the paralysis he felt earlier reached for him again as he stood there, dumbfounded, watching in mute horror as the pool of dark red liquid surrounding the elderly man's head expanded outwards.

'Callum you need to just deal with this...Callum are you listening? Fox!!'

His point of entry was far from ideal; he had forgotten how far east the Waystone would deposit him. Still, anything was better than traipsing across the cracked and dusty relief of the borderlands on foot. It had been many passes since last he recalled being surrounded by such an abundance of flora; despite loathing its inhabitants, the vale was truly a sight worth beholding – even he was able to appreciate its natural beauty, and the future perversions its unspoilt splendour cried out to him for. To the south-west, he could see the Tri-Spires protruding ostentatiously from the southern ridgeline; he hated the unnatural structure, wrought by Mirielle's hands and shaped by her vision alone. The structure was a selfish indulgence, intended solely to visually articulate her ego and ambition. He wanted dearly to tear down the self-serving structure, though he had another – more pressing – calling to attend to. Wiping The Guardian from the board would be a simple task for a Freylarkin of his ability. With The Guardian out of play, Lileah would exact her bloody vengeance and he would have his way with Mirielle alone in private. He licked his lips deliciously in anticipation of the atrocities he would inflict upon her marble-like skin. Though he hated her with a passion, the body of Freylar's queen was like a beautiful uncut gemstone, from which he would produce something wondrous. Those who survived Lileah's devastation would look upon their former queen with horror and fascination after his work was complete, the thought of which sent a pleasurable shiver down his back.

    He followed the southern bank of the winding river, which flowed through the heart of the vale, until he came across a male Freylarkin fishing at the water's edge. Unsurprisingly, the lone Freylarkin failed to notice his silent approach – that is until the moment when he had his victim ensnared in his grasp. Hurriedly he pressed the remaining digits of his left hand to the fisherman's lips. The Freylarkin tried to cry for help immediately, but the sound of his vocal chords died, muffled by the fusing of his lips – a simple trick, one which he had employed many times in the past. The Freylarkin panicked and clawed desperately at his own mouth. He used the distraction to grab the fisherman's rod, which had fallen upon the ground; he swung the thin wooden pole with force towards his victim's head. The impact made a loud thunk and sent the panicked Freylarkin tumbling to the ground. The fisherman writhed slowly in pain, and was clearly stunned by the bludgeoning attack. He immediately got to work, tugging aggressively at his hapless victim's clothes, pulling them free from their owner. After robbing the Freylarkin of his clothes, he fused the dazed fisherman's legs together, then rolled the hapless mutilated body into the river. In hindsight, disabling the fisherman's arms would have been the smarter play, though his insatiable appetite for savouring such moments never afforded his victims a quick release. After a short while the Freylarkin's arms tired, allowing the river's current to drag its impromptu offering down below the surface of the water. He turned his back to the river and hurriedly changed into the stolen clothes, subsequently tossing his old attire into the greedy river.

'Now for the trickier part.' he muttered to himself.

Kneeling down beside the edge of the riverbank, he observed his own wild reflection in the crystal clear water. Pressing his hands to his face, he began to rework his own visage so that it resembled that of his recent victim. For most shapers such feats were extremely difficult to accomplish, and regardless were considered taboo. However, a shaper of his ability had no such concerns; his talent for shaping flesh was unsurpassed, and he repeatedly chose to shirk the laws set by Freylar's queen and her ill-advising council members. Regardless, without a flesh sacrifice the change he wrought upon himself was temporary – yet sufficient enough to accomplish his task. He withdrew his hands from his new face and peered once more into the clear water to observe his altered visage. He licked his smooth lips with delicious excitement as he savoured his latest handiwork; he had a new face – albeit a temporary one – with which he would infiltrate the vale and carry out his will unopposed.

Armed with his newly acquired identity, he continued his journey west along the river's southern bank. The sun was now low in the sky; he needed to quicken his pace for his plan to succeed. Redoubling his efforts, he soon arrived at an aging timber bridge spanning the breadth of the river. Dotted along the riverbank, close to the bridge, were Freylarkai from all walks; each was gathered to discuss gossip or commerce, neither of which held any interest to him. The venerable bridge acted as a hub, linking the rural dwellings of those Freylarkai living in the forest – north of the river – to the heart of Mirielle's corrupt empire. He quietly slid his way past the widespread congregation, hoping to draw as little attention as possible. He was about to step onto the bridge when one of the locals recognised his stolen visage.

'Riknar, good cycle to you!'

He loathed idle chatter; his body urged him to press on, yet his mind stayed his course, warning him of the danger invited by ignoring the irksome local.

'And to you friend.' he replied, offering the Freylarkin a quick courteous glance.

'Fish not biting today eh?' said the Freylarkin tenaciously as he turned to resume his passage across the bridge.

'Something like that.' he said, waving his right hand, effectively signalling an end to their curt conversation.

Hurriedly he crossed the river, seeking to put the worthless tittle-tattlers behind him. The nosey Freylarkin cried something else as he marched across the bridge; some nonsense about a sister – Keshar – though he paid the loiterer no further notice, pretending instead to be out of earshot.

Infiltrating the vale became significantly easier once he entered the forest. Having lived amongst the trees himself – prior to his exile – he knew well the paths less travelled by his former kin. Silently he slipped largely unseen through the forest, until eventually he reached his destination. Breaching the dwelling before him would be easy enough, though misleading its inhabitants would pose a significantly harder challenge. He cast his gaze upwards towards the gaps in the canopy; the light was fading fast, yet there was still time before it abandoned the cycle entirely. Being the creature of habit that he was, it was likely The Teacher had yet returned from the arena. Gingerly, he peered through a small window at the base of the tree. Piles of books littered the floor close to the window, adjacent to which stood a couple of sturdy-looking rocking chairs. Peering further into the gloom, he struggled to discern any signs of movement; perhaps no one was at home, or maybe the occupants were upstairs, he mused. Regardless, he was determined to proceed with his gambit, despite the potential risks incurred. He pressed his hands to his face once more, again altering his visage; his face stretched and deformed painfully, quickly adopting its new arrangement. Satisfied with the revised reflection now staring back at him from the surface of the window, he laughed quietly to himself, confident that his ambition would soon be realised.

'Are you certain?'

'Yes, the knights are all accounted for – we have confirmed.'

'Including The Guardian?'

'The incident took place before her departure.'

'I see.' he replied with a look of concern. 'I need to report this to the Knight Lord. Please continue your observations, and alert me immediately if you discover any further activity.'

'Of course.'

He left the Watchers to their duties and proceeded to find the Knight Lord. Heldran was often found working within the Ardent Gate, engaged in the redoubt's more solitary chores; the Knight Lord seemingly enjoyed spending time alone to marshal his thoughts and unwind. After checking several known haunts, he eventually found the Knight Lord by the stone hearth in the hub. Heldran was alone; he sat on a wooden bench opposite the lit hearth diligently polishing armour belonging to the Order.

'My lord, may I have a quiet word?' he asked as he approached the warm hearth.

Heldran looked over his shoulder whilst continuing to absentmindedly polish a breast plate.

'Of course Vor, my door is always open – so to speak. Come sit with me and tell me what troubles you.'

The Knight Lord slapped his heavy right hand firmly atop the wooden bench upon which he sat, signalling for him to join. He felt a little awkward sharing the venerable knight's perch; he wished that he could relax more in the Knight Lord's presence – like Captain Gedrick or The Guardian – yet his insecurities frequently held him back. For reasons he did not entirely understand, both the Knight

Lord and Captain Gedrick trusted him, well enough even to command the Ardent Gate in their absence. Although the Knights Thranis had no real need for rank or titles per se, nonetheless he was essentially third in command after Heldran and Gedrick, with Loredan taking more of an advisory role within the Order. Yet despite the level of trust afforded him, he continued to worry needlessly about the perceptions of others. He was more than capable – that he knew – though he was unable to convince his soul of that fact. Pushing aside his anxiety, he sat down awkwardly adjacent to Heldran; the Knight Lord's shadow almost swallowed him whole, such was Heldran's immense frame in comparison to his own. He had heard stories of the Knight Lord's combat prowess during the recent meat grinder; it was far from difficult to imagine Heldran beating down his opponents with his enormous great sword.

'My lord we...'

'Vorian, we have known each other long enough now to dispense with formalities. You can call me by my name...so long as you help me polish this armour.' interrupted Heldran, who smiled weakly at him.

'I apologise.'

'There is no need – just relax.'

Heldran passed him a pauldron and a cloth. There was a ceramic pot on the bench between them; he wiped his cloth around the inner rim of the pot and began to work its black paste into the armour.

'Do you mind if I ask you a personal question?'

'Sure – though you may not get an answer.' replied Heldran, who continued to work his breast plate diligently.

'The Guardian – do you miss her?'

'Ha...is it that obvious?'

'I was just curious.'

'As is she...incessantly...but, to answer your question: Rayna is like a breath of fresh air. She is determined, fearless and not afraid to speak her mind – for the most part. I suppose I do in fact miss having her around.' replied Heldran. 'But enough about me...I take it you have something urgent to discuss?'

'Indeed. The Watchers have detected activity across the Waystone network.'

The Knight Lord ceased polishing the breast plate in his hands and laid the armour down gently upon the floor. Heldran turned to look him in the eye. The Knight Lord's weathered face became stony, accentuated by the shadows wrought by the flames flickering in the hearth.

'When did this happen?'

'Late morning, shortly after the gathering.' he replied.

'The Guardian then?'

'That was my initial thought, however, the Watchers assure me that the incident took place prior to her departure.'

'What of the knights?'

'Except for the lost eight, they are all accounted for.'

'Have the Watchers been able to confirm the source?'

'They believe the activity took place along the Narlakai borderlands, however, they cannot be more specific.'

The Knight Lord paused for a moment to consider the facts before abruptly standing up. He too rose, and was forced to crane his neck back to maintain eye contact with Heldran, who stood a full head taller.

'Thank you Vor, for bringing this to my attention. Alert Gedrick and Loredan, have them meet us in my quarters.'

'Us?' he replied, unsure whether Heldran intended for him to be privy to their impromptu meeting.

'A burden shared is a burden halved – Rayna taught me that lesson well. Besides, you are ready now Vor, though you are yet to realise it.'

She woke abruptly. Her breathing was shallow and her skin felt hot and clammy. Her hair clung to the sweat on her back and forehead, and the cloth lining her bed felt damp. She rolled her head gently, casting her gaze towards the room's solitary window; the dying light of the cycle weakly entered the room, bathing it in a shadowy gloom. The air was cool; she felt its tingle against the exposed skin of her right leg, which hung over the side of her bed as a sign of her unrest.

'Trouble sleeping?' enquired a strange voice abruptly.

She flinched, caught off guard by the sudden question; only then did she realise that she was in fact not alone.

'Who's there?! Alarielle, was that you?' she demanded.

Immediately she pushed herself upright, onto her elbows. The familiar face of Nathaniel stepped out of the shadow at the foot of her bed.

'Nathaniel, you made me jump!' she said, quickly recovering from her fright. 'How long have you been standing there?'

Nathaniel said nothing, instead he approached slowly and sat down on the left side of her bed and smiled.

'I experienced another repressed memory. Nathaniel, I think that I killed someone!'

Again Náthaniel chose not to speak. The Teacher merely sat quietly, observing her with a puzzled expression.

'Sorry, I mean released. Nathaniel, I released a person – an innocent! I murdered someone in cold blood!'

Nathaniel's mood suddenly changed as horrid laughter spilt forth from his lips, implying that The Teacher enjoyed her appalling confession.

'Tell me...' said Nathaniel, still laughing in a sinister tone, 'Do you like *my* falchions?'

'Falchions? You are referring to The Ardent Blade presumably? Nathaniel we need to discu...'

'Is that what *you* call it? Interesting...I must confess that I never bothered to name them – indeed I never saw the need.'

'*My father is acting strangely.*'

'Nathaniel, forgive me, but...what is wrong with your voice? You do not sound yourself.'

'Ah, how perceptive of you; indeed I am not myself. Let me show you the truth that this appearance really hides, Guardian!'

Without any warning, Nathaniel pounced on top of her; he grabbed her upper arms and forced her back down onto the damp bed with unnatural strength. Nathaniel's face suddenly twisted and distorted as his eyes, nose and mouth all moved in unison to adopt a completely new arrangement. Shocked and confused by what she was witnessing, all she could do was look on in horror, dumbfounded by the ghastly sight unfolding before her. When finally the ugly metamorphosis was complete, an entirely new face stared back at her. Nathaniel's new visage was weathered and beaten; he now had unkempt long brown hair and an awful pointed tongue which slid across his now cracked lips. Most disturbing of all were his pupil-less black eyes, which reminded her of deep dark wells; they stared unflinchingly back at her, threatening to devour her soul. The grim imposter opened his mouth, allowing its foul stench to claw at her sense of smell. He coughed horridly several times, causing black liquid to ride up his oesophagus and into his mouth. She tried desperately to move, but the thing that was once Nathaniel maintained a vicelike grip on her arms, holding her down tightly. Light exploded from her upturned palms as she summoned forth her inner light, in a desperate attempt to blind her attacker. The light illuminated his face – revealing its true ugliness – forcing her attacker to close his abyssal black eyes. He then coughed again, causing the foul liquid building in his mouth to dribble forth onto her face. She thrust her head left and right in vain, trying desperately to shake the liquid free. Instead it clung to her skin and began to move across her face towards her eyes and mouth seeking a way in. She closed her mouth and shut her eyes tightly, hoping to stave off the vile liquid threatening to violate her body. Her skin crawled as the liquid continued to slide across her face, determined to locate an alternate means of entering her body. Again she tried with all her might – using techniques taught to her by the real Nathaniel – to force her attacker back, yet try as she may, her repeated attempts to free herself were futile faced with such overwhelming strength. Unable to escape, eventually the liquid found what it was looking for. She lay powerless whilst the awful substance crept up her nostrils and shortly thereafter paralysed her body. The light from the room rapidly faded and she felt herself being drawn into the black abyss of her attacker's eyes. Darkness quickly surrounded her, locking her away in its incorporeal prison.

'As you can see, I am not truly Nathaniel.' rasped a horrid voice in her left ear mockingly. 'Let me introduce myself properly; I am Krashnar – at last we meet.'

– www.thechroniclesoffreylar.com –

If you enjoyed Volume Two of The Chronicles of Freylar, I would greatly appreciate an online review from you on the Amazon store. You can also 'Become a Blade Aspirant' on the website and join the ranks of The Blades.

Civilian Freylarkai
Aleska, Valkyrie, Retired
Keshar
Krasus
Larissa, Dressmaker
Riknar, Fisherman

Exiled Freylarkai
Darlia
Krashnar
Lileah

Dire Wolves
Krisis

Orders
Knights Thranis
The Blades

Races
Freylarkai
Narlakai
Ravnarkai

Humans
Austin 'Trix'
Callum 'Fox'
Kaitlin Delarouse
Mr L. Cameron

DRAMATIS PERSONAE

Ruling Council of Freylar
Kirika 'Fate Weaver', Valkyrie
Marcus 'The Blade Lord', Paladin –
Commander of The Blades
Mirielle, Queen

The Blades
Anika, Blade Novice
Lothnar, Paladin
Nathanar, Paladin
Nathaniel 'The Teacher', Blade Master
Ragnar, Paladin –
Captain of The Blades
Rayna 'The Guardian', Blade Adept

Knights Thranis
Falkai, Knight
Gedrick, Knight Captain
Heldran, Knight Lord
Katrin, Knight
Loredan, Knight Restorant
Morin, Knight
Vorian, Knight
Xenia, Knight
Zephir, Knight

Deceased Freylarkai
Alarielle, Blade Adept
Caleth, Blade Lord
Kryshar, Blade Aspirant